BOOK THREE OF THE SONS OF STEEL SAGA

Sons of Steel

Dark Energy

G. L. Keady

ALSO BY
G. L. Keady

DREAMRAIDERS

Sons of Steel Saga

FUTURES END
CYBERWARS

First published in Australia in 2022
by Big Island Productions
Copyright © Gary Keady 2022

Big Island Productions
PO Box 3027, Tuross Head, 2537, NSW, Australia
www.bigislandprod.net

ISBN:
Ebook: 978-1-92303813-4
Print: 978-1-923038-12-7

Edited by: Joan Grady
Cover design: Brandon Evans-Keady
Illustrations: Pierre Jackson. Colourist: Nestor Redulla Jr.

'A sufficiently advanced technology would seem to us
to be a form of magic,'

Arthur C. Clarke.

A wizard deals with magic. A wizard is someone in possession of
highly advanced technology. What is the definition of a wizard?
A man who is believed to have magical powers
and who uses them to harm or help other people.
Etymologically, wizard is a term derived from the
Anglo-Saxon (Old English) term "wysard",
which means: the wise one.'

TABLE OF CONTENTS

CHAPTER 1
PERADVENTURE

I T WAS JUST after 1 p.m. Battered and bruised, with blood seeping through his shirt from a deep cut in his shoulder, Black Alice was behind the wheel of an SUV in a desperate bid to outrun the vehicle pursuing him.

Half a kilometre away the Temple Mount could be seen in all its majesty. Alice was in Jerusalem.

Dr Secta was on the passenger seat beside him, holding an isotopic labelling detection device, or ILDD. He was shaken, unaccustomed to manic car chases.

Mal Function was on the back seat, struggling to read a map. "Take a right up ahead into Ha-Notshrim Street,' he directed.

The rear window suddenly shattered and Mal had to duck the shower of glass fragments. Someone had fired at them from behind.

Alice glanced up at the rear-vision mirror and saw a motorbike tailing them. The ancient street they were traveling was too narrow to go any faster.

With a roar the bike drew level with the passenger side door. They were unarmed – there was nothing they could do. Alice thought of ramming him — he looked across. The rider was wearing a black balaclava. As the bike accelerated and moved ahead, the biker reached behind him, dropped a small device onto the road and scooted off.

Alice immediately recognised what was bouncing on the cobblestones, but it was too late to avoid it. He yelled at the others: "A bomb!"

As the SUV passed over the small device it detonated. The power of the explosion catapulted the SUV into the air. It landed — rolled violently — skidded and stopped, propped up against the side of a building.

When the dust had settled, the mangled driver's side door in the smouldering wreckage creaked open and Alice, face bleeding from the smashed windshield, tried to climb out. He stopped dead, staring down the barrel of an automatic weapon … soldiers had the car surrounded. A shot rang out.

Alice woke with a start, his heart pounding like a drum, mouth parched, body saturated in sweat. He reached out trembling fingers to fiddle with the light switch and flicked it on. In the weak cone of light from the single bedside lamp, he stared at his hands, pleased to find them his — he was half expecting them to be Turk's.

It had been that way for a month, ever since his return from the last time travel event. He'd wake up freaked out, confused, unsure of where or who he was. His dreams had become vivid and chillingly realistic. He had no idea whether they were a glimpse into the future or a montage of images from the past — his or Turk's. He did after all have artefacts of Turk's memory fused with his own. Whatever the case, it was confusing

Alice had been in hiding from the Oceana Government Secret Service since his return. Chief government research scientist Dr Secta, along with his sister and colleague Dr Hope, had him tucked away in their bunker just outside Avalon, not far from Canberra. The bunker had been constructed in the 1960s as sanctuary for government officials in the event of a nuclear attack. Secta had kitted it out and utilized it as a base for the last time travel mission. Hope had set up living quarters in it for Alice, while she stayed nearby at the Avalon Motor Inn. Secta remained in Sydney, in liaison with his sister to coordinate the covert regeneration program that would restore Alice to full health. So far they'd failed to stabilize his atomic structure, and he was still at risk of dematerializing at any moment.

It was critical that the Oceana Government — and, more importantly, Senior Inspector Fanny Honor of the State Security Directorate (the SSD) — were kept in the dark about Alice's existence. They still believed he was missing, presumed dead, after the last mission.

Alice checked the time: it was nine o'clock in the morning. It was easy to lose track of time down in what he affectionately referred to as the pit. It was going to be a big day for him — Secta had finally come up with something he through might stabilize Alice's condition. He'd be arriving with Hope at about noon.

Oceana was still in a state of social unrest. The Octagon Peace Movement, formerly led by Black Alice, remained a constant source of embarrassment to the Oceana government. But with Alice thought dead, the President was confident they were gaining ground over the rebellious dissenters. He wouldn't be able to rest easy, however, until there was categorical proof that Alice was no longer a threat.

In the weeks following Secta's return from the future, Alice's nemesis, Secret Police Senior Inspector Fanny Honor, had been promoted to controller of the newly-formed Oceana Time Travel division — the OTT. Her sidekick, Agent Karzoff, had been elevated to second-in-command. The OTT charter was to secure advanced technology from the future for the strategic benefit of the Oceana Government. With Alice gone, Secta was the official time traveller — but in reality, it wasn't his bag at all. He had other ideas.

With promotion came a new suite of offices for Honor and Karzoff. Located a floor below the President's penthouse at Oceana HQ, it was a major improvement on their former accommodations, deep in the basement bowels of the building.

In a white blouse, prim black office suit, and suitable black pumps, Honor was dressed for her new role. Gone was the austere black uniform she'd worn for years.

Of average height, she did not lack physical stature; she obviously stuck determinedly to an exercise regime, which kept her fitness level an order of magnitude above anything Oceana required from their officers. Her thick raven hair, worn in a bob, hung to her chin and tucked under her jaw-line, highlighting a classic, slender neck. Her Eastern European heritage was obvious in her features and attitude. She was attractive, but one thing detracted from her pleasant physical appearance — her smile. Because she didn't have one.

Honor was having trouble getting her head around having a PA. She was so used to running her own race. The President had personally allocated Viktoria De Cock, a tall, nineteen-year-old South African with short-cropped white hair and a schoolmistress demeanour. Packing a bite even more venomous than her own made Honor see her as a competitor, rather than a subordinate.

On the other hand, middle-aged Karzoff, sporting the crop of short, bright red hair, he was renowned for, fancied his chances with Miss De Cock. He was convinced that below her sombre, unyielding exterior dwelt a wild, sadomasochistic animal.

Viktoria was parked behind the reception desk outside the door to Honor's office. Karzoff and Honor were meeting inside.

"Why is my office smaller than yours?" Karzoff complained.

Honor figured the complaint unworthy of a response. "I vonder vhy zere is a third office," she snarled. "Is ze President expecting to burden us viz anozer pain in ze butt like our PA?"

"I think she adds a lot to the ambience," Karzoff said, with a smirk.

"As long as there are breasts, you are contented Karzoff. Small things amuse small minds."

All of a sudden she sat bolt upright in her chair — something surprising had appeared on her computer monitor. She stood, moved to the front of her desk and began pacing the floor.

"What is it?" Karzoff enquired, twisting his head to follow her.

She stopped, and the thin straight line that made up her lips bent slowly into the parody of a smile. "A breach of security vas reported at ze Avalon bunker a month ago," she said, "So I put it under drone surveillance. I haff just received confirmation of activity." She moved back to her desk and swivelled the monitor for Karzoff to view.

"Vhat do you see?" she demanded.

Karzoff studied the photo. "Hmm," he said. "It looks like Doctor Hope."

The photo, shot from a drone, showed a blonde female entering the bunker.

"Correct," leered Honor. "Zat is indeed Dr Hope. So, now ve haff confirmation zat Secta has been lying. I would put money on zem having Black Alice zere also. I hope so," she added. "If ve cannot nail zis son of a bitch, it vill be a career wrecker for me."

"Oh, I don't think so Honor," said Karzoff, grinning. "The President wouldn't waste a fine big room on someone he intended to sack!"

"You joke at my expense," she snarled, unamused. "It is not funny. Ve need to find out if Alice is zere or not."

Karzoff believed Honor's inability to smile resulted from a lack of sense of humour.

"I suppose so," he sighed. "What do you intend to do?"

Honor spoke on her new mastoid communications implant, or MCI. "Viktoria, requisition a helicopter for three to ze Avalon bunker." She checked her wristwatch. "Collecting us at noon from ze HQ helipad. Passengers vill be myself, Karzoff and a security agent … I vill give you ze agent's name vhen I haff it."

She glared at Karzoff, "Done," she barked. "Now Secta vill get his comeuppance. Arrange for one of ze best agents we haff to join us, and haff him vell armed."

Karzoff bounced out of the chair. "On it!" he cried, sarcastically.

Mal pulled his purple V8 Commodore Ute into the car park of the Avalon Motor Inn. All the way from Sydney, Mal and Secta had been raving about some new drug called 'Flex'. It came as a liquid in a small tube. The user cracked it open and dripped the liquid into one eye. They had sixty seconds to picture a memory they wanted to revisit, then for the next twenty minutes that memory would be vividly recalled, right down to the smallest detail. The user would be so out of it that the drug would have to be used in private.

Originally developed for Alzheimer's and dementia sufferers, it quickly found its way into the recreational drug market. Secta was interested to try it.

"I do worry about the side effects though," he said. "I'd expect anything that dabbles with brain chemistry, especially through the optic nerve, would deplete dopamine levels severely, so usage could well diminish both long term and short-term memory."

Mal was regretting having raised the subject. He wasn't used to having his ear chewed off for hours at a time with scientific jargon he had no comprehension of at all.

Secta was about to ramble on with his encyclopaedic review when fortune favoured Mal. He saw Hope at a window seat in the Motel restaurant.

"There she is," he chirped, and bailed out of the car.

Hope shot them a wave and got up to join them.

Secta climbed out of the car too, stretching his legs after the long drive.

Mal liked Hope dressed in civvies. Her hair was up, and she was all in blue denim with black ankle-high boots, looking like a rock star — a style that appealed to Mal's taste.

She cruised up to them. "Good morning, my boys," she said with a happy smile.

"Morning," grinned Mal, rubbing his hands together. "Aren't you lookin' hot?"

Hope smiled. "I love the smell of country air," she said, inhaling deeply.

"Nice," said Secta. "But it lacks city substance."

"You mean pollution," Mal quipped.

"Needs more methane, you reckon?" Hope asked, heading for the car door.

"You chemist types are all the same," said Secta. "You get off on most anything malodorous."

Clambering back into the ute, they drove off for the bunker.

"We've got a problem," Secta announced grimly. "I received a message from my informant this morning. Honor will be visiting by chopper today."

"What time?" Mal asked.

"Chopper leaves at noon, so I expect it to land at the bunker around 12.30."

"Damn," said Mal, stomping on the gas. "It's 11.30 now — we'd better get a move on!"

"What are we going to do?" said Hope, troubled.

"I'll have to inject Alice immediately," said Secta. "I'm using the updated version of the serum that worked on me."

Hope was worried. "What about the risk of a contra reaction to the original serum?" she asked.

"Granted it's a risk," said Secta. "I think it best for Alice to decide — but to be honest, with Honor on her way, there's not much else we can do."

Fifteen minutes later they were in the elevator, descending to the bunker.

The doors opened and Alice greeted them.

"Hey dudes!" he said, happily. "What's happening?"

"Honor is onto us and on her way here," said Secta, gravely.

Alice whistled. "Okay," he said. "What do you have in mind?"

"I've brought the serum that worked on me," said Secta, holding up his little black bag. "I've refined it somewhat..."

"...But it might further complicate your condition," Hope interrupted, solemnly.

"Yes — but at the same time it might stabilize it," said Secta. "So, it's your decision, Alice."

"And we don't have much time," put in Mal. "The bitch'll be here in twenty minutes."

Al sat on the edge of the bench. Tell me straight, Secta," he said. "What are the odds?"

"They're in your favour Alice," said the scientist. "I've modelled the result a number of times and the results were positive. I'm pretty confident. But — and it's a big but — I can't give you any assurances."

"Well, I've had to trust you a few times now and so far you've come up trumps," Alice growled. "Let's do it."

There were no high fives or fist pumping. All of them were aware of the gravity of the situation. Secta put his bag on the bench, opened it and took out a syringe. He filled it from an ampoule.

Hope sat beside Alice and took his hand.

"At least it's not a bloody great syringe full of that fluorescent green gunk you pumped into me before," Alice cracked.

"No Alice," smiled Secta. "I've refined it into something less lethal-looking." He carried over a small syringe. "Roll up your sleeve, please."

Alice went further, stripping off his black denim jacket. He was wearing only a blue singlet underneath. "No jab in the neck this time?" he grinned.

"No need," said Secta, "This serum is alive — it contains nanobots: microscopic machines. They know where they need to go. So, all you get is a subcutaneous injection in the deltoid."

He'd finished and was wiping the puncture mark with a sterile swab before Alice had even noticed.

"Well done nurse," Al chuckled. "I didn't feel a thing." But suddenly Secta, Hope and Mal nearly jumped out of their skins as he let out an earthshattering, heavy-metal-singer scream

"What? What is it?" Secta yelled.

"Nothing," Al smirked. "I was just testing which scream to use if I needed to."

"Always the fricking prankster," growled Mal, elbowing his friend in the ribs.

"I suggest you sit in the old chair and relax Alice," Secta advised. "It'll take effect in about five minutes."

Al made his way over to the chair he detested so much, with its fishbowl-like apparatus poised above it. He was reminded of saying goodbye to Morri and Turk in exactly the same place — only a month ago, but at the same time far into the future.

"What do you expect to happen?" Al asked.

"I expect you to disappear," Secta said, matter-of-factly.

"Seriously, not again! Where to this time?"

"Don't worry, this time it will be painless."

The long paspalum grass on the open field was bent over, some from the downward draught caused by the blades of the black government chopper, but mostly from the howling near-to-gale-force, icy-cold southerly wind.

Honor, Karzoff and Agent Hillman jumped clear and raced across the field.

To Hillman's surprise, Honor stopped in the middle of the field. "Open, Sesame S-1 override!" she cried. Hillman was even more surprised when a trapdoor opened in the turf, revealing a staircase down. Honor led the way to the elevator platform. Before pressing the call button, she addressed Karzoff and Hillman. "Hillman, you vill shoot on my order," she commanded. "Is zat understood?"

"Yes ma'am."

Garbed in the black Oceana uniform, Hillman was a tall, well-built, Nordic-looking Scot with short-cropped blond hair and a strong accent. He had the ex-rugby player look that attracted Honor.

She handed Karzoff a pair of handcuffs. "Karzoff, you vill cuff Black Alice," she snapped. "Do I make myself clear?"

He took the cuffs between two fingers as though they were something putrid. "Yes," he said, wrinkling up his nose, never fond of being ordered to use brute force — especially against someone with the strength of Alice.

Honor pressed the button. Within seconds the elevator door opened and they stepped inside. Moments later the door reopened to reveal a well-lit lab with Secta, Hope and Mal calmly packing items into boxes.

"Ah, Honor, you must have an override password. I wrongly assumed it was calibrated to my voice only. Pays never to assume when it comes to anything to do with you," said Secta, facetiously. "I trust you're here to help. We could do with a hand."

"Vhere is he, Secta?" snarled Honor, shooting him daggers and speaking through clenched teeth.

"Who would that be, Honor?" said Secta, still loading items into boxes.

"You know exactly who I am talking about!" she insisted.

"I think you mean 'about whom I am talking', Honor. You really do need to work on your English. Furthermore, there is no-one here but we three — plus you three, of course."

Honor stormed to the office area and pointed to the room Hope had made up like a bedroom.

"Very vell," she snapped, "Zen whom has been sleeping in zere?"

"Oh dear no, Honor — this time you mean 'who'," Secta corrected, delighting in getting under her skin.

Hope looked up from loading a box with computer components. "Guilty as charged, Honor," she quipped. "Goldilocks was me. I've been staying here to prep our equipment for transportation back to HQ."

Honor turned on her heel, furious, and strode up to Secta. The sound of her heeled black ankle boots reverberated throughout the cavernous room.

"Vhere is Black Alice?" she all but shouted.

"Your guess is as good as mine Honor," said Secta, leaning back. "Stop shouting for goodness sake. What is all this about?"

Honor, egg on her face, glared at Karzoff, giving him his cue.

"Are we to presume you have been reinstated to a position at Oceana, Doctor Hope?" he asked. "Last we heard you were joining the Octagon…"

"The President reinstated her personally, Karzoff," said Secta, curtly. "Now, unless you're willing to help us pack up, I suggest you buzz off."

"If you vere not our only time traveller, I vould…" Honor bit her tongue.

"Yes Honor?" smirked Secta. "You would do what?"

Honor chose to back down. Without Secta she had nothing. He was the backbone of the entire OTT strategy. Though it irked her, she needed him.

She changed tack. "I have clearance for ze next time travel mission," she snapped. "Zere vill be a meeting at HQ with ze President zis week. I shall send you ze details and see you zere."

With a sharp nod, she led Karzoff and Hillman back to the elevator. Mal, Hope and Secta sat down, relieved.

"Phew, that was close," said Mal.

"Huh," said Secta. "As for her assumption that I will be compliant in being a time-travelling technology mule, she's in for a shock when we meet the President."

Suddenly, to their astonishment, Alice rematerialized in the chair — and what was more, looking as though he'd had a transcendental experience. After a moment, while they all sat stunned, he climbed shakily out of the chair, holding his chest and gulping for air.

Hope rushed over with a glass of water. He took a swig and sat on the edge of the bench. Hope, Mal and Secta waited for him to fill them in.

"I've just experienced the most amazing scene," he said, soberly. The others glanced at each other. Anything Al described as 'amazing' after the adventures of the last few months demanded their unmitigated attention.

"When the drug came on I had the sensation of shooting backwards, just like before," Al said. "Then I saw a light through a sort of smoky haze — I was travelling towards it. As I got closer I could see it better — it was an orb-like thing hovering about a metre and a half above the ground. It was glowing and pulsing with white light — and it had a … a presence. Like it was alive.

"I stopped right next to it … about half a metre in diameter it would've been. Then a voice spoke inside my head. Felt like it was coming from the orb. It said its name was En-Ki and it told me not to worry, everything was all right. The voice was kind of warm, sort of comforting. Sounded like a youngish man, from what I could tell…

"Where am I?" Alice asked.

"You are in a dimension alternate to your own," came the reply.

"Uh … Don't get that."

"A different reality. But that is not important. What is important is that you listen."

"Lay it on me."

"I have been with you all of your life. Manipulating your space-time continuum, leading you to this moment. You have a particular purpose."

"Are you telling me you brought me here, and it wasn't just Secta's mumbo jumbo?"

"That is exactly what I am telling you. Your atomic condition, as it has been altered by Secta's process, has allowed me to open portals or doorways in time for you.

"He then ran me through everything that has happened to me since you first dematerialized me, Secta. It was like I was watching a movie. I even saw things that had nothing to do with me. It was amazing — a replay of my life in a matter of minutes."

Secta was pacing holding his chin deep in thought. He stopped, turned to Alice and questioned, "Did he explain the process?"

Al scratched his head. "He said, that's how I brought you here. My message to you is that you have embarked on a quest … a quest that has intergalactic consequences, and will encounter universal resistance. The nature of this quest will be revealed to you in due course. You cannot stop it. It is your destiny."

… "Next minute I was back in the chair, freaked off my face and wondering what the stuff had just happened," finished Alice. "Was I dreaming it or what?"

CHAPTER 2
DIVINATION

THE LOOK OF perplexity on the faces of Secta, Hope and Mal was priceless.

"So? What do you make of it?" Al asked.

Hope turned to one of the computer terminals that was still operational.

"Who is this En-Ki dude?" Mal asked, while she typed.

"I've got it!" she said. "Says here En-Ki was a Sumerian god. The translation of his name is En meaning lord and Ki meaning earth, so he's Lord of the Earth. According to Sumerian mythology he created mankind. There's plenty on him."

"So, um, I've been talking to God?" said Al, chuckling.

"A pleroma visitation perhaps?" pondered Secta. "You've been given a quest by a Demiurge?"

"Uh … I guess so," said Al. "I dunno what a pleroma or a demiurge is, but this En-Ki cat, if that's who you mean, can't be all that godlike. 'Cause he forgot to tell me what the bloody quest is!"

"I don't know about that, Alice," said Hope. "By the sound of things, this isn't just some aberration. This En-Ki character claims to have been orchestrating your life since you were born. Maybe he embedded your quest in your DNA, like Secta's atomic marker. Maybe you'll instinctively recognise it when you're on the right track."

"That actually makes a lot of sense, sister," said Secta, deep in thought, holding his chin and again pacing the floor. "But it needs careful thinking about. In the meantime, we also need to think about Honor. We can't keep up the charade that Alice is gone for much longer."

The next day Secta was sitting outside the President's office, waiting to be summoned to the meeting. The President's personal secretary, the stunning Miss Vallins, was behind her desk. In a comfy armchair, Secta was gazing out of the big floor-to-ceiling windows at beautiful Sydney Harbour, its waters glistening like flawless diamonds in the mid-morning autumn sun. The canopy of azure blue overhead completed the tranquil picture — tranquil until it was invaded by the ominous grey form of a nuclear submarine, moving through the harbour to the heads. Secta knew it was the sub that had caused all the unrest a few months before, and figured many would be applauding its earlier-than-scheduled departure.

"Can I get you anything, Doctor Secta?" Miss Vallins purred.

"That depends on what you have on offer, Miss Vallins," he replied, suggestively.

Her blue eyes locked onto his and she raised a single eyebrow, "I'm not sure I know your taste Doctor," she smiled. "You appear somewhat... ambiguous."

"Interesting choice of words," he fired back. "Let's just say I'm ... always open to suggestion."

Before their innuendo could go any further, Miss Vallins held up a hand: the President was on her MCI.

"Yes sir," she said, sweetly. "Doctor Secta, you may enter now," she finished, with a lewd wink.

Grinning, Secta walked to the big mahogany double doors that opened into the President's office, where he stopped at a mark on the floor. A laser swept him for weapons, then a loud click announced him cleared for entry.

He looked back at Miss Vallins. "Next time, Miss Vallins," he said, provocatively, and stepped inside. It was all a joke.

Honor, Karzoff and the President were seated in a comfortable lounge setting. The President, dressed in a well-decorated black military uniform, motioned for Secta to sit. "My dear Secta," he beamed. "Glad you could join us. I apologise for keeping you waiting."

Honor's face darkened. She was thoroughly jealous of the respect the President displayed for Secta, who checked the display on the office walls as he sat down. "Have you had any response to the programmable wallpaper?" he asked, lightly.

"Absolutely," said the President. "In fact, only yesterday I had a delegation from South Africa here, and they loved it ... especially when Miss Vallins programmed scenes of Kruger National Park. What a surprise they got. They've already asked how to order it."

"The factory in the Philippines will begin production next month," said Secta, knowing this trivial exchange was irritating Honor and prolonging it just to piss her off. "Should bring us in a lot of money."

"Precisely — and we haven't even begun marketing it yet."

"And I have so many more ideas for its development," said Secta. "Which, now I come to think of it, raises a question ... Are you sure you want to proceed with this time travel project when the means for returning has not yet been perfected?"

A look of surprise broke on the President's chubby face. He shot Honor a look. Her eyes flashed between him and Secta.

"I was led to believe the process was operational," the President snapped.

Secta sat back in his chair. "With respect, sir, I think what happened to Black Alice is testament to the inherent problems with the process," he said. "Which is why such a complicated scientific process should be left to scientists and not SSD agents, perhaps?"

Honor's face reddened to the colour of Karzoff's hair.

"Dr Secta," she snarled, "You informed us vhen you returned from your trip to ze future zat ze process was functioning as expected."

"I said nothing of the sort," he rejoined. "What I did say is that it will ultimately be possible to send and retrieve a traveller safely." He turned again to the President. "Sorry to throw a spanner in the works Ri," he added, glibly. "It might have been more prudent for the OTT to have consulted me before running off at the mouth with impossible plans."

Honor hated it when Secta called the President by his Filipino first name. She felt it was grossly inappropriate, borderline insubordination. Her already brilliant colour deepened.

"You're absolutely right Secta," said the President. "An oversight that will shortly be corrected. Tell me, what do you need to get your process operational?"

Secta was enjoying this. Honor was sinking lower and lower into her chair. Karoff noticed and was also inwardly smiling at her displeasure.

"Well, put simply," Secta continued, "we haven't yet perfected the means of safely returning a traveller in time," he said. "I have, however, been in contact with Professor de Luz, the former senior scientist in charge of operations at the abandoned Desertron Super Collider in Texas. Like Hope and myself, de Luz was working on particle matter transfer, but from a different perspective. I believe some time spent with him could help with an answer to our problem."

"Done," said the President, agreeably.

Honor sat up. "Should I arrange for a visit to ze professor, Sir?"

"I would prefer if only my team met with the professor," said Secta, before the President could reply. "I don't want SSD anywhere near him."

"Agreed," said the President. "I'll have arrangements made. When would you like to leave?"

"The sooner the better."

"I'll arrange an air force transport. How many travelling?"

"Three, sir."

The President nodded. The meeting was over. Secta stood.

"Thank you, sir," he said, with a short bow. He glared at the other two. "Fräulein Honor, Herr Karzoff, auf wiedersehen."

In automatic response to his native language Karzoff inadvertently stood, clicked his heels and nodded sharply.

As Secta left the room, grinning, Honor said, "He said three travellers, sir. Who is zis third? It could be Black Alice!"

"You are obsessed with Black Alice, Honor," said the President. "I am not. I told Secta to sort it out, and he will. Now, go and get on with your work. I want no more of this childish squabbling."

"Yes sir," Honor capitulated, seething inside.

Later that afternoon Secta received a dispatch from the air force, advising of a flight departing Richmond air base northwest of Sydney at eight that evening. It would arrive at the US Defence Department Airport in Irving, Texas approximately 17 hours later, weather permitting. Secta immediately phoned Professor de Luz at his residence in Waxahachie, Texas, to set up a meeting.

Happy to hear from him, the professor committed to collecting the party from Irving Airport and bringing them to his home. Secta contacted Hope to make arrangements.

Al was staying at Hope's penthouse apartment overlooking Coogee Beach, in the fashionable eastern suburbs of Sydney. She was enjoying a glass of wine on the balcony when Al came back from the beach, where he'd been for a swim.

"Wasn't the water cold?" she asked.

"Only to wimps," Al smiled. "It was magic. Last swim I had was in Goulbourn canal — and a whole other dimension."

"Secta called," she said. "We're flying to Texas tonight."

"What — in the States?" Al said, pouring a glass of red and relaxing into a chair opposite.

"Yes," she nodded. "Secta did what he promised — talked the President out of a time travel mission, then got us a trip to visit his old mate Professor de Luz. He's the former operations head from the Super Collider in Waxahachie. Secta thinks his research into dark energy might have the answers we're looking for — might allow us to stabilize the quarks in your atomic structure by reversing their polarity.

"Not that he's told the President that," she went on, smiling. "He's said we're looking into finding a safe way of returning from time travel. Not really a lie, I guess, because we still don't have that sorted either."

"So, who's going?"

"Just us three."

At 7:40pm Secta and Hope boarded an air force transport jet, with Al following behind in heavy disguise. A section of the plane's interior had been configured for passengers, with two rows of three seats on one side of the centre aisle and two rows of two on the other. A female officer greeted them at the plane door.

"Good evening, Doctors Hope and Secta, Mr Function," she said. "I'm Leading Airwoman Marilyn King. Please take whichever seat you prefer, you're the only passengers. Take-off will be on schedule at twenty hundred hours."

Twenty minutes later the big jet was lined up on the main runway, the four Pratt and Whitney F117-PW-100 turbofan engines roaring on either side. The sound in the cabin was substantially louder than a commercial aircraft — the aircraft was, after all, configured for moving cargo, not passengers.

Twenty minutes into the flight the pilot emerged from the flight deck in full uniform and approached Secta.

"Air Commodore Hart, Dr Secta," he said. "Good to have you aboard, sir. Do you have everything you need?"

Secta nodded.

"Excellent," said the AC. "We've got around 17 hours of flight time ahead," he said. "So, if there's anything we can do for any of you, just press the call button."

"Thank you, Commodore Hart," Hope purred.

As the Commander made his way back to the flight deck, Secta grinned at Al. "Hope is attracted to men in uniform," he said, dryly.

"Fairly partial to a uniform myself," Al responded, with a wry grin.

"See Secta, it's not abnormal," Hope pouted.

"Yeah, that Airwoman King is quite something," Al cackled.

"No side effects to the serum, then?" asked Secta.

"None, at all. In fact, I feel terrific," Alice said.

"Excellent, excellent…" said Secta. "Now we need to determine how to keep you that way."

"I'm not gonna just disappear again, am I?"

"No, I think that part of the process is stable now, as it is with me. But we already know that an injection of the new serum will cause you to dematerialize."

"If you inject yourself with the new serum, could you time travel?"

"I don't know. I'm not sure, I want to find out—"

"I would," said Hope. "I'd give anything for half an hour with this En-Ki. Imagine what you could learn about our true history … if he actually is some kind of god, he would know the answer to everything…"

"Finally, we'd all know the meaning of life," Al chuckled.

Neither Hope nor Secta had questioned Alice's encounter. They had enough reason by now to put their faith in him. If he said he'd met a being called En-Ki, then it was more than likely that he had.

It was 9pm and Honor was still at her office computer. There was a knock at the door and Karzoff entered.

"Any word?" he asked.

"Yes, he sent me a photo. Look," said Honor, handing him her cell phone.

Karzoff studied it. "Yes, that is Mal Function," he said.

"Correct. It vas taken by Agent Rees on the flight to Texas only minutes ago. Now look at zis," she flicked to another photo on the device and handed it back.

"Yes, that is him all right, much clearer."

"Look at ze time stamp," she said, with a grin.

"8:45 this evening…"

"Exactly!" shouted Honor. "Fifteen minutes ago — and outside ze Octagon Jungle Bar!"

"That is here in Sydney! So, that is not Mal Function on the flight to Texas?"

"Correct, Karzoff," said Honor, smugly. "I knew it all along. Zat is Black Alice. And zat is ze reason I planted Agent Rees on board. Ve finally haff zem!"

CHAPTER 3
POLARITY

THE PLANE LANDED at Irving airport just under seventeen hours after taking off in Sydney, just as the pilot had said, touching down at 10pm local time. They deplaned into muggy Texas warmth, a pleasant change from the cool Sydney weather. Their diplomatic status meant there was no need to pass through immigration or customs, so they headed directly for the car waiting next to the plane. The door opened and a tall, ageing hippy strode towards them. With a shock of shoulder length, greying hair and beard and moustache to match, together with piercing blue eyes under bushy eyebrows, Professor de Luz reminded Al of one of his all-time favourite metal singers: Robert Plant.

Secta scurried over to the professor and embraced him. "Vic, good to see you," he said, warmly. "You're looking well."

"Well thanks Secta," drawled the Professor. "It's been a while! You haven't changed one iota."

"You remember my sister Hope?" said Secta. "She was at the International Science Convention in Manila with us."

"Of course I do!" boomed de Luz, opening his arms to Hope. "It's wonderful to see you again, young lady!"

"You're as corny as ever, Vic," said Hope. She stepped back from his bear hug and waved Al over, introducing him as Mal.

"Come aboard my wagon," said de Luz, as he and Alice shook hands. "We've got a forty-minute ride to my place in Waxahachie. Plenty of time to talk on the way."

Rees followed them, reporting their movements to Honor back in Sydney. An unassuming man of average height, with a round face and a receding hairline, he was dressed in a black business suit and tie, and had a wretched, squeaky voice.

"We have left no stone unturned," he said. "Everything is bugged — his car, his house, everything, I assure you."

"And his office?" Honor urged.

"He works from home."

"Ven vill you meet ze Home Security agent — vhat is his name again? Holman?"

"Yes, Holman. I think I can see him now — he's waiting at the flight operations centre."

"Stay viz ze surveillance vehicle at ze stakeout Rees," Honor commanded. "And maintain a stream to my office. I am recording everyzing. Clear?"

"Yes sir — Uh, I mean yes ma'am!"

Driving Interstate Freeway Thirty-Five East, Professor de Luz handed Secta a notepad. The message read: 'The car and my house are bugged. We're going to a bar in Waxahachie. We can talk there.' Secta nodded and handed the notepad to Hope and Alice on the back seat.

They kept the chat light and conversational, and Al kept quiet.

After a while the Professor turned into a car park in front of a bar — the little, red brick College Street Pub. There were only a few patrons inside, even though it was Friday night. De Luz led them through the British-style main bar to the veranda out back. They had no trouble finding a table and had quickly ordered a round of Mordelo draft beers.

"It's Mexican," he said with a smile, admiring the waitress's legs as she tripped off to fill the order. "So, tell me. Why in the hell am I being bugged?"

Al figured he was as eccentric as Secta, maybe even more.

"I suspect there are those in our government who don't trust us and want us kept under surveillance," Secta admitted.

"I get that," said de Luz, nodding slowly.

"I guess we better bring Vic up to speed on events," Secta said. Hope and Al nodded.

Outside, a large brown Ford van pulled up across the street. The roof rack was holding a long, white poly pipe, inside which was a directional mic capable of monitoring a conversation two hundred yards away. Inside the van Agent Rees sat with Homeland Security Agent Buddy Holman, monitoring the conversation. The signal was being relayed via satellite to the OTT office at Oceana HQ in Sydney, where Honor and Karzoff were listening and recording. Suddenly, there was a knock at the office door.

"Come!" Honor barked, annoyed.

The door opened and Viktoria entered, carrying a tray holding two cups of piping hot coffee.

"Your coffees, ma'am," she said, apologetically.

"Just put them on ze table," snapped Honor.

In the cramped space, Viktoria brushed past Karzoff, her hips at his eye level. He drew in a deep breath of her aroma. She placed the mugs as ordered busy taking in what they were monitoring.

"Since I retired from the Super Collider, I've been following up on my studies around dark matter or, as some call it, dark energy," de Luz was saying. "I won't bore you with that for now. Let's just say my studies took me from science to ancient history. Here's why…

"There's a theory that the 'Moses' we're told about in the Bible was actually the Pharaoh Akhenaten. Cutting an extremely long story short, this theory says that the Ark 'Moses' used to carry the ten commandments was actually built to specifications provided by an extraterrestrial or supernatural being named En-Ki, using a meteorite as a power source. It's suggested that this power source, when activated, produced dark energy.

"That's real important, because these days while we suspect the existence of dark energy, how to generate it remains a mystery."

"What was the Ark used for?" asked Al, intrigued by the mention of En-Ki.

"A number of things," said de Luz. "But specifically to contact a divine being or beings and as a weapon of great power."

"So … Moses, or this Pharaoh dude, would have used it to contact En-Ki?" Al posed.

"Interesting you should ask that. Yes, I think that's exactly what he used it for," the Professor said.

Back in Sydney, Honor nearly jumped out of her skin. "Confirmation!" she squawked. "It is Alice all right! I vas right!" Karzoff waved her into silence — Hope was speaking.

"Where does Alice fit into this equation?" she asked.

There was a pause, and the sound of clinking bottles. The beers had arrived. No doubt the group was waiting for the waitress to leave before continuing.

Honor suddenly realised that Viktoria was still standing there.

"You may leave now, Miss de Cock," she ordered.

"Yes ma'am," Viktoria said obediently, and left.

"Now pay attention, ve are about to discover vhat zis is all about dear toad."

"Thank you, Stella," de Luz said, winking at the waitress.

She shot him back a sly, shameless smirk.

"Sorry professor, you were saying?" said Hope, pulling him back on track.

"Oh yes," he said. "So — how does Al fit in? Well, I want him to find the Ark of the Covenant."

Alice jumped out of his seat like he'd been bitten on the butt by a spider. "This is it!" he declared. "This is the quest! Recovering the Ark is the quest!"

Honor was astonished. "Did you hear zat, Karzoff?"

"Yes, I did," said her colleague. "But how? Many have sought the Ark, even the Nazis in World War II. It is like the Holy Grail — one of those mysteries no-one has been able to solve. This is the stuff of fantasy … this professor is certifiable."

"But vhat if zey did find it, Karzoff?" said Honor, eagerly. "Vhat vould zey do viz it? Zey vould haff ze most powerful veapon on earth! Ze Octagon would have ze most powerful veapon on Earth! Now ve discover vhat zis is all about! Zey are trying to arm zemselves to destroy ze government!"

"I don't think so…" Karzoff began.

"I need to take this to ze President immediately," Honor interrupted. "Vat vill he zink of his pet scientist now, huh? Caught committing treason!"

Alice sat back down. Secta's phone beeped an incoming text. He checked it and his face paled. He quickly took a notepad and pen from his pocket, scribbled a note and showed them. *My informant in Sydney said Honor and Karzoff are monitoring our every word. They know everything!*

De Luz took the notepad, wrote another note and showed them. *Must be outside — surveillance vehicle. May as well carry on. Don't tell them we know — make it work 4 us. Don't give up informant!*

They all nodded.

"So, how can we track down this Ark?" said Alice, trying to sound normal. "I've seen docos and read stuff about people looking for it, like, forever. They even made movies about trying to find it. What makes you think we could find the damn thing? Got a map or something?"

Inside, he felt sure En-Ki would lead him in the right direction. He was sure finding the Ark was his quest. He felt confident he could do it.

"Yes, well sort of," said de Luz. "I'll show you tomorrow. For now, bottoms up — let's drink to the Ark!"

Honor stood up, walked through to her office and paced. It was 2 p.m. on Saturday. She opened the office door and found Viktoria behind her desk.

"Why are you still here Miss de Cock?"

"I'll be leaving now."

"Before you go, check vith Miss Vallins vhen I can see ze President. It is important."

"Yes ma'am."

Honor joined Karzoff back in her office.

"Make me a recording of zat conversation to play to ze President," she ordered.

"Now?"

"Yes, now, Karzoff!" she snapped.

There was a knock at the door. Honor irritably called out, "Come!"

Viktoria poked her head in. "He can see you now," she said.

"Good. Confirm I vill be zere in fife minutes."

"Yes ma'am. Then I'll be going."

Honor thought for a moment, then said: "Could you stay for a vhile to help Karzoff make extra copies of a recording?"

"Oh. Yes ma'am."

As Viktoria closed the door, Honor smirked at Karzoff. "Get me zat recording."

Tapping the flash drive on her bare knee, Honor sat impatiently outside the President's suite. Miss Vallins came out from the President's office, closed the door behind her and moved to her desk.

"He won't be long Agent Honor," the assistant said, smoothly. "He's in another meeting."

"Perhaps I should come back later," Honor said tersely, and stood.

Miss Vallins didn't reply — she was getting a message on her MCI. "Yes sir, I'll tell her," she said, and turned to Honor.

"He'll see you now Agent Honor, but he has only ten minutes before his next appointment. You'll need to be brief."

Honor blushed. She detested being given that sort of treatment.

The door to the President's office opened and a middle-aged, immaculately dressed woman carrying a black ostrich skin briefcase came out.

Honor stood, straightened her clothing and proceeded to the security checkpoint in front of the big double doors. A loud click followed the scan and she entered.

She didn't expect to find the President with company. The man stood when Honor approached.

"Agent Honor here heads up OTT — the Oceana Time Travel Division I was telling you about," the President was saying. "Honor, this is Gorrick Khan, CEO of the Zen Corporation."

The extremely refined-looking man, dressed in a tailored grey suit, white shirt and thin blue necktie, had close-cropped white hair, piercing blue eyes and stood six foot six.

"Pleased to meet you Agent Honor," he said, cordially.

She recognised the refined accent — Cambridge academic. And… hadn't Zen Corporation offered Karzoff a job a month or so ago? Taking his outstretched hand, she was a little taken aback by how cold it was.

"Mr Khan," she said.

"Call me Gorrick."

"Take a seat Honor," the President said, as she nodded. "I understand you have something urgent for my attention."

"It is a matter of ze highest security sir," she said, reservedly.

"Gorrick here will soon be in charge of government security," he said. "You'll need to get used to him as your new boss. May as well start now."

Honor's face froze. Gorrick sensed her displeasure. "No need to be concerned, Fanny," he said, reassuringly. "Nothing much will change. I very much look forward to working with you. The President has briefed me on your excellent efforts to date."

Honor succumbed to the charm.

After giving them a heads-up on her surveillance operation in Texas, along with her suspicion that Black Alice had returned from the future and been concealed by Secta and Hope, she played them the audio of the meeting between Professor de Luz, Secta, Hope and Black Alice.

When it was finished, Gorrick locked eyes with the President. "I believe the gravity of the situation calls for action, does it not?" he said, sternly.

A smile broke on Honor's face. At last she was gaining traction.

"I agree," the President said.

Gorrick pressed a small remote and a man of similar height and build to him, but with a clean-shaven head, entered the room.

"Agent Fanny Honor, this is Anu Set," Gorrick said. "He will take charge of the hunt for Black Alice."

Honor was devastated. "But Sir, I—"

The President cut her off. Staring at her he said, "I want that Ark and then I want Black Alice dealt with. Efficiently, this time. Do I make myself clear? That is why this man has been placed in charge." He looked at Set. "Neither Dr Secta or his sister should come to any harm. Let me be absolutely clear about that," he said. "They are more important to this government than anyone in this room — including me."

"Yes sir," Set confirmed, sharply, soldier-like. Then, eyes as cold as a shark's, he confirmed the order in monotone: "No harm to Dr Secta or his sister. Eliminate Black Alice after securing the Ark."

"That is correct," said the President, and turned back to Honor. "No expense will be spared to obtain the Ark," he said. "Dismissed, Agent Honor."

Rising from her seat she stood at attention and nodded at the President, then to Gorrick Khan, who got to his feet in a gentlemanly fashion to and acknowledge her. Her eyes met Set's, who was standing stationary. She shuddered. Even to a person as corrupt as Honor, Set seemed like evil incarnate.

Striding defiantly towards the door, she was stopped in her tracks by the President's voice. "Honor, Set will take the other office at OTT," he said. "I expect you to give him total cooperation."

Facing the door and seething she replied. "Copy zat sir."

As the doors closed gently behind her, the President made a steeple of his two index fingers, placed them on his chin and spoke earnestly. "No need to worry about Honor," he said. "She'll come around in due course. She's a control freak and your appointment, Set, threatens her to the core.

"The main problem is that she is jealous of Dr Secta's relationship with me. It goes without saying that relationship cannot continue if Secta is conspiring with Black Alice — and possibly with the Octagon. But I do wonder if Secta's motives may not be as they seem.

"I have known him a long time. He's a reasonable man — a man of science, and a brilliant one at that. No. There must be something else driving him, he's not a revolutionary. Set, make it your duty to find out what that is."

CHAPTER 4
EVANESCE THROUGH THE VEIL

THERE WERE EXPLOSIONS all around him and the ground rumbled and quaked with every blast. Above, the night sky was alight with the bright tails of tracer bullets, shot from drones parked in static hover over the small town. He was too hyped to be afraid. He crouched by the corner of a building and looked through the night vision scope of his Heckler Koch HK MP7A1 submachine gun at the street ahead.

The green world inside the scope seemed almost surreal. Movement. Was it what he was expecting? With every flash, he saw the shadow of it on the wall at the far end of the street. From the corner of his eye he saw more of his troops taking up positions opposite.

Then, out of nowhere, a teenager armed with an assault rifle made a run for it up the street.

He rose sharply and yelled at the top of his voice: "No!"

Hey! That voice isn't mine!

The boy ignored the warning and kept running, sticking to the shadows close to the buildings. But it didn't matter — he was running to his death.

Against his better judgement, cursing himself, he took off up the street after the boy. Ducking from alcove to recess, keeping to the shadows, he was gaining on him. Then he saw what he'd been dreading. From the shadow at the end of the street stepped a cyborg.

No sooner had the seven-foot machine stepped into the street than it raised its arm and fired. The sharp burst of fifty mm rounds sliced the boy in half.

What is this street? Where am I? Who am I?

A hail of bullets ensued, all of them aimed at the cyborg. His backup team had opened fire, but he knew from experience none of it would be effective against this awesome monster.

He was forced to duck back inside an alcove to avoid being hit by friendly fire. As he had anticipated, none of the fire impacted on the cyborg. It just kept coming, its weapon ready to fire at anything that moved. He knew staying still was the only way to avoid its sensors: knowledge gained from fighting them in another time.

Then a second cyborg stepped into the street. Any attempt to take them on would result in death. His men were retreating. He was on his own.

The first cyborg reached the boy's upper torso, bent down, picked it up and irreverently tossed it thirty feet away. It landed in a gory mess, close enough for him to see it wasn't a boy at all. It was a female collaborator from his last venture into the future.

"Nerdo!" he cried out in horror.

Immediately the cyborg's head snapped to glare in his direction, attracted by his voice. It started towards him. Now he was in real trouble.

"Alice!" a voice drummed in his head. "Al, wake up!"

The second cyborg followed the first. Now he was up against two of them.

A hand was shaking his shoulder. When he opened his eyes, he was relieved to find Hope's angelic face staring down at him.

"There you are," she said. "You've been screaming out in your sleep, mate."

Alice's hands were trembling and he was sweating profusely. "Ah damn," he said. "I'm having terrible nightmares, Hope."

Hope sat on the edge of the bed. "How long has this been going on?"

"Every night since I got back from the last event, so a couple of months. They're so graphic — I dunno if they're premonitions or something my mind's concocting out of stuff I've seen."

"What was this one about?"

"I was fighting cyborgs in the street and saw Nerdo get cut in half … it was terrible."

"Nerdo … the first nations girl with all the electronics skills who fought with you and Turk, right?"

"Yeah, it was awful. But it felt like I wasn't seeing through my own eyes."

"It might be what Turk is seeing? You guys were pretty close."

"I wonder if the same thing is happening for Secta … What time is it?" he added, swinging his legs out of bed.

"Just after 6 a.m.," said Hope, with a smile. "Time to get up. Mention it to Secta," she suggested. "It'd be interesting to see if he's experiencing similar dreams. Though knowing him, he might not admit it."

Al cruised into the kitchen in search of food. He opened the huge, double-door refrigerator and found a few slices of leftover pizza. They'd do fine. He put them in the microwave to re-heat.

Chewing on one piece, with the other in his hand, he wandered out through the open patio doors of the hacienda-style single-storey house to the swimming pool patio, where he found Secta and de Luz under a big beach umbrella. The professor looked up and chuckled at the sight of Alice, garbed only in his underpants, chewing on a slice of leftover pizza.

"Al," he smiled. "Good morning."

"Hey prof," Alice returned. "Get some rest?"

"Not really. Getting old — sleep comes at a premium. Never saw that coming!"

"Yeah, I get that," grinned Alice. "You get off the phone and notice the kids have all grown up."

Grabbing a coffee from the pot on the table, Al sat at the table beside the two men. Secta was so engaged in his reading he hadn't even noticed him. He looked up, surprised. "Oh, Alice!" he said. "Sleep well?"

"No actually," Al replied. "Ever since the last event I've been having seriously messed up dreams. Last one I reckon I might have been seeing through Turk's eyes. You seeing through Morri's?"

"No Alice, I'm not."

Al swung his bare feet up onto the table and sank lower in the chair. "Ugh. That's stuffed," he grumbled. "I was hoping it'd be the same for you."

"Al, I've proposed this to Secta," said de Luz, handing over a document. He placed a finger to his lips, reminding Alice they were being monitored. Alice nodded and started to read.

It was 10 p.m. in Sydney. Honor, Set and Karzoff were crammed like sardines into the small OTT monitoring room, listening intently to the conversation between Alice, Secta and the Professor.

"Good morning gentlemen," Hope was saying.

"Good morning gorgeous," de Luz replied. "Grab a coffee and take a chair. You know what?" he went on with a covert wink, "we've got the best waffles in America here in Waxahachie. Any takers?"

"Absolutely!" said Hope. "When does it open?"

"Twenty-four seven my dear," said de Luz.

"Ah, America," said Al. "Everything's 24/7. Excellent."

"You might need to change, Al," Hope suggested with a giggle.

"What?" said Alice, looking down at his undies. "Think I'm overdressed?"

"We need to know what's in that document," said Set.

"Ve should send Rees and Holman in to download everything on ze Professor's computer vhile zey're at breakfast," suggested Honor.

"Good thinking," the man agreed. "Make it so." Standing, he stretched his arms above his head. "This room is way too small," he complained.

"Why don't we just arrest the four of them now?" Karzoff asked.

"Because while we can spy on them we'll gain valuable intel," said Set, coldly. "We need to pick the right moment to make a move. The best scenario would be for Alice to lead us right to the Ark."

"Zen you can kill him — and take it!" Honor agreed.

Having capitulated to working with Set rather than opposing him, Honor found herself attracted to his wicked methodology, his impassive attitude and the inner violence she sensed in him. Karzoff, on the other hand, hadn't made up his mind. But one thing did seem obvious: when it came to emotions, Set and Honor were exactly alike: a pair of cold fish.

Walking from the car park to the Waffle House on the two-eighty-seven highway bypass, de Luz was talking. "I figure they'll be busy trying to crack the password on my home computer, so we'll have time to talk here," he said. "No way they could have the Waffle House bugged, and they won't be outside either. Secta, you wrote me a note about Al's meeting with this En-Ki being. Can you elaborate on it?"

"Hope has researched him," said Secta.

"Then fire away, young lady," de Luz replied.

"According to ancient Sumerian texts, the Sumerian god Anu was supreme Lord of the Sky, ruler of the Anunnaki people of the planet Nibiru, and the reigning titular head of the Sumerian family tree. He had two sons: En-Ki, Lord of the Earth and Waters, and En-Lil, Lord of the Air. The two brothers didn't get along. Critical to their rivalry — particularly from Earth's viewpoint — was the fact that En-Ki had been the first of the Anunnaki to hazard the trip to Earth to begin mining for gold.

"When En-Ki's efforts failed to produce gold in sufficient quantities, Anu sent En-Lil to take command. En-Lil commenced a revised program to mine deep within the Earth. Angered by the intrusion, En-Ki then experimented with Earth's primal inhabitants, creating man in his own image. En-Lil, outraged, seeks to destroy all En-Ki's creations. A battle between En-Lil and En-Ki with his humans ensues, 'til eventually Anu withdraws both of them from Earth and back to their home planet Nibiru."

De Luz stared out of the restaurant window, deep in thought.

"I'd be tempted to dismiss the whole story as myth, if it wasn't for Al's experience," Secta said.

"No, no, no, it can't be dismissed. I totally believe it!" said de Luz, turning back to them. "I've come across En-Ki and the Anunnaki in my own research, and read just about everything ever published by Zecharia Sitchin on the subject. Some of it is debatable, but much is incredibly insightful and well-grounded."

Hope asked, "So was En-Ki an alien?"

"That's the theory," confirmed de Luz. "But look, let me run you through how I think Al can unearth the Ark of the Covenant. It's quite simple actually," he added, pausing for effect. "Al goes back in time to, say, 587 BCE. That's when the Ark was last known for certain to be at Solomon's Temple. Al removes it, hides it, returns to now and we go and retrieve it ... voilà!"

Secta was staring at de Luz, the chunk of waffle on his fork suspended in mid-air. He put it down and wiped his mouth with a napkin. "You can't be serious, Vic?" he said, incredulously. "Physics for the most part repudiates travelling backwards in time."

"In Einstein's theory of general relativity, gravity can bend space-time," the Professor argued. "The bending of space-time through a wormhole travelling faster than the speed of light can be made to produce negative energy density at one end, moving matter in the opposite direction in time if pushed."

"You're talking about exotic matter," Secta said, buying into it. "The creation of a mini black hole and the dimensions ... so the Block universe theory of past, present and future all existing together at the same place in temporal time, by your formula, can be crossed?"

"Yes!" de Luz agreed, "after all, quantum physics theorizes that anything and everything is possible."

Hope chuckled. "So, in other words," she said, "If you can ask the question, there must be an answer. The paper you showed us this morning on colliding positrons — is that related to your idea of retrograded time?"

"Indubitably, my dear. My research proves that a positron collision in a particle accelerator can cause a tiny portal — a wormhole, if you like — to open to any time. Look," he added, as Secta opened his mouth to interrupt, "The reason physics repudiates reverse time travel is because they don't have Alice — or you, Secta, for that matter. I'm not trying to change the laws of physics, my friends. You've done it for me."

The statement hung in the air like the pungent aroma of freshly-brewed coffee, with each of them savouring it in their own way. He was absolutely right. No other scientific research had produced the means to reduce a human to atoms so they could be transported through a wormhole, forwards or backwards in time. Secta and Hope's process had, for the first time in history, cracked the concept of time travel right open.

"Let me get this straight," said Al. "Your research proves that by using a particle collider in a certain way you can open a wormhole to any given time. Is that right?"

"That is correct," the Professor affirmed.

"Yes, but it's just a hypothesis," said Secta. "It's not yet proven or physically tested — at least, I expect not. Vic?"

De Luz shrugged. "The calculations add up, my friend." He removed a notebook from his inside coat pocket opened it and displayed a page of formula to Secta, "See for yourself."

Secta took a sip of coffee and studied the figures.

Al looked out at the cars on the highway. To him the scientific debate had been a blur of mumbo jumbo. The big cerulean Texas sky promoted thoughts of the future dimension he'd returned from two months ago. He pictured the faces of Turk and Morri, and worried about Nerdo's safety. Was it a premonition or just a dream? He knew Turk and Morri would have to take on Animal, Gorrick and Zen. Could that have been what he'd seen? He had no way to know that Animal was on Turk's side after being deserted by Zen.

Alice recalled how Morri could see into the future. Perhaps he was capable of a similar thing: maybe he was psychic. He thought about how some of the ideas in lyrics he had written had come to fruition — might they be a form of premonition? Deep in thought, he watched a brown van pull into the car park and back into a space.

"What do you think, Alice?" Secta was asking. "Alice?"

"Oh. Sorry Secta," he said, snapping out of it. "I was just watching—"

"Vic's calculations look fine to us," Secta cut in. "We need to know if you'd be prepared to try it if it were possible to set up."

"What needs to happen?" Al asked.

"We need an operational particle accelerator for a start," said Secta, sighing. "The only one I know of is the Large Hadron Collider in Cern, on the Franco-Swiss border."

De Luz placed an extended index finder beside his nose and raised his bushy white eyebrows. "I have my own particle accelerator," he grinned. "That's why I've proposed this whole thing. I have secret access to Desertron — the Texas Super Collider."

"But that was never completed!" Secta exclaimed.

"Why do you think I stayed here after it was officially abandoned?" asked de Luz. "It was completed, completed in secret. I'll explain later. What's more important now is that we'll need some kind of certified relic from Jerusalem 587 BCE. It must be from exactly that year. When we collide it with positrons a wormhole will open to that time. It will stay open only a nanosecond, but during that time we use your procedure, Secta, to send Al through." He sat back in his chair, pleased with the concept.

"And ... how would I get back?" asked Al.

That threw the cat among the pigeons. While they looked at each other in dismay, Al looked back at the van outside the window and noticed something wrong — no-one had got out. He grabbed the notebook, scribbled and held it up for the others to read: *Is that van the same one we saw last night?*

They all looked round. De Luz nodded and delicately changed the subject. "Now," he drawled. "Wasn't that just the best waffle you've ever tasted?"

Honor was finishing up for the evening when Set came into her office. He stopped just inside the door. "Finished work?"

"Yes," she said, looking at him tiredly. "It has been a long day."

He moved closer. "They found nothing at the Professor's house."

"Nuzzing on his computer?" she queried.

"Get this," he said. "They were unable to crack the password. How competent is your man Rees?"

"How competent is Buddy Holman?" she snapped back. "I vould haff zought Homeland Security vould be better trained zan Rees."

"Well, it looks like we failed on both counts. But we did get a partial conversation of value."

She stopped what she was doing and glared at him, "Vhat do you mean, 'partial'?"

"It was recorded after Rees and Holman left the house."

"Are you telling me zere vas nobody on zem for ze whole time our men vere in ze house?"

"Yes."

Her face flushed. "Zat is ridiculous! Who ordered zat to happen? It vould not haff happened on my vatch!"

"Calm down," he said, dismissively. "It was just an oversight—"

"An oversight?" she snapped. "Ve do not haff ze margin for error for oversights, Set!"

There was pregnant pause while both of them considered whether to pursue the argument or not. Honor broke the ice.

"Play it to me."

He led her out of the office and into the new, larger, operations room set up specifically for the case. They sat down and Set hit 'play'.

"Vic's calculations look fine to us. We need to know if you would be prepared to try it if it were possible to set up…"

They listened to the rest of the recording, then sat back. "That's all we have, but then again, we don't need much more, do we?" said Set, smugly. "We have their plan."

A grin broke on Honor's otherwise sullen face — she was getting excited. It was a significant breakthrough.

"How does de Luz haff access to ze Desertron?"

"I don't know. I thought all that was left of it was a thirty-mile hole in the ground and a bunch of buildings."

Honor was tapping keys. "Ah, here ve are," she said. "Ze Desertron Superconducting Super Collider project vas cancelled in 1993 due to budget problems. A chemical company bought ze property and facilities in 2012, against some opposition from ze local community." She looked up. "Zere is no evidence zat it is operational, or even partly operational."

"So, it would have to be a black project to exist."

"Must be. Ze name 'de Luz' comes up as ze senior scientist for ze project in '92 – 93, but nussing else."

"I'll get onto my friends at Homeland Security. Perhaps they will tell us more."

CHAPTER 5
ASSIDUITY

I**N HIS SWIMMERS**, Alice was sprawled on a deckchair by the pool like a lounge lizard soaking up rays when Hope joined him. She removed her robe, ready for a swim.

"Aren't you cooking in this heat?" she asked.

He sat up and peered at her over the top of his sunnies. She looked amazing in a brief white bikini.

"Nup, love the heat," he said. "Didn't realise you had such a tasty bod," he added, with a cheeky grin.

She drew him a look, finished tying her long blonde hair back and dived into the pool.

Secta came out and sat in a director's chair under an umbrella. He wasn't fond of sunlight.

"Why don't you get some rays on that scrawny body of yours, Secta?"

"No thanks Alice, I prefer a mortuary complexion to melanoma," Secta replied. "Vic's still on the phone. He's talking to his contacts at the Smithsonian. He's actually managed to secure a fragment of a wooden jug that was unearthed under the Temple Mount in Jerusalem. It's been C-14 dated at 587 BCE. So, things are moving along quite nicely."

"That's great," Al said, rubbing more tanning oil into his thighs. "But I don't fancy spending the rest of my days back in Old

Testament times. I reckon your time would be best spent working on how to get me back."

"Don't worry Alice, I'm on it."

Hope climbed out of the pool, collected her towel from the back of a chair and dried off. De Luz joined them, carrying a bunch of white cue cards. He sat, and held up the first one for them to read. *I have secured the sample. It will arrive tomorrow.*

Then he swapped it with a second card, which read: *We have to accept they know our plan re the collider. The next card said: Worried they'll try to stop us. Ideas?*

Secta waved him closer. He took a card and a pen from de Luz, scribbled and held it up. *Talk about something else, it said. I have an idea.*

"Did you enjoy your swim, Hope?" said de Luz, as Secta scribbled on another card. He held it up: *Set up a false date to use the collider and plan to do it earlier. A.S.A.P.*

Alice signalled for the pen and cards while Hope and de Luz kept up an innocuous conversation about the pool. *You still don't know how to get me back!* he scrawled.

"You know those dreams you've been having, Al?" Hope said. He nodded. "D'you think you can format them before you go to sleep?"

"What, like set the scene then dream it?" Al asked.

"Yes — kind of giving yourself a scripted dream."

"Hmm, don't know," he said, watching her jotting something down on a card. She passed it over. *What if you could talk to En-Ki? Maybe he can bring you back?*

Alice quickly scratched a reply: *Brilliant! I'll try it tonight.*

"Maybe we should give it a try," Hope said aloud, winking at them all.

At dusk, while they were sitting around the pool drinking margaritas, de Luz held up a card: *We need to talk. I'll say we're going to dinner at Catfish Plantation, but we'll go somewhere else. If we move quickly I'll be able to lose them. Nod if you agree.*

They all nodded.

"I'll take y'all for a Texan treat for dinner tonight," he said out loud. "A little restaurant called Catfish Plantation. It offers a veritable corn-u-copia of delicacies."

"Sounds excellent!" said Hope, enthusiastically.

"It's casual, so no need to change. We'll leave in around 15 minutes. Okay?"

Back in Sydney, Honor was already behind her desk when Set entered with Gorrick. She rose to her feet when she saw him come in.

"Good morning," she said, amicably. "Please, take a seat." The three of them sat at the small lounge setting in her office.

"I've asked Gorrick here so we can formulate a plan to counter what our friends over in Texas have come up with," said Set.

"Zat sounds sensible," Honor agreed, relaxing back in her chair and casually crossing her legs.

"We know what they are planning," Set went on. "I've already briefed Gorrick and the President."

Honor scowled at him as though he'd just farted. How dare they go behind my back, she thought. Despite her obvious discontent, Set continued. "We need to establish exactly when they will use the collider," he said.

Honor sat forward. "I zink ve should arrest zem now," she said. "Ve do, after all, know zeir plans. Besides, surely ze U.S. Government will not permit use of ze collider?"

"We don't want to arrest them, Honor," Gorrick interrupted. "It's in our interests for Alice to lead us to the Ark."

"We have already cleared the use of the collider with the U.S.," Set added.

"It is operational zen?" Honor asked.

"Yes."

Again, she hadn't been informed. It was driving her mad. "Vhy are ve haffing zis meeting?" she huffed. "Your plan has obviously already been implemented!"

"We're here to brief you, Honor," Set replied, stony faced.

Honor realised she had no choice but to toe the line. "Very vell," she said. "Vhat else is zere to decide?"

"We need to decide on a course of action," Set replied.

"Zen surveillance must be increased so ve can determine zeir launch date. Zat must be ze priority."

Gorrick and Set nodded in agreement.

De Luz looked into the side mirror at the surveillance van, about ten car lengths behind his Pajero. "Here we go!" he said, turning sharply into a gas station forecourt and waiting for the van to go past. Once he saw the taillights light up he sped through the gas station onto a back road. He took back street after back street for the next twenty minutes, until they arrived at Dallas Highway.

Minutes later the maître d' of Campuzano's Fine Mexican Food Restaurant was ushering them to a reserved table. The manager, Emilio — an old friend of de Luz's — brought the out-of-towners a complimentary pitcher of margarita.

"Okay," said de Luz, once they'd ordered. "Provided you can satisfy yourselves about getting Al back, I'll be ready to access the Desertron on April 30th."

"Exactly two weeks from now," said Hope.

"Yes, at midnight. It'll take approximately two hours to complete the process. I suggest we let the narks think we'll be using it at 5 a.m. on May 1st."

They all nodded agreement.

"Aside from the obvious — determining how Alice is going to return — we'll need a cochlear translator microchip and a new batch of serum," said Secta.

"What … just like that, you're gonna build a translator implant?" Al questioned. "And wait — how will that help me talk to other people?"

"Don't worry, Al," Hope smiled. "Secta's been thinking about this for years … and I expect the implant will include an auto interpreter that converts your words to Latin."

"Latin?"

"Yes, most everybody in Jerusalem at that time spoke Hebrew, Latin, Coptic, Aramaic or Greek."

Al was beginning to feel more and more confident that this was the right path for his quest.

"Are you alright with all this, Alice?" Secta asked.

"Yeah," he said. "It feels like the happening direction."

"Great," de Luz said, emphatically. "I've got everything you'll need, Secta."

Through the window beside their table, they saw the surveillance van pull in.

"Here they are," de Luz announced. "Let's give them what they want to hear."

Honor and Set were in the OTT surveillance operations room, wearing panicked faces. The Texas surveillance team had lost their quarry, meaning they might have blown their cover.

"Do you suppose zey lost zem on purpose?" said Honor. "Zey've gone to a completely different restaurant!"

"I don't know," said Set. "But look — it doesn't matter. We've got them now." He increased the volume, highlighting clinking plates, rattling cutlery, footsteps and the general hum of conversation. Then the focus narrowed and they recognised Alice's voice.

"This is the best Mexican tucker I've ever had."

"Zat's Alice," Honor said sharply, as though she was in control of the directional microphone. "Damn, zey haff already finished zeir meal. Vhat haff ve missed?"

"So, when's D-Day?" Al's voice again.

"Zis is it!" whispered Honor, hoarsely. They listened intently.

"I will have the collider ready at precisely 5 a.m. on May 1st."

"Two veeks' time," Honor whispered covertly, as though the quarry might overhear her.

Set nodded affirmative.

"I'll need to build a translation device so Alice can understand and speak Latin and Hebrew."

"Was that Secta?" said Set. "Can he do that?"

"Yes, zat vas him. And yes, he can," she affirmed, focusing on the receiver. But the conversation had wandered back to Mexican food.

"How will Alice return?" said Set, with a frown. "Did we miss that?"

"Zey must haff ze answer, otherwise zey vould not risk sending him," said Honor.

Set knew she was right, but it didn't make him feel any better. There were no guarantees that Alice would succeed, and even if he did, what was to stop him returning to a secret location where he couldn't be found? He needed better answers — and he needed them fast.

Alice climbed into bed that night determined to contact En-Ki. He'd discussed it with Hope and she'd come up with a way to help him focus his mind through meditation. It was going to be difficult — he had no visual means of reference to concentrate on, just the memory of the glowing orb and the voice. But being a musician, he felt confident he could home in on the unique tones and intonations he remembered.

He lay on his back, staring at the ceiling, and concentrated. He clearly recalled the voice saying: "I have been with you all of your life. Manipulating your space-time continuum, leading you to this moment. You have a particular purpose ... a particular purpose ... a particular purpose..." Gently, he drifted off to sleep.

Early next morning a courier delivered a small package to de Luz. He took it into the living room, where Secta and Hope were busy working. Opening the package, he took out a flat metal container, inside which was a small plastic zip-bag that contained a tiny fragment of wood. Holding it up to the light, he said: "Not much of it, but it'll do just fine."

Secta came over. "You wouldn't want to sneeze," he said. "You'd blow it away. Gosh, it looks just like a chip off any old block of wood."

"It won't be coming out of the plastic bag," said de Luz. "There's a note. It says 'certified 580 to 587 BCE'. This little beauty came from a dig at the Dome of the Rock in Israel, where the most significant finds were about 120 metres to the southeast side. Pottery fragments from the 8th and 7th centuries BCE, animal bones and charred olive pits. Part of a wooden juglet — that's where our piece comes from.

"We know the date's accurate because the timber is from a fast-growing tree indigenous to Jerusalem at that time, now extinct."

"Wow," said Hope, staring at it. "We're lucky to get such a valuable artefact."

"They owed me one," shrugged de Luz. "I've done a lot of freebies for them over the years."

Al wandered over wearing only his underpants, scratching his head and yawning. He'd just woken up. "Morning," he groaned, sleepily. "What's up?"

"The artefact we need has arrived," said Hope, excitedly.

Al peered at it. "Sure they could spare it?" he quipped. "Looks like a splinter!"

"It's all we need," said de Luz with a smile.

"How did it go last night?" Hope asked, pouring a cup of coffee and handing it to Al.

"I don't remember seeing or talking to En-Ki, but one thing I know for certain," he said. "I will be shown the way back. It's more like a feeling than anything else. Pretty much like the feeling that I'm on the right path with the quest, know what I mean? Now. The big question. Is there anything to eat?"

CHAPTER 6
AUTEM CORNU ET ORATIONIS

THE BIG DAY arrived quickly. With only a few hours to go before Al was to be dematerialized, the three scientists were making final preparations. Alice was on the lounge, reading a magazine.

"Alice, can you come here for a moment?" Secta called from the room he'd commandeered as a lab. Al ambled through. He hadn't been in the lab before, and was astounded by all the scientific equipment. Secta was sitting behind a computer, and looked up when Alice entered. "I've made the translation chip," he said. "I'll need to implant it in your mastoid. It works like the organic cochlear stem-cell implant Turk and the others had in the future. Remember?"

"Yeah the OSCI," said Al. "How could I forget?" He sat on the edge of the desk. "Will it hurt?" The question sounded pathetic, even to himself.

"It'll sting a bit, but only for a few seconds," said Secta, standing, a small syringe in his grasp. "Hope!" he called. "Can you give me a hand?"

Hope came in from the room next door. "Got it done?" she asked.

"Yes, finally," he said. "I'll need you to help with the implantation."

"Just relax Alice," said Secta, as he and Hope crowded him. "Hold his ear forward," he added, to Hope. "Good, now..." He inserted the thick needle into the mastoid bone behind the ear, pushing hard. Alice grimaced, but it was over quickly and once Secta removed the needle the pain reduced hugely. "There," said Secta. "Done. And…" he went on, going back to his computer and typing in some data. "… It's activated. You won't feel anything weird, Alice, but when I speak in a language you wouldn't normally know, you will understand — plus you will automatically reply in the same language. Let's give it a try … Comment tu te sens?"

"Je me sens bien merci," said Alice. "But — you were speaking in English."

"No, he spoke to you in French," said Hope. "And you answered him in French, too."

"Wow, I can speak French?"

"More than that Alice," said Secta. "I've programmed thirty-two languages you'll be able to speak and understand."

"How the stuff does that work?"

"It interfaces with the temporal lobe for hearing, then the speech comprehension part of your brain, then the parietal lobe for language comprehension. Then the whole package is simply networked to Broca's area for speech production, all in the wink of an eye." Secta beamed.

"Easy enough for you to say," said Al. "Did you leave enough occipital room for brains?" They chuckled. "It's brilliant, Secta," Al went on. "How long will it work for?"

"Oh, a hundred years or so," said Secta, breezily. "I can update more languages in the future. It's got capacity for around two hundred, but I ran out of time.

"Oh, I also added a little program that allows you to search a preprogramed database of everything I could find about Jerusalem in 587 BCE, plus a limited Wikipedia database. You access it by asking yourself a question. For instance, if you think the name 'Nebuchadnezzar' it'll download a Wikipedia file on him direct into your memory. Now, I think Hope also has something for you."

Al was blown away. He'd always known Secta was a genius but the development of the translator was the crunch. It's no wonder he's so prized by Oceana, he thought. Glad he's on my side now.

Hope took a syringe from the top pocket of her denim jacket.

"Not another injection," Al complained.

"The problem is, mate, when you're dematerialized everything that's not organic will be left behind," said Hope.

"Yes, I left two of my fillings in the chair when I went through," Secta said with a chuckle.

"You'll need to put a marker on the Ark before you bury it, so we can detect it in the future," Hope told him, going on to explain that the marker she'd created was an infused radioactive gold nanoparticle coated with silica. It would be placed inside a sheath made of Alice's own extra cellular matrix, so that once inside his body it would be safe from attack by his immune system. Its organic makeup meant it wouldn't be expelled during the dematerialization process, plus Alice's own cells would mask it from detection.

Once injected into Alice's earlobe, it would feel like a grain of rice. To extract it he just needed to make a small incision, then squeeze the grain free. Being radioactive, the marker would last some five thousand years. Hope and Secta planned to use an isotopic labelling detection device to find it.

"It's basically the same as the ILDD I used to find you last time," said Secta. "It detects the cyclotonic resonance of the marker."

"I just need a little of your blood to create the matrix sheath," said Hope. "Then I'll come back to inject the marker into your earlobe."

Al's mouth twisted. "Okay Vampira," he grinned. "Suck away."

Hope took a vial of Al's blood.

"I'm beginning to feel like a bloody pin cushion," he grumbled. "What else?"

"Just the insertion of the marker from me," said Hope. "Secta will have to inject you with the serum later on."

Al sat silently in Secta's lab, running over what lay ahead. The injections had stimulated memories of what he'd previously been though, and those memories triggered questions like will my body be able to cope with this? He was beginning to feel like a lab rat. He had no real assurances of being able to return from 587 B.C. He had placed himself firmly in the lap of the gods — literally if this En-Ki was who Hope thought he was. To the others he seemed to be trusting that En-Ki would provide him a return link, but it wasn't unequivocal. His thoughts were interrupted when de Luz came into room.

"Al, how are you doing?" the big man asked.

"Alright," said Al. "Just a bit anxious, I suppose."

"I expect so," said de Luz. "I'd be anxious too if I was about to travel in time."

"Ah, it's not the travelling bit that concerns me, Vic," Al replied. "It's the return journey. I'm worried it might be a one-way trip. And if that's the case there wouldn't be any point to it."

The professor moved to the window and stared up at the starry firmament. "Do you doubt that En-Ki will provide you with a portal?" he asked, and turned back to Alice.

"I just don't know whether I was dreaming or not. Sometimes it's tough to distinguish between a vivid dream and whatever."

De Luz walked over to Al and put a hand on his shoulder. "I think maybe you're doubting yourself," he said. "You need to trust your intuition, Al. If you have doubts, call it off. We're relying on your judgement. You're the one at risk here."

Al nodded. The professor was right.

"Look Al," de Luz went on. "I don't know if you're aware of it, but there is such a thing as the fifth dimension. We found indirect evidence of it in Desertron. The theory goes that the result of a collision of subatomic particles is that a graviton escapes from the fourth dimension, leaking into a five-dimensional bulk. In 1993 Gerard Hooft speculated that the fifth dimension is really the fabric of space-time."

"Mate," said Al, "You're speaking a language even my implant can't understand."

"Sorry Al," laughed the professor. "I get carried away. Look, in short, I believe En-Ki may exist in the 5th dimension, and because Secta experimented with you using the holographic space-time principle, you can connect with it ... you see? I don't think you should doubt yourself. This is not some sort of dream aberration, Al. I really believe it is scientifically valid."

"All right Vic, I can grasp some of what you're saying," said Alice. "Like there could be a whole other world around us, just in a dimension we can't see."

"Yes, yes, exactly, um ... quite possibly."

"And that this dude En-Ki might well be in it."

"Perhaps ... perhaps so."

It seemed to make sense to Alice. He relaxed. Maybe it hadn't been a dream after all ... maybe he really had connected with the 5th dimension.

Sydney. 1pm. Gorrick and Set were having lunch at the Hokkaido Japanese restaurant on Loftus Street, just around the corner from Oceana HQ. It was a quiet little piece of Japan, featuring timbered ceilings, wood panel partitioning and sandstone walls, all hidden away in a city basement. There were no other customers — few could afford to eat at high-end restaurants these days. Formerly, up-market restaurants in the city were kept fat by the lunchtime patronage of local businesspersons. But the economic recession otherwise termed the great reset, had sapped all expense accounts, leaving lean pickings and plenty of closures.

A pretty Japanese waitress in a kimono served the two men warm sake. Neither of them showed her any courtesy.

"Alice seriously obstructed our operation in the post-Seven-Year-War dimension," Gorrick was saying. "We cannot afford to let him do it again in this dimension, or our plans will fail to materialise.

"With our current international strategic influence over governments, in twenty years' time we will be in a position to initiate the War. Alice must be stopped if it is to go to plan. And it is essential that we have the Ark."

Set took a slow sip of sake, savouring the taste. He nodded. "There is only one recourse," he said, flatly. "I must follow him into the past, kill him, and plant the Ark for us to exhume. Is there knowledge of the Arc in the future?"

"No," Gorrick confirmed.

"Hmm, that's odd."

"Can any of the Oceana agents be trusted to assist?"

"No. I suspect everyone."

Gorrick looked at him for a long silent moment. "Right," he eventually said. "You know what to do." He smiled superficially, like a politician. Throughout the conversation, neither man had blinked.

"Desertron was reported cancelled back in 1993, but in reality, it has been secretly in operation ever since," de Luz was in full tour guide mode as they walked into the drab, grey main building. "It's the largest particle accelerator in the world, three times larger than the one in Cern. The circumference is eighty-seven point one kilometres with an energy of twenty TeV per proton, whereas the Large Hadron Collider in Cern is twenty-seven kilometres with an energy of six point five TeV per proton."

"Why is it kept secret?" Hope asked.

"The public were worried that a misdirected particle collision could open a black hole that would devour Texas and the world," de Luz chuckled. "But it hasn't so far!" he added, smiling at his own joke. "How did you get on with the marker?"

"Al decided we needed backup, so we put one in each earlobe," said Hope, as they stopped at a security door. De Luz peered into the retinal scanner and the door slid open, revealing a small elevator.

"Alice," said Secta, smirking, "You realise that this time you won't enter someone else's mind?"

"Uh-huh," said Al, warily.

"Well, just like when you arrived back last time, you'll materialise in Jerusalem naked," the scientist sniggered. "We can't send your clothing with you."

"That's great Secta!" Alice cracked. "Let's just hope I don't arrive in the middle of a red light district at happy hour!"

"I'm sure you'll be a crowd pleaser no matter where you land," Hope said, with a wry grin.

The elevator stopped at level eight underground, a depth of one hundred and seventy-four feet.

"How sure are you pencil pushers that this'll work?" Al asked breezily as they stepped out.

"The math says it will," said de Luz, leading them across a narrow corridor and through a door to the central operations complex.

"Yeah well, even Einstein made mistakes," Al countered.

They stopped at a wall of monitors. Secta placed his little black bag on the bench and turned to the worried time traveller, placing a comforting hand on his shoulder.

"I got you back last time, Alice," he said. "I promise I will not let you down on this trip. I wouldn't even be considering this if I had any doubts."

De Luz sat down at the XC-70 supercomputer console and began punching in data.

"Just twenty years ago it would have taken fifteen to twenty technicians to operate this thing," he said. "Now it only takes only one — and all I'm doing is activating the software program. I'm just a spectator with a couple of buttons to push."

Secta stood behind de Luz and rested his hands on his shoulders. "Explain to us in layman's terms how this thing works professor."

"Oh, on a basic level, particle accelerators produce a beam of charged particles — protons — and electric fields are used to speed up and increase the energy of the beam, steered and focused by magnetic fields," said de Luz, all in one breath. "The particle source provides the particles to be accelerated, and electronic fields spaced around the accelerator create radio waves that accelerate the protons in bunches.

"We direct them at a fixed target — in our case the sliver from the juglet — and the collision results in a minuscule wormhole linked to the time of that target — again, in our case, 587 BCE. In that nanosecond, we fire Alice's atoms through the wormhole using a device I created and named Zion. So..." he hit a few more keys, then looked up into Alice's perfectly round-eyed stare.

"Uh – a little more basic, maybe?" said Alice.

De Luz laughed. "It's simple," he said. "The protons zoom around the pipe, accelerating until I press the button. Then they collide with the target and open the wormhole."

"How do you know when to trigger the collision?"

"Good question, Al. And the answer is: it's in the math. I'm uploading that right now. Then I press this button to release the protons, and this other button to release both the target and you. The software and the math do all the hard work," he finished.

"Sounds great," Alice croaked, bravely.

Secta turned to him. "We'll use the ILDD to detect you when you return," he said. "We'll rendezvous close to your exit point. Just make sure you're in Jerusalem. Any questions?"

"How do I get inside the Zion?"

De Luz swivelled in his chair and pointed. "From that booth over there," he said.

"Looks like a vocal booth," Al chuckled nervously. "Well, I've been in plenty of those!"

"Great!" said de Luz. "I've heard you're an amazing singer ... Well, I'm done here. All the calculations have been entered and none were rejected, so the computer is happy with the formula."

"That's comforting," Alice joked.

De Luz look back at Secta, "Time for you to do your thing, my friend!"

"I'll give you a hug now, rather than when you're naked," Hope joked. She embraced Alice. "Basium autem nunc?" she said in Latin. Alice smiled and gave her a kiss.

"Autem cornu et orationis," he replied.

Then he shook hands with Secta and de Luz.

"If I'm not back in a week, cancel my cable TV subscription, will you?" Al joked.

"Okay," said Secta. "Kit off and into the booth."

De Luz turned back to the computer.

Alice stripped off. Hope looked at his muscular body.

"You should have been a body builder," she said.

"Built this one," he quipped back.

Secta opened his black bag and took out a syringe. "Last one, Alice," he said, injecting the serum into a deltoid and leading Alice to the booth. For a moment before he entered, they locked eyes. Alice nodded slightly and gave his signature wave. "Chaa!" he said, stepping inside.

Secta turned to Hope "What did Alice say to you?" he asked.

"Autem cornu et orationis," she said, teary-eyed. "Roughly translated: on a wing and a prayer."

CHAPTER 7
WORLDS COLLIDE

A WHIRRING SOUND commenced as soon as the Professor launched the collider program. The room lights dimmed automatically, making the room feel even more like mission control at NASA during a launch.

The light in the booth allowed Alice's face to be seen from outside through the small plexi-glass window in the door. Hope glanced away from the monitors to check on him — in a blink he disappeared. She'd been expecting it, but she was still shocked. "He's gone," she reported dolefully.

Secta's gaze was transfixed on the array of meters and dials on the control dashboard. "Yes, Vic is loading him into Zion now," he said, unemotionally.

Hope was wringing her hands — the big moment was approaching. The protons were zooming, Alice had been dematerialized into atoms, any second now the computer would trigger an event that would change world history. For the first time ever, someone would be sent back in time.

Hope wasn't sure if it was the hum rising in pitch or her anxiety building up, but she felt like a fuse had been lit and had reached the dynamite. She braced for the explosion.

"Here we go!" announced de Luz, excitedly. The sound reached an ear-piercing crescendo and a single green light changed to red. All sound ceased. The absolute, anechoic silence was deafening.

De Luz slowly swivelled around in his chair. Beaming, he announced: "It's done. He's gone." He wiped away a tear. "My friends," he declared, "It worked like a charm." He jumped up and pulled Secta and Hope into an enthusiastic hug — it was as though they'd just landed the first astronaut on Mars — it was in fact just as epoch-making.

The jubilation ended suddenly when four men burst into the room, three of them brandishing guns. The most unassuming of them and the only one unarmed — a nuggetty, round-faced, middle-aged man with a receding hairline, wearing a black business suit and tie — spoke with a squeaky Aussie accent, saying: "I am Agent Rees, SSD. This is Agent Holman and his colleagues from U.S. Homeland security. I advise you to co-operate. Agent Holman, if you will proceed..."

Holman would have looked more comfortable on a horse punching cows. "Y'all bein' arrested under provision 1021 - 1022 of the terrorist act," he drawled in a strong Texan accent. "That means detention without trial."

"You were on the plane from Sydney!" barked Secta, eyeballing Rees. "You work for Honor? Then you must know I'm an employee of the Oceana Government, and we are on a mission authorised by the President of Oceana. I demand to speak with him!"

"I'm also on mission from the President, Doctor Secta," the little man spat. "And I'm afraid it supersedes yours."

"Shut this thing down, Professor," Holman ordered, and turned to his men. "Cuff 'em," he said.

The smell came first. Alice figured it was manure — and he was right. He was spreadeagled facedown in the dirt next to a huge dollop of it. He rolled over, sat up, looked at his hands and his naked body to make sure all the bits were in place, and chuckled to himself. "Happening," he said, nodding his appreciation.

It was night and there was no one around. A stone's throw away he could see half a dozen mud brick houses, through the windows of which candles were dimly burning. He figured he was on a farm. Off in the distance he could make out enough lights to qualify a small town.

Something touched him on the back and he flinched. Still sitting, he swivelled around quickly to find the provider of the dung: a skinny and unimpressed goat. Then he heard laughter, female laughter. The door to a hut was flung open and a young girl breezed out, carrying a pail. Alice realised she was coming to milk the goat. He didn't want to stand up and give her the full Monty, so he rolled over and played dead. The goat sniffed his bum. "Shoo! Get lost!" he whispered harshly, but it stayed put. A yelp erupted from the girl and footsteps came running towards him. They stopped just short of him. He could hear her panting.

"Mamma, Papa, come quick!" she cried. "Bring a blanket!"

The sound of her sweet voice seemed to resound for miles. Then he heard more footsteps and when they stopped, felt a blanket thrown over him.

"Did you see him? He is a giant!" the girl said.

"Adam!" called a man's voice, "Come give me a hand!"

More feet came running. Hands took arms and legs, picked Alice up off the ground and carried him inside. They laid him on an animal hide mat next to the hearth, which was alight and topped by bubbling pots. He could feel the warmth of the fire and smell the food. He decided to keep faking unconsciousness and listening to what they had to say.

Adam spoke first. Alice estimated from his voice that he was probably late teens.

"Who do you think he is?" he said. "Why is he naked?"

"Perhaps he escaped from the enemy." That was Papa.

"Maybe he is the enemy!" Adam snapped.

"Don't be stupid Adam." The girl's voice. "That does not make any sense."

"What would you know Sabrina? You're only a girl."

"I am a year older than you Adam, so hold your tongue!"

"Stop fighting you two," came a voice that could only be mother's. "Our guest does not want to hear you. Do you, sir?" she nudged him gently with a toe. Since she clearly knew he was awake and listening, Alice, maintaining his modesty with the blanket, sat up.

"Thank you for taking me in," he said. "I'm Alice. I'm not your enemy."

Dressed in a light brown linen, poncho-like shawl with a veil covering her head, Mama was in her late thirties. Papa's more weather-beaten face put him around his mid-forties. Adam had long, flowing black hair and sharp facial features with a square chin. He reminded Alice of one of his road crew — rough and tumbled. In sharp contrast, Sabrina's long brown hair was tied back to show an elegant neck, delicate bone structure and the bluest eyes Alice had ever seen. The angelic face came with an hourglass figure that would have made a catwalk model of her in his time.

Papa offered Alice a hand up, then showed him to the eating area — cushions round a square mat on the floor.

"Will you break bread with us?" Mama asked.

"I'd be honoured," Alice replied, bowing, keeping up his best manners.

Sabrina slipped away and returned with a cream coloured caftan. She handed it to him, then took him by the hand and led him to a small room.

"You may dress in here," she said, shyly, and left.

The room was simple — bare floor, with four basic sleeping mats. Nothing in the way of décor apart from a slip of fabric across the empty window-hole. He changed into the caftan and wandered back to join the others.

Sabrina made room for him beside her. "Perhaps a pair of papa's sandals will fit you," she said, looking at his bare feet.

"You're too generous," said Alice, smiling. "I don't want to abuse your hospitality."

Mama handed him a chunk of bread and pointed to the dishes in front of them. He recognised hummus, and lamb or goat. Copying the others, he scooped up a little hummus with the bread, and knowingly picked up some meat with the fingers of his right hand to make a kind of proto-kebab.

"Are you from Jerusalem, Alice?" asked Adam.

"No, from Athens originally," he replied. It was the answer he'd devised with Hope. They'd sorted out a complete profile for him, in case he had to explain his background.

"You speak excellent Hebrew," Papa said. "But if you prefer your native tongue we will speak in Latin."

"Not necessary," Alice answered. "I can speak many languages. In another time, I was a translator for traders."

"Not a soldier?" Adam queried, looking at Alice's toned physique.

"No, these days I'm just a traveller."

"So. Why does this Greek traveller arrive, naked, on our doorstep?" Papa asked.

"Now, that's not so easy to explain," said Alice. "The last thing I remember I was dressed and carrying everything I owned in a sack over my shoulder. I heard a shout and felt a blow ... and that's it."

"You were robbed?" Papa asked.

Alice felt the back of his head with his fingers, putting on a good act. "I presume so," he said. "I was hit from behind."

"There is too much of that around lately," Papa complained. "Far too many deserters from Nebuchadnezzar's Babylonian army."

"And escaping prisoners," Adam added. "But Alice would know that. He probably had to pass the army to get here."

Alice recognised a loaded statement when he heard one. "Yes, I travelled through the Babylonian lines with a Greek emissary," he said. "We parted because his journey was to finish at the palace of Zedekiah, and I had no wish to go there." Thank God for those rehearsed answers.

"Please do not mention that name in this house," said Papa, grimly. "He is not a favourite of the people."

"He will be dealt with," Adam growled.

"Mind your loose tongue, my son," Papa reprimanded.

"Perhaps I could ask you for one last favour," interrupted Alice. "Could you help me find somewhere to stay tonight?"

The family exchanged a look. Mama spoke up. "You are welcome to sleep in the barn until you find lodgings," she said.

Alice was relieved. He doubted there would be a motel nearby.

"Once again, I am in your debt," he said. "Thank you."

"Babalonii!" The shout from outside woke Al with a start. He rolled out of the hay bed he'd rustled up and rushed out of the barn.

The brightness of the early morning sun dazzled him for a moment, but when his vision cleared he discovered what the commotion was about. Two chariots were driving fast towards the houses making a huge racket, kicking up a wall of dust behind them. Adam was standing outside the house looking very anxious, spear in hand, his father beside him.

The approaching chariots captivated Alice, he felt like he was on the set of some blockbuster Hollywood historical epic, like Cleopatra or Ben Hur.

The first of the three-horse chariots closed on them. It had a bearded charioteer with a warrior beside him, armed with a sword and a bow. The warrior had a striking black beard, square cut at chest level and curly. He was wearing a short-sleeved tunic with a thick belt, and an orange and white fez-like hat. He looked angry to Alice, like an Assyrian warrior he'd seen in history books and on the History Channel. The horses were covered in colourful rigging and armour.

A loud cry from the charioteer brought them to a stop. The second chariot pulled up behind the first. A wall of dust descended, making the horses sneeze and veiling the passengers in a fine red powder.

The warrior in the first chariot handed his bow and arrows to the charioteer who, once the dust had settled, stepped down from the rear of the chariot. The charioteer kept him covered with a drawn bow and arrow, while the man strode arrogantly to Adam and Papa.

"King Nebuchadnezzar II orders you to bring out your women and gold!" he snapped in Aramaic.

Neither Adam nor Papa understood the language. But Alice did.

When no answer came the warrior drew his sword and repeated the order more fiercely.

"King Nebuchadnezzar II orders you to bring out your women and gold!"

Alice took a step towards him and the charioteer fired. *Thunk!* The arrow sank into the ground just an inch from Alice's toes, stopping him in his tracks.

The warrior was tall and well built, with cut arms and a powerful chest. He rushed Papa, a much smaller man, grabbed him around the neck and forced him hard onto his knees.

Adam twitched, clearly thinking of his spear.

"No! Adam!" Alice yelled, "They'll kill everyone! He's asking for your women and gold."

The warrior raised his sword, threatening to strike Papa, and eyeballed Adam.

Adam dropped the spear on the ground.

Alice spoke in Aramaic. "There is no need to hurt anyone here. These people do not understand your language. They speak Hebrew, Latin or Greek."

"Tell them to bring out their women and gold or I will kill the old man!" the warrior commanded.

Alice knew if they got the women and the gold they'd kill them anyway. Before he could speak, Mama emerged, weeping, with her hands half-raised in surrender.

"She is too old!" the warrior growled. "Give me gold!"

"He wants gold," Alice told her. She looked at him helplessly.

"They have nothing," Alice told the warrior. "No gold. These are poor farming people."

The big warrior brought the sword down on Papa's neck, beheading him. Mama instantly collapsed. Adam stood frozen in shock. Alice stared, trying to anticipate what would come next.

A spear flew through the air and impaled the bowman charioteer through the chest. A second spear took the warrior in the chariot behind, right through the throat. The horses reared.

The remaining charioteer yelled savagely. "We are under attack!"

Alice had to make a move or Adam would be meeting his maker. Seeing Adam's spear on the ground, he rushed over and picked it up. He slipped it under his right arm like a lance and, recalling his Anzac Day fight against Spike in the ring, moved menacingly toward the big warrior.

"Back away, Adam," he growled. "Leave this to me."

In the meantime, the attackers who had thrown the spears emerged from their houses and mobbed the surviving charioteer.

The big warrior took guard ready to take on Alice. The wooden spear wouldn't be much of a match for the warrior's sword, but it did have the advantage of length. Alice lunged, but the warrior easily deflected the strike with his sword. Alice knew he was in for it. This guy was a career killer, trained and experienced at fighting with a sword. He, Alice, wasn't. "How the hell am I going to beat this bloke with a pointed stick?" he wondered.

As Adam ran to the first chariot and grabbed the bow and arrow from the dead charioteer, the Babylonian warrior struck at Alice, who parried with his spear. The sharp blade chopped the wooden shaft in two. Now Alice was in big trouble.

Adam loaded an arrow and drew the bow as he walked towards the warrior. When he was close enough he fired. The arrow plunged deep into the back of the soldier's knee. He let out a growl and grabbed at it. That gave Alice the chance to dive at him. He grabbed the man's sword arm and wrestled, relieved to find out he was the stronger man. As he gripped the sword arm to keep it out of action, he smacked the warrior in the face with a series of heavy punches, smashing nose and lips. Then, recalling Turk's chin-jab, he let one go with all his might and it hit the mark. The sword dropped from the warrior's hand. He froze, grabbing at his throat, gasping for air, then collapsed on the ground, coughing up blood.

Alice picked up the sword and slashed, slicing his opponent's head in half. Blood sprayed across his borrowed tunic. The body twitched, went dead. Alice spat on the bloody mess, growling in English: "That'll teach you to mess with Al!"

A loud cheer erupted from the four boys who'd thrown the spears. They surrounded Alice, patting him on the back.

"You handle a sword well for a translator," Adam said.

"A man learns to fight for what he believes in," countered Alice.

Sabrina came out of the house and ran to her Mama, who was still on her knees beside the body of her husband.

"We must collect our belongings and go inside the wall," said Adam. "There will be a reprisal from Nebuchadnezzar over this killing." The other boys nodded their heads in agreement.

"Who are these guys?" Alice asked.

"They are members of the Holiness Code," Adam said.

"What's that? A club, a fraternity?"

"A militant religious order," Sabrina said, standing. "It was devised by the prophet Ezekiel to fight against the rise of the deity Tammuz — he who is championed by our ruler Zedekiah the Unholy."

The name Ezekiel rang a bell. There was something about him — he'd described meeting God inside a spaceship, hadn't he? He could ask his mental database ... on the other hand, he could just ask the man himself. He'd need to find out more about this Holiness Code.

CHAPTER 8
DARK CRUSADE

S ECTA WAS CONFINED to a room with a guard posted outside the door. They were still in Waxahachie but he had no idea where. There was no window, just a single bed, a bedside lamp on a small table, and an uncomfortable armchair. He was wearing out the already worn carpet with his anxious pacing up and down. Unable to determine how much time had passed since Alice had gone, he was beginning to believe he'd be stuck in the room forever. His pacing stopped when he heard the lock on the door unlatch. In came a tall, beastly-looking man, unknown to him.

"Doctor Secta," said the man in a guttural but calm voice. "Please take a seat."

"On that intolerable chair?" said Secta, "I'd rather stand. You may sit if you like." He resumed pacing.

"My name is Anu Set," the man continued, unperturbed. "I am the new supervisor of OTT."

"Ha! I bet that's thrilled the butt off Honor," said Secta with a nasty chuckle.

Resting his hands on the back of the armchair Set gave a thin-lipped smile. "You could say that," he said. "She's certainly no favourite of mine."

"Well, at least we that in common," said Secta, stopping his walk. "Does that mean we're bonding?" He stink-eyed Set. "Look, I asked to speak to the President. I'm sure you know I'm on a mission sanctioned by him."

"Yes, doctor. A fact-finding mission, I believe. Not a mission to send the dissident Black Alice back in time. You realise you have abused the trust the President had invested in you?"

"Hmm. Let's work through that, shall we? Tell me where I'm wrong. As I understand my job description, I am the head of the Oceana Scientific Research Division, which trumps you. I do what I deem necessary for my division."

"Nothing trumps me doctor, not while I hold the keys ... oh, and the gun."

Secta sighed theatrically. "Exactly what is it you idiots want, Mr Set?" he sneered. "All this Mission Impossible rubbish ... It's so unnecessary."

"Then I'll get to the point—"

"About time," Secta put in.

"—a suitable cliché, you will send me after Black Alice."

That stunned Secta. He locked eyes with his antagonist, totally stupefied. "I'm not sure I heard you correctly," he managed. "You want me to send you after Alice? What on earth for?"

"Firstly, I didn't ask you," said Set. "I ordered you. And secondly, because that's what the President wants you to do."

"The President? I don't think so," said Secta. "Who do you really work for?"

"My employer is the Zen Corporation."

That hit Secta like a speeding freight train. He flopped onto the bunk. "You have no idea how much sense that makes," he said. "Good grief. Zen! Next you'll be telling me Gorrick Khan is the boss."

"In fact, he is."

"This is ridiculous," muttered Secta. "Don't you evil buggers ever give up on world domination?"

Set straightened up and sighed. He was over it. "You will send me after Black Alice, or your professor friend will suffer an unfortunate accident," he said. "This is not up for debate, Secta. I'm not going to give you time to think it over, like you see in the movies. Agree now, or I walk down that hall and you never see the professor again."

"Fine," said Secta. "Kill him. Without him no one will be going after Alice." Checkmate, he thought to himself.

Set gritted his teeth.

Secta plunged on. "Your next move is to threaten my sister, I think," he said. "You people are so predictable. What's so important this time? Why take the risk of going after Alice?"

"To make sure he returns with the Ark."

"The President is so keen to get his claws on it that he would resort to these tactics — to murder threats?"

"You could say that."

"Uh-huh. And what's to stop you from killing Alice once he's located the Ark?"

"Nothing."

"Then what's the incentive to send you after him?" Secta challenged.

"You get to continue your work as though nothing has happened."

"And if I don't agree?" Secta asked indignantly.

"Simple. You never work again."

"I don't think the President would agree to that."

"Oh, we would tell him it was collateral damage," said Set, breezily. "Accidents do happen, Dr Secta." He drew a Glock-46-9 mm smart gun from under his suit, took a silencer from his side pocket and slowly fitted it to the muzzle. "Like I said. It's not up for debate."

Secta knew he was beaten. For now.

"Fine," he huffed. "If you're so willing to take the risk, I'll do it."

"The risk is no different than that Black Alice has already taken," Set replied. "If something goes wrong, if I fail to return, there are standing orders in place. They refer to you — and to Dr Hope and the professor. Do I make myself clear?"

"I will need assurances," Secta said, feebly.

"While I'm alive, you have them. Get me there and back and the deal will be honoured, without any repercussions."

"Then I cannot see that I have any choice," said Secta, ruefully. The law of unintended circumstances made him smile. For Anu Set, there would be no coming back.

"It's the Holy Temple," said Adam, as they passed through the huge, heavily-guarded wooden gates in the great wall surrounding the city of Jerusalem.

Alice put down the bag he'd been carrying and studied the structure with its fine, almost ancient Greek, architecture.

The Temple was in a square on a hilltop occupying the middle of the city. The sheer majesty of the entire complex took Alice's breath away. It was over a hundred and eighty feet high. Two great bronze pillars held up the porch. It faced east, and was surrounded on three sides by a pavement fifty feet broad, upon which stood buildings for the priests. The pavement was faced on the inside with a marble rail separating off the cloisters. Outside the building stood a massive altar which, Adam explained, was called The Molten Sea — a huge bronze dish set upon the backs of twelve bronze oxen. A fire burned within.

"Impressive," Al said.

"The altar is for sacrifice," said Sabrina. "Zedekiah, the King of Israel and the house of David, controls the sacrificial system. He brings many offerings."

"And citizens come to watch? What are these sacrifices? People?"

"No silly," laughed Sabrina. "Animals. This isn't Greece!"

Alice quickly accessed more information about the Temple through his implanted database. The search found a reference from crystalinks.com.

The Bible states that in the beginning of his reign, King Solomon of the United Kingdom of Israel set about giving effect to the ideas of his father, and prepared additional materials for the building. From subterranean quarries at Jerusalem he obtained huge blocks of stone for the foundations and walls of the temple. These stones were prepared for their places in the building under the eye of Tyrian master-builders. According to this account, Solomon also entered into a contract with Hiram I, king of Tyre, for the supply of whatever else was needed for the work, particularly timber from the forests of Lebanon, which was brought in great rafts by the sea to Joppa, whence it was dragged to Jerusalem (1 Kings 5).

As glorious and elaborate as the Temple was, its most important room contained almost no furniture at all. Known as the Holy of Holies (Kodesh Kodashim), it housed the two tablets of the Ten Commandments inside the Ark of the Covenant. Unfortunately, the tablets disappeared when the Babylonians destroyed the Temple in 587 BCE, and, therefore, during the Second Temple era the Holy of Holies was reduced to a small, entirely bare room.

Adam led the two goats pulling the small cart he had filled with the family's few possessions into the narrow cobblestoned streets. Mama walked behind, silent and sad. Alice was walking beside Sabrina.

"You look distant," she said, tentatively.

"Sorry," he smiled. "I was just thinking — can anyone enter the temple?"

"No. It is heavily guarded, because it houses the Holy of Holies."

"What is the Holy of Holies?" he asked, even though he already knew.

"The Ark of the Covenant."

He nodded. Of course.

"Alice, this way!" called Adam, breaking his train of thought.

They had reached a very narrow alleyway, hardly wide enough to take the cart. Sabrina turned to Alice, "Mama's sister lives here," she said. "She will take us in."

"What will you do with the goats?"

"We will give them to her to pay for our stay."

"How long will that buy you?"

"Maybe six months."

"Far out!"

"What is?" she asked, looking around in confusion.

He laughed, realising that some of his modern expressions wouldn't translate. "Just my local dialect," he said. "It means … er … excellent. Yes, excellent."

Aunt Edna was a stony-faced old lady. She kept Alice, Adam and Sabrina in the alleyway while she negotiated with Mama. Finally, she agreed on two months for each goat — four months — which included Alice staying there. He was beginning to feel fond of the family, but he knew he'd have to move on. With what he needed to do, he could only bring more danger into their lives.

Edna was older than Mama, and her face told of a much harder life. She lived alone in the four-roomed, mud brick two-storey semi-detached house. The interior was Spartan, just the essentials to sustain a middle-aged lady who had lost her husband to illness a decade before.

Alice was roomed with Adam while the women shared the other bedroom. As Alice lay back on the thin straw bed, hoping to get a little shut-eye, Adam decided to chat.

"There's a secret meeting of the Cabal of Holiness Code tonight," he confided. "Would you like to attend?"

This was the break Alice was hoping for, but he tried not to show it. "Would they accept me?" he asked. "I'm an outsider, after all."

"You have proven yourself in battle, Alice" said the boy. "You have my trust. I will endorse you."

"Fine," said Alice. "I'll come along."

Anu Set was sitting, naked, in the Desertron control room. De Luz was at the console while Secta prepared his injection.

"How are your language skills?" Secta asked.

"I have an implant translator and responder loaded with Latin, Hebrew and ancient Greek."

"Oh?" asked Secta. "And where did you get that?"

"Zen has developed many accessories for the OSCI — the organic stem-cell implant system we use. All Zen employees are fitted with it," said Set.

"I'm familiar with it," Secta snapped, remembering how all civilians had been fitted with a device in Turk and Morri's time.

"I'm surprised you're not fitted with one," Set went on. "Almost everyone else at Oceana is. In fact, I thought it was compulsory."

"Nothing is compulsory in my little corner of Oceana," Secta scoffed. "And never will be," he added, under his breath. He resented Zen for having invaded his sacred scientific turf. It was obvious that them being in bed with the President had diminished his value. Gone were the days of being relied upon as the main man. He needed to change that, or he would soon be redundant.

"So," said Set, breaking in. "Explain to me how I return."

"Right, well, you mark the exact place you arrive, then in exactly ninety-two hours — or four days — we will open a portal on that same spot. You'll use that to return," Secta lied.

"How long will this portal stay open ... in case I'm running late?"

De Luz looked up at Secta, aware of what he was doing, and a raised an eyebrow. Secta was enjoying the game and shot him a wink. "We don't know," he said. "We haven't done this before. But we'll just keep opening it until you make it back through."

The door opened and Hope entered.

Set instinctively covered his genitals with his hands.

"No need to cover up on my account, Set," she said. "See one prick and you've seen them all."

De Luz swivelled in his chair "Time to inject him, Secta."

"I hope you stooges know what you're doing," Set growled, suddenly feeling vulnerable.

"So do we," said de Luz with a chuckle, hoping to increase the man's fear of the unknown.

Secta jabbed the needle unceremoniously into Set's arm. "You will feel a bit odd in a minute or two, but it's best not to throw up or the vomit might fuse with your body," he said, straight-faced. "Did you ever see the film 'The Fly'?"

"Very funny, Secta," Set snarled.

"So I've been told."

Hope led the big man to the booth. He paused at the door. "Remember, Secta, I've left standing orders should I fail to return in ninety-two hours," he said. "You had better make sure this works — or I'll be seeing you in the afterlife." Grinning evilly, he stepped into the booth.

Hope snarled through the small glass window as she locked him in.

"You forgot to tell him he might lose his amalgam fillings," said de Luz.

Secta grinned. "No I didn't," he said.

CHAPTER 9
HOLINESS CODE

SET AWAKENED IN exactly the same place as Alice. Face down, spreadeagled — no dung this time, and no goat. Feeling disoriented, dizzy and nauseated, he struggled to his feet, and staggered to a nearby house. Finding it empty, he curled into a foetal position on the floor and went to sleep.

Alice was sitting alone in a small open space, about a block from where he was staying. He had gone for a walk to take in this very different world. Gazing up at the night sky, he noticed how much brighter everything looked than at home: the stars, the moon, everything. Then he noticed a satellite moving through the heavens. He'd seen plenty before. He recalled fondly one time he'd been night fishing and counted five of them traversing the heavens. People think they're UFO's, he chuckled to himself. Then he sat bolt upright, remembering where he was and when. "Hey, there shouldn't be any satellites up there!" he thought. "So, what the heck is that?"

He searched the sky for more among the firmament, but could only see the one. By its size it appeared to be in a low trajectory. Suddenly he was brought back down to earth by a voice.

"A lot to see, is there not?"

He turned to face Sabrina, bathed in the pale moonlight, looking for all the world like a Greek goddess.

"More than we'll ever know," he said. "Come here."

She tentatively moved closer. He put his arm around her shoulder and turned her gently, pointing at the satellite.

"Can you see that star moving up there?"

"Yes of course," she said, smiling. "That is Betyl. Have you not seen it before?"

"Er ... No," he said. "What does Betyl mean?"

"It means 'House of God'. It has been there all my life. Papa said it first appeared when he was a boy. Ezekiel speaks of a time when he was in the land of the Chaldeans, by the river Chebar, when a great cloud came by — fire flashing forth continually and a bright light around it. In its midst, something like metal, and within the metal, living figures with human form. He speaks of wheels upon the earth beside those figures, and yet appearing as if one wheel were within another. Whenever the beings moved, the wheels moved with them. When they rose again from the earth, the wheels rose also, with a great rumbling sound."

"Wheels within wheels ... Sounds about right," said Alice to himself. "Does Ezekiel believe these beings came from Betyl?" he asked aloud.

"We think so," said Sabrina. "It appeared at the same time as his vision."

To Alice the description sounded exactly like the landing of some kind of spacecraft. He looked back up at Betyl. Wow. An alien craft orbiting the Earth.

"Where is this guy Ezekiel?" he asked. "I need to talk to him."

"He was captured by the Babylonii ten years ago," said Sabrina, sadly. "He was taken to their land. He also foretold the fall of Jerusalem, and the sacking of the Temple. With the army of Nebuchadnezzar approaching, we fear the prophesy is upon us. I think you were sent to help us, Alice. That is why you must go to the meeting tonight."

"I'm happy here at the moment," he said, admiring her every move. She looked back at him as he moved close to kiss her. He closed his eyes and lowered his face to hers … and nearly fell over. He opened his eyes to see her scurrying off. "I guess they don't do premarital kissing here," he thought. "Oh well…"

Later, Adam led Alice through a labyrinth of alleyways towards a rocky hill on the western side of the Temple. About a mile away the great fire burning in the Molten Sea lit up the night.

Adam stopped at the foot of the hill, untied a piece of linen from his wrist and held it for Alice to see. "You understand you will need to be blindfolded?" he asked, tentatively.

"No problem," said Alice. "Go ahead."

Adam fitted the blindfold, took Alice's hand, led him for a few minutes then stopped.

"You will need to bend down here," he said.

Alice ducked and Adam led him onwards. The sound and temperature change suggested they were in a cave. A couple of minutes later Adam stopped and removed the blindfold. It took a second or two for Alice's eyes to adjust, then he saw he'd been right — it was a small cave with a low ceiling.

"We call this place sanctuary," Adam said. "Follow me."

The lad led the way through several small connecting tunnels.

"Why all the cloak and dagger stuff?"

"Being a disciple of Ezekiel is against the law. If Zedekiah's soldiers or the Pharisees were to find us, we would be executed."

"You could have told me that in the first place," Alice groaned. He wasn't fond of being set up.

"Sorry."

It wasn't long before the voices of others could be heard and a light became visible at the end of the long corridor they were travelling.

They entered a larger cavern lit by oil burning torches around the walls. It was occupied by a score of young men. After introducing them to Alice, they all sat on the damp floor while the leader of the group — and the oldest — spoke.

"Welcome brothers, and welcome to Alice, who Adam advises came to us from Athens!" he declaimed. "Alice bravely fought off an attack by the Babylonii soldiers who killed Adam's father. I have prophesised that Jerusalem will fall to the Babylonii. Ezekiel too has prophesised this. We agree that the time is now."

"Who is this?" Alice whispered.

"The prophet Jeremiah," Adam whispered back.

Jeremiah studied his flock. To Alice he looked like all the depictions of Jesus he'd ever seen: long white caftan, long brown curly hair, lightly bearded face … Only the insane-looking green eyes and the dark skin didn't match. "Odd how Middle-Eastern blokes were mostly depicted as white in Renaissance paintings and the Bible," Alice thought, smiling a little.

Jeremiah was speaking again. "We are but few," he said. "We do not have the strength to fight Zedekiah, the Tammuz caliphate or Nebuchadnezzar's Babylonian hoard. This is written. Zedekiah will be taken to Babylon, Jerusalem will fall and burn."

Alice had heard enough. In his mind these dudes were going to preach and rave on while the city perished around them.

"Excuse me for jumping in on your rave," he said, getting to his feet, "But it seems to me there's plenty of saying and very little doing going on around here. If you've known about this for so long, why haven't you prepared for it? Seems to me there's only one solution: we act. We have to take everything of value from the Temple and hide it from Nebuchadnezzar."

A murmur arose from the brothers. Jeremiah began pacing up and down, deep in thought. Alice shrugged and sat back down.

"Our guest speaks like a true orator," Jeremiah said at last. "Adam told me you were a translator, Alice, but apparently you fight like a demon, you have the build of a warrior and the wisdom of ages. You are an enigma, but your words are wise. Please, elaborate." Jeremiah took a seat with the others.

Alice stood back up. "I've done many things in my life," he said. "Far too many to go into now. But this I can tell you: like Jeremiah and Ezekiel I have knowledge that a great apocalypse will befall this city." A flash of impish inspiration struck him. "It comes from the heavy metal, from the Endangered Species!"

A murmur of awe came from the brothers. They of course had no idea what he meant by 'heavy metal', or that 'Endangered Species' was the first album he had recorded back in his own time.

"Does this heavy metal Endangered Species prophesy the outcome of the fall of Jerusalem?" Jeremiah asked.

"Yes, in these words…" Alice burst into song:

"On the streets of Jerusalem town
There's an echo from the underground
Something chills the air
And the cold will last
While the anarchy is there …

High on the hill of Temple Mount
In the room of Holy of Holies
Ezekiel is in despair
Take the Ark away for Solomon's care…

Ahh, from a tower in the dead of night
The heavens will send a blinding light
We will stand hand in hand
Call forth your fellow man
Oh bring your hearts to me now
Oh bring your hearts to me now!

It's the Aries age and you will pray
This will be the judgement day
It's you to blame
But I'm the one to
Fight the flames
Of the fire

When they start to burn higher
They'll scorch and burn
And turn to terrify ya

Oh! bring your hearts to me now
You know the story
Those flames of purgatory grow
Higher, yes they're gonna burn higher
They'll taunt and burn then turn
To terrify ya…
And the world will begin again then
Now you've been warned
The ending days will dawn from Babylon…"

While his full, operatic tones were still reverberating in the depths of the cavern, Alice leered at them in the same way he leered at his audience from the stage. He could tell he had them. His powerful voice, his words and his performance had literally blown them away. Grinning to himself, he resumed his seat.

Jeremiah stood. "I thank you, brother Alice," he said. "You are saying that our city will be handed to the king of Babylon by the sword, famine and plague. But this is what the Lord, the God of Israel, says: 'I will surely gather them from all the lands where I banish them in my furious anger and great wrath; I will bring them back to this place and let them live in safety. Behold, the days come, saith the Lord, that I will raise unto David a righteous Branch, and a King shall reign and prosper, and shall execute judgment and justice in the Earth. In his days Judah shall be saved, and Israel shall dwell safely: and this is his name whereby he shall be called, the Lord our Righteousness: a King Messiah! He will be the good and righteous King who will rule out of Zion.'"

The word Zion struck a note with Alice — it was the name Professor de Luz had given the unit that had despatched him into the wormhole. He was from Zion!

Jeremiah continued, preaching like an evangelist: "The judgment day is coming to Judah because of its disbelief and disobedience. The prophecy of Endangered Species confirms this."

"Is this your prophecy, Jeremiah?" Alice interrupted, "Or does this come from Ezekiel?"

"The Lord speaks to both of us, Alice."

"Does he speak to you from Betyl?"

"I was taken to Betyl," intoned Jeremiah. "I beheld the Earth, and it was without form and void. The heavens had no light. There was no man, and the birds of the air had fled. I beheld, and the fertile place was desert, and the cities in it were broken down by the presence of the Lord."

Oh-kay, Alice thought, Either this guy's off his rocker, or he visited the UFO, or he's pinching stuff from Ezekiel.

Suddenly, a young man ran into the cavern in a panic and stopped, panting, a desperate look on his face. "The Tammuz are coming!" he gasped.

Adam jumped up. "We must take the secret exit!" he cried

"Wait!" Alice ordered. "How many of them are there?"

The young boy looked unsure about whether to answer this newcomer. Jeremiah gave him a nod. "Two," he said.

"Two?" Alice said, incredulously. "I'll deal with them."

"No, Alice," said Jeremiah, quietly. "There will be more of them outside. It's a trap to lure us out. Follow me, and we will all get safely away." He led everyone into a different set of tunnels.

Once outside, Alice could see by the Temple that they were on the other side of the hill.

"Disperse brothers," Jeremiah said. "We meet tomorrow at Beit Ha'am."

"No Jeremiah, that cannot be, not after tonight," Adam protested. "They will arrest you!"

"So be it," said Jeremiah, imperiously. "Now go!" He pulled Alice aside for a moment and said, conspiratorially: "We will talk more of your Endangered Species after tomorrow, if I am not jailed," then turned and scurried off into the night.

The rest dispersed quickly, leaving Alice and Adam alone.

"That was wild," said Alice. "Is it always like that?"

"Yes, but without the arrival of the Tammuz," Adam admitted. "Jeremiah is a radical thinker."

"What is this Beit Ha'am thing?"

"Jeremiah likes to engage in performance art at the Temple during prayer time: Beit Ha'am," Adam explained gravely. "He thumbs his nose at King Zedekiah and the Tammuz. It always brings trouble."

Alice looked up at Betyl. "Yeah, well, I guess we'd better be there to protect him," he said. "You know, I just can't believe that thing up there."

Adam followed Alice's eye-line. "Betyl?" he said. "Ezekiel can tell you more about it. He claims to have been there. I do not believe Jeremiah went there," he added. "I think many of his prophecies derive from Ezekiel."

"I'd really like to meet Ezekiel," said Alice

"He is at the Chebar River, near Tel Abib."

"How long to get there?"

"Two days ride by mule."

"Mule!"

With the caves in darkness, the two soldiers had entered only a short distance before they quickly retreated, as though frightened by something they saw.

On their way back to Edna's house, Alice again accessed his in-built internet. He thought of the caves of ancient Jerusalem, envisioning a reference in his mind's eye: Zedekiah's Cave. He scanned the information and found it was also called Solomon's Quarries: a five-acre meleke limestone quarry running five city blocks under the Muslim Quarter of the Old City of Jerusalem — at least, in his time. He realised these were not the same caves as those he'd just visited. Nor was there any archaeological evidence of the legend that the cave had been the hiding place of King Zedekiah of Judah during the fall of Jerusalem in 587 BC.

CHAPTER 10
THE LIVING DEAD

S ECTA CLOSED HIS little black bag, looked over at de Luz in his chair and asked, "Is there another way out of here, Vic?" De Luz was completing the process of shutting down the collider. "You could always give each of us a dematerializing shot," he suggested with a chuckle. "But if visiting 587 BCE isn't your speed, we could escape through the collider vent."

"I don't fancy being kept prisoner by Homeland Security or visiting Ancient Jerusalem," Secta replied with equal joviality, "So let's try the latter."

"Seriously, boys, what are we going to do?" Hope asked, less insouciant than her colleagues. "Buddy-boy and Squeaky are probably waiting for us outside."

It was a problem they had no choice but to address, otherwise they would find themselves stuck in Texas with Homeland Security on their hammer and no means of support.

"We need to find a way back to Sydney," said Secta. "At least there I could reason with the President, and right now having to deal with Honor seems like the lesser of two evils."

"What about Vic?"

"He'll need to come with us. That all right with you, Vic?"

"Why not?" the big man grinned. "I'm due a vacation."

Secta smiled, "Okay, we'll discuss that once we're out of here. Can you think of a safe place for us to hide, Vic?"

"Let me see," the professor mused. "Ah — remember the little blonde waitress at the College Street Pub?"

"Yes?" said Hope, eyebrows raised, expecting de Luz to admit to a salacious affair.

"That's Stella. She has an apartment near the pub. We could stay at her place for a little while."

Hope's eyebrows raised a little farther.

"She's my niece," he went on. "She won't rat us out."

A look of relief broke across Hope's face.

"Excellent," said Secta. "Now let's move before our friends Squeaky and Buddy-boy decide to check on us."

Rummaging around in the dark, Set found enough discarded clothing to dress presentably. He wandered outside and suddenly bent double, stomach heaving. He threw up violently. "Effects of the time travel process," he thought. Wiping his mouth with the back of his hand, he proceeded to scan the topography. There were no lights showing in any of the other huts nearby, so he assumed they'd been vacated as well. In the distance he could see the glow of a city. Then he noticed the remains of what looked like two chariots, stripped but still recognisable. He was pretty sure they had been recently dismantled. He inspected one of them and found a shallow grave beside it. Taking a piece of the broken chariot to use as a spade, he cleared the sand off what turned out to be a fresh, headless body. On it he found what he needed: a pair of sandals. He stripped them off the corpse and slipped them on. They were a tight fit, but would do for his trek to the city.

De Luz's head popped up out of a manhole in the middle of the Desertron car park. He could see his car, the spy van and two other cars — but no sign of any people. He looked back down at the others and called: "Coast is clear."

The three of them climbed out. It had been a long haul: they'd walked half a mile of narrow dark tunnel then climbed eight floors of metal ladders through a narrow funnel to the surface.

"I'm knackered," Secta admitted.

"Longevity serum might have preserved you, but you'll still need to keep in shape if you want to live forever," Hope jibed.

"Longevity serum? Now that I want to hear about," de Luz said with a chuckle. "You guys take cover over there while I go get the car."

Secta and Hope scurried over to the building de Luz had pointed out and hid behind a rubbish dumpster.

De Luz reached the Pajero and climbed aboard, but as soon as he started it up the sound of the engine attracted a guard from inside. He came running out, brandishing his gun.

The Pajero sped over to the dumpster. Secta and Hope dived aboard and it took off, headed for the front gates.

The big metal entrance gates were closed. De Luz simply ploughed through them, the two Homeland Security vehicles not far behind.

"They'll probably have the Sheriff's office set up a roadblock up ahead," he said. "I'd better make it difficult for them." He turned unexpectedly off the road onto a fire trail. "This comes out at the wastewater treatment plant," he yelled to his two passengers. "It'll be a rough ride, especially in the dark — but we'll surely dodge the ambush. Get a grip, kids!"

It was hard going all right; the rarely-used narrow dirt road was scarred with potholes. A capable off-road driver, de Luz embraced the challenge, but the darkness made it treacherous. Soon they came to an old, narrow wooden bridge over a tributary to Lake Waxahachie. De Luz saw headlights a little way behind them. He knew he'd have to slow down to cross the bridge.

"They'll catch up on the bridge," he said. "But once we get across it and onto Old Italy Road, we'll should get clear. Better duck down in case they fire at us."

"Don't worry Vic, they won't do that," said Secta, confidently. "With Anu Set off-world we're far too valuable to them."

"I guess you're right."

Suddenly a spotlight from above lit up the bridge ahead.

"Damn! A chopper!" de Luz growled.

They watched the chopper descend up ahead.

"He's probably landed on Laguna Vista Road. Damn!" de Luz cursed again.

As the Pajero slowly rattled its way across the bridge, the vehicle tailing them caught up.

"Can I borrow your cell-phone, Vic?" asked Secta.

Struggling with the steering wheel, de Luz reached inside his flak-jacket, retrieved his phone and handed it to Secta.

"Is my number in Sydney on autodial?" Secta asked.

"Yeah, just hit four."

"It's 5pm in Sydney … Oh, hello Viktoria. Yes, we're fine, thank you. Put me through to the President would you? Tell him it's urgent." Secta flicked the speaker on.

"Secta?" it answered.

"Ri, hello. I wonder, could you tell me please, what's going on?"

"I should be asking that of you."

"I don't know what you mean, I'm sure…"

"You haven't been honest with me. Secta. I'm very disappointed in you."

"In fairness, Ri, you haven't exactly been honest with me. Look, you authorized this venture, now all of a sudden there are restrictions on me? It's never been like that before — why the change? Have I ever failed to deliver for you?"

"No-ooo … No," the President's voice came back. "It's this whole Black Alice thing, Secta. Why the hell did you hide him from me? Such deceit was uncalled for!"

"Because of your decision to make me the guinea pig, Ri, "Secta countered. "The OTT decided — with your sanction — that I was to be your time-travelling technology mule. I wasn't even consulted. I'm worth a little more to you than that, surely? Risking my life on time travel experiments? Once was enough, I think.

"Alice is clearly the man for the job," he went on. "But your people — Honor in particular — have personal issues with him. I simply took it upon myself to continue with the program in my own way. You have never questioned that before ... So why now?"

"I have other influences to consider, Secta."

"Such as?"

"Zen Corporation."

"Ah, so that's who's in your ear?"

"They have better means than us to develop this kind of technology."

"You're wrong Ri. Had you taken me into your confidence about them I would have told you of our experience with Zen in the future. They are committed to world domination. In 2087, they had instigated a third world war that had all but destroyed Earth's population. They were building an army of cyborgs to rule over and terrorise the people. And Gorrick Khan was in charge of it all. Not to mention this Anu Set, who threatened our lives in order to chase Black Alice into the past, intent on killing him. What sort of credible government acts in that manner? I ask you?"

"What ... what are you saying, Secta? How do you know Gorrick Khan?"

"He was President of Zen Corporation in 2087," Secta replied. "Six foot five or so, short-cropped white hair, square jaw, Nordic looking, doesn't blink much ... Sound familiar?"

"Are you serious?" The President's tone had completely changed. Secta was getting through. "How can that be possible?"

"Gorrick Khan, Ri, makes Kim Jong-un look like a primary school teacher. Look, just get us back there, I'll tell you the whole story. Trust me," he said, oozing sincerity.

Hope stared at this new version of her brother. She had never heard him speak to the President — or to anyone — in such a manner and with such passion before. She was proud of him.

There were armed men from the chopper on the road ahead, flagging them down with torches.

"All right," the President conceded. "Go to Irving Military airport tomorrow before noon. There will be a plane waiting to bring you home. How many?"

"Three. Professor de Luz, Hope and myself. Thank you, Ri."

"We should have spoken before all this got started my friend," the voice came back. "Goodbye for now."

Secta handed the phone back to de Luz.

"A little difficult to speak when you have no idea what's going on,' he said, grumpily.

"You did so well, bro," Hope said, warmly.

De Luz pulled the Pajero up just short of the men on the road. The vehicle tailing them pulled up inches from their rear bumper. Two men jumped out and rushed the car. The driver's side door was pulled open and Buddy Holman pointed a gun at de Luz.

"Get out with your hands on your head. Now!"

De Luz stared at him blandly. "Or what are you going to do?" he said. "Shoot me?"

The other man was on the phone. Secta smiled at Hope as he said, "Yes sir, immediately Mister President!"

Rees turned to Buddy and spoke quietly. "Lower your weapon, Buddy," he said, dispiritedly. "We're to escort our friends here back to the Professor's home."

De Luz gave Secta a thumbs up.

At breakfast Adam broke a flat loaf of bread and handed a chunk to Alice. They dipped it into a dish of olive oil, and washed it down with a cup of fresh goat's milk. Sabrina joined them.

"You look stunning this morning Sabrina," Alice said, warmly.

"Thank you Alice," she smiled and blushed. "How did the meeting go last night?"

"Informative, I guess. I'm going to see Jeremiah at Beit Ha'am later."

Her pretty smile tightened. "That would be unwise," she said.

"Why, what's the problem?"

"Do you really want to watch sacrifices?"

"No but—"

Adam cut him off. "She is right, Alice. It is too dangerous."

"That doesn't bother me," said Alice cockily. "I should experience your culture while I'm here, right?"

Sabrina gently covered his hand with hers "Please do not go, Alice," she requested, softly.

Alice felt her silky-smooth skin on his and, for the moment, succumbed. "We'll see," he mumbled, with a non-committal smile.

"Why not come with us to the wet market instead," she suggested, her smile restored. "There will be plenty to see there."

"Where is it? I'll meet you there."

"Very near to where we were last night, you will not be able to miss it," Adam told him.

"Come Adam," said Sabrina, standing. "Mama and Aunt are waiting for us."

Once they'd gone Alice made a move, intent on experiencing Beit Ha'am at the Temple.

Outside the sky was a deep blue, its richness and depth a testament to what happens when there are no manmade emissions in the air. Alice knew filmmakers and photographers referred to the time just after sunrise and before sunset as 'the magic hour' because of the clarity of the atmosphere. In 587 BCE, it seemed like it was permanently magic hour. Even the sun on his face felt different, it made his skin tingle under its warmth. No wonder ancient races worshiped it, he thought.

There was a sugary scent of blossoms in the air. There were kids playing in the street, kicking a ball of twine. Women hanging out clothes to dry, old men sitting at their front doors, engaged in conversations with neighbours and friends. It seemed to him that people interacted more than they did back in his own time. He mused about how 21st century society had lost that very human practice, leaving it self-centred and introverted. When these street people looked at him, he felt acceptance: a sense of community, brotherhood — Is that because the enemy is on our doorstep, or is it the norm? Or is it because there are no hand-held devices and social media?

He rounded a corner, still musing, past a fruit vendor who threw him an apple, which he caught.

"Thank you, friend," he called, happily. That sure as hell wouldn't happen back home —at least, not in the city.

He bit into the apple — it tasted totally different than any apple he'd ever eaten before — he munched it up in flash while moving on. He turned a corner and walked into a crowd of people assembled at a landing leading to the foot of the staircase to the Temple, perhaps a thousand or more. They were all looking in the same direction, up at the Molten Sea — and they were all silent. Thinking it might be prayer time and not wanting to be rude, Alice leaned against the corner of a building to watch.

Within minutes a horn sounded a single note, and a procession of Pharisees in lavishly decorated and colourful regalia appeared from the Temple and started down the stairs towards the Molten Sea. Alice counted twenty-three priests, some holding animals on leashes. The leader, a little chubby man, was carrying a staff with what looked like a golden hook fixed at its end.

As they assembled around the twelve gigantic bronze oxen, a voice shouted loudly from behind Alice.

"Hast thou seen this, O son of man? Turn thee yet again, and thou shalt see greater abominations than these!"

He turned and saw Jeremiah. He was stripped to the waist, drenched in blood, a yoke tied round his neck.

"Death is at the gates!" he roared. "The Temple will burn and the dead will rise to seek revenge! Tammuz worship is of the demons Dumuzid and Ishtah!"

The crowd parted to allow Jeremiah through. Alice thought he looked like the local madman. They taunted, booed and chastised him with obscenities, flipping from being peacefully silent to savagely raucous.

Jeremiah reached the base of the steps and stopped.

A hush came over the crowd as a young man with a thin breaded face, garbed in a flamboyant glittering coat of gold and wearing the crown of a king, appeared at the top landing of the Temple.

From the crowd came the murmuring of his name: Zedekiah.

He pointed down at Jeremiah. "I see my counsellor has come to mock me!" he bellowed.

The crowd grumbled their displeasure.

"It is not you I mock, King Zedekiah," Jeremiah roared back. "You are merely a puppet of Nebuchadnezzar … it is Babylonii religion you have embraced that I mock. You stand in the Temple of the Lord, and you worship demons! You do evil in the sight of the Lord, and you will pay! Nebuchadnezzar will betray and imprison you!"

A woman garbed in purple robes drifted from inside the Temple and stood beside Zedekiah. Alice thought it might be his wife. She was exceptionally pretty, and her bearing was regal enough for a Queen.

Seven of the pharisees left the altar and took up positions on the steps leading from Zedekiah to the Molten Sea. The high Pharisee removed the hook from the end of his staff and fixed it on a leash hanging from a ring in the nose of the central oxen.

Zedekiah took the woman by the arm. Her long, shiny black hair waved behind her like a banner in the breeze.

Now that he could see her face more clearly, Alice realised she looked drugged.

"Ishtah made a journey to the netherworld in search of Dumuzid!" Zedekiah shouted. "The seven gates awaited her! She went to the first gate..."

The crowd roared approval. Alice assumed that signalled commencement of the ceremony. He expected the Pharisees to sacrifice the animals next. But he was wrong. The woman began to descend the steps, zombie-like, to the first priest. She stopped, and allowed him to remove her shawl.

"She went to the second gate!" Zedekiah shouted.

She moved to the next priest, who removed the top of her dress, exposing high breasts.

"The third gate!" Zedekiah bawled.

The priest on that step removed one of her sandals, and kissed her bare foot.

"She found her way to the fourth gate," Zedekiah roared.

Just as she stepped down the last few stairs to the waiting priest, Jeremiah rushed up them, yelling madly: "Stop this abomination! Stop in the name of the Lord! It is blasphemous!"

Several armed soldiers Alice hadn't noticed before stepped out from the shadows, rushed and seized Jeremiah.

The fourth priest removed the sandal from woman's other foot, and from a vial of oil anointed both feet.

The soldiers carted Jeremiah off screaming and protesting. As they brought him past Alice, he caught Jeremiah's eye. "We are the endangered species, Alice!" Jeremiah screamed, insanity in his eyes.

Alice considered intervening, but thought better of it. There were just too many heavily-armed guards.

"Ishtah descended to the next gate," Zedekiah cried, taking Alice's attention from the arrest of Jeremiah.

The audience was now deathly silent, transfixed on the woman's descent.

She stepped down again. The pharisee lifted the lower part of her dress and slipped off her undergarment.

"To the sixth gate she went," Zedekiah's voice resounded, building in anticipation.

The sixth priest took a necklace from around her long, slender neck.

"With her Earthly goods gone, she descended to the final gate!"

Before she stepped down, the audience began to shout unitedly: "Turn back! Turn back! Do not sit upon the throne! Turn back! Turn back! Do not sit upon the throne!" Their voices thundered.

"But Ishtah chose not to listen," Zedekiah screamed, lifting the fervour another level.

The woman stepped down the last few steps to the seventh priest. She raised her arms and let him strip off her dress, leaving her naked — and gorgeous, Alice thought. She kept her arms raised and posed for the crowd. Some cheered, but others cried desperately: Turn back! Turn back! Turn back!

Alice was enjoying the spectacle — always partial to a theatrical experience.

"She had arrived in her nakedness at the lower world," Zedekiah announced with a fury. "The throne of Ereshkigal was vacant, and greed drove her to take it!"

The woman sat at the front hooves of the leading bronze ox.

The short fat high priest moved beside her and raised his staff in the air.

"En-Lil, lord of the air and the Earth, guardian of the tablet of destinies, En-Lil of the Anunnaki judged Ishtah a simple woman," Zedekiah bellowed out. "He gazed at her with the eyes of death, because he was the gatekeeper!"

The crowd ripped into a frenzy.

Then Alice found out why. The high priest seized Ishtah, slid his staff up under her arms at the back and dragged her upright. Another priest came and tied her hands.

All of the priests began to hum. Ommmmmm!

To Alice's astonishment the audience joined in. Ommmmm!

Then the high priest gripped the golden hook hanging from bull's nose, moved behind Ishtah and drove it into the flesh of her back. Her knees buckled, her eyes rolled back in her head, her mouth opened and she let out an horrific gasping sound as the hook emerged in a spray of blood between her breasts. She didn't scream, she didn't pass out. She just stared ahead, her eyes fixed on oblivion.

Alice groaned, horrified.

Then six of the priests rushed down the stairs and gripped the rope fastened to the hook, and hauled Ishtah into the air until she was hanging suspended from the nose of the giant ox, blood flowing from down her naked body and puddling on the ground at her feet.

"She became a corpse, hung upon a hook!" Zedekiah bellowed, in conclusion. The performance was over. He turned, made his way back up the stairs, and disappeared inside the Temple.

Stunned by the whole catastrophe, Alice mumbled to himself in English. "These freaks are off their faces."

The Pharisees left the women hanging, legs twitching as her life left her. The priests tethered the animals they had been holding to the legs of the bronze beasts — the crowd would sacrifice them. Their gory ritual complete, they formed a line and scaled the stairs to retreat back inside the Temple.

As soon as the priests were gone the horde stampeded the sacrificial animals. The crowd was out of control. Alice could feel it was about to boil over into a riot. He'd had a gut full of them. These people, whom he'd been so busily admiring, had in one foul stroke degenerated into a bunch of brain-dead troglodytes. People were being trodden under foot, walked over, some were screaming in fear, others in avarice. He turned to make off in the opposite direction and was met by a wide-eyed, equally frenzied throng surging through the narrow alleyway to get to the altar. He was forced to shove savagely to get through.

CHAPTER 11
BEYOND THE STEEPLE

ALICE EVENTUALLY FOUND the wet market. It surprised him that along the way, through some dim alleys where he expected to come across beggars and homeless, there were none to be found.

The market was a thriving concern, a cornucopia of activity and vivid colour. A large area occupied by tents in which everything imaginable was for sale. The people shopping were very different to those he had experienced at the Temple.

It didn't take him long to find Sabrina and the others. She was busy haggling over a colourful piece of fabric.

Someone shouted "Hey!" behind Alice, and he whipped around sharply to find Adam.

"Hey, don't do that," he snapped. "You startled me."

"Sorry," said Adam. "But where have you been?"

"I went to Beit Ha'am."

Adam pulled him aside. "Do not mention that to Sabrina, she will be very angry," he said, conspiratorially. "What happened there? I met a friend a few minutes ago who said Jeremiah was arrested. He will be stoned tomorrow."

"Stoned? On dope?"

"What is dope?"

Alice realised he'd once again used a term Adam couldn't understand.

"Forget it," he said. "So is that, like, a public event?"

"Yes, every Sunday there is an execution."

"You people are sick," Alice growled. "I just saw a young woman stripped naked and hung on a hook like an animal in a slaughterhouse. A priest drove the hook right through her back until it stuck out the front of her," he said wincing.

"Ah, the fall of Ishtah," said Adam. "Yes, I've seen that a few times. The Pharisees would have selected her from the condemned adulteresses. She would have been stoned tomorrow anyway," he added, almost casually. "Better to die on the hook than that. At least the family isn't shamed."

Alice was shocked. "What is it with you people? Doesn't life matter to you?" he said. "Don't you care about other people?"

Even as he said that he had a flash of understanding. Their values were completely different to his. They lived with death on their doorstep every day. It was rare to live past forty years of age. There was no medicine to speak of, only witchcraft. Catching flu was as good as a death sentence.

"When there is nothing you can do about something you just have to accept it, Alice," the boy said, quietly.

"Is that how crime is always dealt with here?"

"The accused is judged by the Pharisee, and if found guilty is put to death," said Adam. "For lesser crimes, stoning or exile. For more serious crimes, public beheading, flaying, burning or strangulation. Theft is not always death — one hand or maybe both cut off."

"Wow," said Alice. "I bet that keeps the crime rate down."

"Indeed it does," said Adam, nodding.

"So, how is someone stoned?" Al asked.

"The accused is pushed off a cliff into a pit," Adam explained. "If they do not die from that, the public throws rocks at them until they are dead."

"If your friend and leader will die that way tomorrow, what are you going to do about it?" Alice probed.

"Nothing."

"You're kidding me!"

"What does that mean?"

"Never mind," he growled. "Get word to the Holiness Code that I want volunteers to meet me at the cavern tonight. Find out where Jeremiah is and we'll get him out."

"That is crazy Alice," Adam said, wide-eyed. "No one would even try that."

"That's what I'm counting on. They won't be expecting it."

"I will do it," Adam said, excitedly. Just as he was about to run off he stopped. "You know, sometimes you use very strange words, Alice," he said.

"That's because I speak a different dialect than you," Alice smiled, hoping the excuse would work. It seemed to, Adam nodded and ran off to spread the word.

A sweet voice came from behind him. "Where have you been, Alice?"

He spun around to face Sabrina.

"Oh, I just went for a wander around town," he said, sheepishly. "What have you bought?"

She unravelled a length of colourful fabric.

"It's like a rainbow," Alice said.

"Yes, that is what attracted me to it," she smiled. "It will make a lovely shawl."

"Anything would look lovely on you."

Sabrina blushed as Mama and Edna arrived loaded up with things they'd bought. Alice took the bundles and they headed home.

On the way, Alice asked Sabrina: "What do you think of Jeremiah?"

"Oh, I cannot make up my mind," she said. "Sometimes he makes a lot of sense, other times he sounds like a madman. One thing is for sure — it is dangerous to be around him outside the meeting place. I think King Zedekiah would prefer to rid Jerusalem of him just as he did with Ezekiel."

"I thought Ezekiel was captured by the Babylonii."

"Many do not believe that to be the case. Though Zedekiah respects Ezekiel more than he does Jeremiah, I think both prophets represented a threat to him."

"To the King or the priests?" Alice questioned.

"Do you mean the Pharisees?"

"Yes."

"That is perhaps a more accurate assessment."

Secta left no stone unturned in reiterating the story of his trip to the future to the President. It had been a future that followed a horrific world war instigated by Zen. A future with no future: the population of the planet purposely rendered sterile by exposure to radiation. A future dominated by an organization with no accountability or scruples, and with the very same Gorrick Khan calling the shots.

"Why was there was no debriefing after the last travel episode?" Secta asked.

The President folded his hands in front of him, focusing on them as though there was a secret beyond the steeple.

"Are you suggesting there are hidden agendas here?" he queried.

"Put it this way," said Secta, "I volunteered, at the risk of my own life and with your knowledge, for a trip to the future to bring Black Alice home safely. While I was busy carrying out my orders, your agents Honor and Karzoff kidnapped and tortured my sister. They also set in motion a plan to arrest Alice on our return. Once I'd successfully made it back, there was no debriefing, no thanks, no nothing … I was asked only for a written report and told that I'd been elected the OTT's official time traveller without even having a vote."

"When you put it that way my friend, I can understand your suspicion," said the President. "But why hide Black Alice from me?"

"Because the hidden agendas were getting in the way of the science," he replied, sitting forward in his chair and speaking with enthusiasm. "We are on the threshold of something fantastic, Ri. Twenty-four hours ago we sent Alice through a wormhole back in time to a specific date. That totally defies the laws of physics! Then, just to prove it wasn't a one-off, we did it again with Set! Do you grasp the enormity of what we have achieved? The potential of it? Do you want to risk all that with Gorrick Khan's Zen Corporation, and the antics of Honor and Karzoff? Do you know what would happen if the U.S. government discovered what we have managed to do, and what it would be worth to them? Ri, can you imagine, after everything I've told you, what would happen if the Ark of the Covenant fell into Khan's hands?"

The President paled. "But why are you still trying to find it?" he said. "Why not destroy it instead?"

"Because we intend to use it."

"Who are you going to use a weapon of such force on, for God's sake?"

"A weapon? It's not a weapon, Ri. Professor de Luz believes it can be used as a communication device to contact alien races."

"What?" The President was open mouthed. "But ... I was told Alice wants the Ark for the Octagon, to wage war against the Government!"

"Ri, Black Alice is a pacifist," said Secta. "The Octagon is a non-violent organization. You're being fed misinformation, fake news. After what I told you about Zen's objective and the fact that Gorrick exists in two timelines at the same age, you must see that you are being skilfully manipulated." He paused and eyeballed the President, waiting for what he'd said to sink in. Then he changed his tone. "If we are to survive," he said, darkly, "If humankind is to survive, we have no alternative but to stop Zen. The Ark and the time travel concept cannot fall into their hands."

Back to studying his steepled fingers, the President slowly opened them and nodded. Secta took a deep breath, relieved. He knew the President. Once convinced by a rational argument, he would initiate an entirely new strategy. Zen would be on the outer.

"All right," the President asked. "How should we proceed?"

"Leave things the way they are," said Secta. "Let Honor believe with Set gone that she's in charge. Order her to let Hope, the professor and myself carry on with our work, on the basis that we will ultimately lead her to the Ark. Tell Gorrick the same, let him continue to think he's got you under his thumb. Keep our plans between us only. When the time comes for Alice to return, we will secure the Ark for Oceana."

"I have already entered into a number of contracts with Zen that I will need to reconsider," the President admitted. "These things are not easy to back out of."

Secta could sense he was mulling over whether to trust what he'd been told. But he knew it was imperative to make a decision. "I cannot understand how Gorrick can be the same person you met sixty years from now," he said.

"I'm not sure he's human, and that's the truth," said Secta.

"And this Anu Set character?"

"We'll let Alice deal with him."

"But they will be able to return?"

"That's the card we have up our sleeve. Alice can return, Set can't. Now. Ri. Give me your word you'll proceed with my plan."

The President slowly nodded his head and held out his right hand. Secta took it: a handshake would suffice. He'd known the President long enough to accept it as ratification of a sworn deal.

Holding an acoustic guitar, Mal hopped off the stage as soon as saw Hope entering the rehearsal room.

"Take a break boys," he said. Hope approached him. "Are you about to serenade me with that guitar?" she said. "How romantic."

Mal played a sweet chord and improvised:

"Oh fair maiden
You've come to give the handsome one
Some news…
Should he find
The news is fine,
Then he won't have
To sing the blues…"

She rolled her eyes. "That'll do, thanks Mal. Your song's beginning to sound a little awkward," she said with a smile. Mal played a suspended chord to finish his ditty, and rested his guitar against the stage.

"Let's go outside," Hope said. "We need to talk."

"Fancy a drink?" Mal proposed, as they went out into the daylight. It was near lunchtime. He pointed at The Clock Hotel on the nearby corner. She nodded, and they strolled through to the courtyard.

Finding a free bench, they sat in the tropical garden setting. Though the courtyard gave the illusion of a peaceful oasis, it was in the centre of busy East Sydney, the hum of traffic and industry providing an urban ambience.

"I want to bring you up to speed on what's been happening," Hope said. "We've been to Texas. And we successfully sent Alice back in time — to Jerusalem, 587 BCE."

"What?" Mal almost yelled, suddenly switched into another unbelievable reality. "You telling me he's gone again, this time *back* in time?"

"Shhh, keep it down Mal," said Hope, worried they might be overheard. "If anyone overhears us they could have us committed," she added, half-joking.

She filled him in, quietly, on every detail, during which he went twice for drinks. By the time she'd finished he was drunk on science, not the beers.

"Bloody hell," he said. "So this Anu Set mongrel has followed Al back in time to nab the Ark and then neck him — and Al doesn't know it! We need to stop that. Can't we get him a message or something?"

"How?" she smiled.

"Yeah, right enough," he said. "That'd be impossible. So what comes next?"

"Well, first you'll need to handle the affairs of the Octagon in his absence."

"Yep, I pretty much assumed that. Go on."

"And he wants you to get word to the band members that he's okay but will be out of town for a couple of weeks."

"Out of town — that's an understatement!" laughed Mal. "So, is this going to be a regular thing?"

"What, his time travelling?"

"Yep."

"I think so. But it must be kept secret, Mal."

"No problem. But d'you know, when he gets back, will he still do gigs? His band will wanna know."

She sat back on the bench. "Only Alice can answer that, Mal," she said. "Now, we need to talk about when he gets back."

The sun was setting, casting a shadow over the deep ravine inside the western rampart that enclosed Jerusalem. Clouds of birds circled in the thermals over it. Standing on the rim, Alice stared down at the tons of rotting garbage at the bottom of the chasm, with gulls, crows and vultures feeding on it. He had to cover the lower part of his face with his sleeve to try to mask the putrid stench rising from the rotting organic matter and the decomposing human corpses that made a horrific part of it. Many were mere skeletons, sexlessly clean, gleaming white with only shreds of flesh left on bleached bones. But most were fresh, bloated beyond recognition, crawling with maggots and obscene in their nakedness.

Many were men, but there were women and children scattered amongst them. It reminded Alice of the hideous human carnage of the Nazi concentration camps during World War II.

"What the hell is this?" he asked Adam, who was standing beside him, also trying to smother the stench.

"I brought you this way to show you the numbers executed by Zedekiah."

"But there are hundreds of them!" exclaimed Alice.

"There are at least twenty executions a week, sometimes more."

Alice could see the slope where the bodies were tipped into the chasm. At the bottom, on the top of the sickening pile, he thought he recognised Ishtah.

"I think I see the woman who was executed this morning."

"Yes, that would be her," Adam said. "Tomorrow Jeremiah will join her."

Alice was beginning to gag. He felt sick to his stomach. Unable to take any more, they headed towards the cavern — about a fifteen-minute walk away.

"Why so many executions?" Alice asked.

Adam thought for a moment. "Let us see..." he said. "Nebuchadnezzar captured Jeconiah, the true king of Judah, during the first siege ten years ago. Ezekiel was also captured then. Nebuchadnezzar put Zedekiah on the throne, with the promise of peace. But over time Zedekiah forged a better deal for himself with the Egyptian Pharaoh Hoprah."

"Okay, so that angered Nebuchadnezzar," said Alice. "Is that why he has the place under siege?"

"Yes, but right now it has been lifted because of the approach of the Egyptian army," Adam explained.

"Are there split loyalties in Jerusalem?"

"Yes, and split religion. Zedekiah executes the opponents of his religion."

"So this time Nebuchadnezzar isn't going to mess about — he's going to destroy Jerusalem."

"Yes, but not in person," Adam said. "The King has gone to confront the Egyptian army. The captain of his guard, Nebuzaradan, leads the army he left behind. He is more ruthless than Nebuchadnezzar. It is believed he has orders to sack the city and burn the Temple."

That made two issues Alice needed to address before Nebuzaradan could destroy the place: save Jeremiah, and find the Ark. He also had a gut feeling he should meet Ezekiel, whom he suspected had a bearing on the quest.

They arrived at the path to the cavern. "There is no need to blindfold you now," Adam said, as they climbed the craggy hill. Stopping, the boy moved a clump of bushes to reveal the small dark entrance to the cave.

"They say from the mud in this cave the Golem was formed," he said.

"Yeah?" said Alice. "And what's a Golem?"

"The word literally means 'shapeless mass'," said Adam. "But Ezekiel moulded a man-shape from clay. It was eight cubits tall, more powerful than any human, capable of ripping an enemy apart. It was released against Nebuchadnezzar during the first siege, and tore many of his soldiers to pieces before it was captured. Jeremiah knows more about it than I. It is said he helped Ezekiel make it."

"Incredible," said Alice, imagining a rampaging giant clay monster ripping Babylonian soldiers to pieces. At the same time, he couldn't help wondering if it was only a myth. It was, however, another reason to meet Ezekiel.

"Did you or your Papa ever see it?" he asked.

"No, it was only used in battle. But Jeremiah talks about it."

"Could it be killed?"

"On its head were sacred letters that gave it life: emet, meaning 'truth'. Removing the first letter forms met — the word for dead — and it would cease to be."

As they entered the cave Adam lit a torch and took Alice over to where the Golem had supposedly been hewn. Alice marvelled at the large outline of a square but recognisably human shape cut from the clay floor. He'd not seen it last time because he was blindfolded. It was also the reason the soldiers that had pursued them had fled. They'd panicked on seeing the giant impression — as you would.

"This thing is huge!" he exclaimed.

"Imagine it coming at you," said Adam. "Scary."

"You sure a bunch of crazy people didn't just dig this out for a laugh?" asked Alice

"Take a closer look," Adam said. "Step into it."

Alice stepped into the metre-deep impression and stroked the inside wall with his fingers. "It's smooth, shiny … rock hard," he said. Intrigued, he tried to gouge it with his fingernail, then tapped it with his knuckles. "Really hard, like glass."

"We played in this cave when we were children," said Adam. "That was before Ezekiel lived here. This wasn't here then."

Alice lay down and was dwarfed by the massive outline. "Huge," he said.

Adam offered him a hand out.

"So, Ezekiel actually lived here?" Alice asked, looking about at the dank surroundings.

"Yes," Adam confirmed. "As soon as Zedekiah was given the throne, his first order was to arrest Ezekiel and hand him over to Nebuchadnezzar."

"Why did Nebuchadnezzar want him so bad?"

"Because he had created the Golem, which they had fought and captured … and because Ezekiel had prophesied the destruction of Jerusalem by Nebuchadnezzar, made necessary by the abominations in the Temple. I think they were afraid of him, in the same way Zedekiah is afraid of Jeremiah."

All of a sudden, in Alice's mind, the Golem had gone from fiction to fact.

CHAPTER 12
DEATH SENTENCE

HONOR WAS FAR from welcoming the report from Agent Rees that the President had stood him down. For Karzoff, watching her pace up and down her office was like being the chair umpire of a tennis match. Rees was seated opposite, wondering what he could say to ease the tension. "At least with Set gone you're back as head of OTT," he squeaked, hopefully.

Honor stopped pacing. Karzoff smiled at Rees, confirmation that he'd made a good call.

"You are absolutely correct Rees," she said, without a smile. "But vhat concerns me is ze President changing ze game plan. Vhy permit Secta and his cronies to continue zeir vork viz zeir treachery exposed? Zey should be thrown in jail!"

"But the President wants them to lead us to the Ark, do you not see that?" argued Karzoff. "I mean, it makes sense to me."

"I suppose so, but our duty is security of ze OTT," snapped Honor. "And vhile Secta valks free, he is a threat to it!"

"Why not adopt a different stratagem this time?" said Karzoff, tentatively. "Take him into your confidence. Sleaze him, so we can accomplish the task with the minimum of fuss. After all, the object of the exercise is the appropriation of the Ark, is it not?"

Honor's stern face slowly lit up. Karzoff and Rees were right. She was in charge, and it was time for her to prove herself once and for all.

She turned slowly to face them. "Zen zat is exactly vhat ve'll do, my friends," she said, wickedly. "Ve vill build zem up as friends, and vhen ze time comes — ve vill *crush* zem."

After an hour or so fifteen Holiness Code members had assembled in the cavern, along with a blindfolded new recruit.

Adam took the role of speaker. "We have a guest, I see," he said. "You may remove the blindfold, Erin."

Erin was a pudgy, round-faced lump of a teenager with a jolly countenance. He spoke with a squeaky voice. "I met this man at Beit Ha'am today," he said.

He removed the blindfold and helped the man to his feet. He was easily well over six feet, a giant by local standards and well built. He had cold, hard eyes and short-cropped blonde hair. He scoured the brothers like he was inspecting something expensive he'd been asked to buy. A small, artificial smile broke on his face. Alice thought it was more like an arrogant smirk.

"My name is Anu Set," he said. "I am here to fight Nebuchadnezzar."

"And from where do you come, brother Set?" Adam asked.

"The city of Petra, in the Kingdom of Edom."

"We welcome you to our brotherhood."

Is that all? Alice thought. No background check? He's just taken on face value? Not the sort of cat I'd be letting mind the kids…

Set sat back down next to Erin.

Adam continued. "It was Alice who asked for the meeting," he said. "So I will let him speak."

Al stood up, glared round at them for a moment, then said: "I was at Beit Ha'am this morning too. I witnessed the hideous execution of a young woman, and the arrest of Jeremiah. When I learned from Adam that Jeremiah will be executed tomorrow, my immediate reaction was to rescue him. So. If you're willing to join me, stand up."

Only Adam stood. They all sat there, shrugging their shoulders. Set rose slowly to his feet.

"You call yourselves a brotherhood," Al snarled. "All of you, with the exception of Adam and Set, can go. You disgust me."

Erin jumped up. "Count me in!" he squeaked.

Al shot him a nod of approval then, body language screaming irritation, watched the rest of them leave.

"They all have families," Adam tried to explain. "And they are not familiar with fighting."

"Where are the guys who helped against the chariots?" Alice asked.

"They failed to respond to the call to meet," Adam said.

"Why are these cowards members of this order?"

"Because they are followers of Ezekiel and Jeremiah," said Adam. "That is the reason for the order. The only reason."

Al folded his arms defiantly. "Well. We'll just have to manage without them," he said. "Where would they keep Jeremiah?"

"I know!" Erin squeaked, excitedly.

"We're going to need weapons," Set grunted.

Alice eyeballed him. There was something he didn't think was quite right with him, but he couldn't put a finger on it. Set returned the stare.

"I know the location of a weapons cache," said Adam, breaking the tension. "Follow me." Taking a burning torch from its holder, he led the way through a small entrance into another cave.

"How many caves are there down here?" Al asked.

"I have never explored, but they say it is a labyrinth," Adam replied.

It was obvious this was where Jeremiah, and Ezekiel before him, had been living. There were rudimentary utensils scattered about, a straw bed, writing implements and a stack of scrolls. Adam took a scroll unfurled it and showed it to Al.

"Here is a prophecy of Ezekiel's."

Al's translation chip didn't include visual conversion.

"I can't read Hebrew," he said. "I can speak it, but not read it."

"Where are you from, Alice?" Set asked.

"Athens."

Al noticed Set's thin-lipped mouth twist into a sneer, and wondered why. In the meantime, Adam found a flat sheet of wood on the floor. He handed the torch to Erin, bent down and lifted a trapdoor. Stashed beneath it in a shallow cavity was an assortment of weapons — swords, daggers, slingshots, bows and arrows.

"Take what you need," Adam said.

They had been collecting weapons for some time, he explained, in an attempt to build an arsenal for the coming battle against the Babylonii. Though none of the members of the Holiness Code had been trained in hand-to-hand combat, Jeremiah had told them that when the time arrived to fight the hand of the Lord would direct them how to strike against the enemy. Al's faith in Jeremiah's sanity took another blow. This certainly explained the lack of volunteers. He figured maybe he'd been a too hasty judging those who opted out. It was one thing to be brave enough to fight, but another to know how. When it came to using these crude weapons in a battle to the death, Al certainly favoured the latter.

Honor returned perplexed from her meeting with the President. As she passed Viktoria at her desk, she feistily ordered her to call Karzoff in.

In front of the large window looking down into the street, Honor hardly moved when Viktoria brought Karzoff into the room. Still watching the world below, she said: "Sit down, Karzoff. I haff interesting news from my meeting viz ze President."

Karzoff obeyed and Viktoria lingered, intrigued.

"It seems our friends Zen Corporation are on ze outer," Honor went on. "I haff been ordered to investigate them." She turned from the window and saw Viktoria still there. Her eyes narrowed. Viktoria picked up the vibe and proceeded coolly to collect a coffee cup and a plate from Honor's desk before striding out of the room. Honor eyeballed her out then, displaying her irritation like a red flag, strode over to the lounge setting, sat opposite Karzoff, crossed her legs and studied her fingernails. Karzoff picked up on it, knowing these were common signs of Honor being on the defensive.

"I haff a bad feeling about her," Honor hissed.

"You feel threatened by another dominant female Honor," said Karzoff, patronisingly. "Do you not know yourself by now?"

"She does not intimidate me, Karzoff," Honor snapped. "But I do not trust her. She is up to somezing."

Karzoff knew not to argue with her when she was in such a mood. She was headstrong, jealous and with a sting in her tail that she used without provocation. He had to be on guard in her company. On the plus side, she was intuitive, dedicated, with a strong will and could never be accused of lacking courage. He changed the subject.

"Tell me about this investigation of Zen."

"Yes," said Honor. "Ze investigation ... Ve haff orders to probe into ze affairs of Gorrick Khan and Anu Set, effective immediately." A corner of her upper thin lip curled fractionally into what appeared to Karzoff to be a carefully constructed sneer. "You vill look into zeir origin, vhile I research zeir immediate history — full due diligence."

"Check," said Karzoff, mirroring her sneer. "And what about Secta and his accomplices?"

"Ve vill continue to monitor zem," she replied. "Haff Rees set up 24/7 surveillance."

"Do we have the budget?"

"Ve haff been given carte blanche," she said, stiffly.

The President had a major conundrum on his hands. He had entered into a number of significant contracts with Gorrick Khan that now, according to Secta, could threaten the security of Oceana. He was seated behind his office desk, searching for loopholes, when his secretary knocked and entered.

"Sir, Mr Khan wants a meeting," she said.

"Tell him I'm busy."

"He says it's urgent, sir."

The President put down the documents he was holding and pinched the bridge of his nose. "When did he have in mind?" he asked.

"Um, immediately sir," she said, distastefully. She didn't like Gorrick. "He's outside,"

Rising slowly to his feet the President growled: "Damn. All right, send him in." He manoeuvred his bulk around his desk and moved to the lounge setting. He flopped into the armchair and then requested, with a sigh: "Bring some of the good coffee, please."

"Yes, sir," said Miss Vallins, heading back to reception.

A moment later Gorrick entered the office. As usual he was immaculately groomed and dressed in a grey business a suit with a thin tie that matched his azure eyes.

"Sit down Gorrick," said the President. "You look unsullied, as always."

The tall man didn't respond. He simply sat opposite the President and crossed his legs. His manner indicated he was annoyed.

"I made way for your urgent meeting, but I don't have much time," the President said, coolly. "So?"

"Your people are making enquiries into my personal life, and I want to know why," Gorrick said, sharply.

"Protocol Gorrick, merely protocol. I order due diligence on all government contracts."

"Pardon my ignorance, but is it not usual practice to do due diligence before contracts are signed, not afterwards?"

"That depends on the nature of the business. I don't see how this is urgent, Gorrick. I'm sure you have nothing to hide."

Gorrick's face tightened. "Why did you not just ask me, rather than setting your incompetent agents bungling about in my affairs?"

"Because this is the Oceana government, of which I am the President, and I don't need to ask your permission," the President replied, unsmiling.

A knock at the door and it opened as Miss Vallins entered carrying two cups of coffee. She placed them on the coffee table in front of them.

"Black, no sweetener for you, Mr Khan," she said, warmly.

He nodded blandly.

"Thank you Miss Vallins," the President said, a little louder than normal, indicating to Gorrick that he lacked manners.

Once Miss Vallins had left the room Gorrick continued. "I don't think you're being up front with me, Mr President," he sneered. "Your attitude has changed — coincidentally, at the same time as the return of Dr Secta."

"Was that a question, Gorrick?" the President asked blandly, sipping his coffee. He looked over the edge of the cup at Gorrick's face. Does the man ever blink? he thought. Secta's claim he might not be human was drumming in his mind.

"I was of the understanding that Dr Secta was under house arrest," Gorrick was saying, impatiently. "But it seems to be business as usual for him and his associates. Why is that?"

"Let me make something perfectly clear here," said the President, placing his cup in its saucer and sitting forward. "I do not answer to you. I do not have to justify my actions to you or to your organization."

Gorrick rose to his feet. "Then I have nothing more to say Mr President," he spat. "Sorry to have taken up your time." He turned on his heel and strode out.

The President wasn't surprised by Gorrick's reaction. He was glad to get it out in the open, but the meeting had left a feeling of trepidation in the pit of his stomach. He felt as though he was dealing with a mafia Don, or the dictator of a rogue nation — Gorrick was someone he could no longer trust.

As the President mused, Gorrick stormed down the steps of Oceana HQ where his chauffeur was holding the door of his stretch limousine open for him. He slipped into the soft leather seat, seething.

As the stretch sped towards the Zen Corporation building, only a few blocks away, Gorrick muttered to himself. "You have just declared war, Mr President. And you will be the first casualty."

CHAPTER 13
THE CITADEL

ARMED WITH DAGGERS under their cloaks, Erin led Alice, Set and Adam to the gate of the Fortress of Antonia, within the Temple enclosure. There were armed sentries either side. Al called his team into a huddle.

"How do we deal with the guards?" he asked.

"We just walk through," said Erin. "Let me do the talking. I'll say we're on our way to evening prayers. Just smile."

It was all too simple for Al. He pulled a quizzical face. If it was that easy to get into the Temple, it was no wonder they'd been conquered so many times. Still, the lad seemed confident. "Fine," he said, hesitantly.

It worked like a charm. After a quick chat with the guards they were on their way.

"I was expecting a bit more resistance," Set muttered to Alice.

"Yeah, me too."

It was dark in the narrow street ahead, and Alice saw they were coming to one of the many high-walled bridges that crisscrossed the city, spanning the numerous canals that brought in fresh water from the nearby Gihon spring.

As they approached the stone bridge, they saw there was another use for it. Spaced at intervals across the expanse was a hideous row of spikes, upon which severed heads were impaled.

They came to the first head, jaws agape in the rictus of death, the severed neck dripping scarlet blood into a gutter.

"Gruesome," Al said.

"What, those?" said Erin, "Oh, you get used to it. Do they not display the heads of the executed in Athens?"

"No."

"I visited Athens last year and some statesmen there were trying to repeal Draco's laws," said Set. "One of which imposed execution for stealing a cabbage. The poet Solon wrote about the Draconian laws … Have you heard of him, Alice?"

Al answered with a grunt.

They passed twenty heads, all fresh, eyes wide, staring unblinkingly into oblivion. It was a powerful warning: heed the rule of Zedekiah.

Adam had noticed Alice's reactions.

"Do not think of Hebrews only as cruel, Alice," he said. "Our enemy, the Babylonii, are notorious for impaling prisoners while they are alive."

The thought rocked Alice even more.

On the other side of the bridge was a citadel between four great stone towers. Erin stopped them short of the dark entrance and spoke in a hushed voice — he sensed danger.

"Prisoners to be executed are kept in the dungeons of the south tower," he whispered, pointing at a three-storey tower to their left. "A friend of my father was formerly a prison guard. He told us the dungeon is two levels down. It most likely has two guards."

"Okay, I think you young fellers should go in first," said Set. "Distract any guards on the upper levels."

"How?" asked Adam.

"If you're stopped, plead ignorance. Tell 'em you're lost, ask for directions to the Temple."

The two lads nodded.

"I don't like these light-coloured clothes," Al complained. Set and Erin were garbed in dark brown, which blended well into the shadows. "Swap with me, Erin, otherwise I'll stick out."

They exchanged clothes, then the two older men waited while the teenagers entered the South Tower. They scurried quietly after them.

Al led Set into a dark stairwell winding down to the second level. He heard the sound of voices echoing through the dungeons, and stopped. Hugging the corner of the landing, Al took a sneak peek at the second floor corridor. Adam and Erin were talking to an armed guard, and from what he could make out the conversation seemed amicable.

He looked over his shoulder at Set. "They're talking to a guard," he whispered.

He turned back at the sound of footsteps in time to see a second, more aggressive-looking guard join the group. He was clearly feeling less hospitable. Both guards were armed with short swords, still sheathed. When the aggressive guard went for his weapon, Al reacted automatically.

"Trouble!" he said, and rushed out into the dimly-lit corridor, Set close behind.

The aggressive guard drew his sword and pushed Erin up against the wall. In one swift movement he swept the sharp blade across the teenager's throat. Blood spurted.

The other guard had seen Alice and Set powering forwards. He also drew his sword.

Alice had no experience of fighting with a dagger, so he simply rushed the soldier before he could react, and punched him with the fist holding it. The blow smashed the man's nose across his face. Meanwhile, the second guard had whipped around and swiped at Alice with his sword. Alice deflected the blow with the dagger. The man drew his arm back for a more accurate strike — and froze. The blade of a dagger exited his chest in a spray of blood. Set stood behind him.

He looked down at the guard Alice had hit and without a second thought, dragged his blade across the man's throat.

"Whoa, you don't muck around do you?" Al growled at Set.

"What were you going to do, bring him along with us?"

Al couldn't answer. He was staring at Erin, who was still standing with his back to the wall, frozen in a silent scream, holding his throat. Blood was gushing between his fingers and running from his open mouth. His eyes were wide with shock. Staring at Alice in disbelief, the dying young man slid down the wall and bled out on the floor.

"No — no!" Adam howled, shaking uncontrollably.

Al recognised that he was going into shock. "Set, get Adam out of here," he barked. "I'll meet you at the bridge. If I'm not there in fifteen minutes, leave."

"But—"

"No buts. Adam is losing it and I owe it to his family to keep him safe. I can handle this. Go!"

Set didn't argue and Adam put up no resistance. There was nothing to be done for poor Erin. One at a time, Alice moved the three bodies into a dark alcove to avoid detection, and stealthily headed down the stairwell to the third level, trusting that Erin had had it right about Jeremiah being there. If there were guards he was ready, armed now with both a dagger and a sword.

It was humid and the air was getting thicker the further he descended. As he rounded what he figured to be the last turn of the spiralling staircase, he noticed a dim, flickering light up ahead. He waited, watching for shadows. Figuring the coast was clear, he stepped out into the corridor. The stench was stifling. Alice covered his nose and mouth with his hand, and took a burning torch from its holder to explore the corridor.

The ceiling was low and the dripping walls were covered in moss. The corridor floor was running with raw sewage: it smelled like he'd arrived in the bowels of the earth. He came upon a cell — rusted bars, locked gate and half a dozen naked bodies lying in their own excrement on the floor, asleep or dead, he didn't know which.

Satisfied Jeremiah wasn't there, he moved on. Four cells later found the prophet, alone, huddled in the corner of his cell.

"Jeremiah!" Al called, keeping his voice down, "It's me — it's Alice … Jeremiah!"

Looking like he was in a dream, Jeremiah struggled to his feet. Al was surprised — he looked okay, considering his ordeal. Though his caftan was filthy, at lease he still had one.

"Alice?" he said in astonishment, gripping the rusted vertical bars. "What are you doing here?"

"I've come to bust you out," Alice replied through gritted teeth, pulling at the mechanism that locked the door. "How do I get this open?"

"Follow the metal rod to your left," said Jeremiah, automatically. "You will find a lever. It will open the door."

As he followed the instructions, Alice asked: "When does the guard make his rounds?"

"He is due."

Alice pulled the lever and yanked the metal rod, unlocking the cell door.

"Is it the same guard from level two?"

"I have no idea," Jeremiah replied, stepping out of his cell. "Thank you for rescuing me."

"You're not saved yet, my friend. Follow me and keep quiet. No talking."

They rushed along the corridor and up the stairs. They made it to the ground floor without incident. Al held out an arm to halt Jeremiah while he checked the exit. He peered around the corner of the staircase. Set was waiting on the bridge some fifty metres away. But something felt wrong. Alice pulled back, muttering to himself. "Why is he standing out in the open on his own?"

"What is the matter, Alice?" asked Jeremiah.

"Just a feeling," Al admitted.

Suddenly the sound of footsteps echoed from the staircase behind them; someone was coming up from a lower level.

"The guard probably found my cell empty," Jeremiah whispered.

"Well, we've got no choice now," said Al. "We'll need to make a run for it. Ready?"

"Ready."

"Follow me," said Al, launching himself in a mad dash to the bridge. With Jeremiah hot on his heels he cleared the tower and was racing across the courtyard when he saw a dozen guards behind him, bows drawn. From the other side of the bridge, a dozen more. They'd kept Set pinned down to lure him and Jeremiah into the trap.

A priest dressed in the regalia of a Pharisee walked out from behind the ranks. As he stopped in front of them, Al recognised him as one of Ishtah's executioners from Beit Ha'am.

"Drop your weapons, or I will order my men to fire," the priest bellowed.

Al complied, as did Set.

Jeremiah, on the other hand, launched into a tirade. "Nasi Abbuthm, bearer of false prophecy!" he roared. "Beware the heaven of a Pharisee who spills innocent blood on the corrupted Temple of the Lord! Hypocrite!"

Jeremiah was digging them all an early grave, and Al wasn't impressed.

"Hey, priest, can we talk this over?" he shouted over Jeremiah's ranting.

Jeremiah stopped and stared at him.

The priest looked down his prominent nose with an expression like he'd just smelled a bad fart. He turned on his heel and with a wave of his hands ordered a man-at-arms: "Take them for Cannis. I will not make a martyr of Jeremiah."

Al frowned at Jeremiah. "Cannis?" he repeated. "Who, or what, is Cannis?"

"Perhaps some form of torture," Jeremiah said, with a mad laugh. "We care little which form of death awaits us, Nasi Abbuthm!" he bellowed after the Pharisee.

"Speak for yourself, buddy!" Al growled.

Set joined them as the three of them were corralled by the soldiers.

"Where's Adam?" Al asked.

"Hopefully home by now," Set replied.

"Quiet!" shouted a soldier, jabbing Set hard in the stomach with a club.

Set doubled over, gasping. "Stuff you!" he growled under his breath.

Alice's ears pricked up. No-one else he'd met in Jerusalem had ever sworn with that word.

CHAPTER 14
MARDUK

HANDS AND FEET bound, cramped uncomfortably into the back of a small, mule-drawn cart, Alice, Jeremiah and Set were being transported to Cannis, a destination unknown to them. They had been in separate prison cells overnight.

"Can't say much for the breakfast," growled Set. "Because there wasn't any."

"I could eat a horse and chase the rider," Alice moaned.

"Even if they give you food, you would be wise not to eat it," said Jeremiah. "The guards urinate and spit in it."

"Oh, lovely," said Al.

At last a pair of big wooden gates opened. They pulled through and stopped. After a conference between the guards and the driver of their transport, they moved again, leaving the guards at the gates. That left only one armed guard next to the driver. If their hands hadn't been lashed between their legs and tied to stays in the floor of the cart, they could have easily overcome him and escaped.

"They are banishing us to the desert, where we will be staked out and our eyes picked out by vultures," said Jeremiah, morosely. "Or worse, they may deliver us to the Babylonii — a fate worse than death."

"Sounds like we've got plenty to look forward to," Al groaned. "Let's talk about something else. Tell me about Betyl. You've been there?"

"I had a vision," said Jeremiah. "Angels came and took me to heaven."

"But in your sermon, the first time I met you, you said you visited Betyl," Al said.

"I was taken to Betyl, I beheld the Earth, and it was without form and void..." Jeremiah began.

"Yes, yes, that was the sermon," Al cut in. "But I want to know more about Betyl. What was it like?"

"I had a vision of war, a time before man..." Jeremiah sighed, staring up at the sky.

Jeremiah, Al figured, had a screw loose. Set pulled a face, indicating he felt the same way.

"Ezekiel witnessed the landing of the great chariot from Betyl," Jeremiah went on. "Ezekiel said: 'As I looked, a stormy wind came out of the north, and a great cloud, with brightness round about it, and fire flashing forth continually, and in the midst of the fire, as it were gleaming bronze. And from the midst came the likeness of four living creatures: they had the form of men but each had four faces and four wings. Their legs were straight, and the soles of their feet were round; and they sparkled like burnished bronze.'"

Al and Set stared at him. "I believe I was taken by the same beings," Jeremiah said, dreamily.

"Sounds to me like a UFO landing," Al mumbled.

"Sounds like a lot of crazy talk," Set said, looking annoyed. "We got ourselves in this position to rescue a lunatic? Why?"

"I'm beginning to ask that myself," said Al. "Hey, by the way, something I meant to ask you..."

"Yeah? What's that?"

"When that soldier jabbed you yesterday, you said 'stuff you'," said Al. "That's not an expression I've heard around here before. Where did you pick it up?"

"It's from my native language," growled Set.

"You also use contractions whereas no-one else does."

Set shrugged his shoulders.

Al knew he was lying, a quick search informed him that the etymology of the swear word stuff derived from 13th Century British. He'd given Set a chance to be straight. Now he'd have to be wary.

It wasn't long before their destination became obvious. Ahead of them were the lines of the massive Babylonian siege. Al was relieved there were no stakes and vultures. He hadn't fancied that at all.

The sheer size of the Babylonian encampment was awe-inspiring — it was like a city.

"There must be thousands of them," Set said.

"Impressive, considering most of the army is supposed to be with Nebuchadnezzar taking on Pharaoh Hophra," Al answered tersely.

Their driver stopped the cart twenty feet from the outer stockade, a good strong one, with sharpened timbers planted facing out as a defensive structure. Beyond it were massive wooden gates and the ramparts of the Babylonian stronghold, ten metres high and enclosing the fortress, with a sentry tower every hundred metres.

"What a set up," Al said, in admiration.

"They say the whole thing is transportable," said Jeremiah, apparently back in the land of the living. "It can be broken down and loaded onto wagons, ready to move, in a day. This heathen army is a sophisticated war machine." Sometimes Jeremiah was perfectly lucid, other times he was totally off the planet. Alice shrugged.

The massive wooden gates creaked open and two warriors, in a chariot drawn by two majestic black horses, drove through. They stopped a few feet away, and the passenger bellowed in Aramaic: "What do you want?"

"Tell Cannis I bear a gift from King Zedekiah, my lord," their guard called back. "The prophet Jeremiah, and two of his priests."

"Priests?" Al almost choked.

"You send your prisoners for us to burn?" the warrior shouted, amused.

"Jeremiah is a high priest, and a colleague of the prophet Ezekiel, whom your King keeps for oracular counsel," the guard yelled back.

"King Zedekiah believed the gift of Jeremiah would give the great King Nebuchadnezzar more access to the gift of prophesy."

"Wait here," said the warrior, dismissively. "I shall speak with Cannis."

The chariot U-turned and re-entered the stronghold.

Al listened to the conversation between the guard and the driver of their cart.

"He didn't seem very impressed," said the driver.

"He may not have heard of Jeremiah," said the guard. "You watch — I will bet you ten shekels he will return for them. They will probably burn the other two, but Jeremiah will be of great value. Nebuchadnezzar likes to have his dreams interpreted. That is why he keeps Ezekiel alive."

This was interesting information. Well, not the bit about being burned alive, but the business of dream interpretation. Alice thought there might be something he could use there.

A few minutes later the chariot was back, with three soldiers following on foot. The prisoners were bundled from the cart, shackled, and led inside the stronghold.

The interior was even more impressive than the outside. It made sense to Alice. When an army laid siege to a large fortified city, it could last years. A virtual city was bound to evolve.

Smoke rose from small fires, and there was a vast number of rounded huts, seemingly thatched. Then tents as far as the eye could see, all in well-defined rows around a large market square. In the central position was a temple with a small coliseum to the side. At the rear were stables and a covered garage in which hundreds of chariots were parked. The market was a hive of activity, with vendors selling everything from fruit to fabric. There were women and children garbed in colourful robes. The shoppers looked different to those at the market in Jerusalem. More flamboyant, better groomed, healthier, fitter … but most of all, wealthier. But the vendors were definitely Hebrews from Jerusalem.

As he was led past the market square, Al noticed that the central point was an edifice for execution. A shiver ran up his spine — he'd been hoping the Babylonians weren't going to be as barbaric as the pharisees in Jerusalem.

"Looks like these Babylonians enjoy a good execution," Set said, chuckling.

"You're sick," Al rasped.

When they stopped next to the citadel the guards separated them. Alice was led inside and imprisoned in a small cell. Still shackled, sitting cross-legged on the floor, he closed his eyes, remained calm. A strong conviction that his quest was meaningful, and that he was being protected from danger by some kind of external intervention, had given him the belief that he wasn't meant to die here, in this time or in this place. Less delusions of invincibility, more a belief that he had a purpose. He simply sat, meditating, and waiting for whatever came next.

Hours later, as the sun was setting, a guard came and took him to meet Cannis. This was the man with the duty of liaising with the enemy. Rotund, with a big round face to match his figure, he was sitting behind a table in a small bland room. Cannis reminded Alice of some kind of ancient Egyptian bean counter, an accountant. His eyes were decorated with black kohl and green eye shadow. He wore an Egyptian headdress, a black wig and a white tunic. Alice estimated by the lines around his painted eyes that he was around forty. But the most dominant feature was his expression. He looked like he'd just bitten into a lemon.

"Who are you?" Cannis asked in Hebrew.

"I am the translator, Black Alice."

Cannis repeated the question in Latin, Greek, Egyptian and Aramaic. Al answered in the same language each time. The fat man raised his painted-on black eyebrows, impressed.

"It seems you have many talents, Black Alice," Cannis said, settling on Egyptian.

"So I've been told," Al replied.

"They said you were a priest."

"They got it wrong."

"I think I will grant you an audience with our King," said the fat man. "He is likely to find you interesting."

"I thought your King was busy fighting your countrymen," Alice answered.

"Hmph," snorted Cannis. "Well informed, also. Yes, I am Egyptian. From Karnak. Like you, I began as a prisoner of war. Now I am chief war liaison, directly responsible to General Nebuzaradan," he finished, proudly.

Alice searched the name in his database, then leaned over the desk and whispered to Cannis: "Better keep it that way, friend, because a little bird tells me Nebuzaradan will soon be famous. It will be he who destroys Jerusalem."

Cannis's eyes widened to the size of dinner plates. He stared at Alice like he was a ghost.

"King Nebuchadnezzar returned from the battlefield today," he whispered. "He wished to consult his advisers on the astrologically-correct time to wage war."

"I can tell him that," said Alice. "I have a connection with Betyl." He pointed sharply up. The action caused Cannis to flinch. He struggled out of his chair and around the desk. He was much shorter than Alice had anticipated, only around five feet.

"You can speak with Marduk?" he demanded.

"I have my ways," snarled Alice, inwardly laughing. "It is called the Happening Vibe, derived from the heavy metal Endangered Species."

Cannis paced the floor, chewing on the end of his thumb. He stopped abruptly. "Guard!"

The door flew open and an armed guard entered. "Go now to General Nebuzaradan," Cannis ordered. "Tell him I have a priest here who can speak with Marduk. Ask if the King would like to give him audience."

The guard said nothing, just turned on his heel and moved off on the double.

"Cannis, I'm not a priest," Al growled. "It's a shame you don't have a phone," Alice said, enjoying the man's reactions.

"What is this ... phone?" Cannis asked, flopping back into his chair.

"A device that allows you to talk to anyone, anywhere, at any time."

"And you have such a device?"

"Don't be silly. There'd be no signal here."

"Signal?"

"Connectivity," Al said.

"Oh, I understand," said Cannis, who clearly didn't.

"Hey, how about removing these?" Al said, holding up his shackled wrists. Again, Cannis stared at him — but Alice felt his fear, not his anger.

Cannis yelled for the guard again. Another soldier entered and was ordered to remove Alice's shackles. Rubbing his red raw wrists, Al said: "I hope you people feed your prisoners. Your enemy certainly doesn't — I could eat the backside out of a skeleton."

"Is that a delicacy from your land?" said Cannis, causing Al to laugh aloud.

Just then a messenger entered the room. "The priest is granted an audience, sir," he said. "You are to present him to the King."

That immediately turned Cannis into a nervous wreck. He began madly brushing down the front of his gown, and flapping around like a butterfly sprayed with insecticide.

The messenger pulled a face. "Follow me," he commanded, abruptly, and stormed out.

This was an audience Alice was looking forward to. He'd always wanted to meet a King. In his time, he'd met and mingled with plenty of stars, dudes you'd call kings of their profession, but this dude Nebuchadnezzar II? Well, he was right up there in the company of

Alexander the Great, Amenhotep and Julius Caesar — the absolute cat's pyjamas of overlords.

It was dark. The markets had closed for the day, all goods and chattels packed out of sight. The messenger walked them across the square into a passageway linked to the coliseum. Beyond the austere arena they came to a building that had been obscured from Alice's view before. It was by far the most imaginative building he'd seen since he arrived in this ancient world.

Built of huge stone blocks, it was three stories high and supported by massive columns capped with a dome. The huge red granite entrance steps led to a pair of exquisite white marble columns on either side of an arched entrance, heavily secured by guards in battledress, armed with gold tipped spears. Their vibrant livery reminded Alice of the Swiss Guards at the Vatican.

Draped from a flying buttress above the columns, all the way down to just above the ground, blood-red, gold-edged banners moved gently in the warm desert breeze. In the flickering light of fires within, two six-foot bronze saucers were balanced on the backs of winged bronze lions with human, curly-bearded heads. The huge metal entrance doors were a portentous yet regal proclamation of imperial power.

Alice wondered if the lion's head was the likeness of King Nebuchadnezzar.

Cannis interrupted his reverie. "When I introduce you to the King, you will prostrate yourself until asked by him to rise," he said, sharply. "If you do not comply, he will order you to be burnt alive. Do I make myself clear?"

"Happy to comply, Cannis," Alice rasped. "I just hope he's got something to eat."

"Whatever else you do, Alice, be wary of Zorlock," his guide replied. "He is personal astrologer to the king, a wicked, jealous sorcerer. Many have fallen victim to his malicious spirit because he saw them as a threat."

CHAPTER 15
NEBUCHADNEZZAR II

THE MASSIVE, COPPER-clad double doors were covered in a patina of verdigris. When Alice was led though he witnessed an even greater display of opulence and majesty than he'd seen on the outside. This king was every bit of what history had recorded. He was the master architect of incredible buildings and monuments, the creator of the famed hanging gardens of Babylon and the world's first museum. Even knowing all that, there's nothing like evidence. The mastery of the man was proven by the magnificence of the engineering that was before Alice. He could hardly wait to meet this king of kings.

A metre-wide golden carpet stretched before them, which they followed to the throne room. The walls were decorated with long tapestries depicting scenes of the great victories of the revered king. Up ahead, Alice could see a gathering of people and, beyond them, a dais upon which stood a magnificent throne. The messenger stopped them and proceeded to the throne. Then came three loud knocks — a staff striking the floor. It was the signal for Cannis to bring the captive forth.

The throng parted for Cannis and Alice. They stopped again a few metres short of the throne. Alice immediately lay spreadeagled on the carpet. Cannis struggled to do same.

"Almighty King Nebuchadnezzar," Cannis intoned face down, "I present for your curiosity this strange priest of Greece! Devotee of the mystic art of the Happening Vibe, prophet of the heavy metal Endangered Species — Black Alice!"

Alice, still face down, grinned to himself.

After a pregnant pause, which passed without a sound, a gravel voice came from the King: "Stand!"

About bloody time, Al thought. I was about to nod off.

"Cannis," the king finished.

Alice twisted his head to look at Nebuchadnezzar.

Sitting on a golden throne was an incredibly regal middle-aged man. He wore a long, curly, raven-coloured beard, cut square at his muscular chest. He was garbed in golden cloth, draped with a purple sash. His head was crowned with a spiralling headdress, under which shone long, beautifully-groomed black hair, and in his hands, he held the golden sceptre of his sovereignty. His fingers were adorned with bejewelled rings.

At his left side stood a powerful warrior with a scabbarded simitar slung from his belt, a golden spiked helmet atop his head of black hair, and elaborately-meshed body armour covering his broad chest. His brown eyes were intense, his nose sharp, thick black eyebrows in a single straight line underlined his brow and he wore a beard similar to the King. This must be General Nebuzaradan.

To the right of the King a tall, thin man in a jet-black caftan stood like a vulture, his face concealed inside a dark hood.

The King's voice rumbled, "Rise."

Alice sighed, at last, then stood. "My lord," he said, with a bow.

"I am told you have a connection to Marduk," said the King. "How be that?"

"I am master of the Happening Vibe, lord King," Alice replied. "In my time, connection with the lords of the air is commonplace."

"In your time?" questioned the King, in his three-packs-a-day voice.

Alice looked at his dark intelligent eyes. This man could take a little of the truth.

"I am a time traveller, great King," he said. "I come from the future." A loud murmur of disbelief rumbled from the assembly. "I can speak any language!" Alice went on. "I can interpret dreams, and accurately predict the future!"

Suddenly, the scowling vulture next to the King straightened up. He pulled back his hood, stink-eyed Alice and declaimed: "This Black Alice of the Happening Vibe is a liar!"

The man's face was almost skeletal, his bald, elongated head framing fierce, piercing green eyes with cat-like pupils. His skin was a rich mid-brown and decorated with mystical symbol tattoos. Around his neck he wore a colourful necklace adorned with astrological charms. His skinny but muscular torso was wrapped in dark bandages, like a living, breathing mummy. Hung from a broad, studded leather belt was an array of ugly weapons: a hook, a scimitar and a dagger. He looked like evil personified.

"Ah! This must be the great Zorlock, a sorcerer of such fame that even in the future his name is revered," Al cried, bowing his head. "I am honoured to meet you, oh great one."

Alice thought if he crawled far enough up Zorlock's butt he might gain approval. The man was certainly taken aback by Alice's rhetoric, and eased up on the aggression. Clearly not fully convinced, however, he said: "The Lords of Overshadow must interrogate this man before he again speaks to the great King."

"That can be done later, Zorlock," the king replied. "For now, I will take food. This man of the Happening Vibe will be my guest. He looks like he could do with some good food — am I correct, Black Alice?"

If looks could kill, Alice would have been vaporized by Zorlock's glare of distaste. It was exactly as Cannis had warned: Zorlock was seething with jealousy and Alice could sense retribution.

"Just Al will be fine, your majesty," he said, bowing to the king. "And yes, I could certainly do with a feed."

When the King arose from his massive throne everybody in the room bowed at the waist and averted their eyes. Alice guessed it was like avoiding locking eyes with a silverback — a show of submission and respect.

After the King had left the room, followed by Zorlock and Nebuzaradan, Cannis took Alice by the arm and rushed him back along the golden carpet. "We must hurry," he panted. "The King does not like to be kept waiting, and we must bathe you and change your garments."

After a wash and a change into a clean white caftan and new sandals, Al looked and felt good as new. Cannis joined him and dismissed the boy slave who had served as both washer and dresser.

"The damage with Zorlock is irreconcilable," he hissed. "Already I have had word that he wants you executed. I warned you!"

"I can't help it if the man is a fool," said Al, shrugging. "I'll deal with him when and if I need to."

"Ah, but now you must also be careful of Nebuzaradan," Cannis replied. "He is a good man, but under the influence of Zorlock. Nebuzaradan will be at the feast also."

"Not Zorlock the warlock?" Al chortled at his own gag.

"No, he will not be there. But you can be sure he will be in the background somewhere, scheming to rid the empire of you."

"Where are my friends, Jeremiah and Set?"

"Jeremiah is waiting to meet with Ezekiel, who is travelling from Babylon and will arrive tomorrow. Set will be executed soon."

"What? There's no need to kill him, he's one of the Happening Vibe," Al protested.

"Then tell that to the King," said Cannis. "But do not plead. The King thinks grovelling is weakness."

"Good advice, thanks … by the way, why are you doing all this for me?"

"I like the concept of the Happening Vibe," Cannis smiled. "Now, before we go, tell me … what is it like in your future?"

Al grinned. "People can fly around the world in huge flying machines," he said. "Man has stood on the moon. We travel on smooth roads in horseless chariots at speeds faster than arrows."

Cannis was awestruck, staring, mouth open. "Better watch out, Cannis," Al chuckled. "You might swallow a fly."

Alice took the opportunity to search the King's name in his translator. He wanted to be armed with as much information as possible, knowing he was up against the power and influence of Zorlock.

"I have travelled many leagues today," said the King. "I am very tired."

In the banquet room, a floor area had been cleared for food and surrounded by large, comfortable cushions. The dishes had been served, one delicacy after another, finishing with a wonderful selection of sweetmeats and fruits accompanied by a goblet of Egyptian mead.

There were only the three of them present, and Nebuzaradan had kept ominously quiet.

"The food was splendid sire," said Al, bowing and raising his goblet in salute. "I am indebted to you. I wonder, may I ask? Who styles your beard? How do you get it to curl like that?"

The King actually laughed out loud. "I do not know that I have ever been asked such an impertinent question!" he chuckled. "I have a slave to do the work, Al. I cannot claim the expertise," he added, smiling. "Now. It is my turn to question you. You will know what I wish you to tell me?"

Alice hummed, eyes closed, putting on a little act for the benefit of the King and his general. Opening them wide, he pronounced: "You will soon bring Phoenicia and the Assyrian province of Cilicia into your empire."

Nebuzaradan laughed, scornfully.

"Something amusing, Lord Nebuzaradan?" Al queried.

"Tell us something new," the General scoffed. "The entire world knows that!"

"I merely offer confirmation, my lord," Al skillfully replied. "I can also tell you that the siege of Jerusalem is almost over. In the summer of this year, you, Nebuzaradan, will lead forces into Jerusalem, destroy the Temple of Solomon and put the city to the torch."

Both men looked more impressed. It would be impossible for Alice to know their plan.

"Who will be my successor?" the King quizzed.

Alice hammed it up again, peering skyward as though to gain a heavenly link, and mumbling happening vibe, happening vibe just under his breath. He locked eyes with the King. "Great King, eldest son of Nabopolassar. reincarnated descendant of the great Nimrod, son of Cush," he intoned. "You will hold the throne for another 25 years. Your son Amel-Marduk will succeed you." He decided not to mention that Amel-Marduk wouldn't be holding the throne for long. He'd be assassinated only two years into his reign and succeeded by his murderer. Maybe not the kind of news the King was looking for.

Nebuchadnezzar rose slowly to his feet and began to pace the room. Alice wondered if he'd gone too far, or not far enough. Suddenly the King stopped. "And what of Nebuzaradan?" he demanded. "Tell me of his future!"

Alice went through his rigmarole for a moment while he mentally looked the soldier up. "He will attach the King's portrait to his chariot when he attacks Jerusalem," he said, at last. "In order that he might always stand in your Majesty's presence."

Nebuzaradan's expression suggested he liked what he'd heard.

"Do you expect this clairvoyance to save your life?" asked the King.

"I had no idea my life was at risk, good King."

"Zorlock calls you a liar," said Nebuzaradan, gruffly.

"A claim made by one who feels threatened by another," Al replied, mildly. He was getting the hang of this prophet business.

"That may be true…" said Nebuzaradan. "Now tell us, prophet, how is it you can see into the future?"

"I come from the future," said Alice. "So my foretelling is about knowing the past."

"Interesting," said the King. "From how far into the future?"

"More than two thousand six hundred years, sire."

The King stared at Alice disbelievingly, "Two thousand six hundred years?" he repeated slowly.

"Yes," Al confirmed. "From a time when men cross the skies in great flying machines. When we have walked on the moon and explored far beyond our own world. When a man has ventured, for the first time, to travel back in time in order to meet a great King."

"And why is it that you have come to meet me?"

"To gain knowledge, sire, not to impart it."

Nebuzaradan jumped up. He'd had enough. "What sort of Hebrew treachery is this?" he snarled. "Zorlock is right, sire. This man is a fraud, a spy!"

"And why do you say that, Nebuzaradan?" The King asked, calmly.

"Because what he professes is impossible," the general said dismissively.

"Just as impossible as some of Ezekiel's predictions, which you also find difficult to accept," said the King. "Predictions, I might add, that have come to fruition. Never fear the unknown, Nebuzaradan, for that is what awaits us all."

Alice was impressed. The King was much more than a bejewelled figurehead. He was a thinker, too.

"I am of the old religion, sire," said Nebuzaradan, backing down a little. "I do not accept this nonsense from the Hebrews. They have proven themselves, over and over, to be untrustworthy. Look at Zedekiah — a classic example."

"I must agree with you there, my friend," said the King.

"But I am not a Hebrew," Alice put in. "I am a time traveller. I come from country that won't even be known by most of the world for another two thousand years!"

The King sighed. "As I said before," he said, "I am tired. We will talk again tomorrow, Al of the Happening Vibe. Guard!"

"Before I go sir, may I ask that you spare the life of my associate, Set. He too is no Hebrew, and has been unfairly treated by Zedekiah."

"I will consider these things on the morrow, once Ezekiel is here," the King replied. "I trust his judgement in matters arcane."

At which point a guard appeared. "Take this man to a secure cell for the night. Do not treat him roughly," said the King.

The guard bundled Alice away.

The room, an old warehouse, was packed to the rafters. A sea of punters all clad in black had come to the Black Alice gig. Ratsso, Blue and Slut were on stage but instead of Alice up front, it was Mal. But that didn't seem to matter, they were all going off big time to a Black Alice favourite, Upside Down.

Mal grabbed the mike and sang, "Everybody's moaning, yeah they're moaning 'bout the times, trapped in their devices, wasting lives on line. Too many options from too many minds. They're questioning reason without validating rhyme. Well yer, so mad, getting all the spam, taking it to dump it in the trash can man. You crack down, rolling on the ground, too much mind control can turn you up-side-down."

With Blue hammering out a powerful beat, Slut launched into a blistering solo.

A lone pretty girl with long black hair dressed Goth was at the bar at the back of the room nodding her head wildly to the beat.

After the gig Mal was seated at the mirror backstage towelling off perspiration. The other band members were lazing about. The gig had been a success, though they missed Al, it was good to play his songs. The door opened and the girl dressed Goth entered.

"Oh hi," she said reticently. "I'm, um, looking for Black Alice."

Mal looked up at her in the mirror and smiled. "Hey babe, he's away so I'm filling in. Like ah, who are you?"

She took a step inside and looked nervously about the messy room.

"Wyetta Walker ... but most people call me Vee. I'm Alice's sister."

Her statement had blown their minds.

Blue glared at her with a frown and said, "Gee, I didn't know Al had a sister."

She coyly bit her bottom lip ... her big almond eyes flicked to each of the bandmembers. "Um, either does he," she said.

CHAPTER 16
CHARIOTS OF THE GODS

THE GRUEL SERVED up for breakfast tasted like its name — a disappointment after the feast of the night before. Al hoed into it anyway, slurping direct from the wooden bowl. He'd just finished when a guard arrived and took him to Cannis.

"Greetings, Alice," Cannis said from behind his desk as Al entered. "Sit down. It seems you made quite an impression on the King last night. He wants to see you again this morning."

"Maybe he liked my jokes," Al grinned.

"On the other hand," said Cannis, "Your request to reprieve your friend Set has made you enemies of Zorlock and Nebuzaradan."

"Why? What's eating them?"

"An interesting expression," said Cannis. "I deduce from its context that you mean what is worrying them?"

"Sure."

"Set was to be Zorlock's sacrificial dedication to Marduk today."

"Oh, I spoiled his show," said Al. "Good. Now what's up Neb's backside?"

"Up his backside … Another interesting expression. I will assume you do not literally mean what is in his anus. Another way of saying what is eating him?"

"I'm full of interesting expressions," said Al, happily.

"It is difficult to say why the general is upset," Cannis went on. "He can be moody, but in this instance, if I was to hazard a guess, I'd say his mood is a contrivance of Zorlock. So, watch your back." His eyes opened wider.

One of the King's personal guards arrived for Alice. He followed the man from Cannis's office across the market square, once more full of colour and life, and along the same corridor as before. This time, instead of following the golden carpet to the throne room, the guard led Alice into a side corridor, where a flight of steps descended to an incredibly exotic-looking bathhouse. He left Alice there.

The pool was approximately twenty metres by six and paved with shiny black and gilt tiles. Skeins of mist rose from the water like gossamer wings. The patio around the pool was tiled with multi-coloured tesserae, with the largest area an incredibly intricate and life-like portrait of the King's head. The transparent domed ceiling provided light for the entire room and amplified even the smallest sound, causing it to echo.

Alice stood, silent and awed, watching coily vapours rise from the mirrored waters. Every few seconds a drip echoed, making the stillness even more perceptible.

"Join me, Al." The King's voice unexpectedly sounded somewhere near Alice's feet. He was sitting, submerged to chin, in the pool.

Al moved to the steps. Seeing the King was naked, he removed his caftan before descending the four tiled steps into the warm water beside the King.

"You have a powerful form, Al," said the King. "More like a Greco wrestler than a priest."

"I have been many things in my short life sire," said Al. "A singer, a writer, a traveller, a warrior — but never a priest."

"After bathing, we shall have an audience with the oracle Ezekiel, who has arrived at my request."

"That I look forward to. I hope he is more ... balanced than Jeremiah."

"Do you question Jeremiah's sanity?"

"I think the stresses of his life have taken a toll, lord king."

"Interesting. I have the same notion. I have known many such visionaries, sorcerers, priests, prophets, astrologers and oracles."

"And which of these do you find the most accurate?"

"Good question," said the King. "That depends — when it comes to matters of the future, the prophet can be useful. When it comes to instilling fear into your enemies, nothing outrivals the power of a genuine sorcerer. But when it comes to matters of the heart, or of one's private life, the astromancer is the most accurate.

"With all of that stated, I have a personal preference for the most curious of the breed: the visionary. It is in this category that I place you, Black Alice of the Happening Vibe. Tell me: at what age will I die, and how?"

This wasn't the first time Alice had been presented a loaded question, and it certainly wouldn't be the last. He knew the answer could be received in a good or bad light, and he had only his gut feeling to go on. That told him to be truthful.

"Your forty-three year reign will be the longest of any king of Babylon," he said, smiling at the King. "You will be forever regarded as the greatest king of Babylon, and you will die an old, old man in the magnificent city of your creation."

The King smiled, much to Alice's relief. "I expect you know the precise year — but I shall not ask it," he said. "Divvits!" he called, causing Alice to jump slightly. A slave came running with a robe. The King stood. The servant held open the robe as the King slipped into and, without another word, both left Alice in the bath. After a few moments, another servant arrived, carrying another robe. Having donned it, Alice was led to yet another room in the palace complex. It was obviously the King's audience chamber. Nebuchadnezzar was lounging back on a giant pillow, chatting with a heavily-bearded, long-haired man seated opposite. The guard left Alice, who waited for the King to acknowledge him.

The room was designed like the interior of the tent of a Bedouin Sheikh: purple drapes suspended from the centre of the ceiling lined the oval walls. The floor was covered with black-and-white animal pelts.

"Ah, Black Alice," smiled the King. "Come sit with us," he said, beckoning him to take a cushion. "This, Ezekiel, is Black Alice. He claims to come from the future."

Ezekiel was no more than thirty-five years old, but his grey hair and bushy grey beard and eyebrows made him look older. Alice was reminded of Charlton Heston's Moses from The Ten Commandments, only with darker skin.

Alice sank into a pillow.

"Black Alice," said Ezekiel. "What an extraordinary name."

"It is a name I was given as a performer," Alice explained.

"A performer? Of what?" Ezekiel asked.

"A singer of music."

"And have you no other name, Black Alice, singer of music?"

Alice smiled. He hadn't thought about it in years. "I was called Daniel sometimes, when I was a child," he said. "It is my middle name."

"Ah?" said Ezekiel. "Then I shall call you Daniel. Did you know that the name means God is my judge?"

"I did not," said Al. "In this time, it seems I am to be judged by you, Ezekiel."

"The King has told me you can interpret dreams. That you are a visionary."

"This is true," said Alice. "And I would like to ask a question related to one of my visions, if I may?"

"Go ahead."

"Have you had contact with Betyl?"

The look on Ezekiel's face hardened. "I shall tell you what I can," he said. "I saw a windstorm coming out of the north, an immense cloud, flashing with lightning and surrounded by brilliant light. The centre looked like glowing metal, and in it were four living creatures.

"In appearance their form was human, but each had four faces and four wings. Their legs were straight; their feet were like those of a calf and gleamed like burnished bronze. They had human hands. Each had one human face, and on the right side the face of a lion, on the left the face of an ox. The last was the face of an eagle.

"As I looked at the creatures, I saw a wheel on the ground beside each creature. I fell to the ground and one of the beings said to me: 'Son of man, stand on your feet and I will speak to you.' It told me it was sending me to the Israelites, a rebellious people. It handed me a scroll and told me to eat it — it tasted sweet as honey. He said: 'Now you have my words. Go and speak them to the people of Israel.'

"I heard from behind me a loud rumbling sound as the glory of the Lord rose from the ground. The being lifted me up and took me to the exiles at Tel Aviv, near the Kebar River. There I sat among them for seven days."

He stopped, looking quietly into nothing. Alice knew there was plenty more to the story, but there wasn't time for the rest of the sermon.

"May I interpret this for you?" he asked.

"You may," Ezekiel said, intrigued.

"Betyl is a craft from another world, orbiting Earth," said Alice, choosing his words carefully. "A smaller craft was sent from it, and it landed near you. The occupants were Anunnaki — you have heard of the Anunnaki, haven't you, sire?"

"Yes," said the King. "The family of Marduk, the creators of man."

"So, when the craft landed, these men descended to the ground," Alice went on. "They were dressed in strange clothes resembling wings, and wearing helmets with three faces on them. They told you to stop the Israelites from worshipping idols. They gave you a pill to swallow — a potion, but in solid form. It gave you the words to say to the Israelites.

"They took you into their craft and flew you to Tel Aviv. There, after talking with the Israelites, you went to Jerusalem, where you used the knowledge given to you to create the Holiness Code, so that when Jerusalem is destroyed, some good people will be saved … Does that sound like your experience?"

"Why, yes it does," said Ezekiel, looking perplexed. "But how is it that you know this?"

"Because in my time, people can travel into space, wearing special clothing and helmets to protect themselves. We have built ships like those you have seen, and invented pills that can help us see and understand things differently. We even have machines that can think, and which provide us with the collective knowledge of millions of minds."

"Are you suggesting that Marduk, creator of mankind, is in a craft that flies in the air?" Ezekiel asked.

"Yes, I am," said Alice. "To you, it would appear as a moving star."

"Can you … speak with Marduk?" the King asked.

"It may be possible, sire," Alice replied. "I would need to know more about him first."

"Marduk is the firstborn of En-Ki," said the King.

Alice's head reeled. Everything was surely falling into place. He suspected that Ezekiel had used the Ark of Covenant to contact Marduk on Betyl — he had after all been high priest of the Temple, and had access to it. Perhaps Ezekiel wasn't saying anything about that because of the King's presence. If the King knew the power of the Ark, he would move heaven and Earth to possess it. Alice had to get to the Ark first. He had to speak with Ezekiel alone. He was about to get his opportunity.

A messenger entered the room, stopped and waited until the King waved him closer. He leaned down and whispered. Nebuchadnezzar grimaced and dismissed the messenger.

"I am afraid we will have to carry on this incredible discussion at a later date," he said. "Pharaoh Hophra has confronted my army at Kadesh, and I am needed. Pray, excuse me." He got up, bowed to his guests, and left.

CHAPTER 17
HARBINGER OF DOOM

EZEKIEL LOOKED AT Alice with all-seeing eyes. "What is it that brings you here, Daniel?" he asked. "It cannot simply be that Jeremiah has been up to his old tricks again."

Alice shifted on his pillow, feeling a little doubtful now that he was about to let the cat out of the bag.

"Ezekiel, we don't know each other and it's unlikely we'll have time to," he said. "So I'll get to the point. I have to trust that, unlike Jeremiah, you are of sound mind and will keep what I will now speak of in confidence."

"I will, Daniel."

"First I must ask: did you use the Ark of the Covenant as a device to speak with God?"

Ezekiel's expression did not change. It was as though he was expecting the question.

"You are a wise man, Daniel," he said. "Yes, the Ark can be used — as Moses used it — to speak with God."

"God, or the occupants of Betyl?"

"They are one and the same."

"I am here to remove the Ark from the Temple and hide it. To keep it safe from the sacking of Jerusalem. The future needs assurance that the Ark is safe."

Ezekiel smiled. "Then you are the one I have been expecting, Daniel. And the time is upon us now."

The fact Ezekiel had been expecting him nearly knocked Alice off his cushion. In his mind, it clarified the connection between Ezekiel and Marduk, and explained why he and Nebuchadnezzar had become allies: Marduk was worshipped by the Babylonians, not the Hebrews. In forming the Holiness Code, Ezekiel had been attempting to unite both religions — much to the distaste of the Pharisees. Aware that his time was running out, Alice continued. "I was hoping to solicit Jeremiah's help," he said. "But his state of mind is too delicate. I cannot trust him."

"You do the right thing," Ezekiel replied. "You must obtain an audience with Zedekiah. Only he can help. You must remember that he is of the House of David," he continued, as Alice drew back in horror. "He is not, in himself, an evil man. He is under the influence of the Pharisees. But he does not want the Ark to fall into their hands, any more than Zorlock's or my King's."

"Why would Zedekiah help me?" asked Alice.

"You must tell him you are Daniel, and that I named you so. That will get you an audience. Then tell him that on my instruction you, and only you, may remove the Ark and be trusted with the secret of its final location."

"Where did the Ark come from in the first place?" Alice asked.

"It was built from specifications given by God to Pharaoh Rameses II," the prophet replied. "Covered inside and out with gold leaf, it became active when a glowing orb delivered by angels was placed inside."

That actually almost makes sense, thought Alice. Specs and a power source from the Anunnaki, and there you have it … a nuclear-powered communication device.

"I really do not know why I was chosen for this task," Ezekiel said, running his fingers absently through his beard.

"I call it the Star Philosophy," said Alice. "You make a leader, then you need only control one person to influence many more."

"Hmm. That is a sensible theory," said Ezekiel. "However now, Daniel, you must leave for Jerusalem, or your enemy Zorlock will put an end to your plans. I believe he is at the root of this siege. I believe he has convinced the King and Nebuzaradan to seize the Ark. I feel sure Zorlock means to use it for evil purposes."

"Why does Zorlock tolerate you?" Alice questioned.

"The King finds value in my counsel. He does not dare oppose me."

"Tell me one more thing," said Alice. "I saw the impression of the Golem in the cavern outside Jerusalem. How on Earth did you give it life?"

"Ha!" chuckled Ezekiel, recalling it. "Remember that I mentioned the scroll — the pill, as you called it — given me by the angels? It also gave me the words that would animate life."

"I see," said Alice, who didn't really but didn't have time to get into it. "And the cavern — did Zedekiah or the Pharisees force you to live there?"

"No, it was my sanctuary," said Ezekiel. "I needed a place to hide my gospels. To bury them forever, if need be. One push on the round rock beside the entrance will seal it all forever."

Just then two guards entered the room and Alice found himself seized.

Nebuzaradan walked along the rampart to the main tower at the city gates. He looked down at the mighty procession of infantry, chariots and cavalry leaving the city, bound for Kadesh. They were travelling in the opposite direction to Jerusalem, which could be seen in the distance, only a few kilometres away. There were at least ten thousand men in the force snaking along the winding road west, their marching feet billowing dust into the rays of the setting sun.

A cheer went up from the hundreds of spectators as King Nebuchadnezzar passed below in a golden chariot pulled by two majestic black Arabian warhorses. Gripping the black leather reins in his gloved hands the King, with his sword against his side, was resplendent in a polished bronze chest plate, with a round spiked metal helmet that reflected the sun's golden rays. He appeared almost godlike. He glanced up at his general, and nodded.

"In a matter of days, the riches of Jerusalem will be ours for the taking," Nebuzaradan said, smiling back at the King who, of course, was too far away to hear him.

"So, the King sanctioned an assault. Good."

"Yes, and at my discretion."

"Even better. I hasten to add we are in terrible danger from the man who has such strength that he can throw his mental force about like careless bolts of lightning."

Nebuzaradan turned to face the speaker, who was lurking in the shadows behind him.

"Of whom do you speak, Zorlock?"

"He who has been given the name Daniel; Black Alice, of course."

Nebuzaradan turned back to the procession.

"Ahh, the Happening Vibe," he sneered. Of course. And just what would you have me do with Black Alice?"

"I shall think of something worthy, my lord," Zorlock purred, malevolently.

"For that I am counting on you, my friend."

"My informant tells me Honor fears there may be an attempt on the President's life," Secta said despairingly to the Professor and Hope.

"By Gorrick?" Hope queried.

"Yes."

Changing — or, more likely, ignoring — the subject, the Professor chimed in. "I've come up with the means for a time traveller to return," he said. "We can't use it this time round, but we'll be able to use it for future events. It's very simple — I'm amazed we overlooked it. All we need to do is send something through the portal to the prescribed time at a set juncture. The portal then opens for the traveller to return."

"How long would the portal stay open?" Secta asked.

"By my calculations, fifteen seconds."

"So, the traveller has a fifteen second window through which to return," Hope said.

"For now, yes," said de Luz. "But we could open and close it as many times as necessary to ensure he succeeded. In the meantime, we can explore a means of keeping it open longer."

"We're talking about a Time-gate here, aren't we?" Hope replied.

Secta got up and began pacing the floor. "You know, if you used a rock from Mars, theoretically you could open a wormhole to the red planet," he said. "Then open a return portal using a piece of the same rock."

"My God," said Hope. "Think of the possibilities."

"Underscores how important it is to keep the President safe," said Secta. "If Gorrick seizes control of the government, our work will be shot to bits."

"Can't say I'm too confident about that," groaned Hope. "Not with those fools Honor and Karzoff in charge."

Secta suddenly stopped pacing the floor. "Only one thing for it," he said, quietly. "We kill Gorrick before he kills the President."

Alice had spent the day confined in his cell and was getting jumpy. With the King away, his support had gone with him.

Eventually the door opened and a guard entered, carrying Alice's dinner.

"I need to speak with Cannis," Al said.

"I only serve food."

"Can you get me someone who knows what's going on, then?"

"I will see what I can do."

Alice ate the slop disguised as food and waited patiently. Finally, another guard opened the door to his cell. This guy was built like the side of a house and armed, unlike the skinny runt who had brought him the plate of gunk.

"You want something?" the guard said flatly.

"Yeah. I want to know what's happening."

"You are in prison."

"I got that," said Al. "But what comes next?"

"You will find out soon enough," the guard growled, then left, pulling the door closed behind him and locking it on the other side.

"Wait!" shouted Alice, rushing to the door. "Send me Cannis, man! I need to speak to him!"

His plea was ignored. He slumped onto the floor.

Alice was awakened during the night when the door to his cell opened quietly and voice rasped: "Alice, it is I — Cannis."

Alice sat up on his makeshift straw bed, scratched his head and yawned. "Ah, Cannis, glad you could come," he said. "Tell me what's going on, will you?"

"You have been selected by Nebuzaradan to fight in the ring tomorrow."

"The ring? Fight?" he said. "Fight what? Fight who? And why?"

"This has the all trappings of Zorlock's influence, I am afraid," said Cannis, shaking his head. "I suspect he waited for the King to leave, then convinced Nebuzaradan to put you in the ring."

"What goes on in the ring?"

"A fight to the death."

"Ah come on, seriously?" said Alice in English, rolling his eyes. "How come I always end up in a fight to the freaking death on these trips? Bloody hell … at least I had Turk to help last time. Stuff it!"

"I am sorry Alice, I do not understand the language you are speaking," said Cannis.

"Ah, sorry," he said, snapping back to reality. "It's all right. I was just having a moan."

"I understand."

"What happens if I win?" Al said, looking on the positive side.

"They will give you another opponent."

"What, they'll just keep sending them out until they run out?"

"Yes. Or until you are killed."

"That's not very fair!"

"It is not meant to be fair," said Cannis. "Gladiatorial combat is important for the people here. They have little else to entertain them."

"Pity I can't put a band together and do a gig," Alice joked.

"What is a gig?"

"A performance … I could sing for them."

"They prefer blood."

"Great. This is great," Al said. "The King is about to enter into an alliance with Hophra, and in the next few days Nebuzaradan will breach the walls and burn Jerusalem to the ground. And I'm stuck here. There must be some reason this is all happening at once."

"I am sorry I cannot help you, Alice," said Cannis. "My hands are tied." He moved to the door, but turned back. "Ezekiel will be taken to Babylon tomorrow," he said.

"What about Jeremiah? And Set?"

"About them I have heard nothing," said Cannis, sadly. "Knowing Zorlock, they will be lucky to be alive. Good luck, Alice."

Alice shot him a downcast smile. "Yeah, later Cannis."

As the door closed, Alice lay back on his straw bed and thought over his life and the people who had played an important role in it. His girlfriend, Stain, murdered by the Oceana Government. He remembered her on stage, dressed in a little, pale blue air force uniform, singing back-up vocals to his song 'Organic Panic'.

Then his old mate, Mal Function. A guy he could always rely on. Then Turk, in the globe arena, holding Duke's severed head aloft, blood streaming down his forearm and Duke's eyes frozen open in the shocked stare of death.

Suddenly the eyes moved to look at him. The mouth opened and tried to speak through blood-soaked teeth, but all that came out was a wet gurgle. Blood bubbled and frothed.

A flash of light, and he was standing alone in the desert, looking up at a moving star. A small object was expelled from it and, like a firefly, sped across the night sky. He knew it was coming for him. The little light increased until it stopped abruptly over his head, a dark triangle the size of a bus, glowing, pulsing … but silent.

A panel slid open in the belly of the craft and a beam of bright orange light streaked from within, forming a spotlight on the ground. A figure slowly descended through the beam to the ground. Once landed, it walked towards him. Is this Ezekiel? Alice thought. The figure stopped in front on him. It was wearing a spacesuit and helmet with a mirrored visor.

"Who are you?" Alice questioned.

The visor retracted to reveal the face of Secta.

"I am the fragile spaceman," he said. The figure morphed into Hope, her radiant smile like that of an angel. Then the face of the President of Oceana, who said stoically: "I am the nightwatchman of the Universe." The unmistakable thud of a shot from a silenced gun sounded. A hole appeared in the President's forehead. Blood trickled from the wound … the spaceman's legs buckled, the suit collapsed and exploded into dust particles. Alice whipped around just in time to see the gunman walking away, the still-smoking gun held loosely at his side. The killer was Gorrick.

CHAPTER 18
TWO BIRDS & A ROCK

ALICE WAS HANDED a wooden sword and a small round shield. He had been stripped of his caftan and fitted with a pair of brief chamois shorts, held up by a leather belt. With his body builder's musculature on display, he was a formidable sight. This was it, there was no way out.

"It is best to practice with sword and shield when you are not a trained soldier," the guard advised, before leaving him in his cell below the coliseum.

Alice agreed. Taking up a fighter's stance, he swished the toy sword through the air, getting used to moving with a weapon.

A few minutes later a young boy entered the room with a pitcher of water.

"Who will I be fighting?" Alice said, with his back to the boy.

"I do not know," the teenager said. "I have heard Nebuzaradan is commander with the King away. He likes animal fights. The King does not … I do not think he even likes the arena, he rarely attends."

Alice turned. "Oh, I thought you were the guard," he said.

"No, just the water boy."

"Tell me son — what happens if I win this fight?"

"Nebuzaradan will decide who or what you fight next."

"What's your name, boy?"

The lad, who had blonde curly hair and a cheeky smile, said: "Yarin. And I know who you are — you're Daniel, named by the prophet Ezekiel!"

"Word gets around, eh?"

"Fast among slaves."

"A slave huh? Where are you from, kid?"

"Jerusalem."

"And how come you're a slave?"

"I was captured when I tried to join the Holiness Code."

"The Holiness Code ... happening. Do you know Adam?"

"Yes, and his sister Sabrina," Yarin said. "It was terrible, what happened to their Papa. I heard how you killed the slayers — ten of them, and you were armed with only a stick!"

"Seems the story has become a little distorted," said Alice, grinning. "As things seem to do in this part of the world."

"Probably because everything gets passed around by spoken word," the lad said. "There is a lot of exaggeration along the way."

"No doubt son," said Al. "Just for the record, I only killed a couple of them. But I did it with my bare hands!" He couldn't resist perpetuating the myth a little.

"How do you get muscles like that?"

"A lot of hard work. I used to be a skinny runt like you. How old are you, lad?"

"Sixteen."

The boy looked sad. Alice wondered how long he'd been away from his family, imagined how tough it would be for him to be away, with little chance of ever seeing them again.

"I have no doubt you will survive the arena, Daniel," said Yarin. "And I will see that the story of your heroic battles will live on in history. I will one day be a scribe." Suddenly he looked nervous, as though he'd lingered too long. "I must go now," he added. "I will come back soon with some food for you."

"Thank you, Yarin. Wait — can you get a message to Adam in Jerusalem?"

He figured a slave might have the means to get messages out through suppliers to the garrison.

"Yes," said the boy excitedly, keen to help his hero.

"Tell him the wall will fall in three sleeps."

Yarin nodded and left.

A little later he returned with a plate of gruel for Alice, who looked down his nose at it. "Pig food," he snarled.

"To be honest Daniel, I would not risk feeding it to a pig," Yarin said, with a chuckle. "But at least you can be sure it has not been spat or pissed in."

"That's some recommendation, kid," Al said, with a laugh.

Alice took the wooden dish, filled to the brim with the sickly porridge. He was so hungry he devoured it in a flash.

"I have passed on your message, Daniel," the boy whispered conspiratorially. "Adam should get it tonight."

"Excellent," Al said, wiping gruel from his chin with the back of his hand.

"Also, I spoke to Tinnus, the longest surviving gladiator here. He said to tell you — wait, let me get this right — strike quick, like the bolt of fire from the sky in a storm. If you hesitate, you will be beaten."

"Thank Tinnus for me. I will take his advice. How long has he lasted?"

"For three games," said Yarin, enthusiastically.

"Three games? I thought you were going to say three years. Three games, damn."

"Good luck Daniel. All of the slaves are praying for you."

"Thanks, son. So, what happens next?"

"They will come and get you when it is time."

Yarin left Alice to wait his turn in the ring. Alice knew the events had begun, because every now and then a loud cheer filtered down to his basement cell from what sounded like a sizable audience above.

It wasn't long before two burly guards came for Alice. He left behind the wooden sword and shield and was walked in silence out of the cell, up two flights of stairs and onto the raceway. He shielded his eyes from the light burning through the gaps in the big wooden doors that opened onto the arena. He'd been in the dungeon long enough to get used to the gloom – his eyes needed to adjust. The guards were standing either side of him, facing the closed doors, each gripping one of Alice's arms. The doors suddenly trembled to a loud bang — a body had been hurled up against them. Through the cracks Alice could make out the naked upper torso of a man, arms spread out, pinned against the doors. Then he heard the spine-chilling growl of big cat: a lion or a tiger — whatever it was it sounded huge. The rapid breathing of the person wedged against the doors became frantic, terrorized. It was easy to tell he was confronting death. A snarl, then a roar from the cat, then a horrific crunch. Blood gushed through the cracks as the man's throat was torn out, and splashed on the sandaled feet of the guards.

The crowd outside let out a raucous cheer.

The victim's silence throughout the ordeal amazed Alice, who was being pulled back from the doors to avoid the blood squirting from the victim's severed arteries as the mutilated body slid to the ground, where it lay silent and lifeless. The only remaining sound was the low vibration of a big cat purring, like an idling V8 engine. A moment later the mangled body was dragged away, no doubt to be further savaged by the hungry beast.

Hope it fills its guts, Alice thought to himself, then it mightn't be hungry enough for me.

A clarion blew one loud, short note. Then came the clatter of chains and the crack of whips. The big cat growled. Two short blasts, and that was it, Alice's time had come. A third guard arrived, carrying a spear and a round wooden shield a metre in diameter with a leather grip on the inside. Alice was handed both. He fitted his left hand inside the shield grip and felt the weight of the spear. It was light, with a sharp metal blade bound to the tip with sinew strapping. If he were to fight an animal the spear would be a better choice than a sword. At least he could keep his distance.

He stepped out into the arena. The first thing he noticed was there was no place to hide. The cat — a lion — was in a large metal cage on the other side. He looked up at the audience. There was a dozen or so tiers around the stadium, and all were full. The arena was smaller than he expected after seeing it from the outside, more like a Greek amphitheatre than a gladiatorial arena. But then again, this wasn't Rome, this was 587 BC.

The crowd roared. Alice readied himself when he realised what the cheer was about: a couple of slaves were winching open the lion's cage. Alice had never thought about how big a fully-grown male lion was until he saw the one he was expected to fight.

Nebuzaradan was watching from the royal box, with Zorlock and Darius the Mede, master of ceremonies, on either side.

A skinny man with a rat-like face, Darius got up, went to the balcony and raised a hand to gain the attention of the crowd.

"Countrymen!" he bellowed over the din. "Our next contest: Daniel in the lion's den! We hope he puts up more resistance than his predecessor!"

A chuckle rippled around the audience like a Mexican wave.

The lion stalked out of the cage, keeping low to ground, its eyes on Alice. His victim wasn't close enough for him to charge yet. Alice recalled a David Attenborough documentary he'd seen about how a lion hunts. He'd called their stalking 'grandmother's footsteps'. The animals normally crept from cover to cover, with an ambush in a final burst of speed at the end. Here, however, there was no cover. How would it change the lion's behaviour? He could tell it had seen him. He chose to keep perfectly still. The sun was beating down on his head, he could feel perspiration trickling down his cheeks and dripping off his chin — but he remained resolutely still and silent, almost not breathing. The beast stopped moving too. A hush came over the audience as they waited for the lion to charge.

"Hey, big fella," Alice spoke softly, in English. He slowly bent his knees, not taking his eyes off the lion, and placed his spear and shield on the ground.

"What is he doing?" Nebuzaradan said, wonderingly.

Alice desperately tried to forge some connection with the beast. I'm your friend, not your enemy ... he thought. I mean you no harm ... see? He spread his arms slowly, palms outward, to show the lack of threat.

Suddenly, he was overcome by a strange feeling of control, as though he'd been touched by the finger of an invisible power. Smiling, he walked very slowly to the lion, stopped in front of it and, to the amazement of the crowd, leaned forward and patted it on the nose. The beast closed its tired eyes and accepted the petting like a domesticated cat. Alice could hear it purring.

"Come on, mate," he said, and walked towards the cage. The huge creature rose from its crouch and followed him. Alice watched the lion enter, then looked up at the slave at the pulley. Yarin was standing next to the men with the rope. Alice gestured, and the slaves lowered the cage door. The lion yawned, and lay down.

Alice walked to centre ring, stopped at his spear and shield and raised both hands in the air. The crowd went ballistic, cheering his name. Daniel! Daniel! Daniel!

Yarin elbowed his friends as if to say 'I told you so'.

Nebuzaradan, Zorlock and Darius were gobsmacked. They'd never seen anything like it.

"How did he pacify the beast?" Nebuzaradan growled.

"I told you he is dangerous," Zorlock snarled. "He used his will ... sorcery!"

"We must do something," Darius complained. "He is winning over the crowd. Listen to them!"

The crowd continued chanting his new name, while Alice turned in a slow circle, arms raised, soaking up the ovation.

Zorlock whispered in Darius' ear. A wicked smile broke on the man's gaunt face.

"Done!" he confirmed, happily, and ducked out of the royal box.

The crowd were still on their feet when the door by which Alice had entered opened again. A burly warrior marched out. He was dressed the same as Alice, except for two leather straps crossing his chest and a metal helmet with a visor obscuring his face. The sunlight glinted off the polished blade of a scimitar in his left hand. In his right, a shield the same as Alice's.

Darius had returned to the royal box to make the introduction.

"Countrymen! Countrymen!" he roared. "Your champion Daniel has placated the lion! He will now display his valour against a worthy opponent... Set, the invincible!"

The crowd roared its approval.

"Is that you under there?" Al asked.

"Yes, it's me all right," came the reply. "I didn't expect it to come to this."

"Me either."

"What should we do?"

"Let's put on a good performance and hope the audience buy it and give us a reprieve," Alice suggested.

"Fine with me," Set said and removed the helmet, casting it aside.

Alice picked up his spear and shield and fronted Set.

They clashed, the blows aimed at each other's shields. It only took a couple of minutes before Set sliced Alice's spear in half.

Yarin reminded his friends that when Alice killed the Babylonian soldiers he was armed then, as now, with only a stick.

The crowd screamed as the two men charged one another again and locked shields. In a battle of strength, they each tried to force the other onto the ground. Alice's shield came free first and he brought it down on Set's sword arm, causing the sword to drop from his grasp.

Alice kept at it, his muscular arms bulging like they were going to burst at the seams. He whipped the broken spear across the back of Set's legs ... dropping the bigger man to one knee. Then he cracked Set across the side of the face with his shield. The blow came close to knocking him out. He reeled backwards.

The crowd cheered wildly.

But Set fought back. From the ground he grabbed Alice's ankle. Standing up quickly, he lifted the leg, thrusting Alice onto his back in the dirt. Quickly, Set snatched up his scimitar and stood over Alice, point aimed at his throat. The crowd hushed. Knowing he was the winner, Set gazed up at the royal box.

"Hey, Set, this is supposed to be an act, right?" Al hissed. But Set had a strange look in his eyes. "Set! Are you hearing me? Snap out of it, man!"

Members of the audience began to stand, slow-clapping. Before long the entire stadium thundered with united slow applause.

Nebuzaradan glared at Darius. "Now what are you going to do?" he growled. "They do not want him killed — this is ridiculous!"

"It is you they look to for a decision, Nebuzaradan," Darius said. "Just give the signal to kill him and it will be over."

"I have no wish to lose my popularity with the citizens, Darius. We need to think of something else — and quick."

"But…" Darius was about to plead but was cut off.

"I have a better plan," said Zorlock. "One in which we can kill two birds with the one stone. Let him live."

CHAPTER 19
MET

NEBUZARADAN STOOD AND gestured for Set to spare Alice. He was rewarded with a thunderous cheer from the audience.

Set withdrew the threatening simitar from Alice's throat and offered him a hand.

"That was a bit too close for comfort," Al protested, glaring at Set with a raised eyebrow.

"I guess we'll never know whether I'd have done it or not," Set replied.

Alice was pretty sure that if the decision had been different, Set would have killed him.

The clarion once more sounded a single blast, and the entrance doors swung open. A guard ran out, carrying a short sword. He handed it to Alice, then turned and hightailed it out of there.

Alice studied the sword, tested its edge. It was sharp, much shorter than Set's, more like a bayonet or long dagger.

"Why have they given me this toothpick?" Al moaned.

Set didn't answer. He was glued to the royal box, wondering what was next.

The clarion sounded two blasts.

"Here we go," said Al.

Darius went to the balcony rail and once again raised his hand.

"Countrymen, we now have two champions!" he bellowed. "What shall we do with them? We will find them a new challenge, of course! Courtesy of Zorlock, chief astrologer to the King, we give you…" A wave of his hand signalled the opening of a large wooden gate behind Alice and Set. They turned sharply to see the three-metre high portcullis being hauled upwards by six men battling an enormous winch.

"What the hell's coming out of there?" Alice growled, crouching, shield and sword ready for whatever might emerge.

When the portcullis was finally locked into place, all he could see was a dark void. Both fighters waited with bated breath, as did the entire audience.

After a pause that felt like hours, Alice noticed movement from within. The spectators burst into oohs! and ahhs! as a monstrosity stepped from the void, ducking to avoid tearing out the shoring.

His gaze widening in horror, Alice recognised their foe. "The Golem!" he shouted, loud enough for Set to hear.

This was the creature Ezekiel had dug out and animated from clay using the sacred words given him by the Anunnaki. This was the creature that had ripped soldiers limb from limb. The Golem was no longer a myth — the Golem was reality. It was over three metres tall, squarely built but recognisably human-shaped, topped by an enormous head with no ears and two goat-like slotted eyes set deep in cavernous sockets. Its face was expressionless. There was hardly any neck. It looked to Alice like a giant plasticine model of a Japanese sumo wrestler. Its massive hands were clenched into fists, its legs were like two tree trunks, anchored with the biggest feet imaginable. Its entire naked, genderless body was of reddish-brown clay, and its body language said it had been programmed to kill any living creature that presented a threat.

It took a sluggish, indecisive step towards them, and a great cloud of dust wafted from the beneath its massive foot. It raised its fists, ready to pound its prey, then marched towards them, one giant, dust-wafting, ground-trembling step after another.

Mustering his courage, Set ran at it and slashed his simitar across its thighs, expecting to create a deep cut. But when the blade stuck the hardened clay it snapped in half, leaving Set holding only the hilt. Before he had chance to react, the Golem struck with one almighty swipe — moving much quicker than expected — and swatted Set away like an annoying fly. A swirl of dust rose up as the man's sliding form cut a deep swath in the sandy floor.

The audience erupted into cheers, and laughter broke out as Set stopped and sat up, blanketed in dust, shaking his head to eliminate the flying stars from his vision.

Alice chuckled, but his expression quickly changed as the Golem turned its attention to him. Racking his brain, he tried to remember the details Ezekiel had given him about animating the monster. Then he remembered that it wasn't Ezekiel at all — it was Adam. The boy's words echoed in his head. *On its head were sacred letters that gave it life: emet, meaning 'truth'.*

Alice could see the letters on its forehead as the massive creature bore down on him. He scowled, trying to remember the rest of what Adam had said … it was getting closer … how do you kill the damn thing? Then it came to him … Removing the first letter forms 'met' — the word for dead … that's how to kill it! He raced to Set, gave him a hand up and pulled him into a huddle. The Golem changed direction and thundered towards them.

They broke from the huddle with the Golem again bearing down. Once again, Set rushed it. When he reached it, he began to run in clockwise circles around its legs. Alice, meanwhile, had followed suit and was running anti-clockwise.

The crowd cheered wildly as the Golem, spinning slowly, tried to follow both men at once. After a half dozen loops, as they crossed behind the monster, Alice yelled: "Now!"

Set stopped abruptly, bent down and cupped his hands, locking his fingers together. Alice rushed forward, put his foot in the cup, and Set lifted with all his might, catapulting Alice onto the Golem's back.

The crowd went ballistic.

Alice threw an arm around the monster's throat and hung there, perilously. He gathered his strength and tried to reach around with his blade. He couldn't stretch far enough. The Golem began to swing its upper torso violently in a desperate effort to fling Alice off. It tried to reach behind and overhead, but Alice was in an awkward spot it couldn't get to.

Alice, gripping desperately, managed to manoeuvre higher so he could stretch over the Golem's head. Once there, holding on for grim death, he reached over and began to hack at the first letter on its broad forehead. Aware of what he was attempting to do, the Golem flailed wildly, flinging itself this way and that in a last-ditch effort to fling his assailant off.

The jerking and bucking lost Alice his grip on one hand. He was in danger of being hurled off.

Set recognised he was in trouble and rushed around in front to distract the monster. The move worked, for a moment the Golem's attention was diverted, giving Alice the opportunity to lock his grip and make the final cut. The letter E was gone. The Golem froze. It was like time had stopped ticking. Alice sat there, clinging to the motionless gigantic statue … he had won.

It took a moment for the audience to realise what had happened, and when they did, slowly, they began to rise from their seats, finally, standing as one while Alice made his way down. Once on the ground, Set embraced him. Both men looked up at the towering giant, now just clay.

"That'll teach you to mess with Al!" Alice growled. And as the last word left his lips, there was a shudder as the Golem crumbled to dust.

When the dust wall cleared, Set raised Alice's arm in victory and the crowd responded wildly, collectively chanting free! free! free!

The only person still seated in the entire arena was Nebuzaradan. "So Zorlock," he rasped, cynically, "Any more brilliant ideas?"

There was a flash of purple cape, as, embarrassed beyond bearing, Zorlock fled the royal box like a giant bat.

"I think we have no choice now sir," Darius recommended bitterly.

To keep face with the crowd, the victor had to be freed.

A little while later, Cannis arrived at Alice's cell and beamed him a broad smile. "Alice!" he exclaimed, "I am so glad to find you alive!"

Reclining on the bed of straw, Alice grinned through his aches and pains.

"They did their best," he growled in his customary swagger, "But it takes more than a lion, a gladiator and a golem to defeat old Al!"

"Your heroics have gained you a reprieve, my friend."

"What does that mean?" Alice asked.

"I have a gate pass here, allowing two to leave."

"Yeah, and go where?"

"Back to Jerusalem — or wherever you wish. You have won your freedom," the rotund little man grinned.

Alice sat up and scratched his stubbly face. "Effective when?" he asked

"Immediately," said Cannis, still beaming. "You may leave whenever you are ready."

"Good," said Al. He thought a moment. He had doubted Set from the beginning. The fight in the area didn't change that.

"I'll take the boy Yarin with me," he said.

"But what of your friend? Set?" asked Cannis, his bushy eyebrows furrowed.

"Freedom was offered to me, wasn't it?"

"Yes, indeed."

"Then I will take Yarin."

"Very well … but allow me to say … he is a slave, you know?"

"Cannis," Al eyeballed him.

The little man wasn't about to argue with the man who had won his freedom. "Alright, alright" he said. "Done. I will make it so."

An hour later, Cannis was bidding Alice and Yarin goodbye at the gates. A donkey cart would ferry them to Jerusalem.

Alice was back in a comfortable, clean caftan. He embraced Cannis. "Goodbye, my friend," he said, "And thank you."

"Proud to call you a friend, Alice," the man replied. "Or should I say Daniel?"

"Nebuzaradan will attack Jerusalem in two days," Alice said. "I would think after that you will be heading back to Babylon."

"I hope so," sighed Cannis. "It will give me time to write my book. I have quite a story to tell now, you know. Daniel in the lion's den, and all that!"

Alice smiled sincerely. He liked Cannis — he had a kind heart. "I have a feeling it will be a big seller," he said, shaking the would-be author's hand. Cannis stood at the gates, waving, as Alice and Yarin drove their cart away.

Alice knew Set wouldn't be impressed when he found out he'd been short-changed on freedom. But at least for now he wouldn't have to keep looking over his shoulder. There was a lot to achieve ahead, and very little time in which to do it. Plus, it made him feel good that he'd be able to return Yarin to his family. Even with catastrophe looming over Jerusalem, at least they would be together.

"You look distant, Daniel," Yarin said. "What are you thinking?"

"Just about the road that lies ahead," Alice replied.

The boy looked at the dusty track. "It leads to Jerusalem," he said.

"Yes it does," Alice smiled, "And that means more trouble for me."

"Why?"

"Because I need to find a way to speak with King Zedekiah."

"That is not trouble."

"How's that?"

"My father works in the palace kitchen," said the boy. He sees the King's servants every day. He could get a message to him from you."

Alice smiled at the serendipity. He had made the right choice leaving Set behind, and been gifted a ticket to Zedekiah.

CHAPTER 20
ZION

THE NEWS SERVICES were bursting with the story that the government was backtracking on contracting the security of the nation to Zen Corporation. In a radio interview with the President, he'd admitted that the deal had been put on ice. When asked why, he'd stated: "More research is required before we can make a commitment one way or the other." The nation had already assumed it was a done deal — and hadn't been happy with the prospect of a private company having so much power over them. Now they were back to worrying about other threats to world peace, like terrorism, North Korea and tensions in the Middle East and the Ukraine, which, thanks to sabre-rattling by Israel the USA and NATO, appeared to be escalating. With Iran's nuclear capability and its alliances with Russia and Turkey, the threat of a nuclear war was ominous.

Secta was weaving his way through a multitude of lunch-break pedestrians, with the incessant rain making his progress difficult. A man of his height had to be mindful of umbrellas to avoid losing an eye.

He was running late for a meeting with the President, and still had a city block to negotiate.

He'd spent the last few days without sleep, working on a means to keep the President safe. Since word was out on the rift between the government and Zen, and after what he'd heard from his informant, he felt the President's life was more at risk now than ever. The thought of Honor and Karzoff being entrusted with the President's personal safety gave him even more reason for concern. The odds of them blowing it were so significant that he had no choice but to act. His solution to the problem was in the bag he was carrying under his arm.

Eventually he made it to Oceana HQ, eyes intact. After an elevator ride to the top floor, out of breath from his rapid walk and looking like a drowned rat, he met Miss Vallins at reception.

"Doctor Secta," she said, smoothly. "Good morning. Can I get you a towel?"

"Yes please, Miss Vallins," he answered, with a slight bow. "It wouldn't be good manners to dribble on the President's floor."

Miss Vallins smiled. She enjoyed Secta's quirky sense of humour. Producing a handtowel from a lower drawer of her desk, she handed it to him.

Secta towelled himself down. "There, how's that?" he said. "Presentable?"

"Gorgeous," she smiled back. "You can go on in, he's waiting for you."

He handed her back the towel, nicely folded. Taking it, she said waggishly, "You'd make someone a splendid wife Secta."

"I'm sure I could," he replied. "But I just don't have the time."

He opened the door, leaving her laughing over his reply.

"Ah Secta, caught in the rain I presume," said the President, putting down a newspaper and reclining in his chair.

"I'm somewhat uncomfortably damp, yes."

"Sit down, sit down. Tell me the latest."

Secta sat in the armchair opposite the President. "A little bird tells me that reneging on the deal with Gorrick has put you in danger," he said.

"Oh, I wouldn't go listening to tweets Secta," the President replied. "It's not like someone's going to barge into my office and plug me … And I don't go anywhere else."

"It doesn't matter, Ri," said Secta, frowning. "Where there's smoke there's fire."

"But I've got loads of security."

"Yes, that's what bothers me."

"Ah Secta, always looking after me," the President said. "Even when I do such a poor job of looking after you."

"All that aside," said Secta, waving a hand dismissively, "It's imperative that you consider my plan."

One thing the President had learned over his years in office was to listen to anything Secta had to say. "First this," said the scientist, digging around in his bag and coming up with what looked like a small laptop. He booted it up. "This is a bug scanner."

"But the room and the lobby are constantly scanned, Secta, you know that," the President said, testily.

"Yes," said Secta. "And by whom?"

"By Zen, of course— ah. I take your point,"

Reading the information on the monitor, Secta continued: "I've modified this scanner, broadening its frequency range. Not only will it detect bugs, it will also locate the transmitter. It covers RF, analogue, digital and any sort of encryption. Checks telephone, AC, Ethernet, alarms and other wires as well as the infrared and UV range … and what do you know? It's showing three bugs in this office!" He looked at the President with a grin.

"Good grief!" the President erupted. "Honor and Karzoff only swept the damn place this morning!"

"The other good news is that by hitting a key — like so — I can disable the bugs," Secta went on. "And yes, I can see that the bugs are feeding to a satellite. I've saved the telemetry and will check it later. So. We can safely assume someone has been monitoring your conversations. I think we can agree on who that would be."

"Say no more," said the President. "What else do you have in that box of tricks?"

"I have not been able to determine where Gorrick Khan was born," Karzoff admitted.

He was in Honor's office, sitting opposite her desk. She glanced at him from behind her monitor.

"How can zat be?" she snapped. "Surely ze Department of Immigration has details of his arrival here?"

"That is precisely what I thought but no, there is nothing."

There was a knock at the door and Viktoria poked her head in, "Excuse me ma'am, but I've got someone in reception to see you."

Honor glared at her. "Without an appointment?"

"He said he's from Zen Corporation and doesn't need an appointment."

Suddenly a hand impolitely shoved Viktoria out of the way and a man barged into the office.

"Hey!" Viktoria protested.

Honor rose to her feet.

The man moved behind Karzoff, who remained seated.

Tall, well built, chiselled from a similar mould to Anu Set, the man had a shaved head, a strong jaw, large eyes, and was dressed in a tailored black suit with a black shirt and a black tie. He looked more Mafia than corporate.

Recognising Honor was angered by the unheralded intrusion, Karzoff decided to stand up and face the interloper as well.

"Vat do you mean by forcing your way in here?" Honor snapped.

The man didn't answer, just fired Honor an icy stare. Then he switched it to Karzoff.

"I, I think perhaps you should leave and make an appointment," the little man stammered. He was quickly cut off.

"Sit down, both of you," the intruder ordered. Without looking behind he added, "You may leave, Miss de Cock. No calls."

Viktoria grimaced and closed the door behind her.

Karzoff sat back down but Honor wasn't going to be dominated. She remained standing, a stony look on her face.

"I am Zanza Kew and I have orders to deliver a message," the man said. He didn't blink and he didn't modulate his voice. Cool as a cucumber, he reached inside his coat, drew a Walther PPQ .22 pistol, and then a silencer from his hip pocket.

Honor slowly reached for the top drawer of her desk, in which she kept a pistol for emergencies.

"You would cause great harm to come to yourself if you touch that drawer, Honor," Kew said coldly, screwing the silencer into the barrel.

Her hand froze. She retracted it angrily, and lowered herself into her chair.

"There is no need for all this…" Karzoff began.

"Shut up, little man," said Kew, smoothly, and pressed the barrel of the silencer against Karzoff's head.

A patina of perspiration formed on Karzoff's face.

"I will say this once," Kew said. "Failure to agree and I will blow Mr Karzoff's brains out and your nice clothes, Honor, will be stained with his blood, skull and brain. Not a lot, because the exit isn't massive, but certainly enough to make a mess."

"Enough theatrics, Kew," snarled Honor. "Say vat you vere ordered to say and get out."

"You're tough when the gun isn't aimed at you, lady," Kew said, calmly.

"On that one we agree," Karzoff muttered.

"This is your one and only warning," Kew continued. "Your investigation into Zen is over. Should I be required to return, blood will be spilt. Are we absolutely clear?"

"Yes, yes, abs … um, absolutely," Karzoff stuttered.

"Understood," said Honor, baldly.

Kew withdrew the gun from Karzoff's red hair, much to his relief.

Calmly unscrewing the silencer and concealing both items inside his clothing, Kew walked silently to the door and left.

"Like hell," Honor hissed, quietly enough to be sure Kew wouldn't hear. "How did he get zat gun past security?" She snatched the desk phone.

"What are you doing?" Karzoff asked urgently.

"Security can arrest him before he leaves ze building."

"Are you that keen to wind up in the city morgue?"

She put down the phone. "It matters not anyway," she sneered. "I vill be haffing ze last laugh."

"Really? And what makes younthink that?"

She checked her wristwatch. "Because vizin ze hour, vun of ze best hackers in Oceana vill come here viz files he has hacked from Gorrick's personal computer."

In the blink of an eye Karzoff's facial expression went from astounded to terrified.

His eyes stinging with sweat, Alice hopped out of the cart. They were safely inside the walls of Jerusalem, and he was keen to get out of the stinking-hot midday sun.

"I'd kill for a drink," he grumbled.

Yarin, wide-eyed and once again taking him literally, said: "Do not say that! You will be arrested! We can go to my family house nearby. There is sure to be food and drink for us there."

They started off through the crowded street, and it wasn't long before the Temple came into view. Alice could see two Pharisees standing on the first landing, making the daily offering to Tammuz, the flock below them humbling themselves on their knees.

"What do you think of religion?" Yarin asked Alice.

"It gives power to fools like the Pharisees, who abuse it."

"Do you think the same of the King of Babylon?"

"Royalty is a different matter," said Alice. "People need leaders. Some are good, some are bad. Nebuchadnezzar seems like one of the good ones."

"So you did not pray when you entered the arena yesterday?"

"No, Yarin, I was thinking about something else," Alice grinned.

"What was that?"

"The way out."

Yarin eventually stopped at a double door entrance to a moderately-sized villa. "This is the house of my father," he said.

"It looks well-to-do compared with others."

"Yes, we have been very fortunate with papa's position at the palace."

"With his influence, why could he not save you?"

"It all happened too quick," said the boy. "And afterwards it was next to impossible to get me back, the garrison had moved on and then the two kings had a difference of opinion." He pushed open one of the doors as he spoke, and led Alice into a courtyard. A fine-looking woman in flowing white robes, her head wrapped in a beige scarf, emerged onto the veranda. Shielding her eyes, she called out to them.

"Hello, can I be of assistance?"

Yarin and Alice stopped to take in her beauty, bathed as she was in the sunlight. Then Yarin spoke quietly, choking back tears: "Mama?"

The women froze for a second, staring at them. Then she threw her arms open and rushed across the courtyard to embrace her boy.

It was an emotional moment for mother and son. Alice turned away, feeling like an intruder. Eventually, they disentangled themselves, wiped away tears, and turned to Alice.

"Mother, this is Daniel," said Yarin. "He rescued me, brought me home."

The woman embraced Alice, and he felt the genuine warmth of her appreciation. He could smell her fragrance, and recognised it as jasmine. Under her headscarf he noticed a lock of blond hair, like her son's. Large, hooped golden earrings adorned her earlobes, and on her wrist she wore a delicate gold circlet. This was the first time he'd noticed jewellery on a woman since he'd arrived. He figured with Yarin being sixteen she had to be in her mid to late thirties, but she looked younger.

"Welcome, Daniel," she said, holding him by both hands. "You may call me Calista. Please, come into our home for food and to quench your thirst."

"Is Papa home?"

"He will be here soon, he had an errand to run."

On closer inspection it was more a portico than a veranda that surrounded the house, the perfect design for escaping the heat of the day. It was decorated with plants, flowers and vines in beautiful clay pots, and as they approached the eating area, there was a pond with water lilies floating on the surface. Unlike the cushioned seating Alice had previously experienced, there was a table and chairs. As soon as they sat down two young female servants brought wine, hummus, olive oil, and bread.

After an hour of catching up on Yarin's life since he went missing, the conversation had just turned to Alice when a man, accompanied by a servant, arrived. Yarin jumped up and threw his arms around the neck of his father, who burst into tears at the sight of his oldest son. Once the emotions had subsided, Yarin made the introductions.

"Papa, this is Daniel."

"He saved our son and brought him home," Calista said, beaming a smile.

"How can I thank you?" Papa said and then hugged Alice. "Please, sit. Call me Razili."

They sat and drank wine together. Once they got through the explanations, Razili said: "It was the Pharisees who banished you my son, not Zedekiah. When I went to him to plead for your release, he knew nothing about your arrest. By the time he tried to act, they had given you to the Babylonii."

"This is a terrible thing, Daniel," Calista explained. "The Pharisees abduct our young men, and exchange them with the Babylonii for favours."

"Nothing surprises me about the Pharisees, Calista," said Al, darkly. "I witnessed Beit Ha'am."

"How can I repay you for returning our son?" said Razli, once again shaking Al's hand.

"I do not want payment Razili," said Alice, smiling at the man. "But perhaps you can do me a favour."

"Anything!"

"Help me get an audience with Zedekiah. I have a message for him from Ezekiel."

"Ezekiel?" he said, shocked. "I thought he was imprisoned in Babylon."

"No, he advises King Nebuchadnezzar," Alice explained. "I was fortunate to meet him with the king only two days ago. He said to tell Zedekiah that he, Ezekiel, has named me Daniel and that the king should give me audience. He said the king would understand."

Alice had presumed the name Daniel was some sort of secret password.

"Can you divulge what you need to speak of with the King of the house of David?" said Razili.

"No, but you can trust me," said Alice. "What I have to tell him is of the utmost importance."

CHAPTER 21
SWITCH

THE AMOUNT OF data Honor's hacker had been able to mine from Gorrick's personal computer was astounding. Sitting in an armchair at home, dressed in a bathrobe with her laptop on her knee, she flicked through one file after another in search of something, anything, to link Gorrick to a plot to murder the President. She had found very little personal information, so was still in the dark as to his origin. There were emails between Gorrick and Zanza Kew, but nothing incriminating. However, her hacker had found a file named Switch that had been well hidden and deeply encrypted. Suspecting it might be relevant, the hacker had spent hours decrypting it. Unfortunately the content made no sense, it was all scientific jargon. But she still believed it had to be of value. She closed the laptop, stood and stretched. It had been a long day. Soon she would retire to bed. Now it was time to shower.

Her city apartment was really too big for one person, but she enjoyed the spatial benefits of living alone. No partner, no pets, nothing to distract her from work.

Her feet were sore from her high-heeled shoes, so she decided to run a bath instead of taking a shower. After adding a few drops of lavender, chamomile, sage, geranium and jojoba oils and a handful of Epsom salt, she slipped out of her robe and into the water. Lying blissfully half-submerged she was trying to meditate when she heard a noise in the living room. Knowing the front door was locked, she ignored it and went back to winding down.

"I did warn you."

At the unexpected voice her eyes opened wide. Kew was standing over her, a gun in his hand.

She tried to cover herself with her hands.

"What do you want?" she thundered, her voice trembling with fear.

In his other hand he held a shopping bag, and under his arm, her laptop. He put down the bag and learned forward, placing the laptop on her stomach in the water.

"No doubt you've backed up the files you had hacked," he said. "An important habit to get into."

Honor knew her laptop wouldn't survive the bath.

Kew picked up the shopping bag he'd left by his feet. "Fortunately for you, there was nothing of value for you in the hack. But..." He held the bag over her. He paused for impact, then upended the contents into the bath — splash, splash. Honor cringed as she realised the bag had disgorged two severed hands. "Got to hand it to you Honor," said Kew, "Nice try. Sadly your handy hacker's hands had to be hacked. I dropped him off at the Citizen's Hospital," he added. "He'll live — but I'm afraid his hacking days are over."

Honor stared in horror at the two bloody hands, jagged flesh at the wrists, leaking blood into the tub.

"Goodnight Honor," said Kew, with a sinister chuckle.

She waited for the front door to close behind him and then jumped from the bath, shaking uncontrollably.

Secta looked up from his computer with a surprised expression. "You're not going to believe this," he said.

Hope swivelled to face him. "What is it?"

"Honor has sent me an email with a file hacked from Gorrick's personal computer," he said. "Apparently she doesn't understand it, and wants to see if we can."

Hope walked across the room to look at the file. After fifteen minutes they had both finished reading.

"We need to discuss this with Vic," said Secta, gravely. "It's incredible."

"I'll give him a buzz, see if he's still in his office," said Hope.

Since they'd arrived back from Texas, Secta had allocated an office on his research floor to de Luz. They all worked odd hours, but this time de Luz was there. Hope asked him to join them.

Secta's private study was homely. In actuality he spent more time there than he did at his Towns Place penthouse at Millers Point. Situated along the hall from his lab, he'd decked it out with a comfy, old-world library setting one might expect to find in a professor's room at Oxford or Harvard. Secta loved being surrounded by walls of knowledge: this was his think tank.

De Luz took a seat. A mug of hot black coffee was waiting for him. Hope and Secta were already sipping on theirs.

Secta explained to de Luz how he'd come by the file, and proceeded with his personal opinion of Honor and Karzoff's effectiveness. This included the situation as it stood with the perceived threat to the President's life. He spoke of how he had perfected a number of security options to better protect the President and how, with this new evidence, the danger had intensified. What they had found in the file named Switch justified all the doubts they'd had about Zen's intentions. Secta handed de Luz a six-page printout and waited for him to read it.

When he'd finished, de Luz whipped off his glasses, pinched the bridge of his nose and shook his head. "Damn!" he exclaimed.

"Yes," said Secta, putting down his empty mug. "That just about sums it up."

"So. Let me see if we all agree here," Hope said. "My reading of this is that Zen is examining a code switch we all have in our DNA, which when triggered basically transforms mankind into zombies."

"That's it in a nutshell, dear sister," Secta confirmed.

"Two things worry me," said de Luz. "One: they have isolated the dormant nucleotides in humanity's DNA code to trigger. Two: they are perfecting the means to broadcast that trigger to the entire human population. It means they don't even have to deliver this thing into the body — they can do it from a satellite or a moon base."

"Agreed," said Secta. "However, if my visit to the future was in the same continuum as this, they failed."

"But that might be because we stopped them now," Hope suggested.

"You could be right, Hope," he replied. "But I can't help thinking this is somehow connected with Alice's quest."

"I think you're on the money there," said de Luz, putting his reading glasses away.

The three of them sat in silence, contemplating the possible ramifications of what they'd uncovered. Secta had witnessed first-hand the devastation Zen had caused the world in the future, with its development of cyber technology. Now, they not only had to prevent that, they also had to put an end to Switch — but how? Secta came back to the idea of taking out Gorrick. But even that raised questions, like how Gorrick could be the same age now as he was in the future? Could he be a clone — and what if there were even more of them? Has Zen developed a longevity serum?

"It seems to me that, between their cyborg development programme and Switch, Zen are striving to create a kind of hive mentality," de Luz posited. "Some kind of controlled, cyborg collective consciousness, a synthesis of man and machine using electromagnetic resonance broadcast from space. Serious stuff. The development cannot only be happening here in Oceana. If that is the case, simply killing Gorrick won't put an end to it."

"Oh God, I hadn't thought of that," said Hope, aghast. "Of course ... Zen's global..."

Alice left it to Yarin's father to arrange an audience with King Zedekiah. He was given a room in the villa and invited to stay as long as he wished, but right now he wanted to visit Adam and his family to make sure they were all right. So Yarin escorted Alice to the house of Aunt Edna.

Only Edna was home. She told them Sabrina had taken her mother to the markets, and that Adam was at a meeting with his prayer group somewhere. Yarin knew that meant there was a meeting of the Holiness Code, so he led Alice to the cavern.

As Alice entered it he stopped at the Golem impression, transfixed. Yarin guessed what was going through his mind and smiled quietly to himself.

After a long pause Alice spoke up. "Hard to believe I fought the thing that came from there," he said.

"Even harder to believe you beat it."

Suddenly, there was a round of applause. Alice looked up at a dozen members of the Holiness Code, clapping wildly. Adam stepped out from among them and hugged Alice.

"We have heard what you achieved," he said. "It is a miracle."

"Not a miracle my friends, just determination and problem solving," he said, "The key to a long life — or so Ezekiel would probably profess."

"You met Ezekiel?" Adam shrieked.

Alice led them further inside. They followed, Adam with his arm around Yarin's shoulders, childhood friends that had found each other after years of separation. The congregation sat, anxious to hear from Al.

"I spent time talking with Ezekiel," Al said. "He is an impressive man. We spoke of many things, but most of all about the future of Jerusalem."

"Why had he been freed from prison?" someone asked.

"It's my impression he is not a prisoner," said Al. "On the contrary, I would say he is a much-valued advisor to King Nebuchadnezzar."

A mumble of discontent went around the flock. Adam spoke on behalf of the others.

"We assumed Ezekiel would not take the side of the Babylonii."

"I expect you assumed that through Jeremiah, huh?" Al said.

"Well, yes."

"You must understand, my friends, Jeremiah is mentally unstable. I know it sort of goes with the territory of being a prophet, but Ezekiel is also a prophet. If you see the two together, as I have had the opportunity of doing, Ezekiel is calm, reasoned, rational. Jeremiah raves like a madman."

Again a rumble of discontent from the assembly.

"Look, in all the time I spent with Jeremiah, I learned nothing," said Alice. "After only a few short hours with Ezekiel I was able to send Adam the message about the attack. It is in nobody's best interests to compare the two, so why don't we just deal with what I learned from Ezekiel? After tonight we have only two days before the attack that will destroy Jerusalem, and there is much to do." he paused and looked around. "Raise your hand if you're prepared to commit to this cause," he said.

One by one, each and every one of them raised a hand.

"Good," said Al, pleased.

For the next two hours, Alice outlined what he needed from the Holiness Code. He selected team leaders to evacuate families, and formed a team consisting of Adam, Yarin and a new, tough-looking lad named Liam, to help him in what he had to do — which he wouldn't know until he'd spoken with Zedekiah.

By the time Alice and Yarin made it back to the villa it was dark. When they entered the courtyard, Alice stopped and glanced up at the clear night sky.

"What are you looking at?" Yarin asked, following Alice's eye-line.

"Betyl," said Alice. "Here it comes now. Look, just over the horizon. See the star moving?"

"I have never seen that before," said the boy. "Why does it move so fast?"

"Because it is not a star, Yarin, it is a ship."

"A ship? In the sky? I do not understand."

"It is a great ship that sails the skies around the Earth," said Al. "It has come from another world."

"Who is inside this ship?"

"Marduk, for one," said Alice.

"Is not that one of the Babylonii gods?" Yarin questioned.

"It is," Al agreed.

Razili heard talking and joined them. "What are we looking at?" he asked.

"Daniel is telling me about Betyl, father."

"Ah yes, Betyl," said Razili. "The house of God."

"So you know it is the ship of Marduk?" Yarin questioned.

"Marduk? Is not that the god of—"

"Nebuchadnezzar, yes," said Al, and got the immediate notion that Razili wasn't impressed with talk about Nebuchanezzar or Babylonian gods. The older man motioned for Alice and Yarin to follow him, and changed the subject on their way to the dining area.

"I have arranged for you to have an audience with King Zedekiah tomorrow, one hour before noon," he said.

"Excellent. What did he say when he got the message?"

"He said Daniel had better make more sense than Jeremiah."

"I wonder what that is supposed to mean." Al mused.

"I would say he is not very tolerant of prophets," said Razili, soberly.

CHAPTER 22
HEPATOSCOPY

IT WAS MORNING, and for Alice there was an ominous feeling in the air. This was the first time he'd noticed overcast skies since he'd arrived in Jerusalem. The sky was normally a great expanse of blue. He was up earlier than the rest of the household, sitting on the edge of the fishpond watching small fish dart in and out of the lily pads. A feeling of otherworldliness suddenly overcame him. He jumped up, head spinning, and braced himself against a column. It didn't feel like the side effects of time travel the way he'd experienced them before. This was more like he'd been touched by something supernatural. He felt the need for fresh air, and walked out into the more open courtyard.

He looked up into the grey sky and took some deep, calming breaths. It was then he noticed something out of place: Betyl. He could see Betyl. In daylight, and with the low cloud cover, he shouldn't be able to see it at all. Its bright light was bigger than before — and it had stopped moving. That meant only one thing. It had moved closer to Earth and was now matching orbits, positioned directly over Jerusalem. The strange feeling had passed, only to be replaced by puzzlement.

Betyl was now a dull red spot in the sky. He wished he could see it through a telescope, then realised it would be two thousand years before anyone invented one. However, if and when the clouds cleared, the sight would be amazing. Then he thought, what if I could make a telescope?

Just then Razili came out into the courtyard and looked up, interested to see what Alice was gazing at.

"Ah, Betyl," he said conversationally. "Seems you are fascinated by that star, Daniel,"

"Razili, good morning," smiled Al. "Yes — but see how it's bigger than it was before … and it is no longer moving."

"I think you are right," said Razili, disinterestedly.

"Tell me, do you know where I could purchase a lens?"

"For reading?" Razili asked.

"Yes, exactly."

"Ah, there is an old man who provides such things to scribes, monks and Pharisees. He takes glass, shapes it, polishes it so it increases the size of whatever you look at. It that what you mean?"

"Yes, exactly."

"Apparently he learned the craft in Egypt. I can take you to his shop on the way to your meeting at the palace."

"I would appreciate that, thank you."

Al sensed there was something bothering Razili.

"Is there something you want to ask me?" he gently urged.

"I am just worried," said Razili. "The siege has taken a toll on the people of Jerusalem, and food is in shortage. Until a few days ago, the Babylonii permitted some supplies to enter. Now they have stopped."

"Are you expecting an attack?" Al asked.

"Yes. But in the meantime the sick, the infirm and the old are starving. Babies are sickening as their mothers' milk slows. You are not seeing it here because I am supplied food from the palace. But soon, crazed people will break into my house and take our food … and all the while the Pharisees have plentiful stocks."

"Are you telling me those priests are controlling the food?"

"Yes. They hoard it and sell it at inflated prices."

"You're kidding me … they're supposed to be servants of God," Alice growled.

"If one challenges them, as did Ezekiel and Jeremiah, it means banishment — or worse," Razili said, sadly.

"Why does not Zedekiah intervene?"

"The King does not know," said Razili. "I only know because of my work. When I requisition supplies from the stores, the workers complain about the gluttony of the Pharisees."

It came as no surprise to Alice that the Pharisees were up to no good. His experience so far had hardly cast them in a positive light.

A little later, Razili led Alice into the shop of Renni Baruti. The old man specialized in magnifying lenses, used mostly for kindling and cauterizing wounds. Renni was probably fifty, which was ancient in this society, with a long white beard and very few teeth. He showed Alice a lens formed from highly-polished quartz. It must have taken years to shape by hand.

When asked what he wanted a lens for, Alice told Renni he wanted to look at Betyl. That seemed to excite the old fella. He wandered off to another part of the dirty and cluttered room, dug around under a dusty old cabinet, all the while mumbling to himself in Egyptian, before suddenly erupting, gabbling with excitement, holding a brass cylinder thirty centimetres long, six centimetres in diameter and clearly ancient.

Renni tried to pop the brass caps clipped to each end of the tube, but his arthritic fingers weren't up to it. Alice took over, revealing crystal lenses at each end of the cylinder. Alice held it up and peered through it. Sure enough, it was a primitive telescope.

"Did you make this?" Alice asked the old man.

"No, no no," he said, grinning toothlessly, "It is from Memphis, the city of my birth! It is said to have belonged to Thutmose the Second.'

The Egyptian father of Moses, Alice's internal database supplied. So many connections — Moses, his father, the Ark of the Covenant and now this telescope, probably the first of its kind in the world. It was doing Alice's head in.

Unconsciously, he squeezed the rice-sized pellet in his left earlobe, and changed the subject. "May I take a look through it outside?"

"Yes, yes by all means," the old man said, excitedly keen to oblige.

Razili and Baruti followed Alice outside and watched him gaze through the scope at Betyl.

It only magnified about ten times, but that was good enough in the daylight. Betyl was definitely not a planet. Alice could see quite clearly that it wasn't spherical, it was elliptical — it had to be a spacecraft.

"What is he looking at?" Baruti asked, quietly.

"The light in the sky," said Razili. "Betyl."

"Would you like to look?" Alice asked.

The Hebrew raised a hand and fiercely shook his head, as though Alice was suggesting something blasphemous. Alice let it go. These were times of strange superstitions, and some things were better left unexplained. He handed the scope back to Baruti.

"Thank you," he said. "Keep this safe — it is a rare treasure." The old man nodded enthusiastically, and Alice and Razili resumed their journey. As they walked, Razili raised a question. "Daniel, while you were with the Babylonii, did you hear of three Hebrews who are advisors to King Nebuchadnezzar? Hananiah, Mishael, and Azariah, otherwise known by their Babylonian names, Shadrach, Meshach and Abednego?"

Alice accessed the story from his database. "I did not hear of them while I was there, but I know the story," he said. "Nebuchadnezzar built a massive golden statue of himself and invited the nations to bow down to it. The three scribes who were his council — Shadrach, Meshach and Abednego — refused to bow and were thrown into a furnace. But they didn't burn. A fourth person was supposedly seen with them inside the furnace. Is that right?"

"Yes," said Razili, sadly. "That was thirteen years ago. I knew them — Abednego lived near my house. I was just wondering if they were still alive. No-one has heard of them in a long time."

They passed by a row of beggars, something Alice hadn't seen before in Jerusalem. They were in terrible condition, starving. Alice knew this was an example of what Razili had told him earlier.

"Apparently the heat from the furnace was so powerful it killed the guards who had thrown the men in," he went on. "So how could they have survived? And who was the fourth person in the flames?"

"They say he was an angel of God," said Razili.

There was no doubt in Alice's mind that this was another example of the Anunnaki intervening in the politics of the times. The fourth person in the fire had to have been one of the spacemen who had visited Ezekiel at around about the same time. Nebuchadnezzar had amassed too much power, and it was obviously getting to him if he was building massive golden effigies of himself. He'd had to be taken in hand.

They reached the outer wall of the Temple Mount. Razili led Alice through a back gate in the Temple wall, and along a narrow passageway to the rear of the complex — Alice took a mental note that the complex was unguarded. They passed through the kitchen where Razili worked, and continued up three flights of stairs to a long, elaborately-decorated corridor.

"The King's instructions were to bring you to the throne room and wait at the entrance until he has finished meeting with high Pharisee Kohen," Razili whispered as they reached two large, gilded doors. Razili listened at the doors then whispered: "The meeting is still in progress."

The door was partially opened by a palace guard. After a quiet word with Razili, he ushered them inside. The throne room wasn't as big as Alice had expected, and only attended by half a dozen guards at the exits and two Pharisees Alice recognised from the Temple sacrifice. Sitting on the throne, glaring down at the world like a ravenous vulture, was King Zedekiah. The Pharisees were bowing and backing away.

Alice had seen Zedekiah at Beit Ha'am, but when he got close he could see the king was a lot younger than he'd expected. Razili stopped short of the throne and bowed. Alice, unsure if he was expected to prostrate himself as he had with Nebuchadnezzar, followed Razili's lead.

"King Zedekiah, this is the man Daniel," Razili said.

"Thank you Razili," said the king. "You may leave us. Speak, Daniel."

"Good King Zedekiah of the House of David, thank you for giving me audience," Al said. "Sire, I met with King Nebuchadnezzar and the prophet Ezekiel only two days ago. After the king left, I held private conference with Ezekiel. He told me to convey this message to you: 'On my instruction Daniel, and Daniel only, may remove the Ark and be trusted with the secret of its final location.'"

Zedekiah sat in silence.

Alice glanced at the wall behind the throne. A fresco of King Solomon in violent battle exuded a coarse, primitive power.

"This must happen quickly," Alice added, "Nebuzaradan will end the siege in two days' time."

Zedekiah didn't know whether to rage at Alice's temerity or laugh at his stupidity.

"I am told that Nebuchadnezzar has three hundred and sixty sorcerers, astrologers, enchanters and magicians," he sneered. "Are you telling me he listened to you? Why?"

"He listens to his personal astrologer, Zorlock, and he listens to Ezekiel," said Alice. "He listened to me because I told him the future."

"I thought only Hananiah, Mishael, and Azariah were interpreters of Nebuchadnezzar's dreams," said the young king.

"I did not see or hear of them while I was there, my lord."

"And now, I am being instructed — instructed — to allow you, whom I do not know and cannot trust, to remove the Holy of Holies and hide it?" he said, with a sneer.

Alice didn't like the way this was going. "Do you think me blind to what lies ahead?" the king went on.

"Sight is often blinded by vision, my lord," Alice countered.

"Are you saying the King cannot see what is under his nose?"

It was another of those loaded and horribly dangerous questions. Alice was standing on the edge of a precipice. He'd be dead in seconds if he gave the wrong answer. He gambled.

"Perhaps so lord," he said. "In the same way you do not see that your subjects are starving to death in the streets while your Pharisees profit from selling your food stocks at greatly inflated prices."

The king rose quickly out of his chair, face burning with anger. "Guard!" he roared. "Bring me Kohen!"

Oh no, Alice thought. Now I've done it.

The high Pharisee had joined Alice in front of the throne in no time. The King had resumed his seat and calmed a little. Before the priest could utter a word, Zedekiah snapped at him. "Kohen! Are you and your kind selling our food stocks at prices the people cannot afford?"

The round-faced, overfed little man let out the pathetic squeak of a rat caught in a trap.

"I asked you a question," Zedekiah insisted.

"Yes, O lord," Kohen managed. "To … to raise funds, for priestly purposes."

"At the expense of the people?" Zedekiah shouted.

"There is no need to upset yourself, lord," said the little man. "We plan to release free food to the people on the Sabbath."

"You sick sycophant," snarled Al. "If you wait that long you will be feeding Nebuchanezzar's army!"

"Who are you?" Kohen whined, looking down his nose at Alice.

"This is Daniel," Zedekiah said. "Sent to me by Ezekiel."

"How can that be? Ezekiel is imprisoned in Babylon!"

"Your powers of prediction are lacking, high priest," said Alice. "I was with Ezekiel only two days ago in the Babylonii camp."

Glaring at Alice, Kohen's mouth formed a thin straight line. His eyes narrowed. "I remember now," he said, pulling himself up to his full and unimpressive height. "This man was banished from Jerusalem along with Jeremiah! Why do you listen to the words of a criminal, my lord?"

"I could ask that too," said Alice, returning serve. "Selling food for profit while the people starve? Not very reverent of you. Criminal, in fact."

"How dare you make such an accusation!" Kohen exclaimed.

"Daniel is here to give me counsel, Kohen, as he did for Nebuchadnezzar. It will be too late to give food to the people on the Sabbath. The siege will end in two days, and you will be in the custody of Nebuzaradan and Zorlock."

"Now, that will be interesting," said Alice. "He is one mean customer, that Zorlock."

"If this man has the gift of prophecy, have him prove it," Kohen barked, defensively.

Both Kohen and Zedekiah cast their eyes on Alice. It was time to perform. He went into his 'future reading' mode, searched his mental database and repeated the information with exquisite care. He was still balanced on a knife edge.

"King Zedekiah, you have reigned for eleven years," he said, slowly. "But the time has come. Nebuchadnezzar will capture Jerusalem. You will try to escape the city, my lord, but you will be captured on the plains of Jericho, and taken to Riblah. There, your sons will be put to death in front of you. Your eyes will be put out, and, loaded in chains, you will be taken to Babylon, to remain a prisoner until you die. Your city will be razed to the ground. Solomon's Temple will be destroyed."

There was shocked silence.

"Hepatoscopy must confirm this, lord," Kohen said, looking decidedly nervous.

Hepatoscopy, put in the ever-reliable database, divination by inspecting the liver of animals.

It's about as rational as any other belief system they've got going on here, Al thought.

CHAPTER 23
SIEGE MENTALITY

❝ SAVE YOUR CHICANERY for your followers, Kohen," Zedekiah growled through bared teeth. "Get out, and distribute the food you have been hoarding — you will not ask for money. Do I make myself clear?"

Bowing obsequiously to his king, the fat man, humiliated to the max, shot Alice a glare of abject condemnation before thundering out of the throne room.

Alice let out a sigh of relief, glad to see the back end of him.

A look of consternation spoiling his handsome face, the King asked, "So these terrible tortures that await me … this is my destiny?"

"I'm afraid so my lord," said Alice. "I am sorry that I cannot be the bearer of more positive intelligence."

"These are not times of joy," the king said, resignedly. "This day has been coming, and I have chosen to ignore it. I have no-one to blame but myself."

Alice could see the pain in the King's eyes. He was at the end of his tether: the thirty months of siege had drained his will. He was a beaten man. He had to think deeply about Alice's request — he was of the House of David and the Ark of the Covenant, the Holy of Holies, was under his watch.

"I cannot let the Ark fall into the hands of Nebuchadnezzar, or worse, Zorlock," he said. "That man makes the Pharisees look like angels. What is your plan, Daniel?"

"Only to remove the Ark to a safe hiding place so it may be exhumed in a safer future," Alice replied. As he was speaking, Alice thought about the death sentence he'd given the King. The man deserved a better explanation.

"King Zedekiah, let me try to help you," he said. "I will tell you the truth as I told Ezekiel. I come from two thousand six hundred years in the future, tasked with removing the Ark of the Covenant to prevent it falling into the hands of the Babylonians. In two days, I shall return to my own time and uncover it from its hiding place."

The King stared at Alice like he was looking at a ghost. And then he spoke as though in a trance: "I have dreamed of you asking this of me, Daniel," he said. "Jeremiah interpreted this dream as being inevitable. As always, I failed to listen to his counsel. I felt he was losing his mind."

"I believe in the cause of Jeremiah my lord," Alice replied. "But his genius and insanity are intermingled."

"That is a fair summation of the man."

"It is how history will see him, sire. And you will be known as a fair man who ruled through troublesome times."

"Thank you, Daniel," said the King. "That is a comfort. But now, tell me a little of your times."

"There is still no peace," said Alice. "Israel still exists and has power, but still fights old enemies."

"So Babylon will be no more in two thousand years?"

"No, sire — not even fifty years. The Persian king Cyrus the Great will take it in forty-eight years' time. In my time Babylon is known as Iraq. It is still a place of social and religious unrest.

"Humans still wage wars — there have been fearful battles in the sky, on the oceans and on land. We have created weapons that can destroy a city in a stroke." Looking at the King's horrified face, he went on: "On the positive side, people live long. We can cure many diseases and help those born differently from others. We have visited the moon, and stood on its surface. We can fly around the world. An invention called electricity lights homes and provides power by which to cook and keep warm or cool…"

Alice went on for at least thirty minutes, giving the king insight into the world of the 21st century. With the horrors that lay ahead for the man, Alice felt he could at least give him something to think about when in less than a week he would have his eyes burnt out with a red-hot poker.

When Alice had finished, the King's mood had brightened somewhat.

He removed a ring from his finger, handed it to Alice and said: "This will get you past any sentry — including those who guard the Holy of Holies."

Alice slipped the chunky gold ring that contained the royal seal onto his finger and stared at it, thinking: this is me, a rock singer, here in Jerusalem in 587 BC and wearing a ring that will open every door in the Kingdom of Judah. He smiled, and bowed.

"Thank you, King Zedekiah," he said.

"Such is all I can do for you and the world," said Zedekiah dispiritedly; a King usurped by the times.

The offices of Oceana had vacated for the day. Only those on nightshift, or the overly passionate about their work, remained behind. Such was the case for the President and Honor.

Miss Vallins had gone home and the President was using the downtime to catch up on some reading. Reclining in his lounge chair, he was thumbing through a document when the office door creaked open. Thinking Miss Vallins had failed to close it properly when she left for the day, he ignored it and went back to reading. Zanza Kew slipped silently into the room. Avoiding the security cameras, he stopped at a predetermined safe position, only two metres from the President. As the President looked up, Kew drew a small, 3D printed pistol fitted with a silencer, aimed and fired once. The .22 calibre bullet struck the President in the forehead. His head recoiled, then slumped forward, leaving him resting his chin on his chest, the document still in his grasp.

Kew pocketed the gun and slipped stealthily from the room.

Honor's implant sounded an alarm. She wasted no time rushing to the President's office.

She entered and found the President slumped in his chair, then immediately called Secta.

It only took him fifteen minutes to get there. She was waiting in one of the lounge chairs.

"Do you think I should reset?" Secta asked, out of breath.

Honor stood. "No," she said, hard-boiled. "I zink ve know vhat needs to be done from here."

Secta took a small remote from his pocket, aimed it at the President, and hit a button. The hologram disappeared.

"I must admit, Secta, I had my doubts about your plan," said Honor, reluctantly. "But it has vorked perfectly."

Secta ignored her admission. "So now we move on to phase two," he said. "That's out of my territory. The President is safe at the bunker with Hope. We will soon, however, need to make arrangements to leave for the Middle East."

"Vunce I haff retrieved ze footage of ze murderer to present to Gorrick, I vill make an arrest," said Honor. "After zat I vill make ze arrangements and let you know. I am avare of ze schedule, Secta."

Secta had fitted out the President's office with an infrared sensor. Once movement was detected, four hidden cameras focused on the violator. The murder had been recorded, and it was only a matter of downloading it to ID the perpetrator. Although they both already knew it would be Kew.

Alice arrived back at the home of Razili and was met in the courtyard by Yarin and Adam.

"Daniel, what happened?" Yarin asked. "Where have you been?"

"We were worried about you!" Adam added.

Alice sat and poured a cup of water from an urn. Even though the sky was overcast, it was oppressively humid. After quenching his thirst, he told them what he'd been doing, and showed them the ring Zedekiah had given him. "This will get us past any sentry," he said, "Including those who guard the Holy of Holies."

"The King's ring!" Adam said, impressed. "That is incredible!"

"Right," said Al. "Now, we have a lot to do. Because tomorrow, just before sunrise, we take the Ark and hide it. Go and ask Liam to join us."

The boys took off to do Alice's bidding. He broke a piece of bread from a loaf on the table and dunked it in a saucer of olive oil. He had left without having breakfast and it was now past lunchtime, he was starving. He was about to dive in for seconds when he heard a loud bang. He jumped up to see half a dozen angry young men rushing towards him, brandishing weapons.

"Hey! Stop!" he yelled. "What's going on here?"

Someone hit him over the head and knocked him out cold.

When he came to, the courtyard was a mess. The invaders were packing all the food they could find into canvas bags. Alice heard screaming. It was coming from Calista, who was being dragged into the courtyard by two guys with a look in their eyes Alice recognised. They had gone over the top — they were now in battle frenzy — anything could happen.

One of them belted Calista across the face, time and again, forcing her to the floor. They were going to rape her. Alice erupted. He jumped up, picked up a chair, ran over to the rapist and belted him with it. The chair splintered apart and the victim crashed to the ground, bleeding and unconscious. Alice was already letting fly at the other guy, smashing him across the face with what was left of the chair. It tore his nose clean off and gouged out his right eye.

Alice grabbed him by the throat, lifted him off the deck and yelled into his bleeding face: "Who sent you? Tell me, or I'll rip out the other eye and eat it!"

Shaking uncontrollably, the young man muttered: "K … Kohen … the Pharisees…" before passing out.

Al had blown his stack. He jumped up and took off after the others as they fled for the exit, trying to escape this marauding madman. As they reached the door it opened, and Razili entered. One of the escaping vandals stabbed him in the gut with a short dagger, dropped it to the floor and then took flight.

Alice caught the last one leaving and tackled him to the ground. He reached down, grabbed him by the hair and was about to deliver a death punch when he realised he was only a boy. "Get the hell out of here!" he yelled in English, and let him go.

Though the boy didn't understand what he'd said he got the idea, and crawled through the doorway on his hands and knees.

Alice went quickly to Razili. He was propped against the wall, covering his bleeding gut with two hands. Alice knew he was dying.

"Daniel," the man gasped through the pain, "I knew this was coming…"

"Shush, be calm," said Alice. "I'll go for help."

Razili leaned his head forward and vomited blood down the front of his white caftan. He looked back up at Alice, blood dribbling from his chin in a string. A tear traversed his cheek.

"No Daniel," he choked. "I will leave you now. I go … to a better place."

Blood was gushing between his fingers … he was bleeding out. Calista rushed over and fell to her knees beside him. She was sobbing so hard she couldn't get a word out, she simply held her dying husband.

Alice staggered to his feet and left them together to say their goodbyes. He knew Razili would die in her arms. After a few seconds he heard a mournful moan: "Oh no, my love…"

Alice sat next to the pond, in tears. All his life this man Razili had done nothing but good. Raised a family, served his King and now he'd been killed for a few bags of wheat, which had been left behind. All he'd died for lay strewn about the courtyard. Two dead, one horribly disfigured, Calista attacked, all for nothing. The futility of it made Alice mad. He wasn't about rest until he'd settled the score.

He got his head back together and calmed down, went back over to Calista. She was still in an embrace with her dead husband. Al gently took her arms and to help her up — then saw the hilt of the dagger that had killed Razili protruding from her breast. She was dead.

Alice slid down the wall to sit on the floor with his head in his hands. "No…" he lamented, "Oh, no…"

Suddenly, everything around him shimmered. The mission went on, and it was almost time to go. He struggled to his feet, dizzy, everything in his vision wavering like a mirage over a bitumen road on a stinking hot day. He walked a few paces, then collapsed.

When Yarin and Adam returned a short while later with Liam, Yarin found his mother and father on the ground in a puddle of blood. He fell to his knees beside them, sobbing.

Adam looked about the courtyard, then saw Alice sitting at the side of the pond, staring at the water. There was a body on the ground near the dining table. It wasn't difficult to make sense of what had happened. He went over to Alice, sat beside him and looked at the water in the pond.

"Are you all right, Alice?"

Without taking his eyes off the water, Alice nodded remorsefully. "I do not think after what just happened I will ever be all right again, son," he said, quietly.

Adam decided it was best to take Alice and Yarin to his aunt's home, while Liam stayed to arrange removal of the bodies.

Sabrina comforted Yarin while he wept. Alice was sitting on the floor in silence, a cup of mead in his hands. No matter what had happened, no matter how badly they felt, the mission would have to proceed before sunrise. There was no choice in the matter, and they would only have one crack at it.

Adam had news. The Babylonian army could be seen massing for an attack. It would come as Alice had predicted, sometime within the next twenty-four hours. "Alice, what needs to be done?" The boy asked. "We do not have much time."

Alice blinked a few times, gathering his thoughts, and took a deep breath. "I know," he said, clambering to his feet. "First, we need to get your family to safety. They will have to go in the opposite direction to Jericho. That is where Nebuzaradan will chase Zedekiah."

"How about Joppa?" Adam proposed. "It is ten leagues from here, on the coast."

"What is that, about fifty kilometres? Good," said Alice. "They must start now."

"Now?"

"Yes. They will need a head start. It will be fine, you three will catch them up by midday tomorrow."

Adam moved closer to Alice. "They will be too scared to leave without protection," he whispered. "Three women cannot travel alone."

"Adam, if they stay here, they will end up like Calista, or worse," said Alice.

"I will tell them," said Adam, face pale.

"Wait!" said Alice. "Why not get word to everyone in the Holiness Code to leave tonight? That way they could travel in a group of ... how many?"

"Fifty or more," said Adam, excitedly. "An excellent idea, Alice. I will go now to spread the word. They will assemble at the western gate at midnight."

"I will use the ring to get them through the gate," said Alice. "Oh, listen, tell Liam to bring two of the heaviest, long-handled hammers he can find, and to leave them in the Golem impression in the cave. It is very important, Adam. Have him do that before he does anything else, okay?"

"Trust me Alice. It will be done."

He moved off, stopped and said, "Alice?"

"Yes?"

"What is oh-kay?"

"Oh!" Alice laughed, in spite of himself. "In my language it is a word for affirmation. It means 'all right', or 'agreed'."

"I see," said the boy. "Good, I will use that — oh-kay?"

Al smiled.

CHAPTER 24
DUPLICITY IN THE CITY

HONOR HAD WORKED into the early hours of the morning to put together a case for presentation to Gorrick, then crashed on the office couch.

Viktoria woke her with a cup of hot coffee. "Good morning ma'am," she said, warmly. "Long night?"

Honor sat up, scratching her head, and said with a yawn: "Yes, but vell vorth it. Zank you for ze coffee. Is Karzoff in yet?"

"Yes, would you like me to send him in?"

"Please. Just give me fife minutes to freshen up."

Twenty minutes later Karzoff was up to date on the attempted murder. Honor swivelled the computer monitor to replay the assassination footage from the different camera angles. Even though they knew it was a hologram being shot, it was still shocking. Honor froze the frame of the murderer turning to leave and zoomed in on the face of the perpetrator.

"One Zanza Kew," she said, with a contented smile. She had a score to settle with him, and now she was armed with what she needed to do it.

"That is him all right," said Karzoff. "What is the next move?"

"Ve are going to confront our friend Gorrick with zis evidence," said Honor. "Then I vill take pleasure in arresting Mister Kew. Vhile ve are doing zat, haff Viktoria arrange three tickets to Jerusalem, leaving tonight, and book a luxury suite for three at ze David Citadel Hotel."

Karzoff was excited. "Who are the three?" he asked.

"You, myself and Doctor Secta," said Honor. "Oh, and haff Viktoria advise Secta of ze schedule, though I suspect she vill tell him anyvay. She is, I am almost certain, his spy."

Standing on the balcony of Hope's Coogee Beach apartment Secta was taking in the view. Hope joined Secta, both were dressed in their civvies. She handed him a glass of red wine.

"Cheers, big ears. You did a great job saving the President."

"How is he?"

"Hates being in the bunker," she chuckled just as a buzzer sounded. She tapped her wristwatch to permit entry.

"It's not Honor is it?" Secta groaned.

"Better not be, I only invited Mal and the prof."

"I'll head back to bunker after we have lunch."

"Good o," Secta affirmed.

Hope left to let in her guests. Secta resumed taking in the view of Coogee Beach, sipping his wine. Footsteps had him turn away from the balcony rail to find Hope, Mal and professor De Luz accompanied by a young lady unknown to him.

"Welcome my friends, and this lovely lady is?"

Mal made the introduction. "Doctor's Hope and Secta and professor De Luz may I introduce Wyetta Walker, known to her friends as Vee, sister of none other than … Black Alice."

They were stunned. Vee was slim, athletic, dark skin and resembled Alice, not only in looks but a powerful countenance.

Secta drifted over to Vee and took her hand. "Alice has never mentioned he has a sister."

Vee smiled, "He doesn't know he has a sister."

"She turned up at my gig last night looking for Al," Mal explained. "I was standing in for him with the band and was as surprised as you when she lobbed backstage and announced who she was. I've known Al longer than any of you and he's never mentioned a sister."

Hope ushered them all to sit at a table.

Once Vee had taken her seat she said, "Our parents went to jail in Perth when Alice was like twelve. Mum was pregnant with me at the time, so I was born inside. After a few months I was fostered out, just like Alice. It wasn't until this year I decided to trace my folks and found out about Rob … Alice. I applied for a gig in security in Sydney, lefty Perth a couple of days ago, lobbed here and decided to look for him. Saw the Black Alice gig poster, so I went to the gig. Didn't think Mal was him."

"Why not?" Mal chuckled. "I sing alright."

Secta asked her, "You said security?"

Mal answered for her. "Get this … she applied for a position with Zen."

"Yeah," Vee added, "They're international. Might give me a chance to travel."

Hope shot Secta a sly glance. "Why not apply to Oceana?"

"I did," Vee declared. "A dude named Karznot or something I think, but he never got back to me."

"Karzoff," Secta corrected with raised eyebrows.

"Why do we not look surprised?" the professor chimed in.

"I can have a word with the President if you like," Secta offered.

Vee was taken aback. "Who? The President? That's going a bit high isn't it?"

Secta took a sip of his wine. There was a lot needed to be explained to Vee. "Well, Alice is very important to the government, I'm sure Oceana would like to have his sister on board."

Mal was nodding. "Anything but Zen."

"Okay, so you guys are all with Oceana?" Vee queried.

While she was topping up her guest's glasses with red wine Hope said, "Are you good at martial arts?"

"A black belt, Dan in TaeKwon-Do."

They all raised their eyebrows. She might be pint sized but the black belt made her a lethal weapon.

She continued, "I don't get it. Why would Alice and you Mal work with Oceana? The organization you're oppose to?"

"You're talking about the Octagon?"

"Yeah. Has my brother changed sides or something? Where is he anyway?"

They exchanged a conspiratorial glance, then Secta spoke up. "He's on a mission for Oceana."

"A mission?" Vee exclaimed, becoming agitated. "But he's a frigging heavy metal singer, what sort of mission could that be?"

"A secret mission Vee," Secta said sternly. "Can't say any more."

That was enough. Vee couldn't take any more and jumped out of her seat. "This is a set-up!" she snarled. "You've got him in prison or something, haven't you? That's what this is all about—"

Mal stood and put a placating arm around her. "Vee, calm down. I'm the leader of the Octagon. I brought you here because these are Al's friends. Sit back down. Secta will fill you in."

Vee reluctantly complied.

"But before his does that we need to validate your relationship to Alice," the professor said.

Now she was really offended. "Excuse me!"

When Secta heard he would be leaving for Jerusalem later that evening, he phoned Hope.

"Just heard I'm leaving tonight with the bookends," he said. "Staying at the David Citadel Hotel."

"Where's that?" Hope asked.

"Not far from Temple Mount."

"Am I to remain with the President?" she asked, dejectedly.

"Yes, I'm afraid so," Secta replied. "I should get more info from Honor following her meeting with Gorrick. If after that she arrests Kew, tomorrow should be safe for the President to return to the city."

"You'd better call Mal — and what about Vic?" Hope asked.

"I'll see Vic in a minute, he's joining me at Café Epiphany for a coffee," said Secta. "By the way I meant to ask earlier at your apartment, how are you getting on with the cryo-eggs?"

"Looking good," said Hope. On top of everything else, she and Secta had been working on a way to de-sterilise the humans of the future. "By the time you return they'll be ready. Has Vic solved the container issue?"

"I think so, I'll ask," said Secta. "So now it's a matter of how to implant them."

"Don't worry, I'll sort that out," said Hope. "Good luck in Jerusalem — and keep safe."

"Thanks sis," said Secta. "I'll let you know when it's done."

His next call was to Mal. "It's on Mal. You leave for Jerusalem tonight."

That put a rocket under him. "Tonight! But—"

"No buts, my friend, you know the drill," said Secta, unmercifully. "I'll text you the ticket details in an hour or so. You'll be booked at the King Solomon Hotel."

"King Solomon, eh? Sounds relatively groovy."

"I don't know about that, it's three star."

"Three out of three? Excellent."

"Er — okay, well good luck," said Secta. "And don't forget to switch your phone to roaming. See you in Jerusalem!"

"Cool. Chaa!"

"Yes … Um, Chaa!"

Secta liked using Alice's customary goodbye.

The plan was in motion, the rest was up to Alice.

Secta sat back in the chair and gazed out of the window of the café at the professor arriving. He wondered what would happen when Set realised he was stuck in the past. He shrugged his shoulders. Who cares, he thought.

Armed with a warrant for Gorrick's arrest, Honor, Karzoff and two armed troopers stormed Zen Corporation. Leading the way, Honor bustled through ground floor security flashing her ID and flagging the warrant about in the air like she was leading a SWAT assault. She knew that by the time they reached Gorrick's penthouse suite on the 50th floor, he would already know about the raid.

When the elevator door opened on the penthouse level, Gorrick was standing there, supported by four heavily-armed guards.

"If you step out of the elevator you will be trespassing, Honor," he said, smoothly.

Karzoff kept his finger on the button, holding the elevator door open.

"Gorrick Khan, I have a warrant for your arrest," said Honor, coldly.

"On what charge?"

"Conspiracy to assassinate the President of Oceana."

"And what proof do you have of that?"

"I am not here to answer your questions, Gorrick. Arrest him!"

As the troopers exited the elevator to make the arrest, Gorrick's guards raised their weapons. It was a Mexican standoff.

"One more step and my men will fire," Gorrick said, casually. "Shall we dispense with this grandstanding and talk in a civilized manner in my office?"

Honor glanced at Karzoff. He nodded.

"Lead the way," she said, and indicated that the troopers should wait. Gorrick's guards waited with them.

Gorrick led them into his huge office space. The room was two storeys high, split level, with a large glass ceiling that let the sky in. In the centre of the room a towering Blue Gum eucalyptus reached up to the skylight roof. The mezzanine was Gorrick's personal office area. The lower level had a large sunken lounge around the trunk of the Blue Gum. A small stream meandered around the room, passing under a small bridge and ending in a waterfall and pond. The sound of the cascading water made the space feel like a tropical paradise. Gorrick led them to the lounge and gestured for them to sit.

"Would you like something to drink?" he asked, cordially.

Karzoff smiled and nodded, hoping for coffee and biscuits.

"Zis is not a social visit, Gorrick," Honor said curtly. "Let's get on viz it."

Karzoff's smile faded.

"I haff sent a video for you to view," Honor added.

Gorrick collected a laptop from a small table beside his chair, opened it and checked his e-mail. He watched the video. When it had finished he looked up, an expression of horror on his face.

"My God, was that…?"

"Yes. Ze assassination of ze President," said Honor. "Do you recognise ze shooter, Mister Khan?"

"Yes. It is Zanza Kew, a Zen operative."

"Vas Zanza Kew acting on your orders?"

Gorrick's voice dropped to growl. "You have got to be kidding," he said. "Why would I want the President assassinated? He must have been acting of his own volition."

"Vhy did he instruct me to stop investigating you, if he vas not acting under your direct orders?"

Gorrick snapped his laptop closed and placed it back on the coffee table. "He had no such brief," he said, offhandedly. Checking his wristwatch, he added: "I'm leaving for New York in a couple of hours. I will have one of my men bring Kew to your office at 2pm today. Can I be of any more assistance?"

Honor stink-eyed the tall man, glanced around the fantastic room, then back at him. The opulence of his office pissed her off even more.

She slowly rose from the chair. "I promise you Gorrick," she said earnestly, "Vhen I am finished viz you, zis opulence will be but a distant memory. You vill be counting ze days in prison."

"You seem to have forgotten that I run the prisons, Honor," was the smooth reply. "Now — if you don't mind…"

In the car on the way back to Oceana HQ, Karzoff broke the ice that had chilled the air. "Did you really expect to arrest Gorrick?"

"Off course not!" she snapped. "It vas only a ruse to make him give up Kew. Do not vorry, Karzoff. Gorrick vill be next. For now, ve haff ozzer fish to fry."

At 2pm that afternoon, as promised, Kew surrendered to Honor and was charged with the attempted assassination of the President. He was finding it difficult to understand why the charge was attempted murder. Honor had decided not to elaborate. It would have greater emotional impact for him to find out later, behind bars for the rest of his life, that his assassination attempt had been thwarted.

Honor wanted badly to arrest Gorrick and put him away as well, but had been advised by the legal office that her case against him wasn't strong enough. They also suggested that Zen Corporation would free Kew within days, because he hadn't actually killed anyone. If he is set free, I vill kill him myself, she thought. Then she brushed all that aside. For now, she was intent on completing the task at hand — and that was to catch Alice on his return, and secure the Ark of the Covenant for Oceana. She was quite prepared to go along with Secta until that opportunity presented itself.

The mead had helped Alice nod off to sleep. Suddenly, the sound of hundreds of trumpets blasted him into consciousness.

"What the hell was that?" he barked, sitting bolt upright, heart pounding.

"It is the qarna," Sabrina called from the other side of the room, where she was helping her mother to bundle their personal belongings.

Alice struggled to his feet. Knuckling the sleep from his eyes, he asked: "The what?"

"The qarna — Babylonii war horns," she explained.

"We have heard them before," said Mama. "There will be another blast soon. After that, the next time we hear it, we will be under attack."

"Is it a warning to us or a signal to their forces?" Alice asked.

"Maybe both," said Sabrina. "But I think mainly they aim to unsettle us. They have many ways of instilling fear."

Alice was trying to get his head around the sequence of events. "What do we expect from them?" he asked Mama.

"If it is the same as the last time, they will first move the siege engines up against our ramparts," she replied. "Inside, there will be archers and spearmen. Below, they will use battering rams to pound the gates open. Our warriors will set fire to the siege engines and pour boiling oil on the men using the rams.

"This could continue for a day, two days ... we do not know, it depends how well our men can defend. But given their state, weakened by lack of food, I think they will not last long. Once the gates are breached the Babylonii will enter. The last time Nebuchadnezzar kept the attack orderly. I do not believe it will be the same this time. There will be much bloodshed." Mama began to weep.

Sabrina hugged her. "Hush now Mama," she said, soothingly, stroking the greying hair. "We must be strong. Only the strong will survive, you know."

Mama nodded her head. "I am sorry Alice," she said, wiping her tears away. "It makes me sad to know that all we have lived and worked for will amount to nothing."

"I have seen evidence of that today," Al said, sincerely. "I understand your pain."

Again the horns of Babylon blared, and the sound chilled Alice to the bone.

Adam and Yarin came rushing in.

"The horns have sounded!" Adam cried, with fear in his eyes. "It is said the attack will come at dawn. The message has been given, Alice. The Holiness Code will meet us at the western gate at midnight."

"And Liam?"

"He will be here soon, he is doing as you ordered."

"Very good. Yarin, are you all right?"

He was concerned for the boy after the ordeal he'd been through. But Yarin was strong.

"I am fine," he said, simply. "Thank you."

They were all on edge. What lay ahead was a game changer. Their world would soon disintegrate, things would never be the same again. That went for Alice as well. The task ahead was daunting. He had no idea how he would get the Ark from the Temple to the cavern unnoticed and unchallenged. The ring was a ticket, but if they had to put up a defence, it was just he and three teenagers unskilled in fighting. After what had happened to Razili and Calista, he was concerned that high Pharisee Kohen could have a trap set for them. And he wasn't completely convinced of Zedekiah's integrity. His request had gone a little too smoothly for his liking. Either the mention of Ezekiel had great influence, or Zedekiah was playing Alice for a mug.

CHAPTER 25
EXODUS TRUST

O NCE LIAM ARRIVED it was time to go. It was going to be a long night for Alice and the boys. The women had their goods packed in bundles and slung over their shoulders.

Alice looked at the size of the bundles. "Are you sure you can carry all that?" he said. "It is ten leagues to Joppa, you know."

"They will be fine," Adam said. "I have arranged for a donkey cart to meet us at the gate. Are we all ready? It is time to go."

Alice noticed a paring knife left on the sideboard. Figuring it could come in handy, he slipped it into his belt.

Edna was having difficulty leaving her house. She broke down in tears.

"I am leaving all my memories behind," she sobbed. "This is where we lived as children, this is where I lived with my Abel!"

"No, no my dear," Mama consoled. "You are bringing them with you. This is only a house. Your memories will live on, in your heart."

Al whispered to Adam, "Did they not have children?"

"No, there was some complication."

Alice nodded.

They left the house and made their way through the oily dark of night towards the western gate. From there a road would lead them to the port of Joppa. It would take around a day, since they'd have to stop for food and water. But even such a harrowing journey would be better than the alternative. Staying in Jerusalem wasn't an option.

It was obvious that the Babylonii were committed to total annihilation.

As they walked the narrow streets, people began coming out of houses and joining them. Their ranks grew. Out in front, with Adam and Yarin either side of him, Al felt like Moses leading his people out of Egypt. He began to sing:

> The light shines down in the hall of the ancient heroes.
> A cloud of dust settles in a ray of the sun.
> Dreams of our land and a dark crusade
> And so we all sing along...
> Oh, show me the way to the sea, my Lord, my Lord
> Such is the price we pay
> for the last crusade
> to be free...

Alice called for everyone to hear: "Sing! Sing with me!" Picking up the chorus, they joined in. The majesty of his voice reverberated throughout the city. It brought people to their windows and doors, and they poured into the street to join the procession, singing with heartfelt passion.

> Oh, show me the way to the sea, my Lord, my Lord
> Such is the price we pay
> for the last crusade
> to be free...

Alice sang on:

> A fanfare plays for our great parade
> On our leaving
> Our armour shines
> As we leave behind our enemy.
> By the sword they live
> By the sword they'll die
> Was it worth the pain

Will you take the blame
For your lord?
For your lord...
With a sword in hand
You're taking a land
That isn't yours
And the price paid
For your dark crusade
Will be your blood...
Will be your blood...

Oh, show me the way to the sea, my Lord, my Lord
Such is the price we pay
for the last crusade
to be free...

The song against the dark crusade of the Babylonian hoard had lifted the spirits of the people. Now, instead of just fifty citizens assembling at the western gate, there were hundreds. Alice had been the Pied Piper, the power of his voice had galvanized the people of Jerusalem and drawn them out of their frightened shells. It gave them the strength and the confidence to leave, knowing that freedom and safety would only be found beyond the western gate.

The gate guards were shocked by the massive procession.

Alice approached. "Open the gates and let the people go," he said.

"Our orders are to not open the gates for anyone," the guard replied. "Go back to your homes!" he shouted at the crowd.

A murmur of discontent rumbled through the assembly.

Alice showed the guard the King's ring. "Now, please ... open the gates," he said.

The guard caught the eye of his partner, who nodded in agreement. The gates were opened and the people streamed out.

Adam hugged his Mama and Sabrina, then finally his aunt.

Alice embraced Sabrina. "I will never see you again," he said. "But I want you to know you will always be in my heart."

"I love you, Alice," she said with tears welling up in her pretty, almond-shaped eyes.

He knew she meant as a brother. Not exactly what he'd have in mind under different circumstances, but he'd take it.

"Will you not come with Adam to meet us on the road?" she asked.

"No. I must return home."

Alice hated goodbyes. He'd said too many as a kid, moving from one foster home, one orphanage to another. After a while it was easier not say it at all. It was one of the reasons he'd gone into his shell when he was young. He'd only been freed from that mental prison by his music. And once again, here, music had brought freedom.

He moved on to Mama and Edna, who were both now in tears.

He took one last look at the three women. "At least you will be safe," he said. "Adam and Yarin will find you later today. I will make sure they do. Goodbye, ladies."

"Thank you Alice," said Mama. "You are an angel of the Lord."

"No ma'am," he replied, with a melancholy smile. "I'm just a traveller in time."

Liam caught up with them after seeing his folks safely on the road. They waited until the last people had passed through the gates, then Alice smiled at the guards.

"Thank you, friends," he said. "You might do well to tell your families to take the road too. They will be safer there from the attack that will come at dawn."

The guards exchanged a quick look of accord, nodded their appreciation, and ran off to do exactly that.

Alice turned to the boys, "Okay fellas," he said. "You did a great job freeing the people. Now we need to free the Ark."

They moved off towards the Temple.

They reached the stairs without encountering any resistance. So far so good, Al thought. But when they reached the concourse, with the great bronze pillars of Boaz and Jachin towering either side, they were stopped by guards.

"Halt!" shouted a big burly guard, armed with a long spear.

Alice confronted him. "We are on an important mission in the name of the King," he said.

"What evidence of this mission do you carry?" asked the guard.

Alice walked closer, hands raised chest-high in submission. The guard pointed his spear to stop him at its length.

"That is close enough!" he growled.

Alice turned his right hand and pointed at his middle finger. "The King's ring," he said. "I am wearing the King's ring. It grants me unconditional authorization to enter."

The guard peered at the ring. "Wait here," he said, and then set the other guard to watch them while he strode into the darkness.

"He has gone to fetch a superior officer," Yarin explained.

"He knew we are no threat," Liam said. "We are unarmed."

"Yes, but you can understand his fear," Adam reminded him. "We could be anyone."

"I suppose so, but not anyone has the King's ring."

A few minutes later they heard footsteps on the marble floor and realised more than just the guard were returning. The boys looked uneasy. Alice shrugged. Whatever was coming, it would be the ultimate test of Zedekiah's righteousness. His face darkened when he recognised Kohen accompanying the guard. The priest leered at him. "What brings you to my temple, Daniel?" he said, spitefully.

"Huh," said Al. "I understood King Solomon built it. How long has it been yours?"

"It is under my guardianship," Kohen snapped back.

Alice bow-fingered the irritating little man, showing off the ring, while regretting that the true meaning of the gesture would go over Kohen's head. "I believe this gives me authority that countermands yours," he said.

The priest's face twisted like he'd bitten his tongue. "The King's ring does not overrule my divine duty," he sneered, and turned on his heel to leave.

"We'll see about that…" Al snarled.

Kohen paused, his back to Alice.

"Guard, I have shown you the King's ring," Al declared. "You know the authority vested in it. Stand aside and let me pass…"

The guard stood his ground for a moment, eyes locked on Alice. Then suddenly he stepped aside. Kohen froze. He turned slowly and glared at Alice, his face bright red.

Then he turned on the guard, got in his face and roared: "Are you prepared to disobey my direct order?"

The guard stood resolute, eyes straight ahead. "Yes sir!" he replied. "I am a royal guard, under the King's command!"

A smug grin broke across Al's face.

"You will pay for this!" Kohen growled.

"Tell someone who cares, Kohen!" Al teased. "Come on boys, we have got work to do."

Livid, the High Pharisee turned and wobbled off as fast as his fat little legs could carry him.

"That showed him!" Yarin exclaimed.

"It is not over yet, lads," Al warned. "You can bet your backside he will be back. He is not about to let us walk away with the Ark. Come on!"

He led them into the Holy Place.

The majestic room was about thirty metres long and three storeys high, the ceiling supported by five columns on either side. Gawking at the enormity of it, Al stopped at the Altar of Incense. Off to his left he could see, in the dim light from suspended oil lamps, several large golden Menorah. Just the sort of loot Nebuchadnezzar's soldiers will be hungry for in a few hours' time, he thought.

"Where's the Ark?" he said aloud, looking around the large room and finding nothing.

"In the Holy of Holies," Adam said. "Follow me."

"Oh, okay, I thought this was the Holy of Holies," Alice mumbled. "But hey, what do I know?"

He followed Adam up a marble staircase and through a veiled doorway into a smaller room. Resting on top of a pedestal was a golden casket with two golden, winged cherubim perched on top.

"The Ark of the Covenant," he breathed. "I'll be…"

As he moved closer he saw a dark mark, like a scorch, on the cherubims' wingtips. It looked as though high voltage had travelled between them. He didn't have time to speculate. Besotted by the majesty of the relic, Alice reached out his fingers to touch it.

"No!" Adam screamed, so loud it echoed around the room and caused Al to flinch.

"If you touch it, you will be struck dead," he warned.

Alice doubted that, but after the stuff he'd seen so far, he wasn't tempted to test it. When it came to seriously weird, this world was full of it.

"Then how are we going to carry it?" he asked.

"Those hoops you can see on both sides?" Adam said, "They are for the carrying poles."

"There," Liam pointed to something at the far side of the room. Propped up against the wall were two long, polished poles. Al took one and Yarin the other — they were about four metres long and heavy. Once they had slipped the poles through the hoops, Al and Liam took the front, resting the poles on their shoulders, while Adam and Yarin did the same at the rear. Together, they took the weight and lifted.

"I thought it would be heavier," Liam said.

"So did I," Adam agreed.

They headed through the veil and back down the stairs into the Holy Place. Alice was expecting confrontation at any moment but it didn't come. At least, not until they reached the pillars of Boaz and Jachin, where waiting for them at the Altar, obstructing the only exit, were Kohen supported by six of his Pharisees, all armed.

"Go no further!" Kohen yelled. "Lower the Ark to the ground!"

Al wasn't going to be intimidated by them. After all, they weren't even fighting men. "No way," he said. "But how about we tip this over to see what is inside? I have been dying to find out."

"We would all be killed!" Kohen bellowed. "Why do that, fool?"

"Because I can!" Alice returned serve with interest. "So stick that in your pipe and smoke it!"

"You rave, Daniel," sneered Kohen. "On my order, my men will kill you."

"If you are prepared to risk us dropping the Ark, fine!" snarled Al. "That is up to you!"

Suddenly, there was a loud scream and a body plummeted from the sky and landed on the patio between Alice and Kohen. It exploded, splashing them all with gore. "Jesus, what was that?" Al exclaimed, staring down at the mess that covered the white marble floor.

"The Babylonii," said Yarin. "They use catapults to hurl Hebrews they have captured over the wall."

Another scream. They looked up in time to see a second man, arms flailing, flying through the air. He landed with a terrible sound next to the Molten Sea.

Alice could see the priest's eyes were flashing about. He was beginning to panic.

"Get out of my face Kohen," he growled, threateningly. "This is your last chance."

Kohen was undecided whether to call Alice's bluff. But one thing was for sure, if another Hebrew was catapulted at them, his priests were likely to desert him.

From the darkness King Zedekiah walked up behind Alice. "Let them pass, Kohen," he commanded. "Priests, go to your quarters and prepare to evacuate. An attack is imminent."

The priests shot off like a gaggle of frightened geese, squawking in fear.

Al decided not to wait around. He just glanced at Zedekiah with a nod of thanks, and carried the Ark off down the Temple stairs.

Once back on street level, he called out to his fellow bearers: "Okay lads, on the double! Jog!"

As they trotted along the dark, narrow, cobblestoned streets, they heard another scream from a catapult victim.

"How long will they keep that up?" Al asked.

"Until the attack," said Liam. "When they run out of men they will hurl women, then children, and then carcasses."

"I cannot say I admire their battle tactics," Al said.

"No. But they are very effective."

CHAPTER 26
TWO EVILS

MAZINGLY, THEY MADE it through the city without attracting attention. The reason was obvious — the citizens who had stayed behind had locked themselves in their houses, too frightened to come out. Most homes were in darkness, no candles or lamps burning inside. It felt as though they were travelling the streets of a ghost town.

It took them thirty minutes to travel the league to the hill of Ezekiel's cavern. All the while Alice had a nagging suspicion something wasn't right. He wasn't wrong. They were being followed.

The sun was rising, and with it would come the full force of the Babylonian attack. The boys were sucking in big ones, so Alice called for a rest at the cavern entrance. Though the Ark felt surprisingly light when they first picked it up, on the haul to the cave it became increasingly heavy. As the lads were regaining their breath, Alice checked inside.

He found the two hammers he'd ordered Liam to leave there. Picking up an oil lamp, he lit it with the two flints beside it, and allowed himself a chuckle at having succeeded thus far. The whole thing was beyond surreal. Then, holding up the lamp, he moved into the meeting area, then the small room Ezekiel and Jeremiah had used as a bedroom and study. He remembered a crate containing scrolls — it was still there. Then he went to where the weapons were hidden under the floor, lifted the covering, and took out four short swords. With the cache nearly empty he filled it with the scrolls, put the swords in the crate, covered it with the hide and lugged it outside. When he reached the boys, he plonked the box down on the ground.

"What is in that?" Yarin asked.

"Swords."

"Do you think we will have to use them?" Liam questioned, timidly.

Al gleaned Liam wasn't a confident swordsman.

"I am better with a sling," the lad said.

"He is the best I have ever seen," Adam agreed.

"Have you got one?" Al asked.

Liam produced a leather sling from under his tunic.

"Like King David used against Goliath," Adam said.

"I used to practice with it every day when I was a shepherd," said Liam, proudly, "Mainly to fend off vultures and crows."

"Good-o!" said Al. "Collect some ammunition, son, because I think we might be needing your skills."

"Are you expecting company, Alice?" Adam asked.

"I am certain we have been followed."

"It would be one of the junior priests for sure," Yarin said.

"Right, this is what we are going to do," said Al. "Help me move the Ark inside."

They did as he instructed, parking it in the Golem imprint and removing the poles.

"Okay, take the poles outside and fit them through the box we left out there."

"Clever … to make a duplicate," Yarin said.

Alice handed him a pole and gave the other to Liam.

"Off you go. Make it look authentic. You stay with me, Adam."

Yarin and Liam left the cavern. Al picked up one of the long handle hammers and handed it to Adam.

"Take the lamp and go to the back way out," he said. "Find a single column next to the exit and smash it down. The ceiling will collapse and cave in, so as soon as you hit the column, drop the hammer and run like hell. Got it?"

"Okay," Adam grinned, happy with his new word.

"Then run around the hill and meet us outside here, alright?"

Adam gave him a sharp nod and rushed off.

Al drew the paring knife from his belt. Pinching the marker in his left earlobe, he dug it out with the point of the blade. He looked at the tiny pellet in his palm, then removed the marker from his right earlobe. He thought of opening the Ark and placing the markers inside, but he wasn't prepared to take the risk, so he jammed one under each of the Cherubim as tightly as he could. Then he picked up the hammer. Just then a loud crash thundered from deep inside the labyrinth. Adam had completed his task. Al was engulfed in a billowing wall of dust, so thick he could hardly breathe or see. Covering his nose and mouth with his sleeve, coughing, he felt his way like a blind man towards the exit. When he came upon the column Ezekiel had told him about, he gripped the end of the hammer and swung with all his might. It struck the column, but made no impression. Then he heard a rumbling sound — it was about come down. He dived for the exit as the entire roof collapsed in a deafening roar, spewing a great cloud of dust and dirt from the cave entrance and, along with it, Alice. He landed on the ground at Liam and Yarin's feet, then sat up, covered head to foot in dust, but sporting a huge grin on his grubby face. He struggled to his feet, brushed down his caftan and checked the entrance — it was well closed off. As Adam arrived, Al gave him thumbs up. Job well done.

Alice made each of them swear an oath that never in their lives — even on their deathbeds — would they divulge the whereabouts of the Ark. This they swore with a pledge to the Endangered Species and the Happening Vibe.

Babylon's armies approached Jerusalem from three sides. Marching to the cadence of blaring horns, regiment after regiment rolled like the thunder in the dark before dawn. Onlookers stood on the walls of Jerusalem, fear in their hearts.

The Tower of David stood proudly beside the main gates of Zion, flying the banner of Judah. Standing alone in the Tower, Zedekiah stared disconsolately at the myriad lights creeping slowly over the plain through the sunrise shadows. The burning torches showed the way for the transporters of the great siege engines, catapults and battering rams. They had half a league to travel before reaching the city. An ominous, low rumble filled the air, vibrating through the timber tower and Zedekiah's body. Soon, hosts of archers would shoot non-stop streams of flaming arrows into the Tower and over the ramparts. The battering rams would begin and Jerusalem's gates would splinter, crack and crumble under the relentless barrage.

The dark veil of death and destruction drifted on the morning breeze, coming from the direction of the rising sun. Zedekiah looked west at the distant line of people snaking along the road to Joppa. In the north, Nebuchadnezzar's cavalry had assembled, he could make out the chariots that would soon thunder through the smashed gates of his defenceless city, wreaking havoc on all who remained. The armies creeping forward left only south to the Plains of Jericho as a possible escape route, but Daniel had forewarned that he would be captured there. He knew Nebuzaradan would pursue him. His conscience told him not to lead the Babylonians west. It would endanger his fleeing people. He knew he had no choice but to flee south.

Suddenly, a thunderous blast from the horns of Babylon shook him to his very sandals. War drums began a synchronous beat. The cacophony of war was sending a powerful message, delivering fear and futility to its victims.

"Guard!" Zedekiah called over the clamour.

A guard arrived promptly and stood with spear in hand. "Yes, your majesty?"

"Prepare the royal family. We will leave by the southern gate. Go now!"

The guard raced down the narrow wooden steps.

Zedekiah turned back to face his demise, peering down at the battering rams below. One was already in position at the Buttress Gate, which led into the Eastern Hill of the city. The other, much bigger ram, which was crowned in the huge, metal, horned head of a bull, was being rolled into place at the main gates. He knew it wouldn't be long before it smashed them open and the Babylonians would swarm in like a plague of bloodthirsty insects, feasting on his remaining defenceless subjects. The remaining citizens of Zion, along with what was left of his army, were outnumbered one hundred to one. Jerusalem had no chance.

Archers were manoeuvring into position on the front lines to begin the firestorm. He could see his remaining soldiers, few in number, still manning the ramparts; most of his army had deserted overnight. Now it was his turn. He turned and faced, for the last time, the city he had ruled for eleven long years. Jeremiah's prophecy echoed in his mind:

The city of Jerusalem will be set ablaze; the Temple of Solomon, the Palace of the King, the houses of the chief princes and principal men, the walls will be broken into pieces and the whole city laid waste, and her appearance will be as a desolate mound.

He regretted breaking his oath of loyalty to the King of Babylon. Ignoring Jeremiah's warnings, he had chosen an alliance with the King of Egypt to throw off Nebuchadnezzar's yoke. Filled with remorse, his eyes wet from the sad reality of this day, Zedekiah made his way down the stairs of the Tower of David, his fate sealed.

Below the tower his family awaited him, his wife and his two sons. Six slaves carrying trunks of gold and jewels expected to leave with them were declined. He told them to take the trunks and proceed to the west, to follow the exodus to Joppa.

A guard led Zedekiah and his family through a tunnel and beyond the city gates. A mule and cart awaited them. The king took the reins to drive his family to the safety of the Jordan Valley.

Word of their escape soon reached the Babylonians. Nebuzaradan sent a detachment in pursuit. It wasn't long before Zedekiah and his family were captured, as the prophecy foretold, on the plain of Jericho, then taken to Riblah on the northern frontier of the land of Cannan.

To the tumultuous roar of thousands of Babylonian warriors pounding their shields with their swords and spears, six chariots thundered past the front line of the advancing army and pulled up in a wall of dust behind the battering ram at the Buttress Gate.

Dressed in a flowing black cape, Zorlock looked like a gigantic bat. "The moment you have long awaited has arrived, Nebuzaradan!" he called.

Resplendent in shiny brass armour and matching helmet, Nebuzaradan drew his sword, held it aloft and shouted triumphantly: "Today I shall write the name Nebuzaradan into the history of the world." He had no way of knowing the battle would go down in history as a great victory of Nebuchadnezzar II.

There came a moment of deathly silence. The calm before the storm, when all that could be heard was the flapping of the Babylonian war banners in the breeze.

A group of valiant soldiers of Zion assembled on the rampart above the Buttress Gate. They broke the silence by pouring flaming oil onto soldiers below. Some of were set ablaze, most severely burnt.

Nebuzaradan ordered the injured and dying to be dragged aside and replaced by fresh troops. He ordered his archers to fire a volley at the soldiers on the ramparts. The air was filled with barbed missiles, which promptly disposed of the opposition.

The ram smashed through the Buttress Gates. Nebuzaradan signalled four chariots to precede him, then entered victoriously into the burning city. Zorlock followed.

Alice and the boys had ferried the fake Ark down the hill and into the narrow street leading to the Temple. A blast from the horns and drums of Babylon stopped them in their tracks. Suddenly, the sky exploded into what looked like a meteor shower — thousands of flaming arrows. Never before had Alice seen war in reality. This was no longer just a prophet's vision … this was immediate, and real.

"It has begun!" Yarin shouted nervously.

"Quick fellas, on the double towards the Temple," Al commanded.

As flaming arrows rained down on the rooftops, setting them ablaze, they rounded a corner and arrived at the forecourt of the Temple. Alice held up a hand. It was the same place he'd witnessed the girl being impaled on a hook in honour of the god Tammuz. Waiting for them at the base of those very stairs were a dozen heavily-armed men. In front of them, looking as bloated and preposterous as ever, Kohen was backed by his armed priests, who were looking decidedly nervous.

"So, the attack foiled your theft," Kohen bellowed, looking at his priests with a smug expression. "The Lord works in mysterious ways…"

"Remind me again which lord you are referring to Kohen," shouted Al. "God? Zedekiah? Tammuz?"

"None of them!" A voice shouted from behind Alice and the boys. "Nebuzaradan is the lord!"

Alice swung around sharply to find Nebuzaradan standing beside a chariot in the alleyway, backed by a dozen soldiers. Out of the darkness stepped Zorlock, shrouded in a black cape and carrying a long staff.

"Well, look what the cat dragged in," Al snarled. "It is Zorlock the Warlock and his staff. Got yourself a day pass out of the asylum for the battle, did ya?"

Kohen's face turned ash grey. He knew it was customary for the victor of a battle to sacrifice the clergy of the enemy. Weak in the knees, knowing the fate that awaited him, he called out: "Lord Nebuzaradan, we worship the same god! We are on the same side!"

Nebuzaradan waved an angry arm, dismissing the cowardly appeal.

"So, this is cosy?" Al said, mockingly. "Both teams want what I have."

Sandwiched between two evils, his mind was searching desperately for an exit strategy — this wasn't what he had planned.

Suddenly the ranks of Babylonian troops parted, and a brute of a man armed with a scimitar stepped through.

Al's mouth curved into a snarl. "Set!" he spat. "I was hoping you were dead."

CHAPTER 27
ASCENSION DISSENSION

S ECTA WALKED ONTO the balcony of his hotel room to take in the view. Even though it was night he could see the Temple Mount in the distance.

"It is only a thirteen-minute walk from here to the Temple Mount," said Karzoff, who had his nose in a guidebook. He looked up. "It is strange to think — right at this very moment, in another time, Alice must be trying to avoid being killed by Nebuchadnezzar's soldiers!"

Secta kept looking at the view. "We walk through pages of history every day, Karzoff," he said, in a bored voice, "even though the actions are invisible to us. Where you are standing for instance … you are surrounded by the ghosts of time. So many have been killed in this city over the millennia, it would be difficult to find a spot where there hasn't been a slaying of some description."

The recognition of a historic environment of murder and mayhem touched Karzoff's sadomasochistic psyche.

"I haff never been able to understand vhy zis is such a fought-over piece of land," said Honor. "Nor vhy ze Jews haff always adopted safety as opposed to defence. Zey promote zemselves as ze victims. In reality zey are ze cause of zeir own peril."

Secta turned and glared at her. "Spoken like a true Nazi, Honor," he said.

The comparison offended her, and Secta knew it.

"It is obvious you know little about history, Secta," she said, coldly. "Ramses rid Egypt of zem. Nebuchadnezzar viped zem out tvice. Ze Romans vanquished zem many times over. Zey vere removed from France and Spain, and ve know vat happened in Vorld Vor II. Even now, since ze British gifted zem Israel, ve haff had nozzing but unrest in ze Middle East. So I ask, are zey persecuted, or do zey invite persecution? Perhaps persecution is encoded into zere psyche from zis religious dogma zat says zey are ze chosen people? You do not haff to be a Nazi, Secta, to ask zese quvestions."

"Tell me Honor, were you born with this dark, distasteful, anti-Semitic prejudice?" asked Secta, "Or is it something you've gone out of your way to develop?" He turned away from the window. "I'm going for a walk," he announced.

"But it is 11pm!" Karzoff squeaked.

"Be careful, Secta, ze streets are dangerous here," Honor smirked.

When Secta reached the lobby he dialled Mal's cell phone.

"Mal, are you in bed?"

"Who's that?"

"Secta, you oaf, who else? I presume you're at the King Solomon?"

"Yes, and there's no way this dump is three stars," Mal complained.

"It's three out of five, Mal," sighed Secta.

"Huh, I didn't know that," grumbled Mal. "Anyhow, yeah, I'm in the sack … there was no way I was gonna get any sleep down the butt end of that bloody plane."

"We'll fly you business class next time," grinned Secta. "Are you ready for tomorrow?"

"Ready as I'll ever be. Hey, the bus driver told me not to drink the water, said it's desalinated. I thought it'd be, like, holy water, coming from the Jordan and all."

Secta chuckled to himself. Mal wasn't dumb as such, just — well, inexperienced in the world. "Just stick to the bottled water in your room, you'll be right," he said.

"Oh, is that for drinking? I thought it was for shaving or something. Cool," said Mal.

"Do you have a bar fridge?"

"Yeah, I've just about drunk that out … it's so bloody hot," Mal complained.

"Haven't you got air con?"

"Yeah, but the hot air comes in the window."

"Close it then," Secta suggested, grinning.

"Good idea. Okay, I'll catch ya in the morrow. 'Night."

"Good night, Mal," Secta said with a smile. Then he dialled Hope.

"Hello," Hope groaned.

"Hope, its Secta are you alright? You sound sick or something."

"It's 7am, Secta, I'm still asleep. Tell me this is a dream."

"Oh, sorry. No, it's not. I must make a note of the time difference."

"Good idea. So you arrived okay? What about Mal?"

"He's fine, just not happy with the flight or his hotel."

"He'll only be there a day or two, he shouldn't whinge."

"It's his first trip abroad," Secta said. "You know what it's like — nothing's ever as good as home."

"Yes, I suppose so," she remembered.

"Is the President still at the bunker?"

"Yes, I don't want to release him. They say Kew will be out of jail tomorrow."

"I agree. Keep him there until we get back. We'll deal with it then."

"Okay. How are the bookends?" she asked, with a yawn.

"Honor seems to have puffed up with anti-Semitism during the flight," said Secta, grimacing. "Karzoff's bearable."

"Never get the Nazi out of that woman."

"Too true. Go back to sleep, Hope. I'll call you when we've got it done."

"Watch out for Honor, she fancies you…" she said, with cheeky laugh.

"Goodnight, Hope," he terminated the call and made his way onto the patio and swimming pool. There were a few people at tables having a late aperitif, and two young women in the pool. Secta pulled up a chair and ordered a cocktail from a passing waiter.

Sipping his drink, he wondered how Alice was faring in the same place on the planet, twenty-five hundred years before.

Alice shouted a warning: "One step closer, Set and I will tip this box on its head! I do not think anyone here knows for sure what will happen if I do."

"You do not frighten me with your empty threats," Zorlock snarled, hubristically, "Opening it would kill you as well!"

"Do not push him Zorlock," Kohen urged, "If he drops the Ark every person within two leagues will be obliterated!"

"Is this true?" Nebuzaradan questioned Zorlock, not at all impressed at being held to ransom.

"It is said to have great powers lord," Zorlock admitted.

"It opened the sea for Moses and the twelve tribes of Israel! It vanquished an entire Egyptian army! It caused the walls of Jericho to fall!" Kohen crowed, as though preaching a sermon.

"Next you will be telling us the story of the three Hebrews that survived the furnace!" Nebuzaradan laughed. But it was an empty laugh, because he knew what Kohen was saying was true.

"I do not have to preach that story," Kohen reminded him. "You already know it — and your king was at the centre of it!"

"Enough!" the general roared. "Put it down, Daniel, or I will order my men to fire."

Four of his men raised their bows and took aim.

Al whispered to Adam, Yarin and Liam: "When I say okay, drop the box and run for the western gate." They nodded. Al fumbled to remove the king's ring and handed it to Yarin. "This will get you through the gate, son."

"But … what about you?" Yarin asked.

"I will—" Before Al could finish the sentence Zorlock rushed forward, long staff outstretched, the pointed end aimed at Alice's face.

With the pole balanced on his shoulder Liam pulled his sling, loaded it and let fly in a flash. The stone smacked Zorlock in the face, rupturing his left eye. Holding it, the contents dribbling down his left cheek, he dropped to his knees, screaming in agony.

The moment had arrived.

"Okay!" Al shouted.

The four of them let go and the box plummeted to the ground. Everyone, with the exception of Al, the boys and Set, hit the deck, trembling, expecting to be vaporised.

That gave the boys the opportunity to take off. Al watched them go. "Chaa!" he whispered after them.

Without looking back, they ran as fast as they could for the western gate. It wasn't until they were well away from the Temple that Adam realised someone was missing. "Hey!" he stopped. "Where is Alice?"

"I do not think he is coming Adam," said Yarin. "I heard him tell Sabrina he will be returning to his world."

Adam nodded his head, sadly. He would miss the man of the Happening Vibe, of the heavy metal Endangered Species. The lads turned together, and continued towards the gate.

Alice was on his way up the Temple stairs, Set hot on his tail. He realised he couldn't keep running, he had to make a stand, so he stopped by the pillar of Boaz, turned and faced Set.

The big man grinned. His chance had finally arrived. He stopped and slashed his sword through the air, flexing his sword arm.

"We can do this the easy way, or the hard way," he said.

"Looks like you did it the hard way to get here," said Al. "What did you have to do, brown-nose Nebuzaradan?"

Alice held up his sword, ready to take on Set. It was way shorter than Set's, but a workman should never blame his tools.

They clashed. Set sliced at Alice with a wicked blow, Alice deflected with his less sophisticated weapon. Their blades locked together.

His face only centimetres from Alice's, Set snarled in English: "Nice parlour trick, Alice … Now tell me where you hid the real Ark!"

Straining to hold back Set's blade, Alice spoke through clenched teeth, "Finally, the truth!" he grunted. "Who do you work for? Zen?"

"Where … is … the … Ark?" Set squeezed out.

They pushed apart, their weapons ringing on parting. Then they stood back and sized each other up again.

"Just tell me where it is," said Set, tiredly. "That's all I need to know."

"And then what, we play a game of cards?" gasped Alice. "Get real, stupid, I know your fricking game! You find out where I hid the Ark, then you kill me … that'd be the brief from your master, wouldn't it?"

Set wasn't going to answer, so Alice charged and let fly with a barrage of blows, forcing the taller man to back up hard against the pillar of Jachin. But no matter how he tried, Alice couldn't get his sword through Set's defences. Instead, seeing an opening, he whacked him on the chin with a heavy elbow jab. The blow rocked Set, and he staggered back like a 3am drunk.

Alice sensed a chance and rushed in for the kill. Clang! Clang! Their swords clashed, but Set still managed to deflect Alice's blows. Then, when Alice was anticipating a slashing blow, Set thrust the scimitar and stabbed Alice's right shoulder.

He felt a hot pain and the median nerve buzzed. The strength dropped out of his arm. He had to back off.

The leader of the Babylonian forces had captured Kohen, and rounded up the other priests. "Take them to the catapult," he yelled at his men.

"No! Please! You have not been listening to me," Kohen screamed. "I can tell you where the royal treasure is! Please! Take the priests but not me! Not me!" His cowardly pleading fell on deaf ears. He was carted away.

Nebuzaradan looked down at Zorlock sitting on the ground with his face in his hands. "Get up," he growled. "You still have the other eye. Get up now, or I will leave you here!"

"But the Ark! What of the Ark?" said Zorlock, savagely.

"I have a battle to fight," snarled the soldier. "You go and find it." He stormed back to his chariot.

Trying to dodge flaming arrows, grasping his bleeding shoulder, with the strength sapped from his fighting arm, Alice was at a terrible disadvantage.

Set seized his opportunity and came after him.

"You can't fight with a wound like that," he said. "Give up. Tell me where the Ark is."

A flaming arrow came directly at Set. With lightning reflexes he sliced it in half mid-air. Al was seriously up against it. He needed to think of something quick, or it would all be over for him.

"How would you know it was the truth if I did tell you?" Alice said, backing up the ramp to the altar, blood oozing through his fingers and running down his arm. The volley of flaming arrows ceased.

"Because you'd have to show it to me," Set growled.

"I buried it," said Alice. "So I can't show you anything. Bad luck."

CHAPTER 28
DIMENSION ASCENSION

A **LOUD SCREAM** interrupted their argument. Alice looked up in time to see a priest flying through the air, arms and legs going every which way, having been fired from the catapult. He slammed into the altar and splattered against its side in a huge splash of blood spiralling out from the huge metal dish.

"Not much of a ride," Al joked.

But Set wasn't in the mood for jokes.

"Listen," he snarled, "Either tell me where the Ark is or you'll be getting a joy ride of your own. Your bones will stay in 587 BCE."

"Answer me this then, how are you expecting to get back?" sneered Al. "I reckon it'll be your bones left here, not mine."

"I only have to return to where I arrived," Set said, although looking uncertain. "That's where the portal back will be."

"Oh yeah? Good luck with that one, buddy!"

"Whatever," said Set. "And how do you think you're getting back?"

Suddenly, the entire Temple began to shimmer. Alice looked around — all of Jerusalem was shimmering like it was in an earthquake. He had to steady himself.

Nebuzaradan's men, rushing up the Temple stairs towards them, suddenly slowed. Alice waved his good arm in front of his face — it moved in normal time. He looked at Set. He was moving in real time as well, but Alice could tell he was feeling the effects of the shimmer.

"Everything moving in slow motion?" Alice asked.

"Yes."

"Must be some kind of time loop. I remember Secta mentioning it could happen."

"It happened yesterday, but only for a moment or two," Set admitted.

"Yeah, same for me."

Then everything slowed to a complete standstill. Arrows stopped mid-air and hung motionless. Kohen, who had been fired from a catapult, froze mid-flight, poised in a deathly swan dive. The Babylonian soldiers had halted mid-stride.

Alice moved down the ramp and walked up to a soldier, staring him in the eye.

"If you look real close you can see they're still moving slightly," he said.

He saw a Babylonian soldier on the stairs about to cut the throat of a Hebrew woman who had run to the Temple for sanctuary. Alice removed the sword from the soldier's grasp and placed it into the woman's hand, aimed at the soldier's stomach.

He looked about and saw more instances where he could intervene. A family of Hebrews had run into the street and were being set upon by unmerciful soldiers. One of the soldiers was holding down a teenage girl. Another was holding the frantic mother so a fellow soldier could stab her. The father and his son had their heads bowed, ready to be beheaded by yet more soldiers, swords raised.

Using his left hand, Alice sliced open the throat of the soldier holding down the girl. He plunged his sword into the gut of the other soldier. He turned to the mother, removed the soldier's sword and cast it aside, then with an almighty swipe severed the head of the assailant. Then he went to the soldiers preparing to behead the father and son, this time striking both at the back of the knees.

Set was watching ruefully, still trying to find his equilibrium. "Have you quite finished?" he yelled.

Gory job complete, Alice whispered something in the father's ear, then turned back to Set. "I'd like to do the whole city," he said, "But I don't know how long the time freeze will last."

Then he noticed Zorlock on his knees, black slime coating his cheek from the dark socket that once held his eye.

"One last get square I reckon," Al said with a wry grin, striding over. With one swipe, he severed both hands at the wrists.

"Won't this look a mess when time returns to normal!" he said, grimly.

Set was over it. He stormed over to Alice, raised his sword and growled: "If you don't tell me where it is, no-one will ever know — and that's just fine with me. One last chance, Alice!"

Suddenly, another shimmer in space and time happened right behind Set. This time it was more familiar — it was the same as the portal that had opened when Alice had visited En-Ki. Right now it was a small vortex, floating a metre off the ground. But it was getting bigger by the second, and he knew from last time it wouldn't last long. He needed to get through when it had opened wide enough.

"Alright! Alright, I'll take you to it," he lied.

Set slowly lowered his simitar. "Then drop your sword," he said, sporting an all-conquering smirk.

Alice obeyed.

"Right. Now lead the way."

Al wasted no time. The vortex was at maximum size and would soon close. He walked to Set's side, being careful to keep the man's eyes on him, then dived at the spiralling maelstrom.

Set realised what was happening and dived at Alice, tackling him around the hips before he reached the portal. Both men crashed to the ground. Alice landed on his shoulder, but pushed through the pain ... he needed to get through the vortex. Time was returning to normal.

He kicked Set in the face, knocking him backwards.

Arrows were beginning to continue their flight through the air. Kohen slowly resumed his death dive. The woman holding the sword was, to her dawning astonishment, driving it into the soldier's gut. Blood was beginning to spill from the throat of the soldier while his teenage victim watched in shock. The head of the soldier stabbing the mother was beginning to roll from his shoulders, and the legs of the two preparing to execute the father and son separated at the knees.

A long, slowed-down scream of agony came from Zorlock as his hands dropped off at the wrists.

Time was about to return in total chaos.

Alice kicked at Set again, and this time connected right on the chin. The blow stunned the man long enough for Alice to struggle to his feet and leap.

Set dived after him and just managed to get a grip of an ankle, disappearing with Alice into the light.

The portal closed on 587 BCE, leaving Nebuzaradan to destroy Jerusalem.

All that was left of Kohen was a red stain on the Temple tiles. Zedekiah and his followers attempted to escape, but were captured as predicted and taken to Nebuchadnezzar in Riblah. Determined to make Zedekiah pay, the Babylonian King had him chained to a chair to witness the execution of his two young sons. It was the last thing Zedekiah would ever see. A red-hot poker was drawn from the fire and placed in his eyes, leaving him in a world of darkness. He remained a prisoner in Babylon until his death a few years later.

Ezekiel lived on in Babylon and wrote his gospels, still hanging onto the belief he had been visited by Angels of God. Jeremiah would write his, too, but with more confused and questionable content.

Nebuzaradan became just a name. Known to have slaughtered fourteen thousand Hebrew prisoners after the fall of Jerusalem, he strode off into history without leaving any other evidence of his life or death. Nebuchadnezzar ruled for another twenty-five years, and built his city into one of the wonders of the ancient world.

Adam, Yarin and Liam caught up with the exodus, and continued preaching the prophet Alice Daniel's Happening Vibe of the heavy metal Endangered Species for the rest of their days.

And Cannis? He spent the remainder of his life in Babylon writing the book of Daniel, a character to whom he attributed every possible miracle his research or imagination could contrive.

Betyl remained in the sky until it finally disappeared after leading three wise men to the birth of a baby boy four hundred and thirteen years later.

Oh, and Zorlock bled out on the steps of the Temple Mount.

It was 6am, and Secta was on the balcony of the David Citadel Hotel watching the sunrise. He hadn't slept, too much on his mind. Mulling over all the things that could potentially go wrong had rendered sleep impossible. Since it was 2pm in Sydney, he decided to give de Luz a call.

"Vic, its Secta."

"I thought you were in—"

"I am," he grinned. "I'm sitting on the balcony of the David Citadel Hotel watching the sun rise over the Temple Mount."

"Extraordinary!" said de Luz. "Listen, Secta, I've broken down some of Zen's Switch formulas, and I think they've got it awfully wrong. There might be a universal strand of DNA that could be triggered to turn us into zombies, but they haven't found the means of activating it. So that plan's off the table, at least for now."

"Well, that's comforting," said Secta. "At least that's one less thing to deal with for now.'

"Yes — but of course, that's not saying they won't ultimately find the correct formula," said de Luz. "But look, they're also working on silicon implants that interface with their OSCI system. From what I can gather the implants are designed to do the same thing as Switch. I can't be certain if it's something they're planning for humans or those damned cyborgs they appear to be designing. We need to put an end to these bastards," he finished. "They can't be trusted."

"You're not wrong Vic," said Secta, frowning. "We need to wipe them off the face of the planet. In the future Alice and I visited, they had a stranglehold on everything. It was a pretty awful world. And they'd deliberately made it that way."

"We've not had much time to talk about that trip, my friend," said de Luz. "When you get back we must put aside some time … there are so many things I'd like to know."

"Put that down as a promise Vic," Secta said. "So, I'm sitting here with an ILDD beside me, waiting for it to signal the arrival of Alice."

"Ha. Knowing you, I bet you haven't slept."

"Hey, who needs sleep? It's a waste of functional time."

"You don't need to worry about that Secta. You took the longevity serum."

"Yes, it sustains the lifecycle," said Secta. "But it doesn't protect against disease — or bullets and bombs, for that matter."

"Ha! Yes, well you're certainly in the right place for all that goddamned crap."

Honor walked onto the balcony in bare feet, wearing a robe. She took in the view, stretched and yawned. Karzoff followed her.

"I'll be in touch, Vic," Secta said, signing off. "Bye for now!"

Honor pulled up a chair opposite Secta and sank into it. "Shall ve order some breakfast?" she said sleepily.

"Never touch the stuff, but I could murder a coffee."

He was interrupted by a beep from the ILDD. He practically jumped out of his skin and snatched the unit off the table. Heart pounding ten to the dozen, he read the meter then looked up at the two agents. "It's Alice," he said, with a big smile. "He's back!"

CHAPTER 29
DATE WITH FATE

ALICE WASN'T IMPRESSED by the exit from the portal. It was positioned a metre and a half above the ground, so he landed hard, yelling at the sharp pain slamming into his shoulder. To add insult to injury, he was nearly crushed to death by the thumping hulk of Set, who'd followed him out.

Both men were naked. Alice surged to his feet, he had to think quick. Seeing a fist-sized rock on the ground, he collected it, staggered over to Set, who was shaking his head, trying to regain composure, and belted him across the side of the head with it. The blow knocked him out cold.

Al took his hands and dragged him into the shade of a shed, out of public view.

There was no telling exactly where he was, or what year it was. He guessed he was still in Jerusalem. It stood to reason he was at the point where he'd first arrived in 587 BCE. He felt something drip onto his bare foot, looked down and found it was blood from the stab wound in his shoulder. The cut needed attention, it was deep and there was nothing he could do to stop the bleeding.

He gazed up at the sun, trying to work out the time. "Hmm, no Betyl, that's a good sign," he muttered. "Looks like early morning..." He looked around. A washing line nearby had clothes pegged on it. He helped himself to an unidentifiable garment that he used to staunch his wound, and covered up in a thawb: a loose, long-sleeved, ankle-length robe. Of course there was nothing to cover his feet. He strode into the nearest alleyway to distance himself from Set.

Moving along the lane he heard a noise in the sky, stopped, looked up and saw a vapour trail coming from a passenger jet.

"Aha!" he grinned. "I'm back!"

As he continued along he found a pair of leather sandals on the back doorstep of a house. They fitted, and he walked on, congratulating himself on his good fortune. Eventually, he came to a road. A car came hurtling by — he never thought he'd be so pleased to see one again. Now there were street signs, billboards, traffic lights — all indicators of modern civilization. It was then he realised what he must look like. Blood from his shoulder wound had seeped through the rough padding and down the side of the beige thawb. He must look like the victim of a car bomb. Suddenly his head was spinning, the dizziness this time caused by loss of blood.

Secta finished texting and climbed into the front seat of the hire sedan. Karzoff was behind the wheel. Honor was already on the backseat. They drove out of the hotel on a mission to track down Alice's genetic signal, which increased or decreased in strength as they got nearer or further away.

Honor was holding an iPad displaying an onscreen GPS map. "Vhy haff you not developed a digital map zat displays ze marker as a blinking light?" she complained. "It vould be much easier to track and locate."

"Good idea Honor, I'll look into it," said Secta. "Are you alright driving on the other side of the road, Karzoff?" The agent tended to drift to the wrong side of the road.

"You know, I thought there was something different," Karzoff admitted, "What with the steering wheel being on this side."

Secta raised a questioning eyebrow at the red-haired man, relieved to see he was joking.

"Let us try turning right on King David Street, tovards Herod's gate," Honor proposed.

As soon as they turned the signal decreased. "Stop," Secta ordered. Karzoff pulled over, and he hopped out.

"Vat is he doing?" Honor growled.

"Be patient, Honor," Karzoff chided.

Holding the ILDD and facing each point of the compass in turn, Secta established the direction of the signal. He leaned back inside the car. "We need to drive south," he said.

Honor consulted the map, "U-turn, Karzoff and head back along King David Street."

Secta hopped back in, Karzoff made the turn. Further down King David Street, Secta noted they were passing the King Solomon Hotel.

"We're getting close," he said. "Take a left and stop."

"At Plumer Square," said Honor. "Take the left onto Sderot Blumfield."

Karzoff made the turn and pulled over next to a small road which, according to a road sign, led to an ancient aqueduct.

Secta scanned the topography with the device. "He's close," he said. "Maybe at the aqueduct, there's a sign over there for a car park. Let's drive in there."

It was a well-treed nature park containing — unsurprisingly — the remains of an ancient Roman aqueduct. At that time of the morning there were no cars, so Karzoff angle-parked to give them a good view of the entrance.

Secta fiddled with the calibration on the ILDD.

"He's here all right," he said. "I'll need to get out and head into the woods over there."

"Best go alone, Secta," said Honor. "If he sees me he might just run away."

"Agreed. Wait here," Secta said, getting out of the car. He walked towards the aqueduct, holding the ILDD in front of him to home in on Alice.

Karzoff saw Honor draw a gun from her coat pocket and check the chamber.

"What do you need that for?"

"Nothing changes, Karzoff," she said. "Alice is still a fugitive. Zis vill ensure he takes us to ze hiding place of ze Ark."

"I hardly think that is necessary."

"I do not remember asking you."

"Argh! You're right, nothing changes!" snapped Karzoff. "Always playing cops and robbers … the man has been pardoned by the President, for goodness sake!"

"That matters not, Karzoff. Ve still haff a job to do."

From Honor and Karzoff's perspective, Secta was looking for Alice. From Secta's point of view, he was losing Honor and Karzoff.

On the other side of the aqueduct was a second car park, and in it a black SUV with its motor running. Secta made a beeline for it.

He climbed into the passenger seat. Alice was out cold in the back.

"Is he all right?" Secta asked Mal.

Dressed like Indiana Jones, complete with obligatory wide-brimmed fedora, Mal certainly looked the part. A two-day growth and a wooden toothpick in the corner of his mouth enhanced the get-up.

"No," he said, curtly. "We're gonna to need to get him to a doctor ASAP. He's lost a lot of blood from that cut in his shoulder."

"How did he get that?"

"He didn't say, when I got here he was pretty much out of it. I got him into the back of the wagon, then you lobbed. But it looks like a stab wound," Mal explained.

"Okay. Head for your hotel."

Honor was becoming restless.

"I am not feeling good about zis Karzoff," she said. "I zink ve haff been double-crossed."

"I think you are right … wait! I can see someone — over there, in the bushes. It might be Alice!"

He pointed. "I zink you might be right," said Honor. "Here, take ze gun and arrest him."

"Me?" Karzoff objected.

"Oh, ve're not going through all zat again, are ve? Here!" she pressed the gun against his shoulder. "Now, take it … I order you to make an arrest!"

"But Alice might…"

"Now, Karzoff!"

He slipped the gun into his pocket, opened the car door and stepped out, muttering to himself. "Why did I mention it? Damn, he will kill me."

The car window lowered "Go now Karzoff," Honor whispered harshly, "He vill get avay! Go, damn it!"

Honor watched Karzoff move toward the bushes. He stepped into the shadows and he too disappeared.

"Vhat is zis?" she grumbled. "Ze Jerusalem triangle?"

Karzoff stopped and called out, hesitantly: "Alice? Is that you? Are you there?"

Suddenly, a man stood up, causing Karzoff to almost jump out of his skin.

Honor was about to get out of the car to go in search of Karzoff when he walked out of the shadows in company of another man. As they got nearer, she recognised the man as Set.

Secta had phoned ahead and, with much diplomatic badgering, arranged for the hotel doctor to be waiting for them in Mal's room.

Bracing Alice, they got him up to the room and onto the bed. The doctor sat down beside him and then opened his clothing. He hesitated. Understandably, he was thinking the injury could be crime-related — it was to be expected in a city where warring factions were the norm.

"The wound is very deep,' the young man said. "It appears to be a knife wound. He has lost a lot of blood, and will need a transfusion. I will arrange for an ambulance," he added, reaching into his pocket for his cell phone.

"No need," said Secta. "I know his blood type — it is the same as mine." He rolled up a sleeve. "Don't worry doctor," he said, in response to the concerned expression on the man's face. "I am also a doctor." He showed his Oceana ID. The doctor nodded, and reluctantly opened his bag and took out a small person-to-person transfusion kit.

Alice's blood was corrupted with things Secta had put there. He didn't want to have to explain them to hospital pathologists.

"These days it is unusual for doctors to carry this," said the young man, as he set up. "But because we have sometimes bombs and shootings here, I find it necessary. In this case your friend is lucky. I will also give him a tetanus shot."

Half an hour later the doctor had gone and Alice was on the road back to normal. He had just finished giving Secta and Mal a basic rundown of his trip, complete with how Set had stabbed him and followed him back through. Secta had explained how Set had coerced them into sending him through the wormhole, and how he hadn't expected him to make it back. They agreed they now had a bigger problem than expected.

Mal brought up what had happened to the president and how Secta had brilliantly thwarted the assassination attempt, though in his opinion, Oceana would be better off without the president and his fascist government. But Secta explained that the alternative — Zen — would be far worse.

Secta, who had been fiddling with the ILDD, got a faint beep. "There we go!" he said. "I'm getting a reading on the Ark!"

"Yeah?" Al took a look at the meter. "Fantastic!"

"Is it close by?" Secta asked.

"I buried it in a cave on a hill about a league from the Temple Mount," Alice said.

"A league?" Mal said. "What the heck's that?"

"Sorry mate," laughed Al. It's about five clicks."

"As the crow flies," Secta said, walking over to the window and opening the balcony doors. "Take a look out here, Alice."

Alice and Mal joined him on the small balcony. "That dome in the distance is the Temple Mount," he pointed. "I can see a few hills, but…"

"Nothing but fricking buildings!" Al complained. "I don't recognise anything!"

"Yeah, reckon it might have changed a little bit in two a half thousand years," Mal quipped.

"You're not kidding. Bloody hell, what's it buried under?" Alice glared at Secta. "We'd better get busy!" he said.

"Are you sure you're up to it, Alice?" the scientist asked. "You can rest for a while, you know."

"Don't be ridiculous, can't rest with that bastard Set on the loose!" said Al. "And what about Honor and Karzoff?"

"They're probably running about like chickens with their heads cut off," Mal joked.

"Alright, if you're feeling up to it, let's go!" said Secta, enthusiastically.

"I'm hungry," said Al, as they headed out the door. "I could eat the butt out of a skeleton."

"Me too!" Mal agreed.

CHAPTER 30
DUPLI – CITY

GUTSING DOWN THREE burgers, three fries, two chocolate fudge sundaes and a large coke, Al sat in the SUV on the hunt for the Ark of the Covenant.

It was just after 1pm. The sky was clear, it was hot, and Al had insisted on driving. Secta was in the front passenger seat calling out readings on the ILDD, while Mal lounged on the back seat trying to make sense of a map and provide street navigation. It was terribly difficult to navigate the car through the quagmire of lanes and alleyways — many were dead ends, not even marked on the map. Plus, the entire two-kilometre zone around the Temple Mount, which fell into the area Alice needed to explore, was so seriously overbuilt it was next to impossible for Alice to recognise anything that could provide a marker.

Ezekiel's cavern had long since been gobbled up by progress. It was challenge enough to find on the map where the hill with the cavern might have been. To make things even more difficult, they had to deal with religious exclusion zones. Secta was becoming frustrated, because the location marker had shown they were getting no closer to the Ark.

Honor, Karzoff and Set were sitting in the office of Colonel Hirum Abraham of the Israel Defence Force. They had explained their predicament and the colonel was contemplating how to assist. A sternly-spoken man in his forties, he was robust but thin-faced, with a receding hairline and an eye patch over his left eye.

They had ascertained from immigration that Mal Function had arrived in Jerusalem from Sydney on same day to Honor, Karzoff and Secta, and was staying at the King Solomon Hotel. From there the colonel had been easily able to discover that Function had rented a black SUV, to obtain the registration number, and to put out an APB for it.

"Once the vehicle has been sighted we will apprehend them," Abraham said, in a strong Israeli accent.

Set looked anxious. "I want them held," he ordered. "I need to interrogate them."

"They haven't broken any law yet, Mister Set—"

Set cut him off. "They will as soon as you give chase," he snapped. "Might I remind you that two of them, Black Alice and Mal Function, are terrorists and extremely dangerous?"

"I would not go that far," said Karzoff. "They are nationals of Oceana, and should be treated—"

"Zat is quite enough, Karzoff," Honor snapped.

"Yes, shut that clown up, Honor," Set barked.

Being humiliated in front of the Colonel didn't impress Karzoff.

The phone rang. The Colonel answered and spoke briefly before hanging up. "The vehicle in question has been seen travelling along David Street near the Wujoud Museum," he said. "That is not too distant from here."

"Let's go!" shouted Set.

"This is good, we're getting closer," Secta said, excitedly. "Keep following this street."

"It's David Street," Mal called out.

Alice looked into the rear vision mirror, and saw what looked like a cop car tailing them. He trod on the gas. In the distance, he could see the Temple Mount.

After a few nervous seconds Secta said, "Hang on, we're moving away from it!"

"Take a right into Ha-Notshrim Street, coming up," Mal said.

The statement sent bells ring in Alice's mind. Déjà vu — Mal had said that before, this had all happened before … A bike, he thought. There's a bike!

There was a loud boom and rear window shattered. Mal had to duck the shower of glass fragments. Someone had fired at them from behind.

Alice glanced up at the rear vision mirror and saw a bike. He was right, and it chilled him to the bone. That gut feeling returned — everything was about to turn sour.

He couldn't go any faster to outrun the bike because the ancient street was far too narrow. All the rapid arm movement in steering had caused some of the sutures to burst open. Blood was seeping through his shirt.

With a roar the bike drew level with the passenger side door. They were unarmed – there was nothing they could do. Alice thought of ramming him — he looked across. The rider was wearing a black balaclava. As the bike accelerated and moved ahead, the biker reached behind him, dropped a small device onto the road and scooted off.

Alice immediately recognised what was bouncing on the cobblestones, but it was too late to avoid it. He yelled at the others: "A bomb!"

As the SUV passed over the small device it detonated. The power of the explosion catapulted the SUV into the air. It landed — rolled violently — skidded and stopped, propped up against the side of a building.

When the dust had settled, the mangled driver's side door in the smouldering wreckage creaked open and Alice, his face bleeding from the smashed windshield, tried to climb out. He stopped dead, staring down the barrel of an automatic weapon … soldiers had the car surrounded. A shot rang out.

As painful as it was for his wounded shoulder, Alice raised both hands in surrender. Three cars skidded to a halt behind the wrecked SUV. People were emerging from nearby houses and businesses to see what was going on.

A soldier unceremoniously dragged Alice from the car.

"Hey, hey, take it easy," he said. "Check that the others are okay!"

"What did he say?" The soldier questioned his comrade in Israeli.

"I said, check that the others are okay," Alice repeated, in perfect Israeli.

With his rifle trained on Alice, another soldier climbed onto the smouldering wreck and helped Secta and Mal out. They were battered, with superficial bleeding, but uninjured.

Six soldiers had their weapons trained on the three of them.

"What is all this about?" Alice asked, still speaking Israeli. "We are the victims here! A terrorist on a motorbike threw a bomb under our car…"

Set pushed through the soldiers and confronted Alice.

"How's the arm?" he snarled.

"You should be bloody thankful to me," spat Alice. "I provided the way back for you — otherwise you'd be copping it from your pals in Nebuchadnezzar's army!" Al noticed Honor and Karzoff at the rear. "Well, if it isn't my old friend Honor the android lover," he said. "And Karzoff. I thought I electrocuted you."

"You vill soon see who vill haff ze last laugh, Alice," Honor snapped.

"Take us to the Ark or I'll order them to start shooting," said Set.

"Hey, go to hell," said Al.

Set moved over to Secta, "You will tell me," he menaced, "Or I'll order the soldiers to take out your left knee."

"But that's my favourite knee!" Secta whined, always a wit.

"Have it your way," snapped Set. "Corporal!"

Alice had experienced Set's callousness. Knowing he'd do it, he conceded. "Tell him, Secta."

As Set moved nearer, Mal drew a fist back ready to lay one on him. Alice caught Mal's eye and shook his head. Mal got the message.

"Fine," Secta sighed, holding the ILDD in front of him. He switched it to audio output and it beeped.

"The ILDD is reading a signal from the Ark," he explained. "Alice had placed a marker in it. As we get nearer, the beep will increase in volume and frequency. Follow me, please."

He walked off, followed by Set, Alice, Mal, Honor, Karzoff and six soldiers with guns drawn and confused expressions. They had no idea what was going on. All they had was a standing order to support agents Honor and Karzoff. But they seemed to be doing what Set commanded, so they went along.

The street had a small incline, which interested Alice. Perhaps it was the hill. They passed houses with the occupants hanging out of windows and doors, watching these strange people parading along the street at gunpoint.

The beep was slowly increasing in intensity, and excitement was growing among them accordingly. Alice knew that as soon as the Ark was located it would be all over for him. Either Set would have him shot or he'd be imprisoned for life. He didn't fancy either, after all he'd been through.

"What did the Ark look like, Al?" Mal asked.

"Just like the pictures, mate," he replied. "A big gold box with two gold angels on top. Wasn't that heavy — four of us carried it out of the Temple Mount."

"I thought you couldn't touch it," Mal said.

"There were wooden poles that went through hoops on either side. We had them on our shoulders to carry it."

"Ah, right … Did you get it open?"

"Nar mate, they reckoned it'd release a killer blast of energy, so I gave it a miss. But I did check out the two angels on top. The wingtips were only a couple of centimetres apart. Looked like an electric charge of some kind had been fired between them — the ends were charred black, like the end of spark plug.

"My guess is there's a power source inside the thing that causes energy to arc across the wingtips. Let it build up enough power and it'd probably discharge a massive bolt of lightning to zap anyone near it. Could also send some sort of beam up into the sky to contact a UFO, I reckon."

"Far out!" Mal grinned. "And now we're gonna dig this fricking thing up, are we? What the hell for? Not right in the head, mate!"

"I'm with you," Al said. "It's probably better left buried. There's already enough bloody weapons of mass destruction around."

Secta stopped, and the entire entourage stopped behind him.

He studied the device in his hand for a moment and then looked up and said, "The signal is definitely getting weaker." He turned around and began walking back the way they'd come.

"Zis could go on for a bloody month," grumbled Honor. "Knowing Secta, he could haff us valking around in circles just for ze fun of it. And my feet are killing me in zese shoes."

"Take them off, then," Karzoff said, curtly. He was still dirty that she'd failed to support him against Set. He caught up with Alice instead. "Alice, where did you actually hide it?" he asked.

"What's that, Karzoff?" Al growled. "Oh – I dunno. I buried it inside a cave called Ezekiel's cavern. But God knows where that is now."

"Yes, but it would stand to reason that there would be no use searching for it lower down," Karzoff said. "So why not take the walkway over there? It seems to climb what remains of a hill."

"Sometimes you actually make sense, Karzoff," Al said.

"Only when I am given the opportunity to think," he replied.

Honor raised her eyebrows.

"Secta!" Alice caught him up and stopped him. "Karzoff suggested we take the walkway over there, it goes up that hill."

"Seems wise," said Secta, and headed towards the walkway, Set hot on his heels.

"You better not be leading me up the garden path Alice," Set snarled, as he passed. "Or I'll make you pay for it."

"Get stuffed … I've already paid my dues," Al snapped.

The ILDD began to register increasing beeps as they progressed.

"What's going to happen if we find the thing?" Secta asked.

"We'll worry about that if and when it happens," Set growled.

Secta and Alice exchanged looks, both thinking Set would be planning on somehow disposing of everybody once the Ark was found.

CHAPTER 31
INGENUOUS CONVERT

BY THE INCREASE in signal, they were getting closer. The walkway they were following snaked up a hill, seeming to join a larger path near the crest.

"Judging by the view back to the Temple, I'd say we're getting close," said Alice, beginning to puff.

"It better be no further, or I vill collapse," Honor admitted.

"I have no idea why we are in so much of a hurry," said Karzoff. "It has been there for two and a half thousand years, it is not likely going anywhere soon."

Set had had enough. He turned on Karzoff. "Listen little man, I don't even know why you're here," he yelled. "You're a pathetic, incompetent clown and should've been left in Sydney cleaning the offices. Now, shut your face or I will!"

After the tirade, once Set had turned his back and resumed his trek up the hill, Karzoff growled at him. "Why should I have to take such talk from him?" he grumbled.

"Because he knows you vill not do anyzing about it, you moron," Honor stated, cruelly.

Karzoff was angry and humiliated. It is time I stood up for myself he thought. I deserve respect.

Secta stopped. "I'm losing the signal," he said. He turned around until he got a better response from the unit. "It's telling us to go this way," he said.

Mal walked over with the map. "Three streets up on the right there's Souk ef-Dabbagha Street," he said. "Looks like it's right at the top of the hill."

"Then let's head that way," Al said.

There seemed to be an ever-increasing number of tourists as they moved up the hill. The street Mal had mentioned was packed with them.

"What the hell's going on?" Al questioned, looking around. The entire street was filled with shops selling religious souvenirs.

Secta hadn't noticed. Eyes focused on the ILDD, he plodded on. "We're getting really close!" he announced excitedly.

"What is this place?" Alice asked Mal.

"Sez on the map that's the Church of the Holy Sepulchre," Mal reported.

They all stopped. The ILDD was emitting one long, single sound. Secta turned in the opposite direction, and it began to beep again. He turned back and pointed it at the Church of the Holy Sepulchre. The sound returned.

He looked at Set, then at Alice. "It's in there," he said.

"Are you saying that the Church of the Holy Sepulchre is built on top of the Ark of the Covenant?" Alice said.

There was a person handing out religious leaflets. Karzoff took one and walked over to Secta, reading out loud. "A stone monument encloses the tomb where it is believed Jesus Christ lay buried for three days," he said.

Alice started to laugh. "This is incredible," he gasped. "I took the Ark from what is now the most revered place of worship for Jews and Muslims, and buried it in a cavern beneath the most revered place in the Christian faith!" He turned to Set. "No-one's going to get the damned thing," he grinned. "The Ark will stay under there until religion doesn't matter anymore. Ha!"

"There must be a vay of obtaining a permit to excavate it," Honor moaned.

"Ha! Impossible," said Karzoff, "This is the Church of the Holy Sepulchre, you fool! They are not going to let anyone dig it up!"

Set lost it. He was staring failure in the face, and the word just wasn't in his vocabulary. He snatched the leaflet out of Karzoff's hand and shoved him away. "Out of my way, idiot!" he yelled. Karzoff fell over backwards and hit the deck hard.

Set grabbed one of the Israeli soldiers who had followed them by the throat, and drew the pistol from of the holster in his belt. Holding the soldier tight, he aimed the gun at Alice.

The other soldiers turned their weapons on Set.

Alice slowly raised his hands hip high. "Put the gun away, Set," he said. "It's done and dusted. No-one is going to get the Ark."

"I've got a job to finish," Set said.

Alice knew he would fire.

"Look Set, listen to me," Honor said, jumping in between Set and his target. It was a dumb move. Her life meant nothing to him.

A shot rang out. Half of Set's face disappeared. Blood, bone and brain matter spattered over the soldier he'd been holding.

They all turned, slowly, to where Karzoff was sitting on the ground, holding a smoking pistol, still aiming at where Set had been standing.

Karzoff was lucky. The soldier Set had grabbed supported his claim of self-defence. The Colonel not only accepted that view, he also provided a military chopper to transport them from Jerusalem to Ben Gurion International Airport in Tel Aviv.

In the business class lounge, with three hours to kill before their flight to Sydney, Honor, Karzoff, Secta and Mal listened intently to Alice's account of his experiences. When he had finished they were left gobsmacked.

Chuffed that he'd been upgraded to business class, Mal had only one question. "Tell me, Al," he said, seriously. "What was the grog like?"

They all laughed. Even Honor.

Once on board, Secta was seated with Karzoff. Honor was behind them, and Alice and Mal were across the aisle. Once the plane was at cruising height and they'd been served drinks, Secta opened a discussion with Karzoff. Normally bitter enemies, Karzoff's actions back in Jerusalem had made a change.

"That was a good shot," said Secta. "I had no idea you were so handy with a gun."

"Oh no, it was totally a lucky shot. Honor will tell you, I am useless with a gun … It was fortunate Honor gave it to me earlier."

"Where did she get it? Surely she didn't travel with it?"

"No, no, Colonel Abraham gave it to her." Karzoff leaned closer to Secta. "I think he fancied her," he whispered.

"Some people have extreme tastes I guess," Secta quipped.

As though aware she was the subject of their discussion, Honor leaned forward in her seat. "Secta," she said, "I need to know vhy you deceived us by meeting Mal Function and going alone to find ze Ark."

"I could ask the same question of you," Secta riposted. "Why did you support Set?"

"I asked first," she said, smugly.

"I was ordered by the President to use my initiative to keep Alice safe and find the Ark," Secta said. "I felt a degree of — shall we say — competitiveness from you in that endeavour. So I chose to go it alone."

"I assure you," said Karzoff, "I had no intention of—"

"Do not be a ferret, Karzoff!" snapped Honor.

"It's a weasel, Honor, not a ferret," Secta corrected.

"Vhatever," she said, dismissively. "Look, ve are all on ze same side here. Ve should co-operate. I can see now zat Set vas no different zan Gorrick, or his assassin, Kew."

"We knew that," said Secta. "He threatened our lives to make us send him after Alice. He wanted to locate the Ark for Zen and kill Alice. Took you a while to work that out, Honor. He was right under your nose, and you didn't even notice,"

"I think it is time for a revision of thinking at OTT," said Karzoff. "Do you not agree, Honor? In fact, I think it needs to begin with you."

"I must admit, I did not expect you to shoot Set," Honor replied, almost smiling. "I did not zink you had it in you to fire, let alone actually hit ze target."

"You see Honor? It is time to revise your thinking," said Karzoff. "Firstly by ending this bad habit of underestimating everybody else, and secondly by ceasing to overestimate yourself."

"Well put," Secta smiled, sipping some champagne.

Honor slumped back in her seat. She had eighteen hours of flight time to think over what Karzoff had said.

Secta sat back in his big, comfy seat, thinking perhaps the days of antagonism between Honor and himself might be over — though deep down inside, he wasn't totally convinced.

Also resting, eyes closed, Karzoff asked: "So, has the President pardoned Alice?"

Secta took a moment. "Yes," he said, finally. "And I think there will be an overhaul of OTT, as you suggest. As a matter of fact, I think the President will be overhauling the entire government. The mess with Gorrick and Zen, with the attempt on his life, has had a profound effect on him. I think he is seeing the people, the country and the future in a much better light as a result."

"Sometimes good results come from bad decisions," said Karzoff. "Do you think he will dismantle the secret service?"

"I'm certain of it, at least in its current form."

"Good," said Karzoff.

In a window seat, Alice was scribbling on a napkin.

Mal was on his fourth beer. So far, none had touched the sides. "What are you gonna do when you get back, Al?" he burped.

"Hmm?" said Alice, putting the pen down for a moment. "I reckon I might do a gig," he said. "It's been a while."

"Didn't you sack your manager?"

"Hah – yeah, I forgot about that goose. I'll manage myself from now on. If I can cut it in 587 BCE, I can cut it in any time."

"And in any key, I reckon," Mal said, with genuine admiration. "What about more trips? You know, into the past or the future?"

"Dunno, mate." He went back to scribbling.

"What you writing?"

"Lyrics for a new song."

"What's it called?"

"Nebuchadnezzar."

"Cool, why him?"

He chewed on the end of the pen and thought. "Interesting question," he said. "Four blokes really impressed me on that trip. Young Adam, Yarin, Ezekiel and Nebuchadnezzar. I reckon I'll write a song about each of them."

"Great idea, man. And what about that other bloke, Cannis? He seemed like a cool dude. And hey, how about the Golem? What a story!"

"No-one would ever believe that one, mate," Al laughed. "But the others I can get away with. It could be a concept album, like Zeppelin or Floyd."

"Killer idea. Any place in there for your old mate?" Mal said, with a huge pick me grin.

"How about a guest vocal?"

"Excellent."

Alice kept scribbling. After a minute Mal asked: "What about the Octagon?"

Alice put the pen down and yawned. "Mate, I think it needs an overhaul," he said. "About time it focused on real issues, like being proactive and communicating with the President's office, instead of demonstrating over anything and everything."

"Spoken like a true politician," Mal joked.

"Mate, don't say that. Anyhow, I'll set it up with the President when we get back."

"I guess things are changing."

"You bet they are."

CHAPTER 32
PHASE TWO

POWERED BY TWO Rolls-Royce BR700 jet engines, the Gulfstream G550 with the Zen ten-pointed star livery on its tail was speeding at Mach 0.85 over the Pacific, en route from New York to Auckland. Relaxing in a beige leather seat in a cabin configured for eight passengers, Gorrick was alone. He was gazing out of the big round window when he received a call on his implant.

"Yes?"

"Kew here, sir."

"They got you released without any trouble?"

"Yes, sir."

"Good. What's the news?"

"Set is dead, sir. Killed in Jerusalem by that idiot Karzoff."

"And the Ark?" asked Gorrick, unemotionally.

"Apparently it's buried under the Church of the Holy Sepulchre, sir."

"There's a strange sense of irony in that."

"Yes, there is, sir."

"Where are they now?" Gorrick enquired.

"You mean the agents, Black Alice and Secta?"

"Yes."

"In the air, ETA Sydney nineteen hundred hours."

"And the President? Where is he?"

"I have no idea sir."

"Find out. Go to phase two. I have a stopover in Auckland for business and will be in Sydney tomorrow. Get me a progress report by then."

He terminated the call and resumed staring unblinkingly out of the window.

It hadn't taken long for Honor, Karzoff, Alice, Mal and Secta to pass through the diplomatic section of immigration and customs at Sydney Airport, but it took an hour to get a taxi outside. The car Honor had ordered from Oceana had failed to materialise. She was livid by the time they got through the queue at the taxi rank — none of it was made any easier by it being peak hour for international arrivals. Then they had to deal with traffic congestion all the way to the city.

By the time she made it to her apartment, Honor had just about had enough of everything. She wheeled her suitcase in, flopped into her favourite armchair, kicked off her shoes and massaged her aching feet.

"You look tired."

She jumped. Kew made his way out of the kitchen, carrying two flutes of champagne. He handed one to Honor. She backed away, so he put it down on the coffee table. He sat opposite her.

"Get out!" she spat, savagely.

"That's no way to treat a guest," he said, calmly. "And this is vintage Verve. Cheers," he said, holding up his glass.

"I haff no idea vhat you are up to, but I do not vant you in my apartment, you are not a guest," she snapped.

He got up and sat on the edge of the coffee table. Putting down his glass, he picked up a foot and began massaging it.

"We might have had our differences, Honor," he said, soothingly, "But believe me, we actually have quite a lot in common."

Honor wasn't sure how to take what was happening. She half-expected him to crush her toes in his hands.

"Work for me," he said.

"Are you asking me to be a double agent?"

"Put it this way," he said, "I was ordered to kill you, but I like you. I could kill you, too. But if you work for me, I won't need to."

"Zat is blackmail," she said. "Vhat happens vhen I am no longer any use to you as an agent?"

"Well, let's hope that doesn't happen."

"And … if I agree?" she asked, coyly.

"You survive to fight another day."

She raised an eyebrow, "I agree," she said, with a deep sigh. "Viz some provisions. I vant money — lots of it. And I vant a personal guarantee from Khan zat my life vill never be threatened again. I am not villing to be an assassin. And finally, if I am caught by Oceana, Zen will provide me a safe exit."

"I can see no reason why those provisions couldn't be met."

Phase two was complete.

The next day, Secta had arranged a meeting with de Luz and Alice at Café Epiphany. He was waiting when Alice arrived. De Luz was running late, as usual.

"Good morning Alice," Secta said. "Sleep well?"

"Like a log," said Al, taking a seat and picking up the menu. "I could eat a horse and chase the rider."

"Order the eggs Benedict," Secta suggested. "It's excellent."

"Good call. Have you eaten?" Al asked, getting up to go order.

"Never touch the stuff," said Secta. "Just get me another coffee. Black, no nothing."

When Alice returned and resumed his seat, Secta detected a look of disgruntlement.

"Are you all right?" he said.

Al sighed. "Dunno," he said. "Just seems to me that all that effort amounted to nothing."

"What do you mean?"

"Look Secta, I put my life on the line a bunch of times on that trip. We were both convinced that finding the Ark and harnessing dark energy was part of the quest. Now we don't have either."

"I understand, Alice," said Secta. "But perhaps as far as the quest is concerned, the object was in fact to hide the Ark so it could never be uncovered."

"But surely someone as hip as En-Ki would have known it was under the Church of the Holy Sepulchre?"

"How? You put it there." Alice was confused. "Think of it this way," said Secta. "Had you not moved the Ark to Ezekiel's cavern, how would it have got there? A whole different reality might exist today."

"So … we rewrote history," Alice tried to summarise.

"Possibly — or changed a future that might have happened. Not to mention the political positives."

"Such as?" Al quizzed.

"I think the entire political topography in this country will change for the better because of our efforts."

Both thought about all the consequences for a moment. It made sense.

"It's imperative you trust the quest, Alice, because the result will not always be obvious to you," said Secta. "But to the overseer — to En-Ki — well, let's just say he's looking at the bigger picture."

Just then de Luz blew in, looking like a tumbleweed.

"Vic," Al said, standing and offering a hand.

De Luz ignored it and gave him a big Texan hug. "Al baby, great to see you made it!"

"You look like you haven't slept in a while, old fella. What's up?" Secta asked, as de Luz slipped into a chair.

"Oh, I've been burning the midnight oil on the question of vitrification embryo freezing," said de Luz.

"Go order yourself a coffee, we'll talk about that once you've got some caffeine in you," Secta said.

While de Luz was ordering, Secta confided: "The main thing is, we pulled it off. We can go either way in time. Think of the possibilities Alice."

"I'm with you, Secta, but right now I have no idea where this quest gig is going to lead me next."

"Don't try and lead it," said Secta. "Let it lead you. That's what Hope always says."

De Luz arrived back, bearing a tray balancing three coffees and two eggs Benedict.

"Speaking of Hope, she'll be back from the bunker today, with the President," Secta said.

"We better meet up with him ASAP," said Al. "There's a lot to discuss."

"I'll arrange it," said Secta. "Now, tell me, Vic: will what I have planned actually work?"

"In a word, yes," de Luz beamed. "The embryo needs to stay in liquid nitrogen, at a temperature of minus 196° Celsius — I've built a flask for the purpose. Hope said she has the embryos ready, so it's just a matter of matching it all up."

"You guys have been busy," Secta said, admiringly. "I've only been away two days and you've achieved all that? Have you sorted Switch out, too?"

"What the heck is switch?" Alice asked, finishing off his eggs.

"Zen has been attempting to develop a process code, which they call Switch," de Luz explained. "It switches on some of the junk DNA that's in everyone."

"And what'll that do?" Al queried.

"They've isolated a particular stand of DNA they believe will switch off the majority of the human senses."

"What! Turn people into fricking zombies? Not again!" Al growled.

"Worse than that, Alice," Secta said. "They're trying to create a hive mentality."

"So we all become drones?"

"Exactly," de Luz confirmed.

"Will these idiots ever quit trying to subjugate mankind?"

"Vic doesn't think they can pull it off," said Secta. "But we both agree we don't like them trying."

"They need to be stopped," said Alice, fiercely. "We know first-hand what these bastards can do."

"Indeed we do," Secta agreed. "But short of having Gorrick assassinated, I don't know where to even start," Secta said.

"With the President," said Alice. "It has to be. That's the all-important question to raise with him at the meeting. Look, if he's going to get his act together, it needs to begin with getting rid of Zen. Agreed?"

"You're right," said Secta. "I spoke with Miss Vallins this morning. We have a meeting scheduled with him for 3pm."

"Are we all attending?" asked de Luz.

"Absolutely. All of us, including Mal, Hope, Honor and Karzoff."

"I thought those two were the enemy?" de Luz asked.

"Karzoff redeemed himself by shooting Set and saving me," said Al, "So for now they're in the good books. But I don't think I can ever trust Honor. Once a slimebag, always a slimebag in my book."

"For the sake of having a team with loyalties beyond suspicion, I wish you were wrong," Secta said, "But I have to say I'm with you on that. She turned on us to support Set far too easily."

"I'm not about to forgive her for ordering the hit on my girl," Al said.

"Have you ever been able to prove that, Alice?" Secta asked.

"What with a trip to the future, then back to stop the collision that could blow mankind away, to tripping off to another future then visiting planet En-Ki, not to mention fighting a three metre Golem, it isn't like I've had the time, have I?" he said.

The three of them chuckled, but Secta was concerned that Alice had indeed been through the wringer over the last six months. That prompted some concern about his physical and psychological wellbeing. It was something he planned to discuss at length with Hope once she was back in town.

"I've been trying to come up with a way of opening a wormhole without using a particle accelerator," said de Luz. "I'm going to need your help with it, Secta."

"We definitely need to refine the transportation medium," Secta agreed. "It's not like we have a billion-dollar collider on hand, after all."

"Yeah, I'm pretty damned sure future access to Desertron will be denied."

Secta thought about it for a moment. "Do we really need such a powerful collision to produce the wormhole?" he asked. "Would we be able to use a Synchrotron?"

"Perhaps, with some amendments…" said de Luz, thoughtfully. "Are you thinking of the 3 GeV radiation facility in Melbourne?"

"Maybe."

"Maybe we should talk with Doctor Robert James," de Luz proposed. "He published a paper on gravitational distortion earlier this year."

"I've heard of him," said Secta, "A Canberra man. He theorised gravitational distortion could tear a hole in space and time to create a wormhole."

"Correct. The paper was mathematically sound, but to my knowledge hasn't been tested past theory."

"Sounds like the guy to speak to," Al agreed. "Seems to me that having a transporter in our own backyard would limit some of the risks — no dealing with foreign powers, for a start."

"You're right Alice," Secta said, taking a mental note. "I'll get onto him."

"Now. Al," said de Luz, turning to him. "Can you describe what happed to allow you to return?"

"It wasn't you?" asked Al, surprised.

De Luz shook his head.

"I dunno," Al said. "I had this kind of gut feeling that something was coming, then there was a shimmer and everything around me wobbled, like a mirage on the road on a hot day … There was a small one the day before, too — and by the way, the same thing happened to Set. D'you think it was En-Ki?"

"Had to be," de Luz shrugged.

"Everything slowed down, sound wound down, then everything apart from Set and me froze. When you looked at folks up close they were still moving, but incredibly slowly. Then a whirlpool cranked up in the air about a metre off the ground. Started about the size of a tennis ball I s'pose, then got bigger. I figured it would close when it got to a certain size. When it was big enough, I dived in."

"Then what happened?" de Luz asked excitedly.

Alice had to think about it. "Everything exploded into tiny stars," he said.

"Did that happen when you went through the Desertron?"

"Nah, that was way different, like going under with anaesthetic — you shoot backwards and suddenly wake up with a headache. When I arrived in Jerusalem, I was really groggy for about twenty minutes. That didn't happen when I came back this time. I was conscious when I fell out of the wormhole with Set hanging onto my legs. Didn't feel side effects, either — well, not like the Desertron or Secta's chair."

"Ah, so that's how Set got back," de Luz said.

"Sorry, I meant to tell you," Secta said. "Yes, Set hitched a ride when Alice entered the vortex."

"Vortex … yeah, that's the word," said Alice. "You scientists come up with cool stuff, sometimes."

CHAPTER 33
FOUNTAIN OF TRUTH

THE LONG BLACK boardroom table reminded Al of a road at night after heavy rain. The surface had a unique finish, like pools of water glistening in the overhead spotlights positioned in pairs every metre, ten pairs in all. Seven of the seats were occupied. The head of the table, backdropped by the Oceana insignia, was vacant. Secta and Honor were closest to the President's empty chair, then came Karzoff opposite the Professor, Hope across from Mal and Alice facing de Luz.

Miss Vallins breezed into the austere boardroom, brightening it up with her cheerful smile and beautifully-tailored suit. She certainly brightened up Mal, he couldn't take his eyes off her.

As usual, Honor glared bolts of jealously at the PA's shapely calves.

"Hi Rita," said Hope, perkily. "You certainly lift the gloom!"

"Thanks Hope," the secretary answered. "The boss will be here soon, he's just finishing a long-distance call. What can I get for you all?" Rita Vallins said.

They all ordered coffees — Secta had recommended the President's favoured exotic blends.

Hope had been brought up to speed on Alice's foray into the past and the events in Jerusalem. A draft report had been emailed to the President, who came into the room before Miss Vallins could return with the coffees. They all made to rise, but a hand signal from him stopped them.

"Please remain seated," he said, taking his chair. He placed a document he was holding on the table in front of him. "I've read the report," he said. "It is truly amazing. You must be commended, Alice, on your remarkable journey into this incredible era, and especially for managing to return unharmed.

"I must also commend Karzoff's bravery in ridding us of Set, and, once again, Secta's genius. Without it, I would undoubtedly be six foot under."

The statement was met with a smile from all, with the exception of Honor, who hadn't been mentioned.

The President continued. "I welcome Professor de Luz to our country," he said. "And I welcome too Mal Function, representing the Octagon, in what I hope will be the prelude to a much closer working relationship. I've had a great deal of time alone in the Avalon bunker to consider many things over the last few days. Isolation, in my case, was a massive wake up call. It cleared my mind — and, I believe, opened it." He paused, and took the time to catch the eye of everyone in the room. The sincerity of his statement was undeniable.

"I am going to change the way the country is governed," he said. "I will listen to the people, and I will appoint Mal Function and the Octagon to give me counsel accordingly. I will change the security system of the country. I am going to decommission the secret service."

Honor and Karzoff exchanged looks of surprise. Honor's face had paled.

"I will convene a committee to deal with Zen," the President continued, "And take advice from Secta, Professor de Luz, Doctor Hope and Black Alice on how best to run a new, streamlined OTT. It will be given a black budget, not subject to any interference from military or government. I hope Professor de Luz will stay and join us on this journey, and help us to employ this incredible technology for the benefit of mankind."

Hope began to applaud. Each of them, one by one, joined in, in acknowledgement of the President's revolutionary ideas. Honor joined in because she didn't want to be the only one not clapping. She was in fact appalled by the President's reversal of direction. The speech had done nothing more for her than to vindicate her decision to become a double agent. What peeved her most was seeing Secta elevated to the principal of OTT, with a bottomless budget, answerable to no-one.

The coffees arrived as the applause died away. The President beamed as he smelled the aroma.

"Oh, this is an excellent brew," he said. "Hacienda La Esmeralda from Panama."

Alice checked it mentally and threw in: "Grown in the shade of guava trees on the slopes of Mount Barú in Panama. The bean is only cultivated in small quantities and is a delicacy in the coffee world — a once in a lifetime must for any coffee connoisseur."

"Brilliant … absolutely brilliant," the President said glowingly. "You know, I am so very proud to be in the same room as people like yourselves. Your bravery, Alice. Hope, the Professor and Secta's sheer genius. Karzoff's quick thinking and Mal's belief and dedication."

Honor, once again, was overlooked.

Gorrick was reclining in an armchair in his plush office listening to the rain. A cyclonic cell had been belting Sydney all day. Gazing at the drops hammering on the ceiling skylight, he was waiting for Kew to arrive. He didn't have to wait long. The sound of footsteps was quickly followed by the man entering the room.

"Kew, take a seat," he said, in a mild voice.

Kew sat opposite.

"Phase two?" Gorrick enquired.

Kew reached to his inside coat pocket, withdrew a flash drive, and handed it over.

Collecting his laptop from the table at his side, Gorrick inserted the drive and began to read. After a minute or two he looked up. "Good," he said. "Yes, we will concede to her provisions. A draft agreement will be ready for your collection upon leaving." He punched a few keys to have his staff draw it up.

"Now," he went on. "I have some concerns about the execution of Set. I had word from Colonel Abraham of the Israeli Defence Force that he was shot in self-defence. Knowing Set, I have no doubts as to the validity of that claim. However, shot by Karzoff? I would not have expected that. What have you learned from Honor about the incident?"

"Set had knocked Karzoff down and taken hold of an Israeli soldier," said Kew. "He was using him as a shield. He'd taken the man's pistol and was about to shoot Alice when Karzoff took him out."

"And why had Set knocked Karzoff to the ground?"

"Honor said he'd been picking on Karzoff. Apparently Set didn't like the man, called him an incompetent pathetic fool, or words to that effect, then knocked him down, humiliating him in front of the others."

"I see," said Gorrick, in an expressionless voice. "Well. Have Honor set Karzoff up. You will kill him. Is that understood?"

"Yes sir. And about Set's body, sir?"

"It arrives in a couple of hours. Now, as regards our outstanding matter with the President. We will sideline the hit on him for a while, let them build up confidence. Once they drop their guard, you will get another opportunity. I expect you this time to make a moral of it."

"Yes, sir."

"Keep up the relations with Honor."

"Yes, sir."

"Good. I want weekly reports on the President and OTT's movements, and a copy of Secta's mission review. You and Honor will report here tomorrow morning at 9am. She will get her signed agreement then."

Kew nodded. "That's all," said Gorrick. "Dismissed."

Kew rose and left.

Gorrick got up and prowled, thinking. He needed to up the ante. He connected his OSCI to the Zen mainframe administration terminal. "Gorrick," he announced. "Schedule an action review of the RF-1 military prototype with the department heads of R&D, tomorrow, 9am. Get me a full status report on Switch by seventeen hundred hours."

The RF-1 was to be the revolutionary centrepiece of Cyborg Rugby, which Zen was developing in a joint venture with New Zealand and Japan. The initial R&D was deemed too risky and expensive for Zen alone, so Gorrick had proposed the concept of an international rugby competition with cyborg players to New Zealand Rugby. They loved the idea. Japan bought into it too, and over the following five years a prototype cyborg had been developed.

Zen had successfully hacked into the knowhow, facilities and finance of its partners to develop a working prototype for its war machines.

Now, with the prototype completed, Zen had withdrawn from the tri-nation alliance. It was ready to move on to the next phase and offer the quintessential RF-1 cyborg soldier for sale to the military forces of every tier-one nation on the planet. At the same time, it planned to take over the domestic security of those same tier-one countries as a condition of the deal.

Unknown to the prospective buyers, every RF-1 would be fitted with Switch hive control, which when activated would put Zen in total control of the entire world's cyborg armies, able to initiate a world war which, ultimately, would put them in control.

The research into human DNA had been a deliberate curve ball, a smokescreen for Zen's actual objective. It was now at a stage where a completed, functional RF-1 was only a matter of hours away. All that was missing was the Switch hive control chip and a fresh human body.

The meeting with the President had left Honor in the darkest of moods. She called Viktoria into her office and waited, standing at the window, watching the deluge outside.

As Viktoria entered, Honor spoke bitterly. "Ze OTT division vill be closing, by order of ze President," she said. "Effective immediately. You may seek a new position viz ze government — I suggest you call Secta. You are, after all, his canary. He may have a place for you. Dismissed."

"Thank you," said Viktoria politely and left, happy to be out of Honor's presence.

Honor sat behind her desk. A private, encrypted message arrived from Kew. It was the agreement from Gorrick, accepting all her provisions. Her thin lips formed into what she thought of as a smile when she saw the sum she'd be paid. Kew had asked for a meeting later that evening. At that moment, Karzoff entered.

"Are you all right?" Karzoff asked, puzzled by her odd demeanour.

"Yes, fine," she said briskly. "Vhat is it?"

"Viktoria said you let her go. Is not that a little premature?"

"Not considering she has been Secta's eyes and ears in our office."

"You cannot prove that, Honor. Besides, he is just as much a part of OTT as you and I. He is entitled to be updated."

"It matters not Karzoff," she sneered. "Drop it."

Karzoff had worked with Honor long enough to know when not to pursue something. Her sting was loaded — no matter what he said, she was going to take it the wrong way. He made for the door, but stopped and turned back to face her before going through. "I think it was a positive meeting," he said. "Only good can come of it."

"I did not join zis organization to vork for ze likes of Secta," she snarled. "He is a joke, a subversive, a puerile clown viz a few smart party tricks. I am an intelligence officer. A planner, a vorker, a leader! Ve are vorlds apart."

"We are all worlds apart Honor," sighed Karzoff. "But we learn to compromise and work together. It is how we get things done."

"A philosophical debate I do not need right now," she sneered. "Zank you, Karzoff."

He turned and left her alone with her mood.

When Alice entered his apartment for the first time in all these months, it felt like an empty shell. He felt disconnected from it, from his former life, as though his incredible experiences of late had caused him to outgrow it. After a penetrating silence, remembering Stain's reflection in the mirrored bathroom door, he sat on the edge of the bed and stared at what remained of his acoustic guitar. He'd smashed it when he jumped from the bed to stop her shooting up. He lay back and listened to the rain, and eventually nodded off.

When he woke it was with a start. It was so quiet. The rain had stopped and it was dark outside, the only light the red flashing neon from outside the window. He got up and walked out. It was enough to have experienced travelling in time — he didn't need to contend with ghosts as well.

He stepped out onto Orwell Street. The cyclone had passed, the street was wet, quiet and still. He wandered aimlessly, like a lost soul, mulling over whether to continue as a time traveller or to go back to being who he'd always been: Black Alice, heavy metal singer and songwriter, chart-topper, performer, beloved of millions.

When he reached Macleay Street he turned right, crossed and headed toward the El-Alamein Memorial Fountain: a place he'd always found solace and, sometimes, the answers to whatever questions were on his mind.

He sat on a park bench in front of the fountain, deep in thought. Now that Mal had made the connection with the President he could run the Octagon, so that would relieve him of one obligation. Being a singer … well, being honest with himself, since Stain's death he'd lost a lot of the passion to perform. He liked to compose, but in reality, if he wasn't going to perform the songs there was hardly any point writing them. So, the big question remained: should he accept the position of the OTT official time traveller? The idea of being on some kind of quest was eating him away. I've got no idea what this quest is, he thought. Then the fountain shimmered.

CHAPTER 34
COGITO ERGO SUM

WHILE SECTA WAS in Jerusalem, as well as babysitting the President, Hope had been working on embryo cryopreservation. Over the last three months, she had harvested three of her own ova and fertilized them with sperm from an anonymous donor. Using a cryogenic vitrification process to freeze the fertilised zygotes almost instantaneously, she'd kept them in storage. Now it was time to come up with a way to transport them into the future.

De Luz was sure he'd found it.

"We're going to the bunker tomorrow, then?" Secta asked.

"Yes," Hope smiled over her mug of coffee. "If Vic's flask is everything he's promised."

They were the only customers of Café Epiphany.

De Luz reached into his bag, took out a metal flask and placed it on the table. "There you go guys," he said. "One cryogenic, time-travelling, embryo transportation module. It'll keep up to three of the little suckers safe for seventy years."

"Excellent," smiled Hope. "I have them ready to go."

"Great," said de Luz. "And while you're repopulating the future, I'll track down Robert James and arrange a meeting, so we can continue our other mission."

"Good," said Secta. "It's critical that we explore building a miniaturized collider here in Sydney. We have the budget. All we need is Mr James's help."

Hope was busily flicking through her cell phone contacts. "There you go!" she cried, triumphantly. "Robert James — we were friends at University. I'll give him a call tomorrow and set up a meeting."

"Serendipity," Secta said, looking out of the window at the city street. "Seren-bloody-dipity."

Honor looked into the vanity mirror in her bathroom, satisfied with her disguise. She was excited by the prospects of her new post with Zen, but there were challenges involved in living a double agent's life. With a last touch up of her blonde wig, and a huge pair of dark glasses, she was ready to go. She strode out into the living room and paraded for Kew, who was in an armchair.

He looked her up and down. A tight, knee-length navy blue skirt, white silk blouse open to her bra, blonde hair, magenta lipstick, black sunnies and stiletto heels and a navy jacket folded over her arm. "Now that is a disguise," he said.

"Zank you darlink," she purred.

They took the elevator to the underground car park, found Kew's 6 series BMW-EV and headed for the Zen building ten minutes away.

Kew took Honor through a secret entrance to an exclusive elevator with only one destination — the penthouse. A retinal and face scan activated the doors.

"Impressive," Honor observed.

The door opened again and Kew led Honor into the reception area of Gorrick's office suite.

"Last time I vas here it vas under very different circumstances," Honor said, tightly.

"I heard," he said, tapping his ear to indicate an incoming message on his OSCI.

"We can go in," he said. "The meeting is just about to start."

Kew opened the doors and ushered Honor into the vast room. Gorrick stood to receive her, holding out a hand to shake.

"Good to see you again, Honor," he said. "Although I must say I only recognised you because you are with Kew."

She shook his hand. "So Gorrick," she smiled, thinly, "Ve are finally on ze same side."

"Yes indeed, welcome," he replied. "I trust your tenure with us will be more fruitful than it has been with Oceana. Please, both of you, take a seat." He waited for Honor to sit, and then sat back down himself and handed Honor a flash drive. "Our agreement, signed," he said. "Plus, a list of what will be expected of you. Nothing beyond your conditions, I assure you."

"Thank you," Honor said, composed.

"When you are in the company of Zen staff, you will be referred to as Pandora. Kew will be your point person, and make all necessary arrangements with you personally."

Just then the door opened and two technicians in white lab coats entered, both Chinese, one a very pretty young woman. Gorrick stood and waited for them.

"Doctors Lissy Li and Xiang Chu, this is Pandora," he said. "And you of course already know Mr Kew. Please, sit."

Doctor Li wore her black hair in a style similar to Honor's under the wig: a blunt bob to her jaw. She was tall and shapely, with an almond shaped face and fine delicate features. She sank into the chair gracefully and crossed her legs. She fired Honor an amorous look, ruby red lips pouted. Honor rather liked it.

Chu, on the other hand, was in his mid-fifties and if it weren't for the lab coat and the introduction from Gorrick, she'd have mistaken him for a cleaner. His looks were seriously unimpressive.

"Doctor Chu is our leading scientist," Gorrick explained. "He and Doctor Li have been up all night, preparing the exhibition I invited you to witness. We are all here, so let us continue. Doctor?"

The little Chinaman nodded in turn to his colleague. Perhaps his English was lacking, Honor thought.

Li stood, donning a pair of spectacles. From her pocket she produced a remote, then faced her audience.

"It has taken nearly half a billion dollars of research and development to get to this point," she said. "But now we are ready to reveal the RF-1— a fully autonomous, cybernetic being. Cyborg tissues structured with carbon nanotubes and plant or fungal cells have been used in artificial tissue engineering, producing new materials for mechanical and electrical uses," she went on. "We experimented with prosthetics and bio-brain implants to determine the correct mix of organics and biomechatronics. Earlier this year a prototype was produced by Japan, at that time still our joint venture partners. It, however, lacked intelligence and employed programming that caused it to walk like a robot from a science fiction film. We nicknamed it Clunky."

There was a chuckle from the audience.

Dr Li continued: "After Zen withdrew from the tri-alliance with New Zealand and Japan, the responsibility fell on our humble division to bring the design to a conclusion. The inclusion of Doctor Chu allowed us to develop neural interface components for the prototype. In layman's terms, a holographic brain-to-computer interface, providing a direct path of communication from the brain to an external device, and vice-versa." She waved the remote in her hand, and paused dramatically. "Mr Khan, Mr Kew and Miss Pandora — I present to you the RF-1."

The big double doors opened with a jolt that caused Honor to flinch, then a six-foot-six monster strode into the room dressed in camouflage military fatigues and wearing a tight-fitting battle helmet and visor. She felt every tiny hair on her arms and the back of her neck rise. This was really scary.

The creature moved fluidly towards them, only slightly robotic when it turned, its arms locked against its sides. It stopped beside Dr Li and, towering over her, looked straight ahead. It had not acknowledged the existence of anyone in the room.

It was a harrowing experience for Honor, one she hadn't expected. She knew this RF-1 cyborg must be a closely-guarded secret, and wondered why Gorrick had exposed it to her. She also knew from Secta's report about travelling to 2087 that Zen had developed the RF-1 much further — although still not far enough to defeat Alice.

"The RF-1 is forty percent organic and sixty percent biomechatronic and carbon nanotubes," Li went on, as though nothing had happened. "It will react to verbal commands or to satellite data streaming. It feels no pain, it is not sentient, it does not think. It merely processes. It can see in the spectrums of infrared and ultraviolet, giving it excellent day and night vision, and is fitted with three-hundred- and sixty-degree sensors that detect movement or ordnance up to one hundred metres. The reaction or response to signal time is one hundredth of a second — this we hope to improve on as faster processors become available.

"Doctor Chu has built a two hundred-millimetre parfocal zoom lens into the retina of one eye. In the future, the lens will be fitted to both eyes, but in this case we had only one to work with. This is the first complete RF-1, because this is the first time we have had a fresh donor body."

"Is it fitted with Switch?" Gorrick asked.

"Yes sir, but still needs refining," Chu said in heavily-accented English.

"Activate reaction please, Dr Li," Gorrick ordered.

Li pressed a button on the remote. Nothing happened.

"Pandora, throw your sunglasses at the RF-1 please," Gorrick requested.

Honor took them from her pocket and flung them hard. The monster snatched them out of the air without even looking at the target, then leaned down and offered them back to her. This thing certainly trumps Secta's Android guard, Honor thought, but she kept that to herself. She had bad memories of that guard.

"Very impressive," she said.

"Have it remove the helmet, Doctor Li," Gorrick ordered. "I would like to see your magnificent work in detail."

Li went behind the RF-1 and undid a connector to free up the helmet. She returned to its side and hit another button on the remote.

"You may order it, sir," said Li. "I've sampled your voice and added it to its protocols."

"Very well," Gorrick smiled. "RF-1 — remove your helmet."

The big creature responded immediately, raising both arms, gripping either side of the helmet and lifting it, visor and all, from its head.

Honor nearly passed out.

Half its face was chrome, shaped with roughly human features but no eye, just a shallow socket. The top of its head was fitted with a chrome skullcap. The rest of the face belonged to Anu Set.

"That ... That is—"

"Indeed, Pandora, you are quite correct," said Gorrick. "We rushed Set's body from Jerusalem expressly for the purpose of reanimating him as our first RF-1. It was not only his wish, it was also in his employment contract."

Honor couldn't take her eyes off him. Neither could Kew.

"It's in my contract too," he breathed. "Isn't he incredible?"

"Does he know who he is?" Honor asked.

"No," Dr Li responded. "As I said, he is not sentient. We have only used his body parts. He does not have his original brain, so no memories or self-awareness."

"Cogito ergo sum," Gorrick stated.

"I think, therefore I am," Honor translated.

"Not yet," said Li. "But in future models? Perhaps so."

As Li and Chu were leaving with the RF-1, Honor waited as Kew had a private word with Gorrick.

"Initiate phase three," Gorrick told him, coldly.

"Yes sir," Kew confirmed.

CHAPTER 35
SEEDING THE FUTURE

PERSISTENT **RINGING FROM** the intercom finally woke Alice. He clambered out of bed and staggered naked to the phone by the door.

"What is it?" he said, grumpily.

"Secta here, Alice!" chirped the reply. "You've got no phone so I came over. Did I wake you?"

"Come up," Al rasped, pressing the entry button.

He rolled into the kitchenette, filled the jug with water, flicked it to life, brushed a couple of cockroaches off two mugs growing pink mould in the kitchen sink and searched for a jar instant coffee.

There was a knock at the door.

"Come in!" he yelled, and only then remembered he was naked. He grabbed a robe and threw it on. It was Stain's, and it barely fitted him.

"Good morning," Secta said jovially. "Have a late one?"

Al frowned at him through squinting eyes. "You're not generally this happy in the morning, Secta," he said. "What's up — someone drop dead? What time is it?"

Secta pulled up a chair and stared at Al's robe. "Nine thirty," he replied. "My, you look pretty in pink."

Alice grunted.

Secta was dressed in civvies, no sign of the ubiquitous lab coat. "You going for a jog or something?" Al said, pouring boiling water into the mugs to flush out the mould.

"Not likely," said Secta. "The closest I get to exercise is riding in elevators."

"Coffee?"

"Yes, black with two sweeteners."

"No sweeteners, so two sugars," Al said, digging a spoon into a coffee jar, trying break up contents that had turned to rock with age. He spooned a few chunks into each mug, sugared them and topped them up with boiling water. Keeping one for himself he handed the other to Secta. He took a sip and grimaced. "Argh! This tastes like crap!"

"Throw on some clothes," smiled Secta, grimacing at the unidentified flotsam in his cup. "Let me buy you breakfast. There's a little café around the corner, on Earl Place."

"Yeah, know it well. Give me a minute."

Fifteen minutes later they were sitting in the alfresco section of the Earl Café, waiting for their breakfast to arrive. It was sunny, the air fresh and clear after the storm. Alice's wrap around sunnies topped off an outfit made up of a blue singlet under a black leather jacket, black jeans and Cuban heeled boots — the rock star look, down pat. There were plenty of clients at the little café, and most of them recognised him, giving him glances and nods.

"Does it bother you, always being recognised?" Secta asked.

"Nar, only time it gets up my nose is if someone says hi and I don't hear 'em for whatever reason," said Al. "If I don't reply they think I'm snubbing them, and sometimes they get shirty. Saying that, it was kind of nice not being recognised in Jerusalem."

The waitress arrived with the coffees and breakfast.

"Thanks Deb," said Al, with a smile.

"No worries Al," she replied, eyelashes fluttering. "Haven't seen you in ages."

"Been in Jerusalem."

"Far-out, how was that?"

"Ancient," Al said with a smile.

"Cool," she said, and waddled off.

"She's a good sort, Deb," he grinned.

Secta seemed to have mustered the courage to bring up the reason he'd called.

"Alice, Hope and I are going to the bunker today," he said. "Would you like to come?"

"Why d'you think I was up half the night?" he said, holding up a flash drive. "I was copying my albums for Morri and Turk."

"So you remembered today is the day?"

"Sure."

"Hope has three fertilized embryos ready to go. They're her eggs, fertilized by a mystery donor."

"Yeah, I know." Al leaned forward. "It's really no mystery," he whispered. "It was me."

"You?" Secta yelped.

"Yep, Hope asked me, so I did the trick before we went to Texas. I was real glad all the little blokes weren't affected by all the stuff you've pumped into me and all that dematerializing gunk."

"I'd just about convinced myself Mal was the donor."

"Mate, the opportunity to be father of the new mankind? Had to be me," Al smirked, reclining in his seat.

"Yes, well it could hardly be me," said Secta. "What with being the sibling of the egg donor."

Alice again leaned across the small table to prevent anyone overhearing. "Last night..." he said. "I went for a walk. Needed to clear my head..."

Secta was getting worried. Alice had been trying to make up his mind about his future. It seemed he had.

"And?"

"All this time travel stuff, having to fight for my life on every mission..."

Secta was wringing his hands under the table, he could feel the crunch coming.

"I mean, I'm not getting any younger, you know? No need to elaborate. I think you get the picture."

Secta untangled his hands and picked up his mug of coffee, but couldn't take a sip. His hand was trembling too much. "And so?" The plaintive squeak sounded pathetic even to himself.

"I absolutely love it!" Al grinned.

Secta reclined so fast he almost toppled out of his chair.

"Oh, good Lord Alice, I thought you were going to opt out,' he said, taking a huge sigh of relief.

Al looked surprised. "You've got to be kidding!" he said.

"I've been concerned about all the pressure you've been under," said Secta. "I thought you were going through the process of making up your mind about your future career. I'm so pleased you chose OTT!"

Alice beckoned him closer. "En-Ki," he whispered.

Secta looked at him wide-eyed and equally wide-mouthed.

"I went to the El Alamein Fountain last night," Al went on. "Used to go there to chill and get my head together. It suddenly shimmered, and time slowed down again. The water went from a spray to slow moving droplets, cars on Macleay Street slowed to a snail's crawl, pedestrians were winding down like clockwork toys. A girl walked through a flock of pigeons that took off and froze mid-flight. It was freaking amazing. I could have sat and watched it for hours.

"But I remembered what happened last time and looked about to see if there was anything going on I could change. Saw this dude lifting a girl's wallet out of her bag as she got out of a cab. I took it out of his hand and put it back in the bag. Then I noticed a big bruiser cruising along with a gym bag over his shoulder. Covered in tattoos, maybe Tongan or Samoan. He'd just crossed the street. So I peeled the bag off him and put it in the hands of the thief, then wandered back to the fountain. There was a vortex forming inside. So, when it was wide enough to enter, I got up on the edge of the fountain and stepped in. The same place as before was on the other side — that glowing orb, hovering just above the floor. And then En-Ki spoke."

Secta took a gulp of his coffee, captivated by Alice's story. "What? What did he say?"

"He said I'd done well. That the Ark was safe, but it was only the start. I asked what would have happened if I hadn't moved the Ark, and he said Nebuchadnezzar would have taken it and history would have changed for the worse. I asked if he could see the alternative timeline, and he said yes. I asked why he'd summoned me, and he said because I was struggling to make up my mind whether to continue with the quest — which was true.

"He said I had to continue, and that I would be kept safe from harm, although not from pain. I couldn't resist it — I asked if he was in Betyl at the time of the Jerusalem siege. Turns out he was. So I asked why he didn't just move the bloody Ark, and he said because then I wouldn't have known where to find it. I called him on that one, 'cause obviously I know where it is but can't get to it. He said it'll soon be needed and I'll discover the way to retrieve it. Then he said I should recognise that my achievements have positively affected the present and the future, and that the next step is coming.

"And that was it. I stepped back into the portal and out at the El Alamein Fountain. It closed really quick, time snapped back, the girl carried on with her wallet in her bag and the big guy saw his bag in the hands of the thief. The look on the thief's face was awesome. I was going to enjoy him getting a walloping when I realised I was standing in the fountain getting drenched. So I squelched my way back home."

"Unbelievable," Secta mumbled, stunned.

"So that pretty well made my mind up for me," Al went on. "But there's one thing I wanted to ask you … how come when I visited En-Ki and returned I stayed dressed?"

Secta reclined in his chair and let out a loud chuckle. "I don't know Alice," he said. "I really don't know … but it's something we need to work on isn't it? Can't have you continually turning up in your birthday suit."

"You know, I reckon we need to tell the President about the quest," said Alice. "He needs to understand the big picture. After yesterday, I've no reason to distrust him."

"Given what he announced, I have to agree with you," Secta said. "So tell me — are you going to give up performing?"

"Nah, I'll do a gig here and there," Al said. "Write songs, record 'em, put out my music … somehow it feels like I'm meant to continue getting the message out. Whatever the message is."

"You have to go with your instincts, Alice," Secta said, nodding. "So far they've been proven right."

"Where do we go from here?" Alice asked.

"Hope is arranging a meeting with a physicist who has theorised that gravitational distortion can open a wormhole."

"And how can that help us?"

"Well, he's local, and if he's right, we wouldn't need a massive particle accelerator to for the job. We could do it with a miniaturised unit right here in Sydney."

"What, like our own Stargate?"

"I suppose so," said Secta. "Is that a TV show or something?"

A few hours later Hope, Secta and Alice arrived at the bunker by chopper. It had been a bumpy ride, low cloud ceiling all the way, enshrouded in a grey void. Secta was pretty shaken.

"Hate those things," he grumbled, as they jumped out and ran to the trapdoor.

"Jeez, how cold is it here?" Al complained.

"Ha, ha, Al," Hope cracked. "I'll have you know that while you've been messing about in the warmth of the Middle East, I've been chilling here, babysitting the President."

"Open Sesame!" Secta called, and the trapdoor opened.

As they entered the lab, Alice looked about. "Well, here we are," he said. "Back in The Pit. All looks pretty much the same as before. Thought you were going to have it all moved to Sydney, Secta?"

"I was," Secta said. "But we needed to keep it intact for today … it is, after all, our only direct link to our friends in the future."

"Right!" said Al. "I supposed you've done all the scientific voodoo on how the embryos are going to survive seventy years?"

"We sure have," said Hope.

"What time is it, Alice?" Secta asked.

None of them were wearing a watch. Alice wondered why Secta had asked him, of all people. "How the stuff would I know?" he growled.

"Because you can access the time via your implant," said Secta.

Alice thought about it for a second and grinned. "It's twelve fifty-nine and thirty seven seconds," he said. "Hmm. That's handy."

"Oh no," Hope groaned. "Now he's got access to infinite information he's going to become mister clever-clogs."

"Alright," said Secta, bringing them back to the task. "Let's get on with it."

Hope took the cryogenic flask over to the crazy, old-fashioned dentist chair, the very same one that had sent both Alice and Secta into the future — and brought them back. She kissed the flask, making sure she left a clear impression of her red lipstick for Turk and Morri to find, then reverently laid it on the seat.

Secta moved in and placed a flash drive beside it.

"The instructions," he explained.

It felt to Alice like they were enacting some kind of religious ritual offering — and in a funny way that made sense, knowing that a replica of Stonehenge stood directly above them in the future. At least it had, until it was blown away by a missile from Zen. The enormity of the task that lay ahead for Turk and Morri, the task of rebuilding mankind, warranted such solemnity. He placed his flash drive on the chair with the other two items.

"What's on that one?' Hope asked.

"All of my albums," he smiled. "They're not readily available in 2087."

"Nice touch," Hope said, warmly.

Job done, the three of them stood back, arm in arm, eyes focused on the chair.

One by one the items disappeared.

"They've got them," Secta said.

Turk and Morri were looking tattered and torn. The battle with Zen in 2087 hadn't stopped once Alice and Secta had left. Turk handed both flash drives to Morri.

"This drive contains the instructions for the flask," Morri said. "The other's got from Alice written on it. Wonder what that is?"

Turk picked up the flask. "It's icy cold," he said. "And look, there's a kiss on it."

He showed it to Morri, who smiled. "That'd be from Secta's sister, Hope," she said. "Although it could be from Secta. He might have liked being me so much he's has taken to wearing lipstick."

They laughed.

Morri inserted the instruction drive into the U-link hand-held computer Nerdo had given her, and read the instructions from the screen. "A note from Secta bids us all well," she said. "He says Alice just returned from a time travel mission into the past — 587 BCE, no less!"

"Incredible," Turk said resting his hulk on the arm of the chair. "They're probably standing in the room with us right now."

They paused a moment while the tiny hairs on their arms rose, chilled by the thought that ghosts of another time were occupying the same space.

Morri snapped out of it. "Okay," she said. "It explains what I have to do. There's a gadget inside the flask that I use to insert three embryos. Secta said the donors were his sister and Alice. Isn't that bizarre? So hopefully, in about nine months, I'll be giving birth to one or more little Alices."

"Well, we know what to name them then," said Turk.

"He says we need to keep well clear of radiation zones for the entire pregnancy," added Morri. "Suggests we should stay down here for as much of the term as possible."

Turk looked around. "He's right. There's so much riding on this."

"We should do it here as soon as possible, he says, because it's a sterile environment."

"Okay — but let's just see what's on Alice's drive first," Turk urged, curiosity getting the better of him.

She ejected Secta's drive and inserted Alice's. "It's an audio-visual."

The first music video was Fighting For You. As they watched, they recognised how relevant the song and visuals were to their fight, and how Alice had understood that. Morri embraced Turk, inspired by the song and the contents of the flask. They were beginning to believe a future for humankind might just be possible after all.

"I don't get how that's possible?" said Al. "They're in the future … we put three things on the chair that wait seventy years for Turk and Morri to collect, but when they take them they just disappear, like magic."

"Just another time travel paradox, Alice," Secta said, offhandedly.

"We in physics-land call things like that time quirks," said Hope. "Can't be explained."

Secta led Alice and Hope to the bunker elevator. As the door opened and the bunker lights extinguished, Secta said: "Alice, I hope you didn't alter too much history while you were in 587 BCE. Did you?"

"Nar Secta, I observed the prime directive at all times."

"The … prime directive?"

"Star Trek Secta — don't tell us you've never seen it?" said Hope.

"No! Do you think I should?"

"Reckon," said Al. "There's heaps of stuff we could learn from it. Not to mention Dr Who."

"Dr Who?" Secta enquired, stepping into the elevator.

"Yeah. Maybe you could make me a sonic screwdriver, I've always wanted one."

The door closed on another chapter.

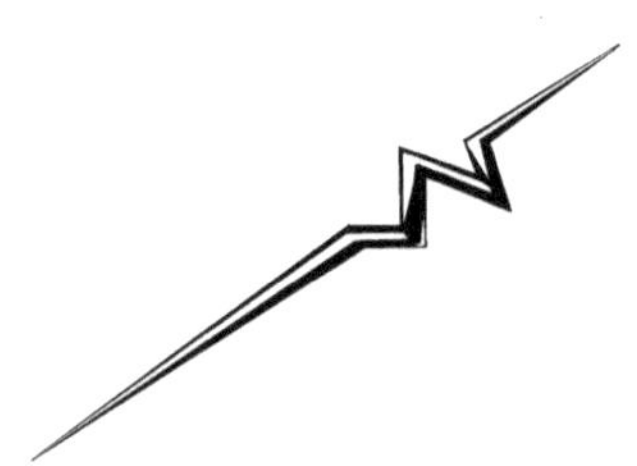

EPILOGUE

Book 4
SONS OF STEEL - BLOCKCHAIN

THE WAR WITH North Korea had left Japan topographically and mentally scarred. After numerous missile strikes, many of the larger cities on the west coast of Honshu had been totalled, ravaged by the resulting firestorms. The attacks had provoked an unparalleled response from the USA.

Twenty-seven years later, a new Japan had emerged, with a fresh, optimistic psyche. The same couldn't be said of the aggressor. North Korea was the scene of the first nuclear strike on a civilian population since Hiroshima and Nagasaki. Pyongyang had been obliterated. The country was eventually invaded by United Nations forces, and after four years of fighting North Korea was finally annexed by South Korea.

The western world had narrowly avoided confrontation with China, after the UN had pressured them to not assist the rebel nation.

The setting sun glistened on the water, like sparkling reflections from diamond facets. Together with the boredom of fishing for three hours without a bite, it was making Doctor Rick Malone feel sleepy. It didn't seem to be having the same effect on Doctor Gensan Hyashi. He was happy whether he caught a fish or not, just glad to be out of the lab for a day to chill in the wilderness of Lake Okutama, a trout fishery that allows fishing under license and a vital source of drinking water for Tokyo.

The appeal of fishing to Malone was simply that in 2047 it was one of the only recreational sports to remain free from the grip of digital technology. As an industrial chemist he was no Luddite, but at times he needed to escape technology — especially living in Japan, where it was ubiquitous.

As the orange glow of the last light streaked across the mirrored surface of the lake, Malone's mind drifted to his younger days, fishing for rock bass with his father in Put-In-Bay, South Bass Island on Lake Erie in Ohio. He rubbed his stubbly brown beard, reminded of when he first arrived in Japan in his late twenties.

Dr Hyashi broke his reverie. "Malone-san, look at the sky!" he cried.

Rick looked up in time to see a meteorite with a long tail streaking through the darkening dome.

"It's going to land right beside us!" he said, excitedly.

Dr Hyashi logged onto the nearest radar through his organic virtual vision retinal implant, OVVA — VV for short. An image of a military radar sweep, only accessible by security cleared users, was projected in real time to his optical vision aid via the retinal heads-up display.

"I see no sign of it on radar," he said.

"It's too small," Rick said. "No bigger than a golf ball, I'd guess."

They both watched the object plunge into the water only a hundred metres away. What they couldn't see was as a small metallic sphere opening and expelling a payload as it sank to the bottom.

Dr Hyashi was speaking excitedly in Japanese to a colleague through his VV. Rick had lived ten years in Japan, but he'd by no means mastered the language. He could, however, pick up the gist. Hyashi was describing what they'd witnessed.

Rick packed up his fishing gear. The event was over, and it was getting dark. Time to call it a day.

Hyashi finished his conversation and began packing his gear as well.

"What did your colleague think?" Rick asked.

"Probably piece of space junk," Hyashi replied. "He will check … there is a registry of all space junk orbiting Earth."

"I know," said Rick, stretching his back. "Aaaah, that's better. Pity there were no fish today — but it was good to get out of the lab."

"I must let the fishing centre know they need to increase stocks," smiled Hyashi. "The last thing we need is casting practice."

Rick chuckled, but his face tightened as he recognised something in the water. "Will you look at that?" he said.

Hyashi looked. There were fish popping up to the surface in numbers, all of them gasping as though they were drowning. Rick walked over to the bank, knelt down and plucked a big rainbow trout from the water. It died in his hands. Hyashi brought over a torch and shone it on the fish. They were both shocked by what they saw — both eyes had ruptured.

"That's incredible!" said Rick, putting the fish down and wading into the water to grab another one, this time a white spotted char. He brought it over to inspect under the light. The condition of the char was identical — both eyes ruptured.

"This must be related to the meteorite," Rick hypothesised.

"More likely radioactive space junk," Hyashi countered."

"Plausible," Rick agreed. "I'll take this back to the lab and analyse them."

Hyashi looked at the lake. "I will not tell the fishing centre they need to restock," he said, quietly. "Look at all the fish!"

There were at least a hundred of them, floating upside-down in the water.

"No," said Rick. "But I think you better let them know what's happened as soon as possible … this is the water supply for much of Tokyo. I'll take a water sample too."

While Hyashi collected his fishing box and rod, Rick filled two flasks with water, put them in his keeper with the two dead fish, and gathered up his gear for the hike back to their cars.

"It'll be interesting to see the results of that water sample."

"I do not think you will find much, Malone-san," said his companion. "Whatever killed the fish will probably be neutralised in a few hours. The real problem will be cleaning up the mess!"

Rick wasn't so sure. A gut feeling told him there was more to it than met the eye.

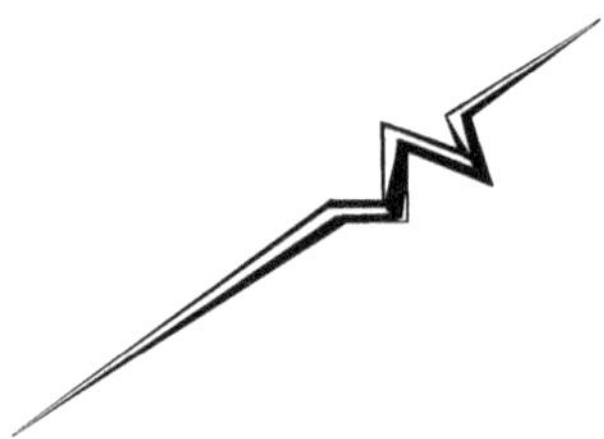